Praise for Mary Daheim and Her Emma Lord Mysteries

"A witty and wonderful story that will keep readers glued to the pages . . . This author should be given a pat on the back considering this is the twenty-fifth novel in the Emma Lord series . . . and each one just keeps getting better and better!"
—*Suspense Magazine,* on *The Alpine Yeoman*

"Daheim injects enough wit and color to make her tale more entertaining than the standard small-town mystery."
—*Kirkus Reviews,* on *The Alpine Yeoman*

"Mary Daheim continues to delight readers with new twists and a wonderful and ever-evolving cast of eccentric characters. Highly recommended."
—*I Love a Mystery,* on *The Alpine Yeoman*

"There are always readers who want to figure out 'who dunnit'; others just enjoy the ride. Daheim offers plenty of challenge for the first group, and a great ride for the second."
—*Reviewing the Evidence,* on *The Alpine Yeoman*

"A core of familiar characters adds charm to all Daheim's 'alphabet' stories. Readers will find this new one similarly enjoyable."
—*The Free Lance-Star,* on *The Alpine Xanadu*

"*The Alpine Xanadu* flows well and brims with vim and vigor, making this one of the best recent installments of the series."
—*New Mystery Reader*

THE ALPINE ZEN

THE ALPINE ZEN

An Emma Lord Mystery

MARY DAHEIM

BALLANTINE BOOKS • NEW YORK

2016 Ballantine Books Mass Market Edition

Published in the United States by Ballantine Books, an imprint of Random House, a division of Penguin Random House LLC, New York.

BALLANTINE and the HOUSE colophon are registered trademarks of Penguin Random House LLC.

Originally published in hardcover in the United States by Ballantine Books, an imprint of Random House, a division of Penguin Random House LLC, in 2015.

ISBN: 978-0-345-53536-8
eBook ISBN: 978-0-804-17748-1

Cover design: Peter Thorpe
Cover illustrations: Peter Thorpe (left and right), Shutterstock/Renee Ciufo (center)

Printed in the United States of America

randomhousebooks.com

9 8 7 6 5 4 3 2

Ballantine Books mass market edition: March 2016

To the memory of Martha Longbrake,
who tirelessly gave of herself.
We are forever indebted to her generous spirit.

This story is set in 2005.

THE ALPINE ZEN

Chapter One

THE MONTH OF June is unpredictable in Alpine. My House & Home editor, Vida Runkel, is not. But this spring and early summer, she's been as changeable as the weather. Vida insists she isn't angry with me, but her long lapses into silence are a sign that all is not well.

Sadly, I know the reason for her behavior. Vida's embarrassed. Her adored grandson, Roger Hibbert, is serving a four-year prison term for contributing to the delinquency of a minor. Or minors, in his case, having been busted for luring teenage girls into prostitution. As a sideline, he had also been dealing drugs.

Lawbreaking isn't new to Roger, though the first time around Sheriff Milo Dodge went easy on the punk for Vida's sake and because he'd ratted out our local drug dealers. However, his recent crimes were more serious. Vida was forced to remove her blinders and see Roger through realistic eyes. That, however, didn't mean she was happy.

Neither was I, but my displeasure was with the weather. A June heat wave in our Cascade Mountains aerie is unusual. Instead of gray skies and intermittent showers, we were having bright sun and unseasonable heat.

"It's not even ten and it's already too warm," Amanda Hanson griped as she brought in the morning mail. "I should write a letter to Vida's advice column asking what she can do to fix it. What happened to our rain?"

I smiled at *The Alpine Advocate*'s receptionist and office manager. "We've had some early morning drizzle," I pointed out. "And it's always good to have had sun for the annual Summer Solstice festivities."

"That was last week," Amanda said, a hand on her bulging abdomen. "If it stays this hot and the baby doesn't come for another couple of weeks, I may explode like a Fourth of July firecracker."

I laughed. "My son, Adam, was born in June on the Mississippi Delta. Think humidity on top of heat. At least we're spared that here in the Cascades."

Amanda gazed up at my small office's low ceiling. "I know. It can always get worse. Are you sure Alison Lindahl's taking my place while I'm on maternity leave?"

"Yes," I replied. "She doesn't teach cosmetology during summer quarter at the community college. Alison came back from her Alaskan cruise Saturday. She's spending a week with her parents in Everett, but if we need her, she can rescue us. She did a fine job when you left to fill in for the post office rush last December."

Amanda suddenly looked dazed. "Where did this year go? So much happened in Alpine. Who says small towns are boring?"

Not me. Last June, if anyone had told me I'd be happily married for the better part of this year, I'd have reserved space for the predictor in RestHaven's psych ward. I didn't even know I was in love until after Thanksgiving. In fact, back then I'd never heard of RestHaven.

"Ahem." Leo Walsh, my ad manager, stood in the doorway. "Are you awake?"

"Yes," I replied, after giving a start. "I was woolgathering. I've decided that my editorial this week should rouse the citizenry to endorse Mayor Fuzzy Baugh's plan to do away with his job and the county commissioners. As usual, everybody in Skykomish County is suffering from utter apathy. Maybe it's the heat."

Leo's weathered face broke into an ironic grin. "Having spent a long weekend recently in Southern California, I feel right at home. Don't worry, boss lady, I have no immediate plans to retire even if I did turn sixty-two in May. But I'll go back to Santa Maria for my son's wedding later this summer."

"Keep saying that," I urged. "It helps dispel my fear of Ed Bronsky wanting his old job back. How are we shaping up for ads this week?"

"Not quite the desired sixty-forty split," Leo admitted. "But we've got the special Fourth of July section coming out this week, which makes up for it. How much copy have you got?"

"Enough," I said. "The insert's front page will be the 1917 photo of the American flag presentation to Alpine for selling the most World War One Liberty Bonds per capita of any Washington city or town. There are two versions of that picture, but we haven't run either of them for the last five years. Our readers never get tired of seeing those shots. Maybe I can use the old-timers as the hook to inspire the locals to get off their duffs and support Fuzzy's government-reorganization plan at the polls."

Leo nodded. "Shame them into it. It might motivate the merchants to buy more ad space." He glanced out into the newsroom. "The Duchess has taken off," he went on, referring to Vida, who insisted she despised his nickname for her, though we all knew better. "Will she ever bounce back after Roger's fall from grace?"

"She has to," I said. "Her gloom can get contagious. Mitch already suffers from that problem."

"Our star reporter's been better since his wife's emotional state stabilized," Leo noted. The previous December, Mitch and Brenda Laskey's son, Troy, had made his second failed escape from the Monroe Correctional Complex, some thirty-five miles west of Alpine. "Oddly enough, I've never heard Mitch and Vida compare notes about their jailbird offspring."

"She's too embarrassed," I said. "I don't know if Vida's visited Roger since he was sent to the Shelton facility. It's a three-hundred-and-fifty-mile round-trip from here."

Leo shrugged. "Just as well. Thank God my kids managed to avoid serious trouble despite my bouts with the bottle and getting fired."

"You turned your life around," I asserted. "I'll admit, when I first hired you, I had my doubts, but you did it."

"Thanks in large part to you." Leo glanced over his shoulder. "Here's Mitch now. Maybe he's got some hot news from the sheriff's office. Later, babe." My ad manager ambled out to greet my reporter.

Apparently, there were no headlines from Sheriff Dodge's crew. The last I'd seen of the sheriff was the back of him going out the side door of our house carrying the garbage and cussing a lot. That was over two hours ago. It was just as well that he and I didn't talk much in the morning. Neither of us was very sociable before we consumed large amounts of caffeine. Maybe that's why our marriage had lasted for over four months.

By ten-thirty I'd made inroads on my weekly editorial. So far, I'd praised the grit, pride, and patriotism of Alpine's early residents. Now I had to rally their modern-day counterparts. That task wasn't easy. I decided I needed more coffee.

I left to seek a refill in the empty newsroom. All that remained from the Upper Crust Bakery run made by my back-shop manager, Kip MacDuff, was a bran muffin and a powdered sugar doughnut. I snatched up the latter and was biting into it when Vida entered, pushing her great-grandson, Dippy, in what looked like a stroller out of *Star Wars*.

To my relief, Vida was smiling. "Amy has an emergency dental appointment," she said, referring to the youngest of her daughters and the mother of Roger. "Short notice, of course, to get a babysitter. I told her I'd be delighted to bring Dippy to work with me. Look— see how happy he is. So many teeth now that he's two and a half. Such a *big* boy!" She bent down and clucked her tongue at him. "What word did Great-Grams teach you today, Dippy?"

"Fool," Dippy said. His watchful eyes, which were remarkably like Vida's, darted around the newsroom. "Old fool. Mud Dudd is . . . old fool."

"Maud Dodd," Vida corrected gently, beaming all the while. "But you mustn't say that to other people."

Dippy turned belligerent. "You do."

"That's different," Vida argued, the toothy smile still in place. "I'm old, you see. You are not." She stood up, one hand adjusting the rhinestone brooch on her felt cloche. "Isn't he amazing? So clever, so quick, so observant."

Except for those watchful eyes, he looked like Roger. Or how his father would have looked had I known the wretch at the same age. I hadn't met Vida's grandson until he was eight. "Dippy seems very alert," I said. "He's grown since I saw him on Mother's Day."

"My, yes," she agreed, wheeling him closer to her desk. "He's almost outgrown his handsome stroller. Dippy has an excellent appetite. Not the least bit fussy. He simply lapped up the casserole I made for Amy and Ted last night. Unfortunately, I can't say the same for Amy—the abscessed tooth made my daughter quite ill."

Vida's casserole would have made *me* ill, though her three daughters and their families must be used to her lack of skills with anything resembling a stove. Maybe

they didn't know any better. To my consternation, I saw
that Dippy had gotten out of the stroller.

"Don't let Dippy hurt himself," I cautioned, fleeing to
my office.

My House & Home editor didn't respond. I could see
her tall, imposing figure standing by Leo's desk, watching Dippy make a beeline for the pastry table. No doubt
the bran muffin was about to become pastry history. I
was lucky that I'd already eaten the doughnut during
Vida's vocabulary exchange with Dippy.

My phone rang just as I settled into my chair at
eleven. "Will you be in your office around eleven-thirty?"
Amanda inquired.

"Yes. Is something happening then?"

"A woman named Irena Rawlings is in Monroe on
business and wants to see you," Amanda explained.
"She's interested in Alpine's history."

"She should talk to Vida, not me," I said. "Tell her
that's fine. We'll probably both be here."

Amanda rang off. I looked into the newsroom, where
Vida was on the phone. There was no sign of Dippy, but
I assumed he was still there, if out of my line of vision.
Twenty minutes later, I saw the little guy scurrying to
his great-grandmother's side while Kip MacDuff en-
tered my office at a slower, if more purposeful, pace.

"How," he inquired, keeping his voice down, "can I
tell Vida to stop that kid from invading the back shop?
He just deleted Mitch's Fourth of July humor piece and
I can't retrieve it. Does Mitch have a hard copy some-
place?"

"He must've backed it up," I said. "Check his computer."

Kip glanced over his shoulder. "Here comes Mitch
now. I'll ask him. Oh, dang—he's being attacked by
Dippy."

My back-shop wizard strode off to the newsroom. I

wondered if I should close my door to prevent the little guy from interrupting the not-so-grand finale of my editorial. But Vida had gotten off the phone and was taking Dippy by the hand to lead him to the stroller. Apparently, they were heading off to drive some other Alpiners to distraction. At least Vida was still smiling.

I finished a draft of my editorial a little after eleven. My writing lacked oomph. Maybe inspiration would strike later. Mitch had re-sent his humor piece to Kip, Vida was still gone, and Leo had talked RestHaven into taking out a larger ad—which Chief of Staff Dr. Charles Woo called a public service announcement. I didn't care if he called it a Bugs Bunny cartoon as long as he signed off on our invoice.

Mitch came into my office to inquire what our lead story would be. "Summer Solstice," I said. "What else? Your events roundup has to go on page one. The annual bash didn't officially end until yesterday with the picnic in Old Mill Park. The locals would riot if we didn't fill up most of the page with their favorite celebration. Besides, we don't have much else in the way of hard news. Unless you want to write about the heat."

"That," Mitch reminded me drolly, "*was* my humor piece."

I felt sheepish. "Sorry. I don't find the prospect of unseasonably hot weather funny. But," I added hastily, "you did a good job with it."

Mitch draped his lanky frame over the back of one of my visitor chairs. "You wouldn't last long in a Detroit summer. I don't miss that part of being in the Motor City, even before it started to deteriorate."

I nodded. "I arrived in Alpine while the town was still suffering from the logging industry's decline. It was very bleak here sixteen years ago, but the opening of the community college helped and now RestHaven has added some jobs, too. Yes, money's still tight when it comes to spending public funds. But SkyCo residents are thrifty by nature."

"That's not all bad," Mitch said. "It keeps government employees from embezzling."

"All thirty of them?" I responded as my phone rang.

Mitch chuckled before heading back to his desk. "Ms. Rawlings is here," Amanda said. "She apologizes for being a few minutes early. Can you see her now?"

"Sure. Send her in." I hurriedly straightened some scattered notes on my desk. When I looked up, I saw a slim, attractive blond woman in a blue- and green-striped summer dress gliding gracefully through the newsroom. Her smile was brittle as she entered my office.

I stood up—not so gracefully, though I hoped with more warmth—and extended my hand. "Hi," I said. "Have a seat."

Her grip was tentative and brief. "You may think I've lost my mind," she murmured, arranging herself in the chair Mitch had been leaning on. "Perhaps I'm on a fool's errand."

I kept smiling. "How is that?"

Her fine features grew solemn. "I should start with my curriculum vitae, Ms. Lord. I hope you don't object."

Her formality was putting me off. "Please—call me Emma. You are . . . Irena?"

She winced. "My first name is spelled *E-i-r-e-n-e*." She pronounced it as "e-RE-nay." "My birth mother named me after the Greek goddess of peace. I prefer Ren. It's less confusing."

"Okay," I said, wondering how long it would take her to get to whatever it was she wanted of me.

Ren cleared her throat. "I'm thirty years old, I live in San Luis Obispo, California, where I'm employed as a public high school art teacher. I've held that position for

THE ALPINE ZEN 9

the past six years. My birth mother, Kassia Arthur, wasn't married to my father. I have no idea if he knows of my existence. They may've parted ways before I was born in Seattle. I should add that I believe one, if not both of them, were hippies. My first name suggests that, along with some poems my birth mother left behind when she abandoned me shortly after the delivery. I was placed in foster care until I was six, when Robert and Helene Rawlings adopted me. They're wonderful people and I consider them my real parents." She paused. "May I have a glass of water?"

"Of course." I started to get up, but felt compelled to stay put. Maybe it was the birdlike nickname that made me think that if I left her alone, she might fly away. "Let me ask our receptionist to get it for you." After relaying the message to Amanda, I asked Ren if my cubbyhole of an office was too warm for her.

She shook her head. "I'm used to it. My real parents moved to San Luis Obispo when I was ten."

Amanda arrived with the water, wordlessly handing it over to Ren, who murmured her gratitude. I waited until my guest had downed almost all of the glass's contents. I didn't want to rush her, but I was getting antsy. "I gather you spent the earlier part of the day in Monroe," I said, hoping to sound casual.

"I arrived last night. As you may know, they have an arts fair in August. During the summer, I sometimes serve as a judge for such events on the West Coast. I've been invited to participate in this year's event." Ren delivered the explanation as if she'd memorized it. Maybe she had.

"We have a small gallery," I said. It was the only pertinent thing that came to mind.

Ren's dark blue eyes showed some life. "You do? I'd like to visit it. Is it close by?"

"Yes, down a block and across the street. I thought

perhaps that's why you came to Alpine." *Hint, hint* . . .
I was starting to squirm in my chair as my office seemed
be growing warmer by the minute.

"No." Ren stared somewhere beyond me. Maybe
she was passing judgment on my Blue Sky Dairy calendar's color photo of Alpine Baldy. "I came to see you
because"—she reached into her straw handbag—"of
this." Ren handed me a sepia-toned photo of a snow-
bound Alpine dated 1915. "It was with my birth mother's poems. Look at the other side. I *think* that's her
handwriting. She wrote her poems in longhand."

I turned the card over, noting the professional imprint
indicating this was a postcard rather than a personal
photo. A scrawled word on the back looked like AUREA.
"Do you know what this means?" I asked.

She shook her head again. "I've researched it, of
course. All I can find is a place in Brazil and an old Italian car. Oh, and a Brazilian female singer. None of that
seems to pertain to my birth mother. But I thought
someone in Alpine might be able to help me."

I felt Ren was overly optimistic. "Unless it's a first
name, I doubt our resident history expert can come up
with anything."

"Who *is* the expert?" Ren asked.

"Vida Runkel, our House & Home editor." I peeked
at my watch. "She's been out for the last hour, so I
doubt she'll be back before one."

I handed the postcard back to her, but she put up a
hand. "No," Ren said. "Please. Keep that. I'll be back
to talk to . . . Ms. Runkel, is it?"

"Yes, but I don't know exactly when—"

"It doesn't matter," Ren interrupted. "I'm not leaving
town. There's nowhere I have to be until August, when
I judge the Monroe art show. Do you have any ads in
your newspaper for short-term rentals?"

"You'll have to ask Ms. Hanson, our receptionist," I

said. "She and our ad manager, Leo Walsh, handle the classifieds. Our next edition doesn't come out until Wednesday."

Ren stood up. "I'll do that now before I visit the art gallery."

"It doesn't open until five," I informed her, also getting to my feet.

"Oh." Ren looked almost stricken, then regained her composure. "I'll explore the rentals then. Be sure to show that postcard to Ms. Runkel as soon as she gets back."

"As I mentioned, I doubt she'll—"

Ren took a step closer. "I told you I was on a fool's errand. A *quest* is more apt. You see, I'm convinced my birth mother was murdered, probably here in Alpine. I intend to stay until I find out who killed her."

Ren pivoted around and left my office in a less graceful—yet much more assertive—manner than she had come.

Chapter Two

"WELL NOW," VIDA said after I'd filled her in about my visitor, "that's a queer kettle of fish. I've never heard of anyone named Kassia Arthur. Are you certain that was her mother's name?"

"Yes," I assured her. "Ren Rawlings *is* a queer sort of woman. She's either a basket case or so caught up in her mission that she's over the top. Frankly, she spoiled my appetite for lunch. But now I'm starving."

Vida looked at the Bulova watch her late husband, Ernest, had given her some forty years ago. "It's after one. You'd better eat something. You won't survive the afternoon without at least a snack."

"You're right," I agreed. "I gather you already had lunch?"

"I did," she replied. "After taking Dippy to Amy and Ted's, I heated the leftover casserole. Poor Amy couldn't chew anything after her long session with Dr. Starr. Dippy and I enjoyed the leftovers together."

Maybe the kid looked so big because his stomach was made of cast iron. "That's . . . nice," I murmured, pretending something had fallen under my desk. I couldn't look Vida in the eye. Unfortunately, I bumped my head on a partially opened drawer. "Oww!" I exclaimed, wincing.

"My, my," Vida said. "Do be careful. Are you sure you're all right?"

"I'm fine, just hungry," I assured her. "I'm going to the Burger Barn now. By the way, did you get your retirement-home copy from Maud Dodd to Kip yet?" It was always wise to remind Vida I was the boss. Many of our readers assumed she was in charge and sometimes even I had to remind myself that was not the case.

"I haven't had time to organize it," she replied. "I'll do that now." She fanned herself with one hand. "My, but it is a bit warm in here. I wonder if Harvey Adcock has any more big fans at the hardware store?"

"Call him," I said, accompanying Vida through the newsroom. "Get two, if he does. The one in my office died this morning."

On that note, I headed out into the sunshine. There were a few clouds hanging listlessly above Alpine Baldy and Mount Sawyer. Neither of the five-thousand-foot peaks had much snow left. Beyond the railroad tracks in back of the *Advocate,* I couldn't see the Skykomish River, but it was running low for this time of year. By the Fourth of July, I probably could wade across it without getting more than my knees wet. Most of the smaller waterfalls along Highway 2 had dried up by mid-May. There hadn't been enough snowpack to feed the little streams above the Stevens Pass corridor. Back in April, we'd been warned of a possible drought come summer. The words echoed in my ears.

After passing the hobby shop and Parker's Pharmacy, I crossed Front Street at the corner of Third. My sunglasses kept sliding down my perspiring nose. I yanked them off as I entered the Burger Barn and collided with a large object that turned out to be my husband.

"Jeez, Emma, take it easy," Milo muttered, grabbing my arm to steady me. "I was going to call you after I got back to the office."

I realized he was holding a Burger Barn bag in the

hand that wasn't still on my arm. "You haven't eaten, either?" I asked.

"No," he replied, looming over me with his thirteen-inch height advantage. "It's your fault I didn't get lunch until now. Come on, let's sit down. At least they've got the ceiling fans going in here."

It was easy to find an empty booth since the noon-hour rush was over. Milo took off his regulation hat, which was no longer the high-crowned style that looked as if Smokey Bear should be wearing it. The sheriff had finally replaced those hats with what I could only describe as an Australian type, more conservative and better-looking. Before I could ask why I had caused him to miss lunch, a freckle-faced waitress whose name tag identified her as Kinsey came to take my order of a hamburger, fries, salad, and a large Pepsi. Milo requested coffee.

"So what egregious thing did I do now?" I inquired as my husband devoured a large chunk of cheeseburger.

He swallowed the mouthful and added salt to his fries before answering. "Some goofball named Ren came to see me when I was about to come over here. She insisted you told her to ask me about her dead mother. It took half an hour to get anything out of her. By then Roy Everson had showed up from the post office with more bones he insisted belonged to his long-missing mama, Myrtle. Is this some holiday for people who can't keep track of their old ladies?"

"I did *not* tell Ren to talk to you. I did not mention your name or your job or . . ." My shoulders slumped. "Damn, I'm sorry you got stuck with her. Worse yet, she's not going away, so I've assigned her to Vida."

"Shit." Milo's expression was wry. "I should've known you wouldn't sic a space case on me." He put the hand that wasn't holding two French fries on mine. "Ren harped on her mother being lured to Alpine by money and then disappearing. Black magic, maybe. Is she crazy or is the weather getting to me?"

"I'm letting Vida determine that," I said. "It'll give her something to do besides mope about Roger's fate. Ren had wanted to visit Donna Wickstrom's art gallery, but I told her it wasn't open until five."

The sheriff's hazel eyes gazed up at the ceiling fan above us. "Maybe Ren—what the hell kind of name is that?—thought our headquarters was an art gallery. She spent a long time studying the Wanted posters."

"Did Ren mention who might've murdered her mother in Alpine?"

Milo waited to answer until after Kinsey delivered my food and his coffee. "No. Only the black magic bit that seemed weird. Ren unloaded that one on me about ten, fifteen minutes into her opening monologue. I'd drifted off by then, reminiscing about the past—like almost a week ago, before it got too damned hot to go fishing or make love to my wife. Why the hell didn't I have AC put in with the rest of the remodeling job on your—*our*—little log cabin?"

"It's not so little anymore," I remarked. "I got lost twice this morning. Again."

"That's because you weren't awake." Milo polished off his burger.

"I assume you don't recall a woman named Kassia Arthur being murdered in SkyCo some thirty years ago?"

Milo looked pained. "As far as I can tell from Ren's long-assed tale, that would've happened in 1975. I'd started as a deputy less than three years before that. There were only two female homicide victims after I joined the department. One was an out-of-work logger who strangled his wife before shooting himself. The other woman was the mother of the Claymore family with the crazy father who offed all six of the kids and

Mom before he put the 22-caliber rifle to his own head and blew himself away." Having eaten his own fries, my husband stole three of mine. "Why don't we check into the ski lodge if it gets as hot as they're predicting? They've got AC."

I glared at him. "Because everybody would know, Vida would put it in her 'Scene Around Town' column, and we'd ruin our hard-earned staid reputation after making lovesick fools of ourselves in public last winter. Got any more dumb ideas, Sheriff?"

He shrugged his broad shoulders. "Guess not. I'd better get back to work since you're being a pain in the ass." He hauled himself out of the booth, but paused to ruffle my hair. "I'll pick up fried chicken at the Grocery Basket on my way home. No point in turning on the stove." He loped away, leaving me with my unpaid bill. That was only fair, I suppose. Washington is a community-property state.

To my surprise, Vida wasn't being pinned to the wall by Ren Rawlings when I returned to the *Advocate*. "No such person has been here," she informed me rather glumly. "Harvey is out of fans, by the way. He expects more by Thursday. Everyone's panicking at the prospect of hotter weather."

"That," I mused, "is a story in itself. Of course, I suppose we have it covered with Mitch's humor piece."

"I can mention in it 'Scene,'" Vida said. "I assume Harvey is taking out a bigger ad than usual this week."

"He should. Talk to Leo about that." I remembered the postcard Ren had left. "Hold on, I've got something to show you."

Apparently Vida's rampant curiosity couldn't be contained. She followed me into my office. I handed her the postcard and explained why I'd suggested to Ren that my House & Home editor should see it.

"The date on the front is 1915," Vida murmured, sitting down in one of my visitor chairs. "Only five years after Carl Clemans began his logging operation here. You'll note that there are very few buildings except for the mill itself."

"Yes," I agreed, "but a lot of snow."

"My, yes," Vida agreed, studying the back of the postcard. "Eight feet on the ground for much of the winter in the town's early years. You can get a sense of that from this photo. No road into Alpine, access only by train. Such hardy people in those days. Aurea . . . what can that mean?"

"That's what I hoped you could tell Ren," I said. "I thought it might be someone's name."

Vida slowly shook her head. "No. No, I've never heard or seen it. The writing looks more recent than the postcard."

"It is, according to Ren. She's certain her mother wrote it."

"Perhaps," Vida allowed. "Is this Ren reliable?"

I made a face. "I thought she was kind of strange. So did Milo. She called on him after leaving here. Ren's a teacher from San Luis Obispo."

"Californians," Vida said in the same tone she would have used for "Satan worshippers" or "Seattle traffic." She stood up, smoothing her black linen skirt. "They have some very peculiar notions. Of course, if Ren wants to talk to me, I'll listen, if only to convince her she's on a wild-goose chase."

"Good luck with that," I said as my phone rang. "I'd better grab the call. It might be news."

It was news of a sort, but not the kind I wanted to hear. "Well? How goes the annulment process?" my brother, Ben, asked in his crackling voice.

I was glad he couldn't see me wince. "Milo is doing his share, but his ex is dawdling. We're supposed to have dinner with Tricia and her new boyfriend, Zach, this coming weekend. If, of course, my husband can get away from all the Fourth of July craziness here."

"How crazy can Alpine get with a bunch of sparklers and some cheap firecrackers? Are the woods so dry that you're all afraid the whole town will go up in smoke?"

"It *has* been a dry year so far," I asserted. "All we've had lately is a little drizzle and it's supposed to get really hot for the long weekend."

"Meaning high seventies? Get real, Sluggly," Ben said, reverting to his childhood nickname for me. "I was sent from El Paso to help out for a couple of weeks near my former turf on the Delta. I'm in Tuscaloosa; the average temperature here in July is over ninety. Why is Tricia or Mulehide or whatever stalling?"

I sighed and put both elbows on my desk. "She insists she doesn't see why Milo needs to get his marriage to her annulled because he's not a Catholic. Tricia isn't stupid, but the Mulehide tag is apt. She's extremely stubborn. She's also balking because an annulment means her three children would become illegitimate."

"Has Milo explained to her that's only in the eyes of the Church? Tricia's not Catholic. Why does she care? Is one of their kids converting?"

I grimaced. "That's another problem. Milo's son, Brandon, is getting married in August to his fiancée, Solange. She's Catholic and the wedding will be at her home parish, Mary, Queen of Peace, over on the East-side in Sammamish. But no, I don't think Bran plans to convert."

Ben chuckled. "Why am I secretly wishing Bran had fallen for a nice Jewish girl? If Tricia's as ornery as Milo says she is, I can see her turning this into an argument against going through with the annulment. She might figure her son would be considered a social outcast if he was illegitimate in the eyes of Mother Church."

"Do you have any real advice for us, Stench?" I asked,

dredging up my old nickname for him. "Or did you call just to needle me?"

"I called to badger you and Dodge to get the annulment process moving," Ben replied earnestly. "Adam and I would like to concelebrate your wedding Mass before I'm too old to stand up at the altar."

"You're far from that," I snapped.

It was Ben's turn to sigh at the other end. "Here's what bothers me—that Milo, not being a churchgoing kind of guy, will get tired of wrangling with his ex and decide it's not worth the hassle. Have you impressed on him how important this is to you?"

"I've tried," I said a bit lamely.

"Try harder. Knowing you, I'd put down money that you've been half-assed about it. Level with him. The poor sap is so nuts about you—though I don't know why—that he'll cave and kick Mulehide's butt."

"Gee, just what I wanted. Deep and thoughtful spiritual advice."

"If you want that, talk to your pastor. Dennis Kelly is damned good at that stuff. I'm not." Ben paused and I could hear voices in the background. "Got to go. Somebody needs bail money. Peace, Sluggly." My brother rang off.

As usual, my irritation with Ben didn't last. He was right, but it wasn't easy to explain to Milo why my religion mattered so much to me. He'd been raised Congregationalist, but hadn't attended church services since he was a teenager. His religion was fishing, a spiritual exercise of a different sort. I understood and so did Ben. Our dad had been an ardent fisherman. But my brother was a priest and had to play by the rules.

"You," Vida said with a frown, "look very pensive. Are you concerned that this Ren person might cause trouble?"

I laughed. "No. I was talking to Ben. He was playing

big brother." Not wanting to fall into a trap that would give Vida a chance to offer a sermon of her own on why the Presbyterian faith was superior to all others, I changed the subject. "Roy Everson has found more bones."

Vida looked disgusted. "I know. My nephew Billy told me." She put both hands on my desk and lowered her voice. "Has Milo mentioned anything lately about Billy and Tanya?"

Back in February, when Milo's elder daughter had been recovering from being shot by her fiancé before he killed himself, Tanya Dodge had sought sanctuary with her father at his house in the Icicle Creek Development. Milo had put the property up for sale, but the market was slow. Meanwhile, Tanya had started dating Deputy Bill Blatt, one of Vida's numerous nephews. In late April, Bill moved out of his widowed mother's home to live with Tanya in Milo's house. As Vida posed the question, I realized my husband hadn't mentioned his daughter and his deputy in the last week or so.

"No," I admitted. "Do you think there's a rift?"

Vida straightened up, her impressive bosom straining at the green and purple polka-dot blouse. "I think my sister-in-law Lila laid down the law about her son living with a woman who is not his wife or, at the very least, his fiancée. I suspect Billy's back home now. Lila is extremely narrow-minded—and inflexible."

In Vida's opinion, most of her in-laws were badly flawed. I knew Lila only by sight, so I withheld comment. "I'll ask Milo," I said.

Vida frowned. "I'd ask Billy, but he's sensitive about personal matters, especially after he broke off with the divorcée who had a child. I was relieved, but Tanya's emotional problems are troubling."

"She's improving," I reminded Vida. "I credit Bill for some of that."

"Well . . ." Vida fingered her chin. "Billy does have more sense than some of the Blatts. I have no idea how that happened." She turned on her sensible heel and exited my office.

I was still smiling, even if Vida wasn't. When Holly Gross, the town tart and Dippy's mother, had been released from jail on bond in April after shooting a drug kingpin, Vida feared a custody battle. Worse yet, she blamed Milo and Prosecutor Rosemary Bourgette for not making a tighter case against Holly in the dealer's shooting death. During a tussle over the gun inside the trailer, the dealer had been killed. Vida had refused to speak to Milo or Rosemary for over two months. She had also given Judge Diane Proxmire the deep freeze. But in April, fate had intervened, allowing Vida to drop her sanctions against the sheriff, the prosecutor, and the judge.

By three o'clock, I'd gotten a grip on my editorial. It didn't exactly hum, but it was what I called positive as opposed to . . . soporific. I hoped. I'd given SkyCo citizens an advance pat on the back for rallying behind Fuzzy's reorganization plan. They might believe they'd actually done something and react with a show of enthusiasm.

Five minutes after I zapped the editorial to Kip, Edna Mae Dalrymple called me. As she often is, the town's head librarian was a-twitter. "My goodness, Emma," she began, "I'm a bit overwhelmed by this young woman you sent to see me. She's requesting copies of all sorts of information, including the area weeklies and dailies going back to over thirty years ago. She seems rather distraught. I'm afraid she'll be here all night!"

I winced. "First," I said, hoping to convey sympathy, "I didn't advise Ren Rawlings to go to the library. I didn't even tell her we *have* a library. She's interested in visiting the art gallery, so she'll probably leave by five. If she doesn't, close down at seven as usual. She has to eat."

"True," she murmured. "I hate being ungracious with our patrons."

"She's from Southern California," I pointed out, hoping that Edna Mae's typical Alpine chauvinism was in play. "She'll get over it."

"Yes, that makes a difference. Not living here, I mean. Thank you, Emma. Don't forget, bridge club is tomorrow night."

"It's also our deadline," I said. "I told you to get a sub for me."

"I did," she replied. "I'd already gotten substitutes for the Dithers Sisters. One of their horses is lame. Then Rosemary Bourgette begged off." Edna Mae lowered her voice. "She has a date. With a man."

"Good for her," I said, and meant it. "Is he local?"

"Not exactly," Edna Mae whispered. "He's a writer and has rented a place at Baring. Oh dear—here comes Ms. Rawlings. I must dash."

I was left hanging, in more ways than one. If we had no late-breaking news, I *could* play bridge Tuesday. I'd done it before, though I preferred not taking chances. I trusted Kip implicitly, but the buck stops with me as editor and publisher. I began performing my editing duties by going over Mitch's lead story about Summer Solstice.

The rest of the afternoon passed without any more reports of Ren Rawlings showing up at places where I hadn't sent her. Vida expressed mild dismay at not having had an opportunity to meet the visitor. I told her it was just as well. Naturally, she didn't believe me.

By five, my office had grown unbearably close. I grabbed my handbag and started through the empty newsroom. My phone rang before I could get to the front office. Amanda was still there, so she answered it for me.

"Yes," I heard her say. "Could you please hold?" Putting her hand over the receiver's mouthpiece, Amanda asked if I'd take the call.

"Who is it?" I inquired.

"She's asking for Kassia Arthur."

I took the phone and heard a disconnect click at the other end.

Chapter Three

"WEIRD," I SAID, handing the phone back to Amanda. "You're sure she told you she wanted Kassia Arthur?"

Amanda looked at me if she thought *I* might be a little odd. "I think so, unless I misheard. I don't know anybody by that name, so it stuck. Is something wrong?"

I explained about our morning visitor. "Maybe," I allowed, "I'm overreacting to Ms. Rawlings, but she struck me as not quite right from the start. What was your impression?"

Amanda's pretty face grew thoughtful, one hand caressing the big baby bump. "It's hard for me to say. She's nice-looking—and slim. All I can think of about now is if I'll ever look that way again. She did seem kind of on edge."

"Did whoever called just now sound like the same woman?"

"Well . . . honestly, Emma, it's hard for me to say. You know how people don't always sound the same in person as they do on the phone."

I knew that was true. Then there was my husband, who, back when I first met him, was so quiet over the phone that sometimes I could hardly hear him. In more recent years, half the time he didn't need to dial my number. I swore I could hear him from almost two blocks away.

"That's fine," I said. "Go home to Walt. Is he barbecuing tonight?"

"I hope so," Amanda replied. "Unless he gets stuck working late at the fish hatchery."

We walked out together, she to her aging red Miata and me to my equally old Honda. I did glance across Front Street to Donna's art gallery, which was open. It occurred to me that I should pay her a call to see if she had any new work by our reclusive artist, Craig Laurentis. She'd received a new painting from him in the spring, but he was experimenting with a different style. It was more stark, almost harsh, and didn't speak to me in the way *Sky Autumn* did. I never tired of looking at the painting, which hung above my sofa. The river seemed to move, tumbling over the boulders and under the vine maple branches.

Milo arrived home fifteen minutes after I did. "They ran out of fried chicken at the Grocery Basket," he grumbled, setting a big bag on the new marble-topped counter. "Jake O'Toole gave me a free side of coleslaw to make up for the long wait."

"Good. Then I don't have to make anything," I said, waiting for my husband to kiss me hello. "Well?"

"Well what?" He removed his hat. "What about spuds?"

"Spuds?" I yipped. "Are you insane? Why didn't you pick up some of the deli's French fries?"

My husband looked genuinely puzzled. Or baffled, given that he's the sheriff. "You can't make them in that little fry cooker?"

"No! You're lucky I don't pull that cast-iron pot over your head. Just thinking about hot grease makes me want to tear my hair."

He snatched up his hat. "I'll go back to the Grocery Basket." Milo slammed the door to the garage behind him.

I immediately felt ashamed of myself. He looked as hot and tired as I felt, having worked an even longer day than I had. I made us each a drink, then leaned against the counter and surveyed my beautiful new kitchen that my husband had paid for. All of the wonderful, amazing remodeling of my once-little log cabin had come out of his pocket. He had refused to let me spend a dime on any of it. If, he'd stated, it was to be our home, instead of just mine, he had to put his money into the project. I was close to tears when he showed up a few minutes later.

As soon as he stepped onto the new dark Pergo flooring, I threw myself against him. He almost dropped the fries.

"Hey," he said, putting his free arm around me. "What's wrong?"

"I'm a beast," I mumbled against his chest. "I hate me."

"I don't hate you," Milo said, managing to set the fries on the counter next to the chicken. "What set you off?"

"Nothing." I looked up at him. "Except the weather. I made drinks."

He tossed his hat on top of the new built-in stainless-steel dishwasher. "You're an ornery little twerp, but I knew that all along." He put both arms around me, the familiar spark in his hazel eyes. "After all those years of waiting for you to come around, there were no surprises. I know what we can do to put us both in a better mood. Tonight after dark, let's go out in the backyard under the evergreen trees and roll around on the new grass Mountain View Gardens put in."

I smiled up at him. "And I used to think you had no imagination."

"Maybe I don't." Milo kissed the top of my head before letting me go. "It took almost a week before I got the idea." He retrieved his hat. "I'll change. You can stop hating yourself by putting more ice in my Scotch. What was in there melted."

Luckily, the sheriff couldn't see me curl my lip. When he emerged from the bedroom, I was seated on the newly upholstered sofa. I loved the brown, white, and green tones that echoed the colors in Craig's painting. I had *not* loved the frayed, stained, and faded sofa I'd bought twenty years ago when I worked for *The Oregonian* in Portland. The rocker I'd bought after Adam was born was also long gone. Milo had seemed to like it— right up until it collapsed underneath him. That was when I realized he'd gained several pounds since we first met.

My husband lowered himself into the easy chair, which hadn't been revamped. I'd bought that item while Milo and I had been going together the first time around. He'd never looked comfortable in the smaller armchair that now sat across the hearth.

"Roy's back at it," he said after lighting a cigarette. "I admit the bones one of the Overholts dug up looked bigger than a bird or a marmot. But it's a *farm*. They've raised every kind of animal except giraffes. The Overholt family has owned that land for sixty years."

"Will you send the bones to the lab in Everett?"

"No," Milo replied. "But I'll keep them until there's a better reason for pestering SnoCo. If Fuzzy gets support to reorganize the county, I might have more funding. You sure you don't want a cigarette?"

I shook my head. "I've gone almost three weeks without smoking."

Milo grinned. "What is this? Your nineteenth attempt to quit?"

"Just about," I admitted. "You're a terrible influence."

"You know I've cut down. Tanya's nagging has had some effect."

"Speaking of Tanya, I hear Bill moved out of your house and went back home to Mother. Is this a sign that the romance is rocky?"

Milo made a face. "I'm not sure. I didn't find out he'd moved out until yesterday when Bill was on duty with me at the Summer Solstice events. You know I avoid getting involved in my staff's private lives."

I was skeptical. "Even when it involves your daughter?"

"Especially when it—" He stopped when the phone on the side table rang. I picked it up and answered.

"I hate to bother you," Donna Erlandson Wickstrom said in an anxious voice, "but the young woman you sent to visit the gallery just passed out. I thought you should know. I called for the medics."

"Good grief!" I exclaimed, causing Milo to stare at me. "Is Ren coming to?"

"Sort of," Donna replied. "I hear the sirens. I'll keep you posted."

I could hear them, too, though they were faint from my vantage point some ten blocks away.

"The nut job took a dive?" Milo asked after downing a big sip of Scotch. "Who was that?"

"Donna. I did tell Ren to go to the gallery," I said, fondling my glass of bourbon. "Now I wish I hadn't."

"Maybe Ren does drugs," Milo suggested. "Where's she staying?"

"I don't know. She intended to find a place for a long-term visit."

My husband ran a hand through his graying sandy hair. "Jesus. She *is* obsessed. Too bad Roy's married. They'd make a good pair."

I only half heard what the sheriff was saying. "I haven't mentioned the strange call I got before I left work," I said, and told him about the person asking for Kassia Arthur and hanging up.

Milo looked mildly interested. "Probably your nut job calling. I wouldn't get into a tizzy over it if I were you."

"I suppose, but," I went on, "I feel responsible for her in some weird way. I wonder if they'll take her to the hospital."

"Gosh, little Emma," he said in mock dismay, "you never told me about your medical degree. Let's eat." Milo put out his cigarette and rose from the easy chair, his almost-empty glass in hand.

"I hate you," I declared, following him into the kitchen.

"Make up your mind. Which one of us do you hate most?" Milo sat down at our new kitchen table.

"That's it!" I yelled. "I'm calling Donna. You can heat up dinner in the microwave by yourself." I stormed off to the living room.

Donna answered on the third ring. "The medics are still here," she said quietly. "Ms. Rawlings is conscious, but seems disoriented."

I almost asked how she could tell. Before I could say anything, Donna spoke again. "Del Amundson says they'll take her to the hospital. I feel I should go along, but I don't like closing the gallery. Clea Bhuj is here from the college with her husband, Allan."

"Stay put," I said. "I'll go. Part of the problem may be that Ren's been so busy she hasn't eaten. I'll let you know when I get back home."

I grabbed my handbag and dashed out through the kitchen. "I have to go to work," I announced over my shoulder. "Enjoy your dinner."

"Hold it!" my husband bellowed, bolting out of the chair. "Where are you going?" He loomed over me, his hazel eyes sparking with anger.

"To the hospital," I retorted. "That's where Ren's headed. It may be a story. Stop being a jackass."

To my surprise, Milo spoke in a normal tone. "Sit

down. Relax. You know how an ER run goes. You won't learn a damned thing for half an hour. Do you really want to sit around and have one of those snotty nurses badger you?"

"I . . ."

The sheriff hooked his arm around my neck, pulled me closer, and kissed me. It was a long and a very hard kiss. When he finally let go, I staggered slightly.

"Why," I gasped, "didn't you . . . do that . . . when you . . . got home?"

"Because I'm a jackass." He took my hand. "Sit down. I heated the food. After we eat we'll both go to the hospital. Maybe I can arrest Ren for creating a disturbance—with us." He led me to the table.

Milo drove us in the Yukon, pulling into a reserved space for doctors in the underground garage. He and KSKY's Spencer Fleetwood were the only two people I knew who had that privilege. Maybe I should have asked—there were three slots and only two doctors in Alpine.

We found Doc Dewey in the ER hallway. He looked weary, and seemed surprised to see us. "If you're here to arrest me," he said to Milo, "make it quick or I'll pass out before you can put me in a cell. Elvis Sung and I've been on duty since four o'clock this morning."

"Jeez, Gerry," Milo said, "is it hot enough for heatstroke?"

Doc shook his balding head. "No, but some damned fools think they're suffering from it. Some will, if it gets to ninety. Now it's mostly accidents, like kids setting off fireworks. Your deputies must be busy."

"Right," Milo agreed. "We're here to check on Emma's new best friend, Ms. Rawlings. Got a diagnosis?"

Doc shrugged. "I'm not sure. I have to wait for the

blood tests to come back." He turned to me. "You know this young woman?"

"She came to see me this morning," I replied, adding the reason for her Alpine visit and summing up where else she'd gone. "My real concern," I concluded, "is that I doubt she stopped all day to eat. She asked for water while she was in my office."

"That could cause it," Doc said. "We can tell that from the tests." Something beeped. Doc reached for his cell, frowning as he listened to the caller. "Got to go. Maybe you should, too, Emma. Amanda Hanson's in labor. You'll have to rustle up a sub." Doc plodded back down the hall.

"Oh, great!" I wailed. "I wonder if Alison Lindahl's in town."

"According to Lori, she wasn't over the weekend," Milo said.

Lori Cobb was Milo's receptionist and Alison's roommate. "I'll try her cell when we get home." I looked up at my husband. "Why did we come to the hospital in the first place?"

"Because you're a pain in the ass," Milo responded, putting his arm around me. "Let's go home and try out that new grass. Nobody can see us with all the big trees. Afterwards we can hose each other down."

I winced. "Sounds like . . . fun?"

Milo shrugged. "Making our own heat sure as hell beats sitting on our dead butts and griping."

I agreed.

Shortly before nine, I'd already reached Alison, who was still with her parents in Everett, but willing to show up for work in the morning. There hadn't been any calls while Milo and I had been rolling around in our backyard. I dialed the hospital, asking for the maternity ward. Amanda was still in labor. Doc Dewey had gone home, but Elvis Sung was on call. After being transferred to the patient floor, my old nemesis, Ruth Sharp, answered.

"Ms. Rawlings is in a room," Ruth said primly. "Are you family?"

Ruth knew damned well I wasn't a relative. "No," I replied, "but she seemed unwell when she visited me earlier today."

"I can't divulge any information," she asserted, sounding smug. "Excuse me. I must make rounds." She rang off.

Milo looked up from the *ESPN* magazine he'd been reading. "You got dissed by a nurse who isn't your pal Julie Canby?"

I nodded. "Worse yet, it was the vile Ruth Sharp."

My husband got out his cell and tapped in a number. Apparently, Ruth hadn't yet gone on her rounds because she picked up on the first ring. "Sheriff Dodge here," Milo said in the tone he reserved for wife beaters. "Give me an update on Rawlings before I call Doc Dewey and tell him you won't cooperate with the law."

I smiled as I watched Milo listen to whatever Ruth was telling him. He, however, was impassive, still in his role as sheriff. "Got it," he finally said. "The next time *Mrs. Dodge* calls, cooperate with her. You got that?" He paused. "Good." He clicked off.

"Well?" I said.

Milo lighted a cigarette. "Want to sit on my lap while I tell you?"

"No," I replied. "You're smoking and I don't want to get close to you. Open up, big guy. And by the way, when I'm working, I'm still Ms. Lord."

"You weren't working at the hospital," Milo shot back. "There was no story." He frowned. "I wonder if I should call Doc."

"Why?" Taking in my husband's thoughtful expression, I grew suspicious. "Give, Sheriff, or I *will* take that cigarette from you."

"Hell," he said, "maybe it doesn't mean anything. Prune Face, or whatever you call that old bat, read off Doc's preliminary findings, which stated the patient was suffering from dehydration, malnourishment, low blood sugar, and nutty as a fruitcake."

"You made up the part about the fruitcake."

Milo acknowledged the comment with a brief nod. "It's the preliminary part I wonder about. Gerry usually goes by the first results. He only digs deeper if he suspects a more serious problem."

"Such as what? Drugs?"

"No. They'd show up right away."

"If Doc's gone home, he won't get the final results until tomorrow."

"Right." Milo put out his cigarette and stood up, rubbing the back of his head. "There's something wrong about all of this." He leaned an elbow on the fireplace mantel. "Maybe I should run a background check on the mother to see if she's really dead."

"Do you want to use my laptop instead of going all the way out to your workshop?" I asked, hoping to sound innocent.

"Nice try," my husband drawled. "You won't sit on my lap, so I won't use your laptop. You'd look over my shoulder." He wheeled around, heading through the kitchen to the new door that led to his man cave.

I'd fix him. I'd use *my* laptop. But it needed recharging. I was still cussing to myself when Milo reappeared, looking bemused.

"I couldn't find any record of Kassia Arthur, dead or alive. What do you make of that, my cute little investigative reporter?"

Chapter Four

Amanda Hanson had given birth to a baby girl shortly after midnight. Vida, of course, found out before I did. Her niece, Marje Blatt, works at the medical clinic and, like her brother, Deputy Bill, is bound to report to Vida immediately, under pain of mortal peril.

"Six pounds, six ounces," Vida announced, standing by her desk like the town crier. "I hope Dr. Sung doesn't send her home this afternoon. All this modern twaddle about new mothers being discharged so soon after giving birth is absurd. Old Doc Dewey must be rolling in his grave. But Young Doc is often prone to peculiar modern notions."

"Do they have a name for the baby?" Alison Lindahl asked.

"Not yet," Vida replied. "It can't be as atrocious as the last two newborns I wrote up—Athens and Nirvana. Really now!" She tromped over to the pastry tray and snatched up a bear claw. "Bear," she said under her breath. "That's what my Gustavson relatives named their baby boy after debating for two weeks. What next? Ocelot? Platypus?"

I headed into my office. Vida was, as she would put it, on the peck this morning. Deadline day wasn't off to a good start. Alison followed me, barely able to suppress a giggle fit.

"Mrs. Runkel's hat," she whispered, catching her breath. "Did she lose a bet or is it really made of sponges?"

"I haven't seen that one in years," I replied, making sure Vida was out of hearing range. "One of her granddaughters in Bellingham made it for her in a crafts class. If you look while she's sitting down you'll see it has no crown. In warm weather, it's probably cool. The sponges are thin."

Alison grew serious. "She seems . . . different from when I worked here last December. Is that because of what happened to Roger?"

I nodded. "She's taken his disgrace hard. She never mentions him." I noticed Vida was heading in our direction, but veered off past Mitch's desk to the back shop. She hadn't even glanced at Alison and me. That spoke volumes. Vida's sharp gray eyes usually darted every which way, including, it seemed, behind her.

My phone rang, so Alison left to assume her front-office duties. I heard Milo's voice in my ear.

"Roy Everson was waiting for me when I got here this morning," he said in a beleaguered tone. "If we don't have any crises, I'll send Dwight Gould and Jack Mullins to the dump site before it gets hot. If nothing else, it'll disprove your wacky theory about Myrtle being buried there next to the Everson property. It might even get Roy off my back until some moron digs up a turkey drumstick."

"Maybe I'll send Mitch to get a picture," I said.

"Of what? Mullins's ass while he's digging through a bunch of garbage? Forget it."

"It'll show how diligent and sensitive the sheriff's employees are," I said in a bright voice. "When will they go out there?"

"I don't know. Why does it matter?"

"Because," I said for what felt like the hundredth time since I'd met Milo Dodge, "today is our deadline."

"It is? Hunh. You'd think I'd remember that by now."
He actually sounded sincere.

"Guess what? For once, *I'm* hanging up on *you*." I
banged the phone down.

The good news was that by eleven o'clock, most of the
copy was in to the back shop. The bad news was that if
it hadn't been for the Summer Solstice festivities, the
front page would've been deadly dull. Not that the past
few issues had contained earthshaking news, but the
previous edition featured a five-inch, four-column photo
of an overturned eighteen-wheeler that had jackknifed
on a hairpin curve two miles east of Alpine. Miracu-
lously, the driver had escaped with only minor cuts and
bruises. Mitch had written the upbeat copy that went
next to a photo of the sheepish Wenatchee man who'd
been heading home.

I was coming back into the empty newsroom ten minutes later when I heard an all-too-familiar voice call my
name. "Hi, Ed," I greeted my former ad manager, who'd
done almost nothing in the early years of my tenure and
nearly put the *Advocate* out of business.

"Hot enough for you?" Ed asked, never one for an
original turn of phrase. Apparently the relatively pleasant morning was too hot for him. He was stuffed into
plaid Bermuda shorts and a sleeveless T-shirt embla-
zoned with the words *Remember de Bronska*. The allu-
sion was to the so-called villa Ed had built with a large
inheritance from an aunt in Iowa. He'd managed to frit-
ter it all away in a few short years before finally selling
the property to the rehab facility now known as Rest-
Haven. The T-shirt had been made for the booth Ed
had set up in Old Mill Park to sell souvenirs from his
villa during the Summer Solstice celebration.

"It's not supposed to get really hot until the end of the
week," I said, perching on the edge of Leo's desk. I had

no intention of getting stuck in my office without an escape route.

"Right, right," Ed murmured, staring disconsolately at the now-empty pastry tray on the other side of the newsroom. "Say, Emma, you got some room on the front page?"

Of course I did—or could, but not for Ed. There wasn't room for Ed in a lot of places, given his girth. Before the advent of cell phones, I'd always wondered how he dealt with a phone booth. Or the rides at Disneyland, where the Bronskys had made their first splurge after his aunt's money landed at the Bank of Alpine.

"We're pretty tight," I said. "Summer Solstice, you know."

Ed winked and pointed a chunky finger at me. "You got it! A tie-in."

"What," I inquired, trying not to sound leery, "do you mean?"

"Well," Ed began, looking as if he'd like to sit down, "I didn't sell as many souvenirs as I hoped over the weekend. And we didn't have very good luck with the Mr. Pig float this year."

"Yes," I agreed, "having your float break down at the start of Saturday's parade was a blow."

"It sure was," Ed mumbled. "Everybody missed the spectacle."

"A real shame," I noted. Except there had been some entertainment involved in the fiasco. Two of the float's real pigs from the Overholt farm had run away. They hadn't been found until the next morning, eating out of overturned garbage cans not far from the site of Ed's souvenir stand. But the only spectacle was when someone threw a firecracker into the float's cardboard silo and it blew up all over the hood of Mayor Baugh's aging Cadillac. "I'm glad you weren't badly hurt when you fell off the float, Ed."

"I'm tough. Just got kind of bounced around," he said.

"Bounced" was an apt word for Ed. Before I could say anything, he continued on a brighter note: "I did sell four copies of my autobiography, *Mr. Ed.* They were all tourists, so they had no idea about my life and times in the limelight, especially the Japanese TV cartoon version, *Mr. Pig.* Too bad nobody over here ever got to see it. So how about it? If you need art, I can whip up something by deadline."

I felt I'd missed a beat. "What did you have in mind?" I asked.

"More description of Casa de Bronska's souvenirs. You know most people here have no idea about different kinds of antique furniture. Take my racuckoo escreetor, for example. How many folks in Alpine—"

"Your what?" I couldn't help it. Usually I can translate Ed's mangling of foreign words, but this time I was stumped.

"You know," he said, scowling. "My personal writing desk. Or maybe you never saw it in my private study."

"You mean . . ." I still wasn't sure what Ed meant, but I took a wild stab. "A rococo escritoire?"

Ed nodded, the scowl still in place. "Isn't that what I said?"

Luckily, I didn't have to answer. Alison stood in the newsroom doorway, telling me the sheriff was calling. Even Ed could take that hint, though he sighed—heavily. "Guess I'll have to wait," he mumbled, waddling off. "You might have more room next week after . . ."

I couldn't hear the rest of what he said from the safety net that was my office. "News?" I asked my husband in an overly eager voice.

"Not exactly," Milo said. "Mullins and Gould are going to the dump site after lunch. If you want a picture, tell Laskey. What I want—besides you—is a big

T-bone tonight. I'll barbecue it, but you buy it. Get those baked potatoes to zap in the microwave, but no topping glop on mine. I made two grocery runs last night." Not surprisingly, *he* hung up on *me*.

Five minutes later, Vida showed up. She looked remarkably cheerful. My evil self wanted to ask if Roger had been let out on bond.

"It's official," she declared, beaming at me in her toothsome manner. "Bobby Lambrecht is the Bank of Alpine's new president."

I could practically hear a blare of trumpets. Vida's longtime friend, Faith, was the mother of Bob Lambrecht, and the widow of a minister who'd served for several years at First Presbyterian Church. Bob had been born and raised in Alpine. He'd gone to high school with Milo, but later had moved on and up in the banking world.

"Can we announce his new post?" I asked.

Vida nodded, the sponges bobbing above her silver-rimmed glasses. "Yes, it's official as of July first, but Bobby and Miriam won't arrive until after the holiday. However, I understand they're ready to put money down on a condo in Parc Pines. They're considering the purchase of a house, but even if they eventually move into a house, they'll keep the condo for the children's visits. I must call Faith. I do hope she goes ahead with her plans to move here from Spokane. So hot there in summer, so cold in winter."

And not the least like Alpine, I thought. But then heaven would probably disappoint Vida. "How did you hear the news?"

"Andy Cederberg," she replied. "He'll stay on. Frankly, he's relieved. His wife, Reba, told me Andy's lost twenty pounds since he took on the job of running the bank. He never wanted the responsibility after Marv Petersen retired."

"What about Rick Erlandson? Is he still in as second in command?"

"Oh, yes. No one will be let go," Vida asserted. "Goodness, I wouldn't want Ginny's husband to lose his job with three children to support. She might want to come back as our receptionist. Ginny can be rather gloomy. If anything, the bank's been shorthanded. Alpine has grown in recent years with the college and RestHaven." She frowned. "I do hope we don't get overcrowded. Look at the mess Seattle and its suburbs are in. Why, my daughters in Bellingham and Tacoma can't believe the changes where they live. The freeways are impossible."

"I doubt SkyCo will burst its seams," I said dryly. "We're still holding at a little over seven thousand."

Vida wasn't reassured. "It's creeping up on us. Growth, I mean. Look at Monroe. Every time you turn around, they've added two hundred people. My, my!" She adjusted her glasses. "I must call Faith."

I decided I should ask Andy for an official statement even if I had to make up one for him. The acting president was just fine when it came to banking, but he wasn't the most articulate guy in town. On the other hand, I could never balance my checkbook.

After calling Andy and putting words in his mouth, I took the brief article to Kip. We could get a picture of Bob from the Bank of Washington in Seattle for next week's edition. Mitch returned from wherever he'd been, so I told him about the dump site photo op. I also had to reiterate what Milo called my wacky theory about Myrtle Everson's body being buried there. In nineteen years of searching, no sign of her had ever turned up after she'd gone berry picking. The Eversons' futile search had gone on since then, with every bone they found handed over to the sheriff for DNA.

By noon, Vida was still on the phone, presumably

chatting with Faith Lambrecht. I was hungry, especially for a turkey sandwich. Milo should never have mentioned the word "drumstick." Maybe I'd walk to Pie-in-the-Sky at the mall. My office hadn't yet become a sauna, so I hoped the outdoor temperature was still benign.

I was right. There was a slight breeze ruffling the nasturtiums and ageratum in Mayor Baugh's concrete planter boxes along Front Street. The odor of gasoline hung on the air from a Blackwell Timber truck that had passed me as I exited the *Advocate*. A train whistled in the distance, and by the time I was passing the sheriff's office, I could hear the warning bells signaling for traffic to stop at the crossings between River Road and Railroad Avenue. I was almost to the corner of Second when Milo yelled my name. I turned around and saw him heading toward me.

"Where are you going?" he asked. I told him. He glowered at me. "You'd let your husband starve?"

"I assumed you were having your usual grease fest at the Burger Barn," I said. "Why aren't you?"

"I'm sitting out front for Mullins," Milo replied. "Jack wanted to eat before he started digging up the dump site. Get me corned beef on rye, butter, mayo, mustard, lettuce, potato salad, two bags of chips, and a slice of . . ." He paused. "Banana cream pie. Oh—two dill pickles."

"You expect Little Emma to carry all that without a wheelbarrow?"

"You can get one at Harvey's Hardware," he said with a straight face. "I wouldn't mind some of Pie-in-the-Sky's good coffee."

"As opposed to the paint thinner you drink at headquarters? Give me a break, Dodge. I don't have enough money to cover all this."

He let out a big sigh as he reached for his wallet. "For a kept woman, you sure are broke most of the time."

"I'm not a kept woman," I declared. "I'm your wife."

He handed me two twenties. "You're right. But unlike the first wife I had, I'm keeping you. You're too damned cute to send back."

I looked up at him. "Someday I'll stay mad at you for . . . hours."

"I'll wait." He started to turn around, but stopped. "If they don't have banana cream, get boysenberry."

I growled low in my throat and headed for the mall.

The line was long, and to my dismay, Vida's despised sister-in-law, Mary Lou Hinshaw Blatt, was in front of me. She, too, is a big woman, and just as opinionated. Also like Vida, she seems to have eyes in the back of her head.

"Hello, Emma," she said, turning to stare down at me. "I drove by your house the other day. You certainly put a lot of work and *money* into the remodel. The newspaper must be raking it in."

I felt the two twenties in my wallet might catch on fire. "Milo paid for all of it," I said in sort of a squeak.

"Oh?" Mary Lou sidled up a place in the line. "I heard the sheriff was letting his daughter stay at his house in the Icicle Creek Development with my nephew Bill. I'm glad Lila put an end to that. It's reassuring to know one member of the Blatt family has good sense."

The barb at Vida rankled, but I held my tongue. Luckily the line split in two as a second person showed up behind the counter. Mary Lou barged in front of a hapless dark-haired girl who looked like a college student. I stayed put. Ten minutes later, I entered the sheriff's headquarters where my husband was still working the front desk.

"Where'd everybody go?" I asked, glancing at receptionist Lori Cobb's empty chair.

"Lori's grandma had a stroke this morning," Milo said. "The old girl's at least ninety. Maybe she misses her husband. He's been dead for six months."

I began unloading the box with the bold brown PITS logo, an unfortunate acronym for an eatery. "I thought she was dating."

"They broke up. Lori's grandma said the guy cheated on her—at Bingo." Milo grabbed the corned beef sandwich. "Jack's at lunch, Dwight's on patrol, Doe Jamison and Sam Heppner are breaking up a fracas at Rest-Haven. Where are my pickles?"

"Your . . . *what* fracas?"

Milo didn't answer until he'd swallowed a big bite of sandwich. "The drug and booze rehab unit chief, Iain Farrell, called a few minutes ago. A couple of patients got into it. It's not the first time."

I glared at the sheriff. "It's not? You've never informed *the press* about any such incidents."

Milo found his damned pickles. "The set-tos were in the log."

I was puzzled. "Then why didn't I notice? I always go over what Mitch takes down every day."

"Let me check something." Milo popped a couple of potato chips into his mouth and went to flip through the log on the counter. "I'll be damned," he muttered. "You know we list only addresses with domestic disturbances that don't require a citation or an arrest. Those Rest-Haven bastards changed their address from River Road to Bonneville Way. They must be using the medical rehab center as the address instead of the main entrance. If the change is official, I wonder how much mail Marlowe Whipp has lost for them."

"Not much more than he usually drops," I murmured. "I've never liked Farrell, but Woo seems like a good guy. I've only met him twice."

"Right." He shrugged and sat back down. "Maybe

some of the nuts were getting loose and going through the mail in the lobby. They tend to give their patients some freedom, as long as the doors are locked."

My mind flew back to February when a psych ward patient had escaped and died of a heart attack before he could be found. I glanced at my watch. It was five after one. "I should head for the office. Are you still stuck here in the front?"

"I am until Doe and Sam get back. Want to sit on my lap?"

"Are you insane?" I shot back, gathering up what was left of my sandwich and bag of chips. I'd already finished the Pepsi and dumped the can in the recycling bin. "We're a staid married couple now. Don't ruin our image." I stood up. "By the way, does Tanya like working at the Icicle Creek Ranger Station?"

"So far," Milo replied, also getting to his feet. "It's only been a little over a week." He moved closer and cupped my chin with the hand that wasn't holding the pickle he'd finally found. Just as he leaned down to kiss me, Jack came through one of the double doors.

"Oops! Sorry, boss, didn't know you were . . ."

Milo's hand fell away from my chin and he almost dropped the pickle. "Damnit, Mullins, why aren't you at the dump site?"

"I thought I'd check in to tell you I was on my way," Jack said. "I have to get my cruiser to meet Dwight out there because . . ."

I left them to the rest of their exchange. I could've sworn that Jack's twinkling eyes gave him away. He'd probably seen us through the glass in the door. Mullins might be the flakiest of the deputies, but he was probably the smartest and had a puckish sense of humor.

As soon as I got back to work I called the hospital to ask if Amanda was still there. She was, and answered on the first ring. "Oh, Emma," she said, after I offered congratulations, "she is the sweetest thing! Walt just left for the fish hatchery, but we had her in the room for over an hour."

"Are you going home today?" I inquired. Vida would want to know—if she hadn't already been informed by one of her numerous sources.

"No, not until tomorrow," Amanda replied. "I didn't get settled into bed until almost two last night. But she's worth it."

I was smiling into the phone. "Have you picked out a name?"

"Yes." Amanda paused. "Emma."

"What?" I said. "I'm still here."

She burst out laughing. "That's her name, after you. If you hadn't helped me get my head straight last fall, she wouldn't exist."

"Oh, Amanda!" I was stunned. "I almost fired you!"

"That was part of it," Amanda said seriously. "I admired you for raising a son on your own. When you told me about his father and how he was stuck with his disturbed wife and after she OD'd, you planned to get married, but he got killed . . . well, I thought you were heroic. So did Walt. But we don't have a middle name. We thought about our mothers' names, but Emma Linda and Emma Barbara don't go together. Besides, the name we didn't use would make the other mother feel bad."

I was so overcome by Amanda's kind words that I didn't take in all of what she'd said. "You almost made me cry," I declared. "I'm going to kId's cOrNEr after work and buy whatever you need most. What is it?"

"A house," Amanda retorted—and laughed again. "We're pretty well set after the shower you and Vida gave earlier this month. Disposable diapers come to mind. You can never have too many."

"Done," I said. "I'll wait to deliver them after you get

home. I'd come to see you now, but it's Tuesday and I
may have to play bridge tonight."

"That's fine," Amanda assured me. "Ah! Here comes
Vida."

We rang off. I wondered if I should call Edna Mae to
see if I had to fill in for Rosemary Bourgette. Then it
dawned on me that I ought to find out more about the
writer our prosecutor was dating. That might be a feature story for next week. Rosemary, however, was in
court, but would get back to me. I called Edna Mae
next to ask if she'd found another sub. She hadn't. I suggested trying Rosemary's mother, Mary Jane, who
often filled in for absentees. Edna Mae hadn't, but
would inquire after she coaxed Crazy Eights Neffel off
the top shelf of the Humor section. She obviously didn't
find anything funny about our local loony.

Around two-thirty, Milo called before either Rosemary or Edna Mae did. "Okay, you're half right, my
little smart-ass. Gould and Mullins found a body at the
dump site."

I practically leaped out of my chair. "You see? My
hunch paid off." I paused. "What do you mean, half
right?"

"It's not Myrtle," he replied. "As I remember, the old
girl wasn't six feet tall, and she sure as hell wasn't a
man. Got to go." He hung up on me. Again.

Chapter Five

I TORE OUT THROUGH the newsroom to look down Front Street at the sheriff's headquarters. The black Yukon wasn't as easy to spot as Milo's previous vehicle, a red Grand Cherokee. But the new SUV was big, and I saw it pulling away from the curb. If the sheriff was going to the dump site, so was I. Mitch was at the hardware store, interviewing Harvey Adcock, who was in charge of the civic fireworks display. That wouldn't take long. I'd call my reporter after I got to the dump and assure him there was a definite photo op. My expertise with a camera was limited to asking which way to point the blasted thing.

Just to prove how inept I am with any kind of mechanism, my car was overwarm. I hadn't thought to leave any windows partly rolled down. The morning's balminess had lulled me into self-defeating inertia. Thus, once I got out of the commercial area and hit the Burl Creek Road, I drove very fast. I wasn't afraid of getting a ticket. The sheriff and all the on-duty deputies were at the dump site or back at headquarters. I slowed down only when I got behind a rusting white pickup truck.

I crossed the old Burl Creek wooden bridge, which badly needed reinforcement—if only the county could afford it. Our earlier breeze had blown itself out somewhere in the vicinity of Spark Plug Mountain. The cottonwood trees alongside the road stood motionless; the air coming through my open windows offered no comfort. Roy and Bebe Everson's house was on my right, though I didn't notice any sign of life. He'd be at the post office and his wife apparently wasn't around. I slowed down to pull in behind Milo's Yukon and the two cruisers. Before getting out of the car, I called Mitch. He'd just gotten back from the hardware store and would be on his way immediately.

Dwight Gould was standing at the edge of the road. He saw me, but didn't speak until I was a couple of yards away. "Damned gawkers," he grumbled. "You'd think we'd dug up a treasure chest. Hell! Here comes another one." He motioned for the midsized sedan to move on.

I did the same, seeing Milo and Jack jawing by a big mound of dirt. I picked my way through the junk that people had randomly discarded. The official county dump was out of town, where River Road ended. West SkyCo residents found it easier to toss their unwanted items on the vacant lot after the original owner had abandoned the property.

As I got closer, I heard Carroll Creek gurgling just beyond the dump. A blanket lay on the ground, probably covering the hole Dwight and Jack had dug. Being squeamish, I thought that was just as well. "What's going on?" I asked as Milo finally noticed my arrival.

"We're waiting for the ambulance," he replied. "They're up at the ski lodge. A guest keeled over in the lobby."

I gestured at the blanket. "You need an ambulance here because the body's not really dead?"

Milo removed his sunglasses and shot me a withering look. "I don't want the stiff going to pieces on us. Literally. We have to try to ID him."

"Are you sure it's a man?" I asked. "Some women are six feet tall."

"We've got evidence to the contrary," he said, wearing the impenetrable mask even I couldn't rip off.

Jack chuckled. "Give it up, Emma, unless you're going to drug him at home tonight."

I glared at the deputy. "As if. I don't suppose Sheriff Go-by-the-Book will let me say he thinks it's a man?"

"*Possibly* male," Milo said, looking beyond me to the road. "Is that Laskey's car?"

I turned around to see the Taurus pull up in front of the first cruiser. "Yes. He's here to take pictures of your blanket. I don't suppose you can give me an estimate of how long whoever this is has been dead."

"Nope," the sheriff responded, stepping away from the hole. "You do the picture honors, Mullins."

"Sure, boss," Jack said. "I can show it to Nina to prove I actually do something besides loaf on the job."

"That won't prove it to me," his boss drawled.

Mitch nodded to Milo and Jack, but approached me first. "How gruesome is it in terms of our readers' sensibilities?"

"Don't ask me," I replied. "I haven't looked. I'm at the top of the list for getting queasy over . . . remains."

Mitch laughed. "I'm from Detroit. I've seen it all. I'll ask Dodge."

Warily, I watched my reporter and my husband. They weren't on the best of terms. Mitch hadn't liked Milo's attitude in the aftermath of Troy's escape from prison in December. The young man had come down with pneumonia and been brought to Alpine Hospital. State law enforcement officials had intervened, ordering the patient's removal to the infirmary at the Monroe Correctional Complex. Milo had to comply, but Mitch felt the rules should have been bent—that happened sometimes in Detroit. I'd told him this was Alpine and Sheriff Dodge didn't bend rules. My reporter hadn't been happy with me, either.

"Skeleton," Mitch called out. "Think Halloween, not Fourth of July."

I hesitated, then looked at Milo. He was still doing his impassive sheriff bit. "Okay," I said, "I'll see for myself." I covered the twenty feet to the hole and pretended I wasn't bothered by looking at the . . . remains.

What I saw wasn't as bad as I feared, but wasn't as good as I hoped. The skull still had some fair hair attached and the skeleton wore rotted clothes. I noted what was left of a blue denim shirt and jeans. The brown leather boots and wide leather belt were decaying, but the silver buckle was in fairly good shape. I was uncertain about running the photo. A partially clothed skeleton was more gruesome than one that was unadorned. I said as much to Mitch.

He shrugged. "I don't have a problem with it."

I appealed to Milo, Jack, and Dwight, who had left his post by the road. "What do you guys think?" I asked.

"Nina will throw up and faint," Jack replied. "After she recovers from seeing my picture, she won't mind the stiff."

"I've got no problem," Dwight put in.

Jack narrowed his eyes at his fellow deputy. "Of course not. You aren't married to my wife."

"Cut the crap," Milo ordered. "I say go with it. There's the one-in-a-million chance that a local might recognize something about the stiff that'd help ID him." He looked out to the road. "Here's the ambulance. And Fleetwood. Damn. I want all you media people out of here. Now."

I didn't argue. Mitch and I met Mr. Radio by his BMW. "You're late," I said, mustering a wry smile. "I helped find the body."

Spencer Fleetwood rarely evinces surprise, but he did now. "Good grief, woman, has the missing Mrs. Myrtle been found?" His dark eyes glanced at the adjacent Everson property. "Where are the relatives?"

I stopped smiling. "It's not Myrtle. It's a man. I was wrong about Myrtle, okay? Where were you? Your station is just down the road."

"I was wooing advertisers along the Highway 2 corridor," Spence replied self-righteously. "One or two of them may be willing to go co-op with the *Advocate*. I assume you got the jump on me by using feminine wiles to coax your favorite bear."

I paused before answering, realizing that Mitch had withdrawn from the encounter between Mr. KSKY and Ms. *Advocate*. My reporter was heading for his Taurus, no doubt anxious to get the photo to Kip. There were pictorial changes to make and news copy to write.

"I have no feminine wiles, as Milo has been telling me for sixteen years," I said. "But I can nag. I've been trying to get him to dig up the dump site since early spring."

Spence nodded absently, his gaze fixed on medics Del Amundson and Vic Thorstensen, who were talking to Milo. "This may take some time," Mr. Radio murmured. "In the interest of cordial relations and advertising revenue, would you share what you've gleaned here?"

I decided not to be perverse, which I often am by nature. "The sheriff isn't in a talkative mood. Big surprise. All I know is that it's probably—and I quote—male. He's been reduced to a skeletal state."

Spence stroked his hawklike nose. "So decomposition may've taken awhile. Well." He sighed. "I suppose I should do a remote."

"Touché," I muttered. "I'll go put out the dinosaur of a newspaper."

I trudged to my Honda, realizing I'd started to perspire. How could it have gotten so much warmer and I hadn't noticed? Maybe, I thought, it was the dead man, lying for who knew how long in that deep, cold grave at the dump site. There was no dignity in that. Despite what misguided optimists tell us, there is nothing digni-fied about death.

I'd given Mitch a thumbs-up on the story, which we'd squeeze onto page one. The picture would go inside to keep us from looking too ghoulish. The cut-line would ask that any information about the dead man be re-ported to the Skykomish County sheriff. As for details, we were on hold until Milo returned to his office.

In the pressure of deadline and breaking news, I'd for-gotten to find out if Ren Rawlings had been released from the hospital. By good fortune, Julie Canby an-swered the patient floor phone.

"She hasn't been discharged," Julie told me. "Doc Dewey doesn't have the final test results and Ms. Rawl-ings seems unsteady on her feet."

I tried to translate Julie's discreet comment. "Is she disoriented?"

"Well . . . somewhat. Do you know her very well?"

I explained my brief acquaintance with the patient.

"That's odd," Julie said. "She is running a low-grade temperature. That, along with thirst, sounds as if she might have contracted some sort of fever, but that should've showed up in the first tests."

Guilt tugged at me. "I feel I should call on her, but we're up against deadline and I may have to play bridge tonight. Poor Ren doesn't know anybody here in town."

"Oh yes, she does," Julie said with a smile in her voice. "Mrs. Runkel visited with her for half an hour. Got to go over charts. It's time to change shifts. Take care, Emma."

I looked out into the newsroom. Vida was at her desk. She must have come in while I was on the phone. I hurried to plunk myself in her visitor chair. "Well?" I asked. "Did you interview every hospital patient?"

My House & Home editor took me seriously. "Not quite. Hortense Cobb is still in the ICU. Amanda was the only one in maternity and two of the ward patients were unconscious. Or seemed to be. I did drop in on my niece Lynette Blatt—kidney stones, so painful—and Darla Puckett—hernia repair from a previous surgery, no doubt the removal of her brain, which she hasn't used in years anyway." Vida paused for breath.

"You left out Ren Rawlings," I gently reproached her.

Vida scowled. "I was saving her for last. She's definitely unhinged. I'm not surprised her mother was a hippie. Though with that old postcard, I did think back to who might've been considered a hippie in Alpine thirty or more years ago. Frankly, there weren't many. People here have too much good sense."

"But there were *some* hippies?" I prodded.

Vida made a dismissive gesture. "Pretend types, really. The young following a fad they saw on TV. There was the drama group that tried to put together a performance, but burned down the Little Theatre instead. They scurried away in disgrace. That was just before the environmentalists began to make a fuss, but they came from out of town."

I pointed out that Ren's mother might've been among them. Vida allowed for the possibility. "Most of those people came to protest and then moved on," she explained. "If Kassia Arthur had stayed here, I'd have heard about it."

That was indisputable. Vida knew everybody who had spent more than a week in Alpine. I was surprised she wasn't on a first-name basis with all the college students. Of course, 80 percent of them were from Skykomish County, so she had a good start.

"So why," I inquired, "do you think Ren's unhinged?"

Vida adjusted her glasses. "'Unfocused' may be a kinder description, though she is very skittish. It's difficult to get direct answers. I asked four times if she knew what her mother looked like, before she finally admitted she had no idea. There were some sketches, but only of vague landscapes. I suggested the poems might include personal, even physical allusions. That made Ren think. A pity she didn't bring them with her. I wrote down phrases she remembered." Vida paused, rummaging in her purse. She rarely took notes. Her memory was phenomenal, with more room than a computer chip. She removed a wrinkled Venison Inn napkin, which I assumed was the only thing she had for jotting down Ren's recollections. "Hair," Vida began. "Quote, 'raven wing strands.' I should add that the strands were on a man's bare thigh." She quoted again. "'Cerulean reflected back at me, pure as the heaven that'—whatever. Kassia's eyes, perhaps. There was also an alabaster mention, which might have been her skin."

"Ren's fair-haired and blue-eyed," I said, "but her skin isn't pale."

"All that California sun." Vida made a face. "Impossible to tell what kind of complexion people from there really have. Imagine living every day with heat and no rain."

My expression was sardonic. "I don't have to imagine it right now."

Vida bridled. "You know what I mean. This weather won't last."

It was pointless to argue. "Did Ren say anything else of interest?"

"Only that she knew her mother was murdered," Vida responded. "I pressed her as to why she was so sure, but she had nothing to support her suspicions. She simply *felt* it. Whatever *that* means." Vida ruefully shook her head, the gray curls bobbing under the sponges.

I stood up. "I forgot to ask—did you see Amanda and Walt's baby?"

"Yes, but she was asleep in the nursery," Vida replied. "Still a bit red in the face, spiky dark hair, very difficult to tell much about features. Like most new parents, Amanda insists she and Walt can discern resemblances going back three generations on both sides. Ridiculous."

I smiled and went back to my office. Maybe Milo had returned from the dump site. It dawned on me that Vida hadn't asked where I'd gone. The omission was unlike her. On the other hand, if she'd just gotten back from her hospital tour, she wouldn't know I'd ever left. I was on my way to update her, but she was on the phone.

"Yes, yes," she practically shouted, "I'll be right there." Replacing the receiver, she stood up. "My sister-in-law, Ella, has fallen. A neighbor found her. I must rush over to Parc Pines. Why am I the only one who has to deal with my family's problems?" Not expecting— or needing—an answer, she grabbed her purse and rushed out of the newsroom.

Edna Mae hadn't called me back, so I dialed her number. Naturally, she apologized for being remiss. "I've been so caught up with our summer reading program," she explained. "With people going on vacation, we can only choose four books. Why would some of our readers prefer *The Da Vinci Code* to *The Plot Against America*?"

I gathered she expected an answer. "Because it's more popular?"

"But it wasn't one of the Top Ten Best Books," Edna Mae responded. "I like to keep up the library's standards."

"That's commendable," I said, then cut to the chase.

"Is Mary Jane Bourgette going to substitute for her daughter?"

"No, they have to babysit grandchildren tonight. Oh dear, I should've let you know sooner. I'm so sorry. It's at the Driggerses' house."

I tried to sound pleasant. "Okay. I'll see you there. Bye, Edna Mae." I hung up.

The afternoon was ebbing away. Rosemary had never called back so I could grill her about the date. Maybe she was in a dither at the prospect of finding an eligible man in Alpine. In any case, I didn't intend to run the story about him—if there was a story—until next week. But it was going on five and no word from Milo. I was on the verge of calling him when I decided that should be Mitch's job. He was at his desk, so I told him to rattle the sheriff's cage.

My reporter looked puzzled. "I already did. I got back from his office just as Vida roared off in her Buick. Dodge didn't have much more to say than what he knew at the dump site. I sent the story to you five minutes ago."

I held my head. Mitch had a knack for making me feel inept. "I'm sorry. I'll check it right now."

Mitch was right. The sheriff merely elaborated—wrong word to use, but he was my husband, so I'd give him the benefit of a doubt: an adult male, approximately thirty-five to fifty years of age, probably Caucasian due to light hair color, no ID, cause of death unknown, investigation under way. Kip, who is in charge of our website, had already posted the bare bones. I grimaced again. Either the skeleton or the heat was getting to me. I couldn't seem to think about this story in any way that wasn't grisly. But the possibility of death by homicide was worse.

Chapter Six

VIDA CALLED FIVE minutes later to tell me she'd had the medics check out Ella, who might have broken some ribs. "Tony Lynch took her to the ER, so I'm here now waiting to see what happens next. I hope they keep her overnight. I wonder if she's had another small stroke. She insists she didn't, but kept babbling about being frightened. Such a ninny. I have all my copy in, by the way. I must dash."

I wished Vida luck. Before I spoke with her again, she'd find out what had happened at the dump site and be very angry with me. My excuse that there'd been no opportunity to tell her would go for naught.

At five, I went to the back shop to make sure everything was going smoothly. Kip assured me it was. I shut down my computer and left to pick up Milo's dinner requests at the Grocery Basket. He'd be unhappy when I told him about the bridge game, so I bought the biggest T-bone I could find. The bill for my smaller steak, two baked potatoes, and three ears of corn came to forty-one dollars and change. It was a good thing my husband was paying our monthly bills or I couldn't afford to feed him.

When I got home, the temperature inside was over eighty, but the evergreen trees would provide shade on the new patio. I opened all three doors and the kitchen window, which now looked out into the garage instead of my old carport. Frankly, I missed seeing the greenery that used to be part of the view.

Milo arrived five minutes later, obviously out of sorts. I summoned up my courage to tell him about the bridge date, but he spoke first. "I have to fill in for Bill Blatt tonight," he said, removing his hat and hooking an arm around my neck before he kissed me. "I won't have time to start the grill. Can you broil the steaks?"

"Yes," I assured him as he let go of me. "It works better for me, because I have to play bridge. The seven-thirty start would be cutting it close. Rosemary Bourgette has found a man."

"Shit," Milo muttered. "I hate young love. Tanya invited Bill to dinner at Le Gourmand so they could talk."

I laughed. "The four people you refer to aren't really that young."

Milo got out glasses and the liquor. "They *seem* that young. At least Bill and Tanya do. If Lila Blatt kept her mouth shut and hadn't made Bill move back home with her, there might not be a problem."

"I don't think the Blatt women *can* keep their mouths shut," I said. "Ella had a fall today and Vida went with her to the ER."

"So that's what the late-afternoon scanner call was. Let's sit outside. How long for you to make dinner? I should be back at the office by six forty-five. Tanya didn't know Bill had the evening shift and didn't think to ask him about his schedule."

"Relax," I urged, running my hand up and down his arm. "It takes fifteen minutes to fix dinner. Less, if you'd eat your meat rare like I do."

Milo put his big hand over my much smaller one. "Stop petting me, woman. Or do you want to skip the food?"

Fool that I am, I hesitated. "No," I finally said. "I won't go to bridge club on an empty stomach. But I've always liked your arms. They're starting to tan and they're so strong and—"

"Quit while we're still upright," he growled and led the way outside.

The patio was small, only a third of what level ground I'd had before. The rear of my property sloped up the face of Tonga Ridge. Milo's new workroom occupied the rest of the flat area. My first question after we settled into my old steel outdoor chairs was if the Eversons knew a body that wasn't Myrtle had been dug up at the dump site.

"Yeah," Milo replied after lighting a cigarette. "Gould stayed after Mullins and I left. Bebe showed up to ask what the cruiser was doing by the site. He told her in his less than tactful way. She burst into tears and then entered the state of denial. She's probably still there."

"Roy will really pitch a fit," I said, batting at a mosquito. "So will the rest of the family. I'll bet they'll want to see the skeleton. Are you sending it to the Snohomish County lab for a full autopsy?"

"Maybe." Milo's gaze followed a Steller's jay's flight into a tall hemlock. "Doc ruled out a blow to the head or strangulation. Skull, ribs, and neck bones undamaged. Assuming—got that?—it was foul play, it was probably a gun, knife, or poison."

I waved off two more mosquitoes. "Damnit, I'm being attacked. Why don't they bite those big, brawny arms of yours?"

"Because I'm smoking," Milo asserted. "You want one?" He proffered the pack of Marlboro Lights.

"Yes!" I leaned over to snatch a cigarette. "Light me up, Dodge."

The sheriff's hazel eyes twinkled as he clicked his lighter. "I thought you gave up trying to seduce me."

"I did," I said after taking the first puff. "Now I'm starving. I also think one of those damned bugs bit me."

To prove it, I scratched my ankle. "The deerflies will be early in this heat. They're worse than the mosquitoes. Maybe," I went on, hitting on a better way of discussing the skeleton, "Mr. X was chewed to death by our flying wildlife."

"Who buried him?" Milo asked. "Carpenter ants?"

"It wasn't Al Driggers," I shot back. "Which, by the way, is where the bridge club meets tonight. If you never ID Mr. X, will Al get the job of burying him at county expense?"

"Damn," Milo said softly. "He was already buried. If we'd left him there we could've saved the county some money. Maybe Driggers Mortuary will give us half off because the stiff's being reburied. You might ask Janet about that tonight. Do it before they all get tanked."

"I think I'll avoid the topic." I checked my watch. "It's almost six. I'll start dinner. Stay outside. The kitchen may get warmer. We'll eat here." I carried the rest of my drink and the half-smoked cigarette inside.

I was only off four minutes in my estimate of prep time. As we ate—and I dueled with the bug life—I asked Milo who was filling in while he took time out for dinner.

"Gould," he responded. "He'll get paid for it."

"Say," I said, "you never told me what went down at RestHaven in the rehab wing. Did you send someone to straighten them out?"

Milo shook his head. "The combatants had cooled off when my deputies got there. That's what happened the first time around in May. Iain Farrell's so damned uptight about patient privacy that he wouldn't call us if the staff was being held hostage. But the psych ward's maven, Rosalie Reed, convinced Woo they needed help. Maybe she's running scared after her nutty husband escaped and ended up dead last winter. Anyway, Farrell's not in charge of security since they hired a full-timer."

My eyes widened. "They did? Nobody told us about

it. What's wrong with Kay Burns? That's her job as their PR person."

He shrugged. "Maybe she and Gould are still getting it on and she's distracted. They *were* married. I don't ask my staff about their personal lives, though I'd like to tell Mullins to shut up when he bad-mouths Nina. He knows she's the best thing that's ever happened to him."

I agreed, but I wanted to stay focused on RestHaven. "Who's in charge of security? And why hasn't Spence broadcast it since he's sleeping with Dr. Reed?"

"I don't know," Milo replied. "Maybe Woo put a lid on his staff. They've been operating like the CIA ever since they opened up. The only reason I know about it is because I ran into Sid Almquist this morning at Cal's Chevron. He started at RestHaven June first. I was happy for the guy. He's had a rough time."

The name rang only a vague bell. "Was he the one who was living with his wife and their new baby under the Icicle Creek Bridge when we were going together the first time around?"

Milo nodded. "He'd been laid off at the old Cascade & Pacific Mill after that horse's ass Jack Blackwell bought it out. He and Mary Jean moved to Snohomish, where he worked security for a regional group of banks. The Almquists always wanted to come back here, so he applied for the job and they hired him."

"How did that slip under Vida's radar?" I asked, aghast. "Of course, she hasn't been herself since Roger went to jail."

"At least she's speaking to me again," my husband said after devouring the last bite of his giant steak. "I guess that's good news. I'd better go." He stood up and leaned down to kiss the top of my head. "Good luck with the card-playing winos."

I'd finished cleaning up from dinner when Vida called. "Honestly," she said without preamble, "Ella is such a ninny! She fell in Parc Pines' underground garage as she was about to go to Safeway. She shouldn't be driving. Why doesn't Milo pull her license?"

I sat on the sofa. "He can't. That decision has to be made by the Department of Motor Vehicles when her current license expires. Ella hasn't had any accidents or violations, has she?"

Vida harrumphed. "No. She rarely goes over ten miles an hour and is terrified to leave the residential area. She didn't break anything, but Doc's keeping her overnight because her blood pressure is very high. She might still be lying in the garage if Walt Hanson hadn't pulled in after visiting his wife and baby."

"Does Ella know why she fell?" I asked, checking my watch. It was seven-ten, plenty of time to drive to the bridge-club get-together.

I heard Vida utter an exasperated sigh. "She insists she saw a pervert lurking by some of the other cars. Naturally, she refused to give details. Too shocking, she told me."

"It wasn't Crazy Eights Neffel?" I asked, only half-teasing.

"Ella's used to Crazy Eights, even when he's naked. I can hardly blame him in this weather. It was probably someone visiting another Parc Pines resident. Cupcake needs bathing. He's starting to molt."

I left Vida to tend to her canary's toilette. After applying lipstick and brushing my shrublike hair, I set out for the Driggerses' home in The Pines, Alpine's version of an upscale development. Janet and Al had downsized to a smaller, if newer, house after their grown children moved away.

It felt cooler when I got out of the car. The Pines had been known as Stump Hill thirty years ago before the property was converted into a residential area. Over time, homeowners had planted various types of flora, including a woebegone palm tree. Vida had told me that a couple from Santa Barbara tried to California-ize their property. They'd spent just two years in Alpine, apparently realizing they hated snow. I marveled at the palm's will to survive, but it certainly didn't thrive.

Janet welcomed me at the door. "You're early!" she cried. "We thought you'd still be entwined with your big stud. Come in, we're almost all here." She lowered her voice. "As usual, some of them aren't all there."

I smiled at the five familiar faces in the tastefully decorated living room: Darlene Adcock, Charlene Vickers, Dixie Ridley, Linda Grant, and, of course, Edna Mae. They all smiled back, some more genuinely than others. Linda was the high school girls' gym teacher and Dixie was married to the boys' coach, Rip. Neither had ever been part of my rooting section. Linda was rumored to have had an affair with Milo after his divorce. I'd tried subtly to ask him if that was true, but he'd evaded the question. Or maybe he forgot. It happened before my arrival in Alpine.

"Who's missing?" I asked.

"Lila Blatt," Janet replied. "She usually plays with a spin-off group from the Burl Creek Thimble Club. Take a seat. It's never too early to start drinking." She picked up a large bottle of pink wine—maybe a rosé—and began filling glasses set on the two card tables. "Okay, ladies, let's do the next best thing to screwing. Besides using your vibrators, of course."

No one looked shocked. We were all used to Janet's ribald mouth. I figured it was her way of dealing with death at the funeral home. She also took the edge off of that grim business by working part-time at Sky Travel. As Janet put it, she was sending the locals somewhere at both places, but a few of them never came back.

The doorbell chimed as Janet finished filling the last

glass. I was standing not far from the door, so I volunteered to let in the newcomer.

"Mrs. Dodge?" Lila Blatt said with a slight squint.

I smiled. "Yes, come in. I'm still Ms. Lord at work. Call me Emma."

She smiled back in a fixed sort of way, as if she were out of practice. I recognized Lila from sightings around town. She was the youngest of Vida's Blatt in-laws, probably in her early sixties. An average-sized woman, she had short, steel-gray hair, piercing blue eyes, and chiseled features. If memory served—and it often didn't with all the branches on Vida's family tree—she'd married Rupert, the youngest of the Blatt brothers, who'd suffered a fatal aneurysm not long after he hit fifty.

Apparently, Lila knew the others, especially Charlene and Darlene, her fellow Burl Creek Thimble Club members. We immediately addressed the evening's agenda by drawing cards for partners. I ended up with Dixie; Edna Mae and Lila were our opponents. The coach's wife had drawn the highest card among our foursome, so she was the first to deal.

Dixie was also the first to take a dig at me. "We're all anxious for you to host us at your remodeled log cabin," she said, fingers snapping out the cards with the finesse of a Vegas pro. "Milo never lavished that kind of money on his home with Tricia."

"That's because Milo and Tricia had three children," I said in a pleasant voice. "After he stopped paying large sums for child support, he was able to save money and invest wisely."

Lila, who wore her half-glasses on a long gold chain, squinted at me with those piercing blue eyes. "I didn't realize the sheriff made such a large salary. My son Billy certainly couldn't support a family on what he makes. He can barely pay me room and board to help make ends meet."

I shrugged. "Tell that to the county commissioners.

They set the salaries for the sheriff's department. If Mayor Baugh's plan goes through to eliminate his own job and the three commissioners, there might be more money to spend on law enforcement."

"*If*," Dixie said archly. "I dealt and I pass."

As usual, it took Edna Mae some time and much scrutiny of her cards to make a bid. "One diamond," she finally twittered.

We'd played a few hands when Lila turned to me. "By the way, I wish your husband would stop making Billy work so many nights. I'd planned to have him install the new TV for my bedroom this evening. It wasn't delivered by my nephew Ronnie until almost five-thirty. Why does UPS come so late?"

I probably looked stupid. "I've no idea about UPS," I replied, realizing that Lila didn't know Bill was dining with Tanya at Le Gourmand. "As for Bill's schedule, all of the deputies are on a set rotation."

Somehow, by the grace of God or Charles Goren, we got through the first table without any more awkward episodes. Shortly before ten, we were on the last round. I was partnered with Janet, facing off against Linda Grant and Lila Blatt. By this time, almost everybody was semi-blitzed, except me. And maybe Lila. Unlike me, she seemed to keep up with the rest of the crowd, but her rigid demeanor didn't change.

"Good Lord," Janet gasped, "I'm free of Char and Dar and their giggle fits! If they wet their pants on my upholstered Amish chairs, I'll strangle them with some of our bondage ropes."

"Where *is* Al?" I asked, hoping to distract my hostess.

"He's in bed," Janet replied, taking a sip of white wine. "He went to the hospital first." She hiccuped and bid a spade.

"Is he sick?" I asked after our opponents passed and I'd responded with two hearts.

Linda passed again. Janet said four spades to make game. "No," she said to me while I laid down my cards. "He got a call from an out-of-town woman who's in the hospital and insisted he come to see her. Maybe she's dying and wanted to make arrangements. Who knows? We can use the money. I didn't get a chance to talk to him when he came in the back way a little after eight. Okay, we've got this one in the bag. Not the body bag, of course . . ." She began to play out the hand.

The final half hour passed without incident except for Linda Grant making a crack about how *wise* it was of Milo and me to spend so much time getting to *know* each other before *finally* getting married, and Lila looking as if she never wanted to see any of us again. I wanted to ask Janet more about the hospital patient, but she seemed on the verge of passing out. Being first out the door was my priority, lest some of the other players crash into me in a drunken stupor.

When I pulled into the garage, I was surprised to see Milo's Yukon already parked there. I was also alarmed, wondering if something was wrong. I hurried inside, finding him in the easy chair watching baseball wrap-ups on ESPN.

"Why are you home before midnight?" I asked, sitting on the easy chair's arm.

Milo kissed me lightly and chuckled. "Blatt showed up in uniform around ten. His old lady thought he was on duty. She'd gone somewhere for the earlier part of the evening, so he took his work clothes with him when he went to dinner with Tanya."

I laughed. "Lila was at bridge club. She mentioned Bill was working tonight. I wondered what was going on. How did their dinner go?"

"Hey," my husband said, "I told you I don't interrogate my staff about their off-duty time. He looked happy, though."

"Bill's mother is demanding," I remarked. "Any on-the-job news?"

He shrugged. "A couple of fender-benders in town. Doe Jamison made quick work of those. I only had to make one call."

"That sounds like a . . ." I frowned at him. "I thought you were working the front desk. Why'd you have to go out on a call?"

Did I detect hesitation on Milo's part? "It was from Jeannie Hobbs," he said. "There was some guy hanging out by her house. Her husband's out of town, so she asked for a male officer to come by. I was it."

I slid off the chair's arm. "Really? How *is* your former girlfriend?" I asked in a voice I tried to make light-hearted.

"Loosen up," my husband said, obviously not fooled. "Jeannie Clay's been married to Dale Hobbs for three years. The only time I see her is when I get my teeth cleaned every six months."

Luckily, the sheriff had good teeth. *Great* teeth, actually. "I know. I'm not jealous. I never was. Your romance with her didn't last long."

Milo laughed, revealing his amazing teeth. "You were jealous as hell. It was a rebound fling after you dumped me. It pissed you off because she was so much younger. I couldn't figure it out. By then, you were panting for Cavanaugh to pop the question."

I flopped onto the sofa. "You know why. Then I got snarky about your affair with the Irish widow. That was even weirder, because Tom and I were engaged. I always felt you were *mine*. I didn't want to share."

"You got that right." He stood up and stretched. "Since you're home safe from the local sots and pervs, I'm heading for bed."

"Was there a pervert at Jeannie's house?" I asked as Milo mussed my hair on the way out of the living room.

He paused in the hall doorway. "The flowers were trampled by a bedroom window. I told Jeannie not to mess with it. I'll have a deputy check for footprints tomorrow. It might be kids. She didn't get a good look except seeing a male run through the yard." His hazel eyes sparked. "Maybe I'll drop in tomorrow after work to find out if she remembers more details." My husband disappeared into the hall.

I refrained from gnashing my teeth. I might damage one and have to go see Dr. Starr—and his assistant, Jeannie. I stopped acting like a jealous wife and checked in with Kip to make sure everything was going well at work. He assured me it was—except for a phone call he described as creepy.

"How creepy?" I asked.

"It was some guy asking for what I thought was the rent," Kip replied. "I told him we didn't pay rent because the building had been included in the price of the newspaper. That seemed to confuse *him*. Finally, he explained he was looking for somebody named Ren or Rent who'd given him our number as the one to call in Alpine. I told him there must be a mistake."

I realized Kip didn't know that Ren Rawlings had paid me a call. My back-shop wizard often enters his high-tech world and doesn't emerge for hours at a time. I filled him in.

"Dang," he said under his breath. "Now the guy who called thinks I'm nuts. His number showed up only as out-of-area."

"Don't worry about it," I consoled him. "We may never see Ren again once she's let out of the hospital."

"Right," Kip agreed. "It all sounds pretty weird."

On that note, we both rang off. Of course what sounded weird on Tuesday would feel downright sinister before the week was over.

Chapter Seven

VIDA HAD REVERTED to her more prickly self by Wednesday morning. "What's wrong with those RestHaven people?" she demanded, re-pinning a froth of white net covered with tiny green satin bows that passed for a hat. "This is the fourth time I've invited one of them to be on my radio program and they always refuse."

I was pouring my first cup of coffee. "They must not realize that *Vida's Cupboard* is don't-miss-listening in SkyCo. Who is it this time?"

"Iain Farrell," she replied before blowing on the hot water she drank every day at work. "First it was Jennifer Hood, the medical rehab nurse. Her excuse was the escaped patient and not wanting to draw attention to the facility. Then it was Dr. Reed, who claimed to be a grieving widow. I had words with Spencer about that. The grapevine has been rampant with talk of his affair with Rosalie, dead husband or not." She stopped speaking as Alison arrived with the Upper Crust pastries.

"My second day on the job," our fill-in receptionist said, opening the lavender box. "I'd forgotten how much fun it is to pick out the morning goodies. The cinnamon rolls are still warm from the oven."

Mitch, who was already working at his computer, practically vaulted over to the table. Leo hadn't yet arrived, but Kip must have caught the baked goods' aroma. He'd already informed me that this week's *Advocate* was ready for delivery. I kept my distance from the men. Mitch's lanky frame never showed any signs of the damage he could do to pastry. Sometimes I wondered if Brenda wasn't a very good cook.

Vida was keeping her gimlet eye on the pastry tray as Mitch and Kip moved away. "So fat-making," she murmured, looking as if she were arguing with herself. "I was particularly annoyed with Kay Burns. Not only is she their PR person, but a native Alpiner who's returned to her roots. That's the subject I wanted to discuss with her. I didn't intend to ask about her failed marriages to Dwight Gould and Jack Blackwell before she left town thirty years ago. That's old news."

I kept a straight face. "Yes, I'm sure you could've had an interesting segment about why former residents like Kay and Sid Almquist come back to Alpine. I forget. What was her excuse?"

Vida sighed. "Kay claimed that being PR for Rest-Haven, she'd be taking away from the facility by discussing personal reflections. Twaddle, of course." She suddenly lurched forward in her chair and stared at me. "Did you say Sid Almquist? What do you mean?"

"He's the full-time security person at RestHaven as of June first," I replied calmly. "Milo told me last night." Seeing Vida's gray eyes shoot daggers at me, I hastily added that he'd only found out by accident.

"You see?" she shrieked. "That should've come from Kay! That's her job. What's wrong with those people?"

"It's all about patient privacy," I said. "You know how touchy they've been from the start. That's probably why Farrell declined."

Vida fell back in her chair. "It's absurd," she murmured, looking not unlike a big red, white, and blue burst balloon in her striped summer dress. "They may be in Alpine, but they're not *part* of Alpine."

"They provide jobs," I pointed out. "Jennifer Hood helps at the clinic when they're shorthanded and even Iain Farrell pitched in when Elvis Sung visited family in Hawaii over Memorial Day weekend."

She sniffed. "My niece Marje told me Farrell only saw two patients."

"But he was available," I said, noting that Mitch had discreetly left the newsroom. No doubt he didn't want to get caught up in Vida's maelstrom.

"I think I'll grab a cinnamon roll before they're all gone," I mumbled. "I need a coffee refill anyway."

I walked over to the table, noting that of the half-dozen rolls, only two remained. I changed my mind, taking a sugar cookie instead. "Alison got petit fours," I informed Vida, knowing she had a weakness for them because they were, as she put it, *petite*.

"I'll see," she murmured, staring at her computer screen.

Leo arrived five minutes later, looking pleased with himself. He sat down in my office holding on to his faux-leather ad case. "It only took me eleven years, but I finally got Jack Blackwell to take out something bigger than his standing two-by-two ad. Call me cunning."

I grinned. "What did you do? Threaten to set fire to his mill?"

Leo's expression was roguish. "Before I paid my routine visit, I was thinking about the lack of rain and the threat of forest fires. That gave me an idea for a sales pitch. I told Black Jack that as the only mill owner in town, he should man up." Leo paused to light a cigarette.

"You challenged his manhood and survived?" I said in surprise as I got out the ashtray I kept in a drawer for smokers like Leo, Milo—and me, when I fell off the No Nicotine Wagon.

Lee nodded. "But I did it in a macho kind of way. You

know, just between us aggressive, enterprising good ol' boys. He fell for it. I went on to say we need a timber-industry type to stand up for the forests. I suggested what amounted to a public service ad, warning locals, visitors, passers-through, and any other two-legged life form about the dangers of starting fires around here. I used the Fourth of July as the hook."

I was still smiling. "You are a sly fox," I said. "How big of an ad?"

"A full page," Leo replied, his well-traveled face smug. "Will the sheriff cancel his subscription?"

"What subscription?" I shot back. "Like the mayor and the county commissioners, Milo gets a courtesy copy. Which, I might add, he rarely reads. The freebies go back to the days of my predecessor, Marius Vandeventer, and Milo's former boss, Eeeny Moroni."

Leo shook his head. "I still can't get over how things that happen today in Alpine have roots from thirty, forty, even eighty years ago. How long have Dodge and Blackwell gone at it? I remember you telling me about Jack running against Milo when the sheriff's office was elected."

"That was spite on Blackwell's part," I said. "Their history goes way beyond that, to Jack's arrival from California when Milo was still a deputy. A basic personality clash, as my husband describes it."

Leo chuckled. "In other words, Dodge didn't like Blackwell trying to push him around."

"You got it. And Jack didn't like Milo pushing back."

Leo put out his cigarette and stood up. "Your better half has to admit that Blackwell runs a decent mill."

"Milo grants him that much," I assured my ad manager. "It's Jack's personal life that's always been a shambles. You know Patti Marsh's sad story," I added, referring to Blackwell's longtime main squeeze.

"Right," Leo said. "She's never turned him in for

beating the crap out of her." He glanced over his shoulder. "I'd better get a cinnamon roll before they're gone. Mitch just nabbed the next-to-last one."

"Do that. And congratulations on the full-page ad. That's huge."

Leo grinned. "Guess my job's safe from Ed Bronsky for another week." He turned to head for the pastry tray.

I leaned back and contemplated next week's issue. We were already in good shape, especially with Leo's advertising coup. The holiday festivities would offer plenty of photo possibilities. It might be our lead story unless Milo came up with something new about the buried body. Given the circumstances, he should be so lucky. So should I.

Shortly after Alison brought the mail in around nine-thirty, Rosemary Bourgette called to ask if we could go to lunch at her brothers' 1950s-style diner, The Heartbreak Hotel. She sounded rushed but upbeat, so I assumed she wanted to tell me about her date. Naturally, I agreed to join her.

Just before ten, Kip dropped off our advance copies of the paper. "Looks good," I said to him. "Any chance we can run color next week with the fireworks-show photos?"

He grimaced. "Maybe. It's your call. How's the budget?"

I told him about Leo's coup. "Let's think about it," I said.

"Sure." He grinned at me in his still-boyish manner before heading off to deliver the rest of the advance copies.

Two minutes later, Vida screamed. I leaped out of my chair and ran into the newsroom. Leo and Mitch were gone, but Alison had rushed in from the front office. I stopped within six feet of my House & Home editor's desk. Except for looking a bit flushed, she seemed fine.

"What's wrong?" I asked, still shaken.

Vida held up the *Advocate*'s front page. "This is what's wrong! Why didn't you tell me about the dead person at the dump site?" She tossed the paper aside, yanked off her glasses, and began rubbing her eyes in a familiar gesture of deep distress.

I hurried to sit in her visitor chair, noting that Alison had discreetly withdrawn to her post. "Vida," I said, "I never got a chance—"

"Nonsense!" she interrupted, still pummeling her eyeballs. As always, I thought I could hear them grind and squeak. "You don't trust me anymore! I've fallen out of your esteem." She eased off on the cornea assault. "I thought we were friends as well as colleagues." Dropping her hands into her lap, she stared at me with reddened eyes. "Ever since you got married, you've relegated me to a second-class citizen."

I held my head. "Oh my God," I said under my breath. "I don't know what to say."

"There's nothing *to* say," Vida replied stiffly, putting her glasses back on. "Please leave so I can finish reading the dump-site story. I do not like to be uninformed."

I hesitated. Of course I'd expected her to be angry, but I hadn't envisioned anything this drastic. I could only surmise that her wrath wasn't entirely spontaneous, but that resentment had been building for some time. It had never occurred to me that she'd be jealous of Milo's role in my life. Then I shrugged, stood up, and walked away.

Sitting down at my desk, I wondered if my wedded state really was the source of her outburst. The key remark was about not trusting her. Vida and I had never discussed Roger's fate except for the facts that had to go public. Later, I'd been reluctant to bring up the subject, knowing how it embarrassed and upset her. I assumed there was guilt, too, for spoiling the jerk and turning a blind eye to his many faults. And while Vida might use every tactic short of electric shocks to elicit personal data from others, she turned mute when it came to her private life. She might say—even believe—my marriage had erected a barrier between us, but I suspected Roger was the cause of her current state of mind. It had always been that way with her grandson. I supposed it always would be. I picked up my copy of the newspaper and started scanning it for typos. They, like Roger, are always with us, no matter how carefully we try to avoid them.

Having managed to keep my distance from Vida for the rest of the morning, I started out of the office before noon to meet Rosemary. Alison stopped me at the front desk, but looked furtive. "Where's Mrs. Runkel?" she whispered.

"In the back shop, I think," I replied. "Could you hear what she was saying earlier?"

Alison nodded, her pretty face troubled. "Is she having a breakdown or a meltdown?"

I kept my eye on the newsroom in case Vida returned to her desk. "Maybe neither. She's still in shock from Roger's arrest. I wish Buck Bardeen could provide more support for her. In fact, she hasn't mentioned him lately. Maybe they had a falling-out over Roger."

Alison frowned. "I remember when I worked here in December that Vida's . . . friend thought Roger should join the marines. She hated Colonel Bardeen's idea. But it might've kept her grandson out of prison." She paused, glancing down the hall. "Mrs. R. just went into the rest room. I knew Roger when I was a little kid. We were in kindergarten together before my parents divorced and I moved to Everett. He used to do some really disgusting things, including make himself throw up."

"Roger's idea of humor never matured much beyond that," I said, heading for the door before Vida came out of the rest room. "I should be back by one o'clock."

It took less than five minutes to drive to the diner, which was located east of Alpine Way between Railroad Avenue and River Road. As I turned into the parking lot, I glimpsed the old steel bridge over the Sky, where a sorry chapter in Roger's disgrace had unfolded in April. I shook my head as I got out of the car and walked into the diner.

Terri Bourgette, Rosemary's youngest sister, was greeting an older couple I recognized only by sight. Seeing me enter, she waved a handful of menus. "Be right back, Emma," she said.

I waited, staring at the antique Wurlitzer jukebox. Cal Vickers tramped past me—and stopped. "Hi, Emma. You're due for an oil change. Or did Dodge already tell you?"

If Milo had mentioned it, I'd forgotten. "Right, Cal."

He moved on in his grease-stained work clothes and beat-up Chevron cap. I assumed he was joining someone who was already seated.

A moment later, I felt a tap on my arm. "I'm late," Rosemary said. "Is my bratty little sister ignoring you?"

"No," I replied, smiling. "She's . . . here's Terri now."

Terri handed us each a menu. "Let Rosie find a table for you," she said. "She'll want one with complete privacy so she can dish about her hot new boyfriend."

"You should be so lucky," Rosemary shot back good-naturedly. "The last guy you went out with had horns."

"That was hair gel," Terri retorted, but put on a big smile for whoever was waiting behind us.

Rosemary led the way to the opposite end of the diner. She always moved briskly, whether in court or in chambers, as she likes to say mockingly of her small, cluttered office between the county auditor and the county clerk. She selected a booth across from a young couple who were so absorbed in each other that they wouldn't have noticed a pair of okapis sitting on the opposite side of the aisle.

"Now I feel old," Rosemary remarked, glancing at the duo.

I looked at the three framed photos on the wall: the TV cast of *Father Knows Best* in a family pose, looking happier than they should be; a sullen James Dean posturing on a movie poster for *Rebel Without a Cause;* the famous photo of Marilyn Monroe standing over a New York City subway grate with her skirt blowing, as Vida would say, "up to there!" I might've smiled at the thought, but I couldn't.

"*You* feel old," I said. "I was born in that era."

Terri reappeared. "Let me take your orders," she said. "We're short a server today."

Rosemary hadn't looked at the menu. She probably knew it by heart. "The Eddie Fisher Oh My Pa-Pa-Ya fruit salad and a Diet Coke."

I saw the special. "Make it a Rosemary Clooney Half As Much Reuben for me. Oh—I'll have lemonade. Thanks."

Terri hustled away. "She's great," her sister declared. "I'm lucky. I come from a family where we all like each other. Mom and Dad did a terrific job of raising six kids. I could never do that. Maybe that's why I've stayed single so long."

My expression was wry. "I waited to get married until I was past having more children. Tell me about the date."

Rosemary's piquant features lit up. "Yes, the date." She looked off to one side, as if collecting her thoughts from the corner of the booth. "He's not drop-dead gorgeous," she finally said, "but he *is* attractive. To me, anyway. His name's Desmond Ellerbee and I met him Sunday at the Summer Solstice picnic. He thought I was stealing his car."

"Were you?"

Rosemary laughed. "No. He has a Toyota Avalon that's the same model and color as mine. It was getting so warm and so loud around five o'clock that I wanted to sit away from everybody and collect myself. Chasing four preschool nieces and nephews for a couple of hours wears me out. I went over to the parking area and opened the car door. I admit, I vaguely wondered why I'd left a SkyCo map on the front seat, but I just wanted to crash. The next thing I knew, a man was yelling at me. It turned out to be Desmond. I felt like an idiot."

"Was he mad?" I asked.

"A little," Rosemary said, pushing a strand of dark brown hair off her cheek. "But when he saw I wasn't some ditzy teenager trying to steal his Avalon, he asked what the heck was I doing behind the wheel. I told him I was contemplating a midlife crisis. He laughed."

"Great meet-cute story," I said, smiling. "I stumbled over my own feet when I introduced myself to the sheriff. I bet you revived."

"You got that right."

She stopped speaking as Terri brought our beverages. "Your orders will be up in three minutes," she said, then leaned closer to her sister. "Have you gotten to the first kiss by the donkey engine in the logging museum?"

Rosemary's brown eyes snapped. "That did not happen! I have a reputation to maintain. Go away!"

Giggling, Terri left us. "Where was I?" Rosemary asked, blushing.

"Somewhere between the Toyota Avalon and the donkey engine," I reminded her.

She nodded. "Right. Des had come back to his car to

get mosquito repellent. We introduced ourselves, then he asked if I was coming or going. I told him neither— I was recovering from chasing small children. He asked how many I had. None, I informed him, and . . ." She clapped both hands to her cheeks. "I noticed he wasn't wearing a wedding ring, so I said I wasn't married. Does that sound pushy or desperate?"

"Neither one," I asserted. "I might've said the same thing. I gather the answer didn't scare him into taking a dive in the river?"

Rosemary smiled. "It did not. We walked around the park edges for maybe fifteen minutes, getting acquainted. He's forty-eight, married once if briefly when he was in college, no kids, born in Miles City, Montana, spent one year at Montana State in Bozeman. Dropped out not only because he wasn't sure what he wanted to be when he grew up, except not married to his nineteen-year-old bride. That's when they split. Des moved to L.A. Eventually, he studied writing at UCLA. Now he's working on a film script about the early days of logging, which is how he ended up here." She stopped as Terri appeared with our orders.

"Donkey engine," she murmured and spun off down the aisle.

"Grrr," her sister said. "Yes, we went through the logging museum. Des had seen it a couple of weeks ago. He moved up here—near Baring, actually—in May. As he put it, he's still getting his Bearings." Rosemary's dimples showed as she laughed. "There wasn't any action on the donkey engine, but that's when he asked me out to dinner at Le Gourmand."

An odd, strangely sinister memory tickled my brain. "Where is this place he rented?"

"I haven't seen it yet," Rosemary replied, "but it's off the road, more like a cabin than a house. It's small, but it has a hot tub. That's what sealed the deal for him. He loves to soak and come up with ideas."

I hurriedly swallowed a bite of my Reuben. "That's where Crystal Bird lived. When she was murdered several years ago, the property went to her estranged husband, Aaron Conley. I haven't seen him around here in ages. Is he still the owner?"

Rosemary looked surprised. "I never thought about that. My family moved here before Crystal was killed, but I never knew her. In fact, she hadn't lived there very long, had she?"

My brain filled up with all sorts of emotions and images: me, wanting to strangle Crystal for her virulent broadsheet attacks on my role as newspaper publisher; Milo, briefly considering me a suspect; Vida, jealous of a new woman friend I'd made; and all of us caught up in the wreckage that had been Crystal's life after returning to her native turf.

"Crystal was here just long enough to make enemies," I said. "Father Den found her body."

Rosemary speared a pineapple chunk from her salad. "I definitely remember that. He offered prayers for her at Mass, though she wasn't Catholic. It happened before I became prosecutor. I'll have to fill in the background for Des and ask if Conley is his landlord." She turned wistful. "He plans to stay only for the summer. Oh—he's not Catholic."

"Neither is Milo," I pointed out. "Are you engaged already?"

Rosemary almost choked on her pineapple. "No," she finally sputtered. "But he's the first guy I've gone out with in ages that has *possibilities*. We had such a good time last night. Our reservation wasn't until eight and we were the last ones still there when they closed at eleven. We had so much to talk about."

"That's a good sign," I said. "At first I felt Milo and I

had little in common. But we always talked a lot from the start. It didn't dawn on me until I married him that what we had together was Alpine itself."

Rosemary's eyes twinkled. "That figures. He's the law around here and you're the voice of the people. You're icons. Have you forgotten the gossip you two caused when he kissed you on a street corner?"

I looked askance. "That was so dumb I still can't believe it, especially at our age. We're more like relics then icons. When are you seeing Des again?"

"Friday," she replied. "Maybe a movie and then a late supper at the ski lodge. Des hasn't been here long enough to get frustrated by the lack of places to go on a date or just out for an evening. Besides, being a writer, he likes the relative quiet. I guess L.A. can get overwhelming."

The conversation drifted off along the lines of how contemporary courtship had changed and yet remained the same, why it was so hard to find the Right Person or any person, and being thankful that neither of us had been stupid enough to get married when we weren't yet grown-ups. I was tempted to mention Vida's outburst, but opted for discretion. Rosemary already knew from her own experience how touchy my House & Home editor could be, especially when it came to Roger.

Not only had it grown warmer when I stepped out from the diner, but I dreaded going back to the office. Worse yet, I was resentful of Vida for making me feel that way. So many Alpiners thought she ran the newspaper and I worked for her. That's always bothered me, but it's understandable, given her high profile in town and her longer tenure with the *Advocate*. My other concern was that her attitude would contaminate the rest of the staff. It was already making me feel sick, at least at heart.

To put off the inevitable, I pulled up in front of the

sheriff's headquarters. Maybe there was some news. Jack Mullins was on the phone and Lori either wasn't on the job or else hadn't returned from lunch. Jack winked and gestured at the sheriff's open door.

"Where'd you come from?" Milo asked, looking up from his monitor.

I fell gracelessly into one of his two visitor chairs. "Vida pitched a five-star fit and I'm upset."

Milo seemed unmoved. "So? It's not the first time."

"This is different," I asserted. "She doesn't think I trust her and feels I've broken our friendship by marrying you."

Milo just looked at me. "She thought you'd marry *her*? Things have gotten a little weird in the last few years, but even if you women want to marry each other, isn't she kind of old for you?"

I slapped my hand too hard on his desk and winced. "It's not funny!" I yipped.

"You've done this before with her," he said. "If you're really pissed, fire her. You know damned well that job means everything to her, especially now that Roger's in the slammer. She'll come around."

"But she'll still be mad at me," I protested, rubbing my sore hand. "I don't want to turn the newsroom into a toxic waste site. When she got mad before, the rest of my staff got upset."

The sheriff sat up straight in his chair. When he spoke, he used the voice he reserved for public events and recalcitrant felons. "Your biggest problem is that you never let her know you were in charge. Yes, you told me how she mentored you and eased you into taking over from Vandeventer after he was out the door the minute your check cleared. You're more like a fourth daughter than a boss. Over the last few months, this has been building with one damned crisis after another. It's up to you to sit her down and make her fish or cut bait.

Don't get me mixed up in this. She's tried to run my job, too. It took me a while to tell her to butt out, but I did it. Maybe she's too old to change. If she is . . ." He shrugged. "Then it's time for her to retire."

I hesitated. "I can't imagine the paper without her," I finally said.

"You can't seem to get along *with* her. Your call." He leaned back in his chair. "That's all I'll say. If you're interested in new developments about the stiff, there aren't any. But I'd like you to look at something."

"Okay," I said, annoyed with myself for dumping on my husband at his workplace. "What have you got for me to see?"

Milo reached behind him for a plastic evidence bag. "This is from what was left of the guy's clothes. The only label was on the jeans—Lee's. The boots were probably Frye's. Doc can't tell how long the stiff's been dead, so I'll have to ship what's left of him to Everett." He paused, putting on a pair of latex gloves before removing the silver belt buckle from the bag. "What do you make of this?"

"It's a peace symbol," I said. "The dead guy might've been a hippie."

Milo nodded. "The longish hair indicates he may have stuck to his beliefs and the lifestyle." He chucked the buckle and what was left of the belt into the bag. "Go away. If you don't, I'll make you sit on my lap."

I stood up and checked my watch. It was almost one-thirty. "The paper's out by now. You may hear from someone who has information."

"Dubious," he said, removing the gloves. "Let's eat out tonight."

"I could make a shrimp louie," I offered.

Milo was back at his computer. "Get real. That's not dinner."

I left. When I walked into the newsroom, I saw Vida's

grim face. She ignored me and I did the same. Surely she couldn't stay mad at me. Or, I wondered, was she really mad at herself? Worse yet, was there an intangible threat in the overly warm mountain air that was a danger to all of us?

Chapter Eight

AFTER I SAT down at my desk, it dawned on me that I hadn't checked on Ren Rawlings. I'd intended to call the hospital earlier, but knew neither Doc Dewey nor Elvis Sung would officially release her until around eleven. Then the confrontation with Vida had knocked Ren out of my mind.

Julie Canby was on duty again. "Ms. Rawlings was discharged shortly before noon," she informed me. "The second set of lab results didn't show anything alarming."

I supposed that was good news. "How did she seem?" I asked.

It took a moment before Julie answered the question. "Vague? Uncertain? Maybe a touch of apprehension?"

"That could be her usual MO," I said. "Do you know where she's staying? Ren never told me."

"The ski lodge," Julie replied. "She had to give a local address before she could be released."

"Did she say if she was leaving town?"

"I didn't have a chance to ask," Julie said. "They'd brought Hortense Cobb from the ICU and I had to help get her settled."

"Okay. I might try to reach Ren later on. Thanks." I rang off.

A few minutes later I saw Vida leave, purse in hand.

Mitch and Leo were both on the phone, but my ad manager hung up almost as soon as I approached his desk.

"Welcome," he said glumly, "to the chilliest place in SkyCo. Except it isn't in this weather. Why does Vida have to go off on these tangents? Is it all a plot to force me into early retirement because I smoke?"

"Don't ask," I said, sitting down in the chair next to his desk. "The only advice I've gotten about her is from Milo, who thinks I should can her. Or give her a choice to snap out of it."

"The Duchess is the most stubborn woman I've ever met," Leo declared, glancing at Mitch, who'd ended his call. "Has she taken your head off yet today, Laskey?"

"Only twice," he replied, getting up from his chair. "I'm considering another humor piece, this time about small-town tyrants."

"That's funny?" I retorted.

Mitch turned thoughtful. "No. Nothing's funny in here. I think I'll go nose around for something that is." He ambled out of the newsroom.

"Switch gears," I said to Leo. "Do we still have Ed's old clip art file?"

Leo grinned. "You're so desperate for a laugh that you want to bring back Bronsky?"

"Ed was never a laughing matter," I asserted. "Unless you count him being a joke as an ad manager. I want to look up peace symbols."

"How come?" Leo inquired. "You're going retro?"

I explained about the dead man's belt buckle. "It might look familiar to someone around here if we run a picture of it. I mean, in terms of identifying the dead guy."

Leo shrugged. "Seen one peace symbol, seen 'em all. I take it there's nothing unusual about this one?"

"It's silver. Well, silver-plated, I guess. It's kind of tarnished."

"That'll happen if the peacenik's been buried for a long time in the dump site," Leo noted. "I assume there'll be an autopsy?"

"Yes," I replied. "Doc's resources are too limited, so it's up to SnoCo to bail us out. If they're piled up—literally—it could be days before they get back to the sheriff. Not that there's any rush."

Leo tapped ash from his cigarette. "I suppose Dodge would know of anyone who'd gone missing since he's been on the job."

"He would," I asserted. "When it comes to his work, Milo's memory is flawless. Taking out the garbage is another matter."

"I did that a couple of times when I was with the family in May." My ad manager looked faintly sheepish. "I kind of liked it. Liza referred to my household chores as communal living. But she laughed when—Say," he interrupted himself, "were there any hippie communes around here back in the day? This whole area is perfect for that kind of setup."

"Vida would know—of course," I said. "Maybe I'll wander down to Milo's office and ask him. My office is starting to overheat."

Leo chuckled. "Can't keep away from the guy, huh?"

"More like I'm trying to avoid Vida," I responded, lowering my voice. "She's so unpredictable these days."

"She doesn't talk as much," Leo allowed. "That's not all bad."

A couple of moments later, I headed on my way, pausing only to wave at Alison, who was on the phone, apparently taking a classified ad. Vida's Buick wasn't in sight, but Milo's Yukon was in place. When I walked into headquarters, a tearful Lori was seated behind the counter with Jack Mullins patting her back.

"Her grandma just died," he said, sounding unusually solemn. "Her mom called. They'd moved Grandma

Cobb out of the ICU because she wasn't responding. She was ninety-two. No real surprise. Right, Lori?" He kept patting her. "Go home. I'll hold down the fort."

"No," Lori said in a small voice, wiping away the tears. "Mom and Dad are taking care of everything. I'll probably have to take time off for the funeral anyway." She pulled a tissue out of the box on her desk and blew her nose. "Grandma and Grandpa are together again. That should make me happy. But it doesn't."

"It will," I assured her. "The only good thing my brother and I could hold on to when our parents were killed in a car accident is that they were with each other." Never mind that even as Ben grieved as much as I did, he'd told me that was lousy theology. We would all be with God was as close as he could come to envisioning life after death.

Jack finally stopped patting Lori. Maybe his arm was tired. "You here for the big guy?" He nodded at Milo's closed door. "Your old man is seeing another woman."

"Who?" I asked.

He shrugged. "Lori and I didn't recognize her. Whoever it is told us she'd been in here Monday talking to Dodge. She's kind of a dish. You sure you can trust him?"

"After sixteen years?" I paused, thinking of my reaction to his call from Jeannie Clay Hobbs. "Yes. I think I know who his visitor is. How long has the door been closed?"

Jack looked at Lori, who'd composed herself. "Twenty minutes?" she said. "She got here quite a while before Mom called about Grandma."

I considered how long Ren could natter. The picture could wait, I supposed. On the other hand, if Vida was back at the office, I preferred to stall. "Say," I finally said, "do either of you know what's happening with Bill and Tanya? We old folks are out of the loop, especially since your boss doesn't like his staff bringing their personal lives to work."

Jack shrugged. "That doesn't bother me. I don't have a personal life. I'm married to Nina."

"Jack . . ." I began, but saw Milo's door open. Ren was in front of him and he looked as if he wanted to kick her rear end all the way to Front Street. To expedite her departure, I dove behind Jack so Ren couldn't see me. She walked by the three of us without a glance. Lab results or not, I still wondered if she was on drugs.

"Well?" the sheriff called to me after his visitor was out the door. "What now?"

"Gosh," I said, "I've got a question for you."

"No shit," the love of my life growled. "Let me grab a coffee refill."

"I get it," Jack said under his breath when Milo disappeared. "It was his charm that won you over."

"Right," I muttered. "Along with his sunny disposition." Seeing the sheriff enter the open area behind the curving front counter, I headed for his office and sat down.

Milo returned with a mug of the swill known as coffee in the Skykomish County sheriff's headquarters. I'd never figured out what it would be known as in other parts of the civilized world. Maybe Tricia couldn't make good coffee. What really bothered me was that my husband didn't seem to notice the difference between decent brew and dreck.

"My query is," I began, "were there ever any hippie communes along the Highway Two corridor?"

The sheriff sipped his sludge before answering. "Yeah, I vaguely recall at least one somewhere outside of Sultan. That was probably about the time I got drafted right out of high school. It may've been gone by the time I got back from Nam and headed off to Everett to study law enforcement. What's your point?"

Annoyingly, the sheriff's response was understandable. "The guy's hair wasn't gray, was it?" I countered.

"So what? Neither is yours."

"That's a family fluke," I retorted. "Ben's older and has only a few gray hairs. You already stated the dead man was under fifty."

"Right," Milo agreed, leaning back in his big swivel chair. "Let's consider the hippie angle, if only because I'm worn out from listening to your California caller. We'll get back to her later. For the sake of argument, let's say the guy was under fifty, but not by a lot." The sheriff paused to light a cigarette. "You want one?"

I shook my head. "Why do you say 'not by a lot'?"

Milo looked vexed. "Doc said what hair was left *might*—get that?—indicate the stiff was balding."

"Were the remaining hairs hippie-long?" I asked.

"No. Just longer than average. And don't ask—like Ren did—if hair and fingernails grow after you're dead. That's an optical illusion turned into a myth and a lot of bad horror movies."

"I'm not Ren," I huffed. "Why did she ask you that?"

Milo held up a big hand. "Back off. Stay on the subject. Doc and I guess the guy was in his forties when he died. Except for the manner of body disposal, there's nothing to indicate death was unnatural. I'm emphasizing this because you'll post some of it online, right?"

"If," I replied haughtily, "I find it newsworthy."

Milo stared at me without blinking, a favorite tactic he used on perps. "You're such a pain in the ass. Go ahead, you do the math."

"What math?" I asked, genuinely clueless.

"Damnit," he said, shaking his head, "you're not only cute, but you're smart, right up until you get a case of the dumbs. You're lousy at numbers. I'm talking about a forty-year-old dead guy who's wearing a hippie belt.

Maybe he kept wearing it because he never shed his early politics."

I still looked blank. "I'll take your word for it. You're the sheriff."

"So I am." Milo sighed wearily. "What do you intend to put online?"

"Nothing," I replied. "It *is* speculation. I don't like going public with guesswork, either. Now tell me about Ren."

The hand that wasn't holding the cigarette held his head. "She read the story in the paper after she got back to the ski lodge. Ren thinks the dead guy's her father. She wanted to see the stiff. I told her it had gone to Everett. For all I know, she hightailed it over there."

I felt like holding *my* head. "Wouldn't he be too young?"

"Not if he was late forties when he died. Hell, even if he hasn't been dead for ten years, he could've knocked up her mother in his teens."

"Did she have any reason to think he'd ever been in Alpine?"

"That postcard," Milo replied. "She wonders if her father gave it to her mother. That could make sense. Or else they came here together."

I considered the possibility. "Why such an old postcard? We've had SkyCo postcards forever. And where did they get it? It's ninety years old."

"I'll be ninety years old before I figure out what's going on with Ren," Milo grumbled. "I asked if she was sticking around. She thought so—if the atmosphere stayed positive. Don't ask me what that meant."

I stood up. "Who else can she pester? Ren's talked to both of us and to Vida. She's scoured the library sources, which probably included the *Advocate* along with other area publications. Unless she does personal interviews of random residents, Ren's at a dead end." I winced. "I shouldn't have said that. Digging into the past is a risky business."

He nodded. "You should know. It's a good thing you married me. You've got police protection."

"True." I gave my husband a bleak smile and left, hoping I wouldn't need protecting in the foreseeable future.

As I trudged back to the office, I realized that the one visit I'd left out in recapping Ren's tour was the art gallery. I felt remiss, given that was where she'd collapsed. The gallery opened at five, but Donna was usually there by a quarter to. The old iron clock by the bank said it was going on four. I'd leave work early. Vida's parking slot was still empty. Maybe she'd succumbed to her disgust with me and gone home.

Alison provided the answer as soon as I stepped through the door. "Vida called to say she'd heard from an old friend's daughter who's married to the new bank president. Mrs. Lambrecht is in town looking over the two vacant Parc Pines condos. Vida was meeting her to offer advice and have supper at her house."

I made a face. "That might make Miriam Lambrecht decide to stay in Seattle. There ought to be a city ordinance that our House & Home editor should never be allowed within ten feet of a stove."

"If she puts all those recipes in the paper and gives helpful kitchen hints, can she really be such a terrible cook?" Alison asked.

"In a word, yes," I stated without hesitation. "And I'm not saying that because she and I had a spat this morning."

Alison grimaced. "Do you think she's sick, but won't talk about it?"

I'd never thought about Vida being ill. Except for a rare cold or touch of flu, she was as healthy as she was opinionated. Which was saying a lot about her iron constitution. I admitted to Alison that a physical ailment hadn't occurred to me.

"The problem is," I went on, "she'd never admit it. Nor could I worm anything out of her daughter, Amy. She, along with her sisters, guard their mother's privacy as if she were the Queen of England."

"She *is* the Queen of Alpine," Alison said with a wry smile.

I nodded. "That's another obstacle for me. I may be her boss, but she considers me a pretender to the throne."

Alison's phone rang. I paused, giving her a questioning look to see if the call was for me. She shook her head, so I headed to my office, which had grown uncomfortable. I wondered if Harvey Adcock had received his shipment of new fans. Feeling enervated, I decided to go into the larger and better-ventilated newsroom. Maybe I could spend the rest of the workday researching Alpine in the hippie era. It'd be more comfortable sitting at Vida's vacated desk instead of in my airless office.

I pulled out the 1967 volume for starters. I'd been thirteen during that year's "Summer of Love" and living in Seattle's blue-collar neighborhood of Wallingford. Back then, I was more interested in dealing with zits than reading about sit-ins at San Francisco's Golden Gate Park.

Apparently, Marius Vandeventer wasn't any more intrigued with counterculture than I'd been. Except for brief wire service stories he'd plugged into the back pages, there was nothing hippie-related. I moved on to 1968. Still nothing, nor did 1969 or 1970 yield any SkyCo references to what was by then a waning movement. The only hint of hippie politics was Marius's staunch pro–Vietnam War stance. It was quite a switch from the Socialist-Labor leanings in his early Alpine years.

Yet the hippies hadn't evaporated in a puff of weed. Their spirit had remained alive, as the dead man in the dump site might have attested. They'd evolved into protesters of many things, including environmental abuse. I flipped through the 1970 and 1971 editions. For the first time I saw some local young people with longer hair and hippie-like attire. Along with progressive ideas, fashion statements take a long time to reach isolated small towns like Alpine.

A glance at my watch told me it was almost four-thirty. Mitch and Leo had come and gone and come back again. My reporter finally asked me what I was doing. Realizing he hadn't been here when Ren had visited the *Advocate* on Monday, I filled him in.

"So what's the tie-in?" he asked. "Is she a developing story along with hippies? Or is Ren a suspect in the long-ago murder of a man she thinks is her father?"

I sighed. "Unfortunately for our front page, I doubt she's either one. For all I know, she may be headed back to California."

"But Dodge doesn't think so?"

"Sometimes he likes to think the worst," I replied. "If Ren turns out to be a story, she's all yours." Aware that my reporter was touchy about divisions of labor, I added that so far all we had was a curious flake seeking her roots.

Mitch didn't agree. "That's a feature, with so many people getting interested in their ancestors. I noticed that back in Detroit not long after this country's bicentennial. Do you want me to take a shot at her if she's still at the ski lodge?"

It wasn't the worst idea he'd ever had. In fact, Mitch had plenty of good ones. After the giddy, enthusiastic Carla Steinmetz Talliaferro, the good-looking yet journalistically raw Scott Chamoud, and finally the disastrous, mad-as-a-hatter Curtis Mayne, I wasn't used to a savvy, veteran reporter like Mitch.

"Go for it," I said. Better him than me.

"I will," he responded, taking a quick look at his watch. "Maybe I'll head for the ski lodge now."

"Good luck," I said—and meant it.

Shortly after four-thirty, I decided to peruse only one more volume before heading to the art gallery. More hippie fashions, more beards on men, more long hair on both sexes. Yet no editorial allusions to the politics that had created the movement. No snide comments from Vida about nontraditional attire—she hadn't started working for the paper until 1980. I was about to quit halfway through 1973 when a wedding picture caught my eye. The 18-point type read STANLEY-DODGE NUPTIALS. I let out a shriek just as Leo came out from the back shop.

"What's wrong?" he asked, halting halfway to his desk.

I'd started laughing. All I could do was point to the photo in the bound volume. Leo took one look and laughed, too. "Jesus," he said. "Is that really the sheriff?"

I tried to control myself. "I . . . think . . . he still had . . . that suit . . . when I first met . . . him," I gasped between gusts of hilarity.

"Hey," Leo said, "I had three of those with the wide lapels and bell-bottom pants, along with the two-button look. I thought I was one cool-looking ad dude."

"But you didn't wear them after 1980," I pointed out.

"I might've," he said, no longer amused. "That's about the time I started hitting the sauce too hard. Man, does he look young—and sort of scared. Mulehide or whatever is really into the hippie thing. Pretty girl. I can't believe she's the same woman who came to see you back in February."

"Tricia hasn't aged well." I took another look at the photo. "The hippie bride look was in, even here. Rose-anna Bayard had carried an artichoke instead of flow-ers, and Buddy's hair and beard were all over the place. Back in the day, our future photography-studio owners were into composting and growing their own vegeta-bles."

"Milo's clean-shaven," Leo observed. "Was he al-ready a deputy?"

"Yes. After he got back from Nam, he went to Everett Junior College to get his criminal justice degree. He was hired as soon as he finished. Somewhere in there, he met Tricia. She's originally from Sultan, but was working in the ski lodge gift shop."

"I see her real first name is Patricia," Leo noted, scan-ning the copy. "Married in the Sultan Community Christian Church by the Reverend J. C. Peace. Real name?"

"Good question," I murmured. "It sounds as hippie-like as Tricia's long, flower-covered hair, baggy gown, and love beads. I wonder . . ."

"What?" Leo asked, noting I'd drifted off to some other place.

"What?" I echoed, giving a start. "Oh. The annul-ment." Suddenly, I was excited. "You may know this, but if you're married in a Protestant church, the cere-mony has to be conducted by an authorized Christian minister or it's not recognized as valid by Catholics."

Leo smiled. "You're looking for a loophole?"

"You bet I am," I replied. "Tricia's dragging her feet. Meanwhile, Ben's pressing me to get it done. Milo and I have to talk."

"After seeing this picture of him, I thought maybe you were considering your own divorce."

I stared again at the tall, lanky young man standing somewhat ill at ease beside his beaming, bright-eyed bride. "I think he seems kind of sweet. But age has greatly improved his looks."

"I'll grant that much," Leo conceded. "But sweet, he's not."

"That's good," I asserted. "If he was, I'd never have married him."

Leo just shook his head and wandered off to his desk.

I set aside my research. After telling Alison I was leaving early, I headed for the art gallery across Front Street and four blocks east. I found a parking spot near the corner of Eighth. The CLOSED sign was on the door, but I could see Donna inside. She hurried to let me in.

"I was going to call you," she said, smiling. "I sold Craig's new work today to a man from Longview. He liked it a lot better than you did."

"He probably knows more about art than I do," I said, a trifle chagrined. "I can only respond on a visceral level. Most of Picasso's works are a total mystery and the Pop Art movement looks like junk."

"Some of it was," Donna agreed. "I'm no expert, but I studied art in college and I try to keep up with what's current. This," she went on with a sweeping gesture, "is more personally rewarding than running the day care. There are only so many diaper changes and nose-wipings you can do in a day before you need something more aesthetic. Of course I couldn't afford to run the gallery if it wasn't for my day job."

"Does Craig know you've sold the painting?"

"I left a message on his cell," Donna replied, re-arranging two pairs of ceramic candleholders on top of a display case. "He'll get in touch when he feels like it. You know time and money mean nothing to him." Her gratified expression changed. "I heard Ren Rawlings got out of the hospital today. Do you know how she's doing?"

"Well enough to pay Milo a call," I replied. "She's still trying to track down her mother—and her father. That's why I'm here. I wondered what sent her into a swoon in the first place. Do you have any idea?"

Donna's pretty face grew earnest. "She'd only been here a few minutes. I spent most of that time with Clea Bhuj and her husband,. Allan, who came as soon as I opened. I left them mulling over antique bookends to ask Ren if I could help. She said she was an art teacher and was judging a Monroe art show this summer. She thought her mother had visited Alpine years ago. I gave her my brochure so she could see the kind of art I feature and what I've sold. Clea called to me, so I excused myself. Moments later, Ren collapsed. She knocked over a Nez Perce carving of Chief Joseph. Luckily, it's made of wood. No damage done."

I sorted through Donna's account. "I gather there wasn't any indication of what upset her? No squeals or gasps?"

Donna shook her head. "Nothing. Clea saw her fall. She said Ren dropped to the floor like a rag doll. Have the doctors given a diagnosis?"

"Nothing much showed up in the lab tests," I replied. Noting it was almost five, I told Donna I'd leave her so she could finish getting ready. Maybe Ren was merely the skittish type. That was a much less pejorative word than "unhinged" or "goofy." But I still felt uneasy. For some reason, the word "dangerous" lurked somewhere in the back of my brain. Unfortunately, I didn't know if Ren was in danger or if she posed a danger to someone else. Eventually, I'd find out. The seeds of discovery had already cast their long shadows over all of Skykomish County.

Chapter Nine

I'D STOPPED AT Cal's Chevron to get the oil changed and fill the tank. Milo hadn't yet arrived by the time I got home at five-thirty. I immediately opened all the doors. Both bedrooms' windows were already up as far as they could go without letting a bear crawl inside. I didn't make drinks, figuring we'd probably eat at the air-conditioned ski lodge, maybe in the bar. With its Norse decor and the little waterfall off by the serving area, the Viking Lounge always seemed cool.

By ten to six, I was getting antsy. The sheriff was usually home by then, unless he was working a big case. I wondered if something had come up that he hadn't told me about. It wouldn't be the first time Milo had neglected to keep me posted about what he called "the job" and I called "breaking news."

Two minutes later, he rushed through the front door. "Emma!" he shouted. "Are you nuts?"

I jumped off the sofa. "No. Why?"

He snatched off his regulation hat and tossed it on the easy chair. "There may be a perv loose and you've got the doors wide open?"

"You're taking this perv thing seriously?" I asked.

He grimaced. "Dustin Fong took the impressions from Jeannie's garden today. We got a good one. It's not any kind of sportswear, but more of a dress shoe. Scratch the teen punks. I stopped by to let Jeannie know. Now she's really upset. On top of that, Grace Grundle called to say she thought she had a prowler. Dwight went over to check about an hour ago, but couldn't find a sign of anybody except Marlowe Whipp walking through a flower bed to deliver Grace's mail."

I felt myself stiffen. "When's Jeannie's husband coming home?"

"Friday night," Milo replied, starting for the bedroom. "Dale works for the state fish and game commission, so he's gone a lot. I'm going to change. Are you ready?"

"Yes," I called after him, heading in the other direction to close the back and side doors. Just what we needed, I thought—a head case on the loose with the temperature supposed to hit over eighty before the weekend. Maybe we should close the windows, too. Fleetingly, I wished Jeannie's husband didn't travel so much. She might require further protection from the sheriff. That thought made me want to kick myself. Was I turning into a typical, irrational wife? Of course I wasn't, I told myself—and slammed the back door shut.

Milo was ready by the time I'd set up the morning coffee and watered the kalanchoe plants on the kitchen windowsill. We headed out into bright sunshine for the ski lodge. Henry Bardeen greeted us at the door. I inquired after the guest who'd passed out the previous afternoon.

"An older man from Morro Bay, California," the ski lodge manager replied, looking uneasy. "Mrs. Fowler thinks it was food poisoning. They'd just checked in, so he couldn't have gotten it here. But you know how rumors start."

I nodded. "Was he hospitalized?"

Henry shook his head. The obvious toupee stayed in place. "Dr. Sung diagnosed it as colitis—a chronic condition. You'd think his wife would've realized that. He was up and about today."

Milo grabbed my arm, apparently impatient to move on. "Any openings in the bar?" he asked.

"Yes," Henry replied, "but with AC, we're busier than usual."

"Right," the sheriff said, hauling me off through the lobby. "Thanks, Henry," he called over his shoulder before lowering his voice to speak to me. "Do you have to start yakking at everybody you run into? I'm starved and I could use a drink."

"It might've been a story," I protested as he propelled me into the bar. "If nothing else, a 'Scene' item for Vida."

"Like what? Old coot gets gas?"

Henry's daughter, Heather Bavich, was coming our way to seat us, so I didn't answer him. I noticed she was pregnant with her second child and congratulated her.

"Due date is November," she said. "I hope it's early in the month so I'm not out of commission for Thanksgiving."

"Just be glad you don't have to worry about Christmas," I responded as she showed us to a corner table.

"I am," she said. "Trevor's birthday is December first. He hopes it's another boy. I'd prefer a girl this time."

I smiled. "Good luck with that."

Milo was staring at the bartender, who looked like a college student. "Tell whoever's slinging the drinks to bring us a Scotch-rocks and a Canadian water-back, okay, Heather?"

"Right," she said. "Enjoy."

"You did it again," the sheriff muttered after Heather hurried away.

"Hey, jackass, I've got an image to keep up around here," I retorted. "I'm the neighborly newspaper snoop. Besides, Henry's an advertiser."

Milo shrugged. "What are you having? I'm going for the Trondheim cod." He looked up at the typical blond waitress whose name typically began with a *B*, in this case, Blythe. "We'll order in ten minutes," my husband informed her as she set our drinks in front of us. "Thanks."

"I think you scared her," I said. "I'm having a double order of the gravlax and a side salad. Why are you so grumpy?"

He frowned and put the menu aside. "I got a call from the Everett ME while I was changing. Ren was there and said I sent her."

"To view the corpse?" I asked in surprise. He nodded. "What did you tell whoever called?"

"It was Colin Knapp," Milo replied, relaxing a bit after taking the first big sip of Scotch. "I told him she'd come on her own, but to let her have a look. Maybe it'll scare her and she'll take off for California. Knapp figured she was screwy."

I put my hand on his. "Cheer up. I should be the one who's grumpy. I didn't get a kiss when you came home."

He grimaced. "Damn. Why did you marry me? Mulehide was right. I'm a lousy husband." He moved his hand to put it on my neck and leaned over to kiss me . . . gently. The young couple at the next table stared. Luckily, I didn't recognize them. "That better?" Milo asked.

I smiled. "Yes. Though you did give me a good laugh today."

He looked puzzled. "When?"

I told him about seeing his wedding photo. Milo actually turned faintly red. "Oh God! Now you know why I burned all the wedding pictures Mulehide left behind when she took off with Jake the Snake."

"I liked it," I declared. "You looked so young—and endearing."

Milo took a really big swig of his drink. "Endearing?

I looked like an idiot. I *was* an idiot back then or I'd never have married Mulehide."

"She looked very pretty. But," I went on, "that wedding coverage gave me an idea."

"What?" he asked sharply. "You want to back out of ours now?"

I scowled at him. "I mean the annulment. Pay attention. What do you remember about the minister who married you?"

He grimaced again. "Not much. I was really nervous. It was Mulehide's church, so you'd have to ask her. Why does it matter?"

It took me until our meals arrived to explain once again the Church's reasons for granting annulments. Milo digested the information along with the rest of his Scotch. He asked if I'd talked to Ben or Father Kelly about what I suspected regarding the Reverend J. C. Peace.

"No," I replied. "I only saw the wedding story just before I left work. We'll have to get a copy of the church registry to see if the minister signed it. Tricia might know if he was legit."

Milo shook his head. "I doubt it. She didn't go to church much after she got out of high school. Her folks went once in a while, though."

I realized how little I knew about Tricia Stanley Dodge Sellers. I'd met her for the first time back in February, when she'd come to ask if I'd help Tanya deal with her PTSD. "Are both Stanleys alive?"

"Yeah," Milo said after swallowing a mouthful of pickled beets. "In fact, they still live in the family home. They liked me, especially her dad. I was employed." He forked in some cod.

I licked at errant crumbs from the hard bread under my gravlax. "Have you seen them recently?"

"Oh . . ." He gazed up at the white pine ceiling. "Last

winter when I went steelheading at Reiter Ponds. I drop by when I'm fishing that hole near Sultan. Ralph still fishes. They're nice folks, even if they did spoil Mulehide rotten. She was the only girl among their four kids."

"You've never mentioned anything about your ex-in-laws before," I said with a tinge of reproach.

Milo shrugged. "Why would I? You don't know them."

"I'd like to know them now," I asserted, leaning closer. "They may be able to help us. Or are they gaga?"

My husband turned thoughtful. "Their minds are still sharp. Madge got a new hip last summer, but she needs the other one fixed. Ralph's in decent shape, though he moves slower than he used to." He paused. "They might like to meet you. They've been nagging me to find another wife for years. I doubt they know we're married." He grinned. "Wait until they see what I got."

I couldn't help it. I simpered. It's a wonder I didn't say, "Aw, go on!"

Instead, I stopped grinning back at Milo and asked when we could pay them a call.

"If we go to Bellevue over the weekend, we could stop by on the way back," he said after a pause. "They always like hearing about their grandkids. Mulehide isn't good about keeping them in the loop. She doesn't visit her folks very often, especially since her last divorce. I guess she's embarrassed."

"Do you think you can get away from work to have dinner with Mu . . . I mean, Tricia?"

"Probably," Milo replied. "The big to-do for the Fourth is on Monday, so we should be able to go Friday or Saturday." He shot me an inquiring glance. "Are you nervous about seeing Mulehide in her natural habitat?"

"Not really," I said. "Curious, though. I know what

the house looks like from the outside because I saw it on TV during the standoff with Tanya's late fiancé."

"It's nice inside. But," he added with a gleam in his hazel eyes, "she doesn't have all new appliances like you do."

I simpered again.

Except for a flicker of eyelids behind the big glasses, Vida didn't acknowledge my arrival Thursday morning. It was a bad start to the workday, but I told myself I might as well get used to it. A few minutes after I settled behind my desk, Mitch showed up with the bakery goods. I emerged to get a powdered sugar doughnut and asked him to come into my office. He looked wary. But my reporter often did.

"I haven't checked the sheriff's log," he said, placing his coffee mug on my desk and holding a knish on a napkin. "You think there's news?"

"No," I said. "The only so-called news I heard from the sheriff last night was that Ren Rawlings went to the SnoCo ME's department to view the remains of what she thinks might be her father. I wondered if you tracked her down before she left town or after she got back."

Mitch frowned. "She was already gone by the time I left here. I didn't try later on. I don't like leaving Brenda alone at night unless I have to, for county commissioners' and school board meetings. I'll check after I go to the sheriff's office and the courthouse."

"That's fine," I assured him. "The ancestry angle might turn out to work with some other residents. In fact, we've had more diversity here since the college opened. As you know, the president, May Hashimoto, is Japanese and there are at least three or four other faculty members who have Asian backgrounds."

"Good angle," Mitch said, brightening as he always did at the prospect of an interesting feature. "How about the old-timers? All those Scandinavians, at least one Greek family." He glanced over his shoulder and lowered his voice. "I wonder if Vida would help me with the locals?"

"She might," I replied. "It's right up in her wheel-house. And she's not mad at you."

"Yet," Mitch said under his breath.

I merely nodded.

I wasn't in the mood to research possible hippie pro-testers. In fact, I was in a faintly pugnacious mood, no doubt triggered by Vida's antagonistic stance. However, she wasn't wrong about RestHaven's reluctance to be-come part of the community, especially releasing news of interest to SkyCo residents. I decided to call Spencer Fleetwood to get his reaction. Early on, Rosalie Reed had leaked items to him, which had infuriated me. Then I discovered they'd been lovers long before Dr. Reed had come to Alpine. But in the past few months the leak had been plugged. I suspected someone—probably Dr. Woo—had reprimanded Rosalie for not holding the in-stitutional line.

Spence answered in his usual mellifluous voice, but immediately went on the defensive before I could say anything. "If you're calling about Almquist's hiring at RestHaven, I did not know about it until I read it in the *Advocate* yesterday. We may both be sleeping with our sources, but Rosalie's lips are as sealed as your favorite stud's."

"Damn. You read my mind," I said. "Now I'm really annoyed. What's going on up there? Is Kay Burns earn-ing her money by *not* releasing news?"

"So it would seem," Spence replied. "It's one of those off-limit topics with Rosalie. You understand—akin to you making demands on Dodge about ongoing investi-gations."

"Right. I get it. Is Woo the one who's so touchy or is it Farrell?"

"Both. Patient privacy." Spence sighed. "I've actually talked to Woo about it, but he's politely adamant. Discretion is his middle name. By the way, what's Vida doing for her show tonight? She hasn't yet told me."

I stiffened in my chair. "I don't know, either. Maybe it's a surprise."

There was a brief silence before Spence spoke again. "You sound tense. Is the Queen of the Alpine Airways still a cloud of gloom?"

"Yes. Good luck with her tonight."

"Oh God!" Spence exclaimed, no longer mellifluous. "What now? Never mind, I shall gird my loins. Got to dash off to do the hour-turn news. Not that I have much of it this morning." He rang off.

I decided to pay Kay Burns a call. It was better than staying in my office, where only a tight-lipped Vida remained at her desk. But when I was halfway to the newsroom, she spoke to me.

"I'm writing about Miriam Lambrecht," she announced as if she were handing out Order of the British Empire medals at Buckingham Palace. "She's not only a charming, well-bred woman, but extremely kind and friendly." Vida turned her back to me and resumed typing.

In other words, I thought, as I trudged out of the newsroom, *the opposite of me.*

RestHaven might have changed its mailing address, but after parking my Honda, I went through the main entrance, half-expecting to see an armed Sid Almquist in uniform barring my way. But access was effortless and the rotunda was unchanged. I went up to the main desk, asking for Kay. The solemn young Samoan woman told me she'd check with Ms. Burns. While she spoke to

Kay, I mentally added the receptionist to the list of ethnic possibilities for Mitch's proposed feature.

I was informed that Ms. Burns would see me. Did I know where her office was located? I didn't. She pointed to a door on the right at the rear of the rotunda. My footsteps echoed as I walked across what had once been called the Bronsky ballroom, but in reality was where the family played Ping-Pong on rainy days while waiting for a mammoth delivery from Itsa Bitsa Pizza.

Kay rose when I came into her comfortable office. "What a surprise, Emma!" she exclaimed. "I haven't seen you for over a month. Do sit. Coffee?" She pointed to a Starbucks Verismo model on a mahogany table.

I declined. "You might want to have some booze on hand to put in that coffeemaker after I tell you why I'm here."

Kay, who was in her mid-fifties, but looked much younger, kept her composure. "Oh dear. What have I done?"

"It's what you haven't done," I said, trying to keep my voice light. "Both Spencer Fleetwood and I are frustrated over the lack of coverage we're allowed to have of RestHaven. Vida's upset, too, because all her requests for staff members to be on her radio program have been turned down. Even you refused, though you knew she wouldn't ask embarrassing or intrusive questions on the air." In private was another matter, but of course I didn't say that.

"Well." Kay ran a hand through the short black hair that was styled to set off her fine features. "In my own defense, I realized Vida probably would talk about not only my life since I came back to Alpine, but my earlier years before I moved away. Frankly, I wanted to avoid that. It wasn't a happy time for me with two failed marriages. Vida does have a way when it comes to wringing information out of other people. It could've been embarrassing."

"She has her methods," I conceded, wondering if Vida had given her the third-degree before leaving Alpine. I almost had to agree with Kay's refusal to be interviewed. "I can see your point," I continued, "but that doesn't explain the other three who bowed out. I know the reasons Farrell, Reed, and Hood told her, but it still seems uncooperative. As you must know, it isn't good PR. RestHaven is part of the community."

Kay folded her hands and waited a moment before responding. "Let me explain the culture here," she began, her blue eyes fixed on my face. "There's no mystery about the medical rehab section. At the moment, half the patients are local. Vida probably knows who they are. They'll recover from whatever problems they have and return to their lives. The addiction unit is very different. Some of the patients register under an alias. They want privacy. Surely you and Vida and Spencer understand that."

I nodded. "Of course."

"The same holds true of the mental health ward," Kay went on. "Let's be frank. While society is changing its attitude toward mental illness, it's still a very sensitive subject. Not only do the patients want to avoid being stigmatized, but so do their family members. Until mental illness sheds its taboo status, we must protect the people in our care."

"I realize that," I allowed, "but when Dr. Reed's husband escaped, keeping his identity—even his physical description—a secret was detrimental to finding him until it was too late. Nor was it fair to SkyCo's residents. They had no idea if the missing man was dangerous. That caused some panic, especially among parents and the elderly."

Kay finally looked off toward a framed print of Marc

Chagall's *Amoureux de Vence*. I was glad it wasn't Edvard Munch's *The Scream*.

"Let me give you an example," she said, leaning forward in her chair. "This morning a patient admitted herself, insisting on using a false name. She didn't want anyone—including her parents, whom she implied might be deceased—to find out she'd come here. She's ashamed. Frightened, too. How can we not respect her feelings? It would be barbarous of us to do otherwise."

"That I understand," I asserted. "But it's not what I'm talking about. Hiring Sid Almquist, for example, *is* news here. Good news, given what happened to him and Mary Jean before they left Alpine."

Kay looked blank. "I don't know anything about that. I've only a vague recollection of Sid and none of Mary Jean."

I stood up, smiling ironically. "Kay, I hate to say this, but I think we're deadlocked on this issue. Mitch Laskey has been asking for months about the groundbreaking for the Alzheimer's wing. We understood that would happen in the early spring. Now we're into summer and still no date's been set. Is it going to happen or has the idea been shelved?"

Kay looked pained. "The architect, Scott Melville, hasn't yet finalized his plans. That is, the input from our administrators is still being evaluated. There is some concern about those power lines that would go right over the proposed site. Aesthetic and emotional impact on both patients and staff, you see. This isn't for publication, but we might have to add on out back instead of to the east."

I nodded. "I only hope that when it comes to this kind of news that doesn't violate patient privacy, RestHaven will be more forthcoming."

Kay had also gotten to her feet. "I hope we can do that," she said quietly. "I don't want you, Vida, and

Spencer to be angry with me." She smiled. "I like Spencer very much. He's a charming man. And I know you mean well. By the way, what did happen to poor Sid before he left town?"

My smile widened. "I can't tell you that. I'm protecting his personal and professional privacy."

I felt smug as I walked out into the rotunda. But I was also curious, a natural condition for me. I wondered if the young woman who had admitted herself was Ren Rawlings. My musings were interrupted as I neared the exit and saw Iain Farrell come out of his office. He took one look at me and went back inside, closing the door behind him.

That made me more than curious. Now I was also suspicious. Maybe Farrell was afraid I'd ask embarrassing questions. Or maybe he was just afraid of something I couldn't guess.

Chapter Ten

BACK AT THE office, I forced myself to flip through early 1980s' *Advocate*s. By then, the counterculture hippies had morphed into the pro-environmental yippies. During my tenure with the *Oregonian*, my beat had mainly involved human-interest features in the Tri-Met area around Portland—Multnomah, Clackamas, and Washington counties. I'd rarely been assigned to hard news during my later years on the paper. The big environmental headlines in the eighties came out of the Willamette National Forest, where anti-logging protesters allegedly used vicious tactics that went beyond tree hugging. Ultimately, the protesters won out, creating economic devastation for the timber industry. Oregon's Lane County had never quite recovered.

The *Advocate*'s environmental coverage picked up dramatically as the movement invaded western Washington. By 1985, Vandeventer was practically apoplectic in his editorials. He almost went over the edge vilifying three of the protesters by name, all from the Seattle area. Their gravest sin was putting a clown mask on Carl Clemans's statue in Old Mill Park. I guessed that Marius had lost his sense of humor. From what I'd heard of Mr. Clemans, he enjoyed a good laugh, even at his own expense.

Halfway through 1984, I surrendered. Vida had been on the paper for almost four years. If Kassia Arthur had ever made news in Alpine, she would have remembered her. Still, that postcard nagged at me.

I looked up to see Kip in the doorway. "Hey," he said with a grin, "I'm all the way up to 1967 putting the back issues on discs. Do you want me to rush the job?"

"No," I replied. "Save it for your spare time."

He nodded before glancing over his shoulder into the empty newsroom. "I wanted to make sure Vida wasn't here," he said, no longer grinning. "She turned in a weird story about the new bank president's wife a few minutes ago. You always go over her copy, right?"

"I do, but I rarely make major changes. She does have her own chatty style, and even if it's not always good journalism writing, readers seem to like it. What do you mean by 'weird'?"

Kip frowned. "It's hard to explain, except that it's . . . kind of personal. I'll zap it to you now." He left for the back shop.

I had a feeling I knew what Kip meant. Two minutes later, the House & Home–page feature appeared on my monitor. The opening graf was fine, at least for Vida's homey style. But after a quote from Miriam Lambrecht saying how happy she and Bob were to be moving to his hometown, the piece started to go downhill.

"Miriam is a delightful woman," Vida wrote, "who will be a welcome addition to the community, particularly among her peer group. It's so refreshing to be in the company of a wife and mother who feels no need to be in the workplace, where she can flaunt her authority over employees who are helping put food on her table."

There was more in little snippets, such as Miriam being the kind of person "who one feels can be a true and loyal friend," and of course an endorsement of the entire Lambrecht family as members of the Presbyterian Church, "to which she will bring her selfless attitude and tireless efforts on behalf of those less fortunate."

I raced off to the back shop. "That second graf's out," I told Kip. "I can defend the editing on the grounds that it insults Betsy O'Toole, Janet Driggers, some of the college faculty, and several other women who have families as well as employees. I don't care if Vida blows up and lands out on Front Street. The rest of the article can stay, even if it's a bit much."

Kip's laugh was ironic. "The Lutherans won't like the church bit."

"Neither will the other churches," I said, "but they can write letters, send emails, or call her on the phone to bitch."

"Are you going to tell her what you're doing?" Kip asked.

"No," I replied. "I've edited Vida's copy before, especially when she does news stories. I don't recall her ever complaining."

"Maybe she never reads the articles after they appear in the paper."

I shrugged. "That's possible. I suspect Vandeventer may not have edited her copy. Judging from some of the articles he wrote, he didn't edit his own." I gave Kip a forlorn smile before returning to my office.

A few minutes later, I saw Mitch enter the newsroom. I went to his desk, waiting for him to pour some coffee. As soon as he sat down, I reeled off more ethnic possibilities for his roots feature.

"Diversity," he murmured. "Not exactly Alpine's middle name, but it's a start. By the way, the Ren bird has flown the coop. She checked out of the ski lodge early this morning. Is that story a dead end?"

I winced. Should I mention the new patient at Rest-Haven? Kay Burns hadn't named names nor had she sworn me to secrecy. From a personal point of view, I no longer had Vida to co-speculate about odd occurrences in Alpine. Thus, I confided my conjecture about Ren.

Mitch was on the scent. I gave him a thumbs-up sign and was about to go back to my office when Jack Blackwell stormed into the newsroom. He glanced at Leo's vacant place, glared at my reporter, and headed in my direction as if he intended to mow me down. I held my ground. "What now?" I asked as he stopped a mere two feet away.

"You and Baugh should be run out of town," Black Jack declared, shaking a fist. "How does that senile old bastard have the nerve to ask for a vote on reorganizing the county's government? If that's your idea, think again, you silly little tramp!"

"Hey!" Mitch called out sharply. "You ever heard of free speech?"

I didn't know whether to be more surprised by Jack's outburst or Mitch's defense. They were both six-footers, but the mill owner carried another twenty pounds and was in decent shape for being close to sixty.

Blackwell whirled around to face my reporter, who had gotten to his feet. "Keep out of this, Laskey," he snarled, his dark, saturnine features making him look every inch the villain. "You work for her, you're just a stooge like Walsh." He snapped around to face me again. "Where is that son of a bitch? I want my money back for that ad!"

I'd stepped a few feet away from him. "You're out of line," I said, relieved that I sounded so self-assured. "Would you rather I wrote an editorial about you being an asshole who beats up women?"

Jack slashed at the air with his hand. "I'd sue your fancy little ass off! And don't try to threaten me with Dodge. Everybody in town knows that bastard's been screwing you for years. You're the two biggest hypocrites in Skykomish County."

The only thing bigger than Blackwell's mouth was his ego. He was so self-absorbed that up until recently he hadn't known Milo and I had ever dated. I waited for a moment, then held out my left hand with the gold band and its twin circlets of tiny diamonds. "That's *Mrs.* Dodge to you, Blackwell. When are you going to make an honest woman of Patti Marsh?" I jerked my hand away from his curious eyes. "Who's the real hypocrite now?" I demanded. "Get out before I call the sheriff and every damned deputy he's got on duty."

If Jack's scorching black eyes could have killed, Mitch would've had to call Al Driggers to take me away. But the jerk wasn't giving in—not quite. "You and Dodge haven't heard the last of me," he declared, striding out of the newsroom. "I run the county commissioners. I'm his boss, and don't you and that antique of a mayor forget it!"

"Good God!" Mitch gasped as if he hadn't exhaled for at least a minute. "What got into him? Blackwell's all business whenever I've dealt with him. I thought that full-page ad was great PR."

I flopped down in Mitch's visitor chair. "It was. It is." I shook myself. "That can't be the real problem. I don't get it." I smiled weakly at my reporter. "Thanks for defending me. He might've slugged you."

Mitch shrugged. "You think I covered my crime beat in Detroit without knowing martial arts? Self-defense is practically a requirement for Motor City reporters— including the ones on the women's page."

I laughed. "I didn't know that. Was it included in the résumé you gave—" I stopped, seeing Alison hurry into the newsroom.

"You're both okay?" she asked, her blue eyes wide. "I could hear most of that. I almost called the sheriff!"

"No need for that," I said. "Mitch is my secret weapon. Or so I just found out. You grew up mostly in

Everett, so you don't know Black Jack's reputation other than as a law-abiding mill owner."

Alison looked askance. "I heard you say he beats up women. Why don't they report him?"

"His longtime girlfriend and favorite punching bag, Patti Marsh, apparently loves the guy," I said, trying to explain the unexplainable. "The rest have been short-timers or got back at him in other ways."

The phone rang in the front office before Alison could respond. She rushed off as I got to my feet. Mitch had finished his coffee, announcing he was headed for Rest-Haven. He almost collided with Alison, who was in the doorway, telling me that the sheriff was on the phone. I scurried back to my desk to take the call.

"News?" I inquired brightly.

"Not for you," Milo replied. "I should be talking to Laskey, right?"

"He just left. I'm the editor, remember?"

"Oh, right." My husband sounded beleaguered. "As far as the autopsy wizards in Everett can tell, the dead guy died of natural causes. That doesn't mean he did, though."

I made a face. "So what's your official statement, Sheriff?"

"Damned if I know," he said. "Make one up."

"I can't do that," I retorted. "Come on, give me some real information. How long has he been dead? How old was he when he died?"

There was a pause. I suspected Milo was studying the official ME report. "Three to six years, with the recent warmer winters hurrying decomposition. Age between forty-five and fifty. Caucasian, fair-haired, original but discolored teeth with some dental work, evidence of a broken ankle before he was twelve, broken arm in his twenties. No tattoos."

"That's pretty thorough," I said, "but you went too fast—wait. You're kidding about the tattoos, right?"

"Yeah. I just wanted to see if you were still alert." Milo yawned in my ear. "I'd meet you for lunch, but I can't."

"Why not?" I asked.

"Tanya got to me first," he replied. "God, I hope she isn't breaking up with Blatt. I haven't seen much of him today. He's out on patrol. I'm going to hang up on you now."

"Wait—have we reached a new plateau in our relationship that you're announcing a hang-up in advance?"

"Huh?" Milo sounded faintly startled. "No. Maybe I'm waiting for you to tell me what you're going to post on your news site. We've gotten only four calls from locals who think it could be somebody they knew who disappeared five to twenty years ago. None of the missing males were from SkyCo, though. Oh—Averill Fairbanks stopped by to say it was an alien named Leroy from the Great Red Spot on Jupiter. Mullins told Averill he was right—he'd seen Leroy go into the Icicle Creek Tavern in April of 1999. Now don't you wish I *had* hung up on you?"

I laughed. "Can I put the ME's findings on the site?"

"Hell, yes. Isn't that what you wanted to know in the first place?"

He rang off before I could answer.

Five minutes later, I left for the courthouse. Maybe Blackwell was ahead of me, on his way to berate Fuzzy Baugh. The clock in the faded redbrick tower stood at twenty to twelve. As I reached the top of the stone steps, Rosemary Bourgette emerged through one of the swinging double doors.

"Emma!" she cried, beaming at me. "Des is making me dinner tomorrow night at his place." Her eyes rolled heavenward, blinking at the bright sun. "I wonder how well he can cook. He mentioned pasta. Does that mean spaghetti?"

"Let's hope not," I said. "I call that survival food. It's a far cry from Le Gourmand. But it's definitely another date."

"I need date-worthy summer clothes," Rosemary declared. "I'm off to see if Francine Wells has anything at her Fabulous Fourth summer sale. Wish me luck."

I complied and waved her off. It'd been a while since I'd shopped for clothes. Except for buying a new winter parka on sale in the late fall, I hadn't splurged on my wardrobe in a long time. Maybe I should check out the sale. On the other hand, I was already beginning to sweat. Besides, unlike Rosemary, I had a husband. What I really needed was more bath towels. On that practical note, I walked toward the mayor's office and announced my arrival to his secretary, Bobbi Olson.

"He'll see you," she informed me with a dour expression. "He locked himself in his office when I told him Jack Blackwell showed up a couple of minutes ago. What's up with *that*?"

"Jack's being a jackass," I said. "Where'd he go?"

Bobbi shrugged. "Out the back way."

She buzzed the mayor. A moment later, Fuzzy stood—a bit stooped of late—in the doorway, smiling benignly. "A welcome sight for these tired old eyes," he asserted with a touch of the Bayou in his voice. The mayor bowed slightly as he ushered me inside and closed the door. "To what do I owe this pleasure?"

"Black Jack," I replied, sitting down in the comfortably cushioned chair across the mahogany desk from the mayor's even more luxurious model. "I assume you barred the door to him."

Fuzzy chuckled. "Valor is more difficult than discretion in my advanced years. Commissioner Blackwell did not take kindly to my proposal of abolishing his county job. May I hazard a guess that you've already suffered his wrath?"

I nodded. "When will you call for the special election?"

"At the Fourth of July picnic," the mayor responded. "What patriotic citizen could object? I'm content to surrender my own position. Surely Jack would like to unburden himself of his frustrating government duties. It can't be easy, given that the two other commissioners are so elderly and no longer capable of making sound decisions for our fine county." The faded blue eyes held a hint of life. "A stroke of genius on your part, my dear, to run the flag picture on the front page of the special edition."

"It seemed appropriate," I murmured modestly.

"Indeed. Which," he went on, folding his liver-spotted hands on the desk, "is why I'll propose that the election be held Tuesday, September sixth—immediately after the Labor Day weekend. It's time we put this county back to work." For emphasis, he unfolded his hands and caressed the arms of his chair. "How does that strike you, shugah?"

"Canny," I remarked. "Maybe I should have Milo's deputies pat down Blackwell if he shows up for the Labor Day event. Have you told Spencer Fleetwood about your plan for the Fourth?"

The mayor leaned back in his chair. "All in good time. Had you not been so concerned about my welfare I wouldn't have told you until it happened. You will be in attendance?"

"Yes," I assured him, standing up. "Meanwhile, keep Black Jack at bay. No doubt he's still on the prowl. I assume you're not armed?"

Fuzzy gingerly rose to his feet. "I'm not afraid to walk the streets of Alpine without a weapon." The blue eyes flickered. "My lovely wife is licensed to carry and conceal her Taurus PT-25 pistol. Irene never leaves home without it." He made another bow. "Do give my regards to your valiant husband. As always, it's been a joy to visit with you."

Joy or not, I felt uneasy as I left the courthouse and heard the noon whistle sound at Blackwell Timber. I half-expected to espy Jack hiding in the shrubbery surrounding the venerable old building. Instead, I saw Milo loping out of his office a block away to get into the Yukon. I assumed he was meeting Tanya for lunch at the ski lodge.

I didn't feel hungry, so I decided to go back to the office and order some towels from Penney's online site. By the time I arrived, only Alison was there to man the phones. Since some people ignored the sign on the door that said we were closed during the lunch hour, either our receptionist or Kip stayed around to take calls. My back-shop wizard usually brought his lunch, so I was faintly surprised to see Alison in place. I asked her why she hadn't gone out to eat.

"Chili MacDuff called just before noon," she replied. "She thought someone was hiding in their garage. Maybe everybody's nervous because there were those reports of a lurker in the paper this week."

"All two of them?" I said.

Alison shrugged. "I'm glad Lori Cobb lives with me at Pines Villa. Mrs. Runkel says her sister-in-law, Ella, is gaga, but maybe she did see someone suspicious in the Parc Pines garage next door. Just in case, I look around our underground parking when I come and go."

"No point in taking chances," I said. "Go ahead and have lunch. I'm going to stick around. This weather kills my appetite. I can stay up front while I do some online shopping."

Alison slid off her chair. "Okay. I won't be long."

I found two sets of towels on sale. Feeling at loose
ends, I went into the newsroom to take another look at
Milo and Tricia's wedding write-up. Having been overcome with mirth from seeing my husband as a lanky,
anxious groom, I'd only skimmed Vida's predecessor's
account of the wedding. Maybe I could find some details about the Reverend J. C. Peace. Grasping at straws
is second nature to journalists. A mere mention of interest can spawn ten inches of copy on an uneventful day.

Lugging the volume back to the front office, I flipped
to the June 1973 issues. Tricia's maid of honor was a
cousin named Valerie Stone of Arlington; Milo's older
brother, Clint, had been his best man. I'd never met
Clint, whose residence was listed as Pullman. No doubt
he'd been finishing his doctorate in biology at WSU
back then. All I knew about my brother-in-law was that
he and his family lived in Dallas—and Milo never had
anything good to say about him.

After the two other bridesmaids, flower girl and ring
bearer, there was a brief note about the minister: "The
ceremony was conducted by the Reverend J. C. Peace of
Arlington."

I sat up straight. Coincidence that Cousin Valerie and
Minister Peace both resided in the same place? Arlington was another former logging town, but now three
times the size of Alpine. Its location just off the I-5 free-
way had turned it into a virtual suburb of Everett. But
back in 1973, it had been much smaller. On the other
hand, I knew nothing about Tricia's maid of honor.

Unwilling to give up my curiosity about the reverend,
I put his name into the computer. Nothing. I narrowed
my search to *The Seattle Times*. Another blank. Finally,
I tried *The Everett Herald*. Zip. Maybe the newspapers'
online sites didn't go back that far. Or maybe I was nuts
for thinking J. C. Peace was the answer to a prayer for
an annulment.

At five to one, Vida was the first staffer to return. She looked startled to see me. I said hi and tried to smile.

"Where's Alison?" she inquired in a tone that suggested I might have beat up on the poor girl and booted her out onto Front Street.

"Lunch," I replied, then dared to ask *her* a question. "What do you know about the Reverend Peace?"

She scowled. "Who?"

I stated his full name as given in the wedding article.

Vida was magnanimous enough to look thoughtful. "Y-y-yes. The peculiar person who performed Milo and Tricia's wedding. Ernest and I did attend, even though it was in Sultan."

At first I thought she'd said it was "insulting." Which it had been, as she had already told me, because the ceremony hadn't been held in "one of Alpine's nicer churches." She'd probably said the same about Princess Elizabeth and Prince Philip's wedding at Westminster Abbey.

"I believe," she continued, digging deep into the gold mine that was her memory, "the minister was later arrested."

"For what?" I asked.

"Some sort of protest. Antiwar, perhaps. Or was it over charges filed against another of those do-good groups from thirty years ago?" She shook her head. "It didn't happen in Alpine. Seattle, perhaps." Vida dismissed civil unrest with a shrug and stalked off into the newsroom.

In other words, the reverend was just another do-gooder typical of his era. But I wasn't giving up on him yet. In mid-May, Milo and I had gone to Bellevue to celebrate Tanya's birthday with the rest of the Dodge family. My husband had insisted on taking us out to dinner to spare me from his ex's mediocre cooking. Being ignorant about Eastside eateries, he'd let Tanya choose the restaurant. The first explosion from Milo had come when she emailed him to say we'd meet at Bison Main. Convinced we were having buffalo burgers for dinner, he'd grumbled for hours until I figured out that the restaurant's name was Bis on Main. I gave up trying to explain what that meant, but the food was good. At least Milo thought it was after he realized he could order steak. Two steaks, in fact, because they were filet mignons and looked small to him. He'd also picked up the hefty check.

But dining *en famille* in a public place hadn't been conducive to discussing Tricia's role in the annulment process. We didn't stop at her house, so after shelling out seven hundred bucks, my beloved wanted to get the hell out of Bellevue and hightail it back to Alpine. The dinner had been a bit of a blur to me. Three strong MacNaughtons on the rocks can have that effect when I was feeling anxious about facing the rest of Milo's family as the second Mrs. Dodge.

The first thing I did when I got back to my office was to call my husband. "What," I asked, "do you remember about the Reverend Peace?"

"I already told you," he replied, sounding testy. "Not much. He was young, had a beard, long hair, typical hippie. Hyped on love and all that bullshit. He spoke so damned softly that I couldn't hear him if I'd tried."

"Don't hang up on me," I warned him. "Who's Valerie Stone?"

"Val?" Milo sounded startled. "A cousin. Why . . . oh, right, she was Mulehide's maid of honor. What about her?"

"Never mind. Is she still in Arlington?"

He paused. "Maybe. Tanya might know. Ask her."

As I expected, he hung up. I felt frustrated. Vida was on the phone. Dare I call Tanya at work? She was new to the job, so that wasn't a good idea. I didn't know what she and her father had talked about at lunch. Was she in distress over Bill? I sat grim-faced, drumming my fingernails. Then I bit the bullet and called Tricia.

"Emma," she said in a voice that conveyed surprise, if not pleasure. "Is something wrong?"

"No," I replied, hoping I exuded warmth. "It's about the annulment. I have a couple of questions. I'm not prying, strictly informational."

Tricia's laugh seemed forced. "Well . . . certainly. I really don't understand the process, but I gather it means something to you."

"It does," I declared. "Who chose the minister who married you?"

"I did," Tricia responded. "He was a guest speaker at the church's young people's group in Sultan. I was very impressed by his vision of how our society should evolve, being a bit of a rebel back then. In fact, Milo's cousin Val knew him. After I moved to Alpine and went to work in the ski lodge's gift shop, she and I became roommates. That's how Milo and I met. You might say Val set us up. I eventually forgave her for that."

I ignored the remark. "Is his real name J. C. Peace?"

"Well . . . that's how he signed the church's marriage certificate."

"Do you still have it?"

She laughed. "My, no! I left all that behind when I moved away. Milo told me he threw it all out. He would, of course. That's so like him."

I gritted my teeth. "Would the church have a copy?"

"The church is now a Boys and Girls Club," Tricia replied. "My parents only went there for special occasions. We weren't a religious family. I respect your own beliefs, though I don't understand all the rules and regulations Catholics have. It seems very complicated. It isn't as if you and Milo aren't already married."

It was pointless to explain why the annulment meant

so much to me or why the minister's status mattered. I tried another tactic. "I've never heard Milo talk about Val. Are you still in touch with her?"

"Not often," Tricia replied. "Val never stopped trying to change the world. After she graduated from high school, she joined the Peace Corps and was sent to Jamaica. It sounded like a vacation to me, but she insisted the island wasn't all rum and calypso. Then she came back to Alpine, but only for a short time. Val surfaces every so often, by phone or email. I think she's in India now. She blogs and writes poetry. I've never known how she makes her living. I suspect she lives off of whatever man she's with for as long as she can put up with him—and vice versa. Don't get me wrong," she added hastily. "I've always been fond of Val, but she's an idealist and a blithe spirit."

"I don't recall Milo mentioning her," I said.

"Oh?" There was a defensive note in the response. "She lived with the Dodges for a few years. Val's parents on Milo's mother's side divorced. Frank was an alcoholic and after the marriage fell apart, Peggy Stone had a complete breakdown. Val was fourteen at the time and already kind of wild. The Dodges took her in. She lived with them until she turned eighteen, the same age as Milo's sister, Emily. I assume he's told you she died of cancer in her thirties?"

"Yes," I replied, though it had been Vida who'd given me the account of Emily's brief life. Milo had, however, referred to his *sisters* upon occasion, which had puzzled me, but I'd never pressed him for details. "I hope we can make it for dinner tomorrow night," I said. "That is, if the invitation is still open."

"Oh, it is," Tricia responded with enthusiasm. "I want you both to meet Zach. I think I've finally found Mr. Right. He's so sensitive, pleasant, thoughtful, easygoing—everything I always wanted in a man."

In other words, not much like Milo. "I'm very happy for you," I said. "We'll be there unless some crisis doesn't come along before we take off."

"Yes." Her tone hardened. "So often during our marriage, Milo had a crisis. Maybe you can put up with it. You don't have children. I did."

"I have my own work crises," I said. "They're inherent in both of our jobs. Is there anything I can bring?"

"No, but thanks for offering," Tricia replied. "I have everything I need." Her last words sounded smug.

I felt sorry for her. After twenty years, she was still bitter. She'd walked out on her marriage and into the arms of a man who'd betrayed his wife. From what little I knew of Tricia, she was a decent, well-meaning woman. She loved her children. And, yes, she'd had the heavier task of raising them. Milo had done his best, but the job always came first. I wondered if Tricia had regrets. I had my own, especially wasting thirty years waiting for my son's father, Tom Cavanaugh. I didn't judge Tricia. Life's full of what-ifs.

But the chat left me wondering. Who was Valerie Stone? She'd lived in Alpine and apparently been a hippie. Val was a poet, a free spirit, and the right age to be Ren's mother. Kassia Arthur was on the birth certificate. Like J. C. Peace, the name struck me as an invention.

If Tricia and Milo didn't have the answers, someone else might. I went into the newsroom to do what everyone in SkyCo did. I'd ask Vida.

Chapter Eleven

"VALERIE STONE," VIDA repeated. "Yes, of course, she was Tricia's maid of honor. A slim, dark-haired girl with a bit of a wild streak. Nice-looking in an exotic sort of way. She had a great deal of nervous energy, unable to stay still for very long. I recall stopping by the ski lodge reception desk when she worked there. Valerie never seemed to have the time—or the focus—for a friendly chat."

In other words, Val had evaded Vida's interrogation techniques. "You've never talked about her," I said. "Neither has Milo. But she sounds hard to forget."

Vida fingered her chin. "Well now. She wasn't in Alpine very long. Once she graduated from high school, she went into the Peace Corps. She mailed some articles about what she was doing in . . . Jamaica, I believe. That, of course, was before I started working here."

Prehistoric, I thought, in terms of the *Advocate*. "But she came back to Alpine, right?"

"Of course," Vida asserted, implying that any sensible person would do the same. "Not directly, though. I believe she spent some time in Seattle. Valerie wasn't raised here, but in Arlington, where Milo's aunt and uncle lived. You know about their divorce?" I nodded. "Peggy Stone never recovered. She died in the Sedro Woolley asylum. Her ex-husband, Frank, simply disappeared. He drank. I suppose he's dead, too."

Encouraged by Vida's civility, I considered passing on my latest crazy idea about Ren's mother. But she turned away. "I must answer two more letters asking for advice about wayward spouses. If these women didn't whine so much, perhaps their husbands wouldn't stray. It takes two to ruin a marriage. By the way, Ella is out of the hospital. There's nothing wrong except extreme muddle-headedness." She began typing in her usual *rat-a-tat* manner. For some reason, it reminded me of a machine gun. Maybe she'd like to shoot me. But our nonconfrontational conversation was heartening. Or maybe I was grasping at straws.

Yet I hadn't been enlightened much by Vida's recollections of Tricia's attendant. I'd hoped for a tale about Val leaving town to have an illegitimate child. Maybe I should put thoughts of Ren Rawlings aside. Assuming she had checked herself in to RestHaven, Ren might be there for weeks, even months. Her story intrigued me, but in terms of news value, the most I'd probably get out of it would be Mitch's human-interest piece about Alpiners' roots.

The afternoon wore on, overwarm and soporific. It was the last day of June. What would July and August be like? I pondered the question as I drove home at five, noting a heat haze rising above the indolent Skykomish River. The first thing I did when I arrived was to open all the doors and windows. If the lurker showed up, he could stand around and lurk. He probably didn't have any more energy than I did. Milo could grill. I had hamburger in the freezer and my little cooker to make the blasted French fries. I'd toss a salad and call it good.

The sheriff arrived at five-thirty, looking irked. After he gave me a perfunctory kiss, I asked what was wrong.

"People," he said, tossing his regulation hat onto the peg by the front door. "I'm going to change. I sweated so much the past two hours that this shirt's going straight to Mrs. Overholt." He headed out of the living room and into the hall.

I hadn't known until after we started living together that one of the Overholt women had been doing the sheriff department's laundry and cleaning for years. It was one way to make some extra money. Their farm barely provided subsistence living. I'd been relieved, wondering how I'd ever get a decent crease in Milo's pants. Ironing was never my strong suit. If it didn't wash and wear, I didn't buy it. Except, of course, for my rare splurges at Francine's Fine Apparel. That part of my wardrobe went to the dry cleaners next door to the *Advocate*.

"So," I said when my husband reappeared in the kitchen and I'd informed him he had to start the grill, "what's wrong with people now?"

Milo gulped some Scotch before answering. "We've had more calls today from as far away as Moclips, all swearing the stiff must be a missing husband, son, brother, or their village idiot. Worse yet, Roy Everson isn't giving up. He insists the skeleton's Mama. He told me she was taller than she looked."

"But no possible IDs?" I asked as we headed outside.

"Not really," he said after sitting in the lawn chair. "When you pin down the callers, they either have a description that doesn't match, the wrong time frame, or a different part of the state." He paused to light two cigarettes and handed me one. "Here's your bug repellent."

"I need it," I murmured, waving off a pair of caterpillar moths. "Maybe you'll have a serious hit by deadline."

"Tuesday?" my husband said, looking puzzled.

"We haven't changed it," I shot back with a glare.

Milo nodded absently. "Are we going to sit here until the sun goes down or do you plan to feed us tonight?"

I gave him my best wide-eyed look. "You haven't started the coals."

"Shit," he growled, getting up. "I have to do all the work around here. Go pour me half a Scotch and get some of your scrunched-up editorials I haven't had a chance to read."

"Jackass," I muttered as I went by him. "Why did I marry you?"

"My brawny arms," he called after me. "Bring some real matches while you're at it. My cheap lighter's about to fizzle."

After grabbing his glass, I grumped my way into the house. The phone rang as I was pouring Milo's Scotch. I hurried into the living room, but when I picked up the receiver, I didn't hear anyone at the other end.

"Hello?" I repeated, a bit louder.

"Ms. Lord?" The voice was barely audible.

"Yes. Who's calling?"

"Ren. Ren Rawlings, from RestHaven."

I was so startled that I sat down on the sofa. "How are you, Ren?"

"I'm . . . sick. Can you come see me? Not tonight." Her voice had gained some strength. "Visiting hours are over. Tomorrow, maybe?"

"Yes, of course. Late morning?"

"That should be fine. You see, I'm frightened."

"Why is that?" I inquired.

"Dr. Reed is very kind," she replied. "So are the other people here. But . . . I think someone is trying to kill me."

Paranoia? I wondered, for lack of a clinical diagnosis. "You mustn't worry about that. You're safe at Rest-Haven," I assured her. "Try to sleep."

"How can I be safe?" Her voice was shaky. "But my mother's spirit is in Alpine. I feel her near me. I must hang up. I'm sleepy."

I heard her fumble with the phone before she rang off. Ren was fanciful, maybe delusional. She recognized her own fragile emotional state. That was good. But fear for her life wasn't. Did she have a logical reason to be afraid? Maybe, but I had no idea what it might be. I decided I needed another shot of MacNaughton.

"Now what?" my beloved bellowed when I finally reached the patio. "You couldn't find any matches?"

Ren's call had made me forget. "Damn!" I set down our refills and turned to go back inside, but Milo grabbed my wrist.

"Sit," he said. "I finally got it started. What took you so long?"

I related Ren's call. The sheriff shook his head. "I wish you didn't get mixed up in stuff like this. Send Vida. It'll get her out of the office."

"Ren asked me, not Vida," I said. "The poor girl doesn't know anybody here. What if she's not crazy? I mean, what if someone *is* trying to kill her? She already ended up in the ER."

Milo folded his arms across his chest, a sign that he didn't want to argue. "Your call."

"Damned straight," I murmured. "Hey, tell me what Tanya had to say about Bill. I assume that was the topic of your lunch conversation."

"Some of it," he allowed. "Bill's between a rock and a hard place. Lila's always guilt-tripped him since his dad died. She doesn't pull that on Marje, maybe because she's a girl. The Widow Blatt wants a man around the house. She's never worked, so she only gets Social Security and her husband's small pension. I guess she's strapped for cash."

"She's hard-up—and hard," I remarked. "Vida was right when she said her sister-in-law's inflexible. Is this a deal-breaker for Tanya?"

Milo smiled slyly, an unfamiliar expression for my straightforward mate. "I suggested that since Lila had a spare bedroom and needed money, Tanya should offer to move in and pay room and board. Bill can figure out what fringe benefits he gets from that setup."

I reached over and punched Milo in his brawny arm. "You cunning devil! That's devious. Would Tanya even consider it?"

"You bet," he replied. "I'll say this for my daughter—she's damned near as stubborn as her mother. And she likes a challenge."

"She *is* getting better," I said. "She must *really* like Bill."

Milo nodded. "She does. Damn. I can hardly believe it. Her other guys were disasters. Maybe almost getting killed by the last one set her head straight." He glanced at the barbecue. "I think we've got gray coals. Bring on the burgers. You can skip the bug repellent. The smoke drove the flying insect squadron over to the Nelson place."

"Good," I said, getting up. "I hope they chew that rotten bunch into itty-bitty pieces. I'll bring the radio outside. Even if Vida's being a pain in the butt, we can't miss her program."

Milo grunted. "We can't? Maybe she's going to trash you."

"Then I *will* have to can her. Damn." I kept going.

As it turned out, *Vida's Cupboard* was not only benign, but bland. She'd recorded a chat with Miriam Lambrecht enthusing about the move to Alpine, which conveyed a certain down-to-earth charm. Following the commercial break, Vida apologized for "technical difficulties" involving an attempted recording of her phone conversation with Miriam's mother-in-law. Thus, our House & Home editor gushed for the remaining five minutes over the possibility of Faith Lambrecht returning to Alpine. Apparently the minister's widow was on the fence. Vida closed the *Cupboard* by tactfully suggesting that her old friend would have to be mad as a hatter not to return even if she had to crawl three hundred miles from Spokane.

"Shit," Milo said in disgust after I turned off the radio. "Why didn't Vida ask how happy Miriam's husband, Bob, will be to go fishing again?"

I shook my head and went back into the house. Some people—including Milo and Vida—often had one-track minds.

The evening passed in lazy, drowsy bliss, lying out on the sweet-smelling new grass and watching the stars come out over Alpine Baldy. The old moon was riding high above Maloney Ridge and Skykomish. Sniffing the clover next to my cheek, I nestled closer to Milo. We ignored an owl's hooting and I fell asleep in his arms. Neither of us woke until the sun had risen and we were both damp from the morning dew. If this was marriage, I thought, watching my husband rub his eyes and shake himself like a big, rumpled dog, I liked it.

Vida had the bakery run, so she hadn't yet made her appearance. Alison was in place, along with Leo and Mitch, who were staring at the still-perking coffee urn. Having gotten up earlier than usual, I'd eaten a real breakfast for a change. After greeting everyone including Kip, who'd come from the back shop, I went into my office to call Janet Driggers. I'd forgotten about Al's visit to the hospital until I saw his wife's Audi parked outside of Sky Travel on my way to work.

As sometimes coincidentally happens, Janet called me before I could pick up the receiver. "You're not Vida," she said after I answered. "Where's Mrs. Know-It-All-Alpine?"

"She's not here yet," I replied. "Can I help?"

"No," she said. "First, I swear on Al's always eager body that I'll never let Lila Blatt in my house again. She's toxic. No wonder Rupe died young. If Al hadn't buried him, I'd swear he ran away from home."

"Lila's a pill," I allowed. "What's your real reason for calling?"

"Tell Vida Mrs. Cobb's funeral won't be until Thursday because of the long weekend," Janet replied. "Would you believe Myron Cobb asked if we could give him a discount because both of his ancient parents died within a six-month period? Good Lord, for over thirty years Alf Cobb milked the county as a commissioner for more money than Al and I'll ever see."

I refrained from comment. "Baptist Church? What time?"

"Ten," Janet replied. "They'll keep it short so they won't have to serve lunch—just stale cookies and booze-less punch. Remember how cheap they were for Alf? You expect more for Hortense? She was merely the commissioner's wife."

"Milo and I were absent. We were still recovering from almost getting killed just before the funeral started."

"Thoughtless of you to survive," she remarked. "We could have started off the new year in a big way. Oh, well."

"Say," I said before Janet could go off on another tangent, "who did Al visit in the hospital Tuesday night? I'm not snooping. It's a news-related question."

"It is?" She sounded surprised. "You must be hard up for the next edition. Speaking of hard—"

"Stop," I broke in, seeing a sour-looking Vida arrive with the pastry box. "Was it Ren Rawlings?"

"Yes. Al says she's not playing with a full deck. You know her?"

I kept it simple, explaining how she'd come to see me

on a quest for her roots. "Does that have anything to do with her summons for Al?"

"Exactly," Janet responded. "Ren's a morbid sort. She wanted to know if Al or his father had ever buried an unidentified or unclaimed female corpse. Never happened, of course. How could the funeral home collect? We're not a freaking charity."

"That's it?" I said, noting that Vida was filling the goodies tray only with various types of muffins. No wonder Mitch, Leo, and Kip were hanging back.

"You expected Ren's bio?" Janet retorted. "Ah! Here comes Carrie Starr. I love her. She always wants to go somewhere with or without Dr. Bob. Let me know if you and Dodge decide to have a honeymoon. Some people figure you've been on one for at least ten years. Why not? I'm damned envious." She greeted the dentist's wife and rang off.

". . . more wholesome and much healthier," I heard Vida lecture my trio of male staffers. "You may be slim, Mitch, but you must consider your arteries." With that, she adjusted the beribboned straw boater and stomped off to her desk.

Great, I thought, *now my employees will not only be glum, but they'll mutiny.* I felt like Captain Bligh.

Leo, however, was undaunted. "Say, Duchess, what kind of technical difficulties did you have last night on your show? Couldn't Fleetwood help you out?"

"Fie on you, Leo," Vida snapped. "Spencer wasn't at the station. Presumably he was comforting Rosalie Reed."

I leaned back further in my chair as both staffers moved off to their respective desks. I heard Leo ask why Dr. Reed needed comfort. Vida replied that things were a bit unsettled at RestHaven, but added archly that she wouldn't dream of prying. Leo shut up.

Even if I'd been hungry, my perverse nature wouldn't

permit me to partake of Vida's muffins. I've nothing against muffins, but in an ornery-off, I can give my House & Home editor a run for her money—or her muffins. I did, however, have to inform her about Hortense Cobb's funeral. I emerged from my office and marched to her desk.

"Thursday?" Vida said after I'd relayed the message. "Very well. The rest of the Cobb family must be poor at organization." She turned to the stack of mail Alison had just delivered.

I went back to my office. Mitch showed up at nine-thirty to tell me what I already knew about the sheriff's log. He asked for my take on what he termed the Stalker. "Is it a story," he inquired, "or hysteria?"

"Stalker?" I echoed. "That's a bit strong. He's been reported as lurking, though. Did the sheriff have anything new about the guy?"

Mitch shook his head. "Nothing solid. Mrs. Everson thought a man had been following her in an older model van. She couldn't give a decent description of him or the vehicle. It happened last night when she was coming home from a meeting at the Methodist Church."

"Bebe Everson is prone to hysteria," I said. "Especially if it involves anything to do with her long-missing mother-in-law, Myrtle Everson." I lowered my voice. "Ask Vida why things are unsettled at RestHaven. I'm already off to a bad start with her. By the way, are you going to do the native-roots series?"

"If you think it'll play," Mitch replied. "I started putting together a list of locals who have different ethnic backgrounds. So far I've got five blacks including your pastor Father Kelly, six Asians—Deputy Fong being one of them—nine Hispanics, mostly college students, and the longtime Irish, Greek, and Italian families."

I nodded. "Then go with it. Buddy Bayard is French, by the way. So is Crazy Eights Neffel, whose real last name is Neville, but I suspect he'll tell you he came from outer space and is really a Neptunian."

"I'll leave him off the list," Mitch said. "Do you think it's a series? Three stories, maybe?"

"Why not? It's good filler and you can use family photos."

My reporter started to turn away, but stopped. "Got a question on the Greek family—Doukas. I've heard Vida mention the name, but I found only a listing for Simon Doukas, the attorney. Are there any other Doukases still around? I got the impression the family was a bunch of big movers-and-shakers at some point."

"Simon's the son of Neeny Doukas," I explained. "Years ago the family was quite large and owned half the town. Neeny's been dead for years, though he was still here when I moved to Alpine. His first wife had died and he remarried before moving to Palm Springs. I don't recall any children besides Simon." I grimaced. "I'm not on good terms with him. We got off to a bad start." There was no point in mentioning that Simon had called me a whore because I'd arrived in Alpine with a son and no sad story of a former husband.

Mitch gestured in Vida's direction. "So I go to the primary source?"

"Who else?" I said. "There may've been other kids who moved away. Like a lot of rich, powerful men, Neeny was hard to get along with."

"Right," Mitch said. "Coming from Detroit, I'm well acquainted with robber barons and corrupt labor leaders." Upon that note, he headed straight to his desk, apparently disdaining the muffins.

Since Mitch was doing the ethnic series, I figured I might as well take on Desmond Ellerbee. Not wanting to pester Rosemary, I called Directory Assistance for the number and was rather surprised that he was listed.

I thought an L.A. film-script writer might seek anonymity while the creative juices were flowing.

"I'm flattered," he declared after I introduced myself. "I didn't think anyone up here in this woodsy world would care about Hollywood types."

"We had a movie filmed here several years ago," I said. "A local young woman was the costar. We're not completely primitive. I thought perhaps I could stop by this afternoon."

"Yes," Des said in his pleasant voice. "Why not? I'm making dinner for Rosemary, but it'll be a simple meal, fresh and organic."

I translated that as something my husband would proclaim fit only for goats to munch in the backyard. After assuring Des that Rosemary would be delighted with Southern California cuisine, we settled on two o'clock for the interview. He asked if I needed directions; I told him I'd once visited a previous occupant. I didn't add that my hostess had been murdered shortly after I'd left. I'd leave that detail to Rosemary over glasses of California Pinot Grigio.

Shortly before noon, I noted that my staff was on hand, so I made an announcement. Summoning Alison from the front office and Kip from the back shop, I informed my curious employees that I was breaking precedent by not opening the office on Monday, the Fourth of July.

"Don't worry," I went on, seeing Leo looking puzzled, Mitch faintly bewildered, and Vida staring at me as if I'd lost my mind, "you'll get paid for the day off."

No one spoke for at least thirty seconds. I was about to return to my office when Vida broke the silence: "Well now. I suppose you and your husband are taking the weekend off for your long-delayed honeymoon. Am I correct in assuming next week's edition will be only eight pages?"

"No, on both counts," I asserted. "We'll go at least twelve, maybe sixteen. Milo has to work this weekend." I turned on my heel and beat a retreat to my sanctuary. I heard someone—probably Leo, being the only one who'd dare—utter a stifled laugh.

Damn, I thought, sitting back down at my desk. *Nothing cheers Vida these days.* I thought she'd be pleased to have a free day with Dippy or Buck or just working in her garden. Maybe I'd have to crawl to her on my hands and knees before she'd come around. What really troubled me was that even the most abject apology might fail. I vowed I'd do whatever it took. The status quo was untenable. *The Alpine Advocate* without Vida was unthinkable.

Thus, I tried not to think about it. But of course I could think of little else.

Chapter Twelve

THE MORNING HAD taken its toll on my appetite. I'd do my good deed for the day by visiting Ren Rawlings at RestHaven. I'd interviewed emotionally disturbed patients a few times when I worked on *The Oregonian*. Generally, my subjects had been more cheerful than their austere surroundings. At least the local facility was new. For comic relief, I could always recall its days as Casa de Bronska.

Upon arriving at RestHaven, the first person I recognized was Iain Farrell, who was heading toward the entrance. He paused a few feet away, looking puzzled. "Ms. Lord?" he said, sounding unsure.

"Yes," I replied. "I'm here to see Ren Rawlings. How is she today?"

His heavy, dark eyebrows came together. "You're a friend?"

"I know Ren," I said, feeling my face tighten. "She called last night to ask me to visit her."

"I see." Farrell's gray eyes veered off toward the main desk. "Very well. I must ask you to keep your stay brief. Nor should you excite her. She's in a very fragile place."

I refrained from asking if that "place" was made of French crystal or English bone china. "Is she on medication?"

He made an impatient gesture with his right hand. "A mild sedative. Merely to calm her while we ascertain the proper treatment. Excuse me, I'm late for a luncheon engagement." He brushed past me in his haste to exit the premises.

The serious young Samoan woman had been replaced by a freckle-faced young man with overlarge ears. "Unit Six," he said, checking his monitor. "Please turn left on the second floor."

I thanked him and headed for one of the two passenger elevators. As lazy as the Bronskys were, I marveled they'd never thought of installing one for themselves. Or maybe an escalator in case they all couldn't fit in the elevator. The other elevator door opened. To my surprise, the sheriff got out—and started walking right by me.

"Milo!" I called sharply.

He turned around. "Emma." My husband didn't look pleased to see me. "Okay," he said, moving closer. "I'm guessing you're here to see Ren. Good luck with that. I'd rather interrogate Crazy Eights Neffel."

"Why," I asked, ignoring the stare of the young man behind the front desk, "did you interrogate her? I was invited, as you may recall."

He sighed. "She called my office saying somebody was trying to kill her. Yeah, I know she told you the same thing, but Mullins took her semi-hysterical call a half hour ago. I figured it was either send Dwight Gould or go in person. You know Dwight—he's not Mr. Tact."

"Well? Is there cause for concern?"

Milo had taken off his regulation hat and was scratching behind his ear. "Hell, I don't know. Ren's definitely scared of something. Farrell came in when I was there and gave her a shot. She started to calm down after that. For all I know, she may have gone to sleep."

"I saw Farrell when I arrived," I said, lowering my voice almost to a whisper. "He's a real jerk."

The sheriff nodded absently. "He started giving me

some guff, but I told him to stick it before I arrested him for interfering with an officer of the law. He backed down fast. I don't trust that guy. Didn't he give you a bad time when you interviewed him last winter? Too bad we weren't married then. I could've busted him for lipping off to the wife of a law officer."

"Is that an actual crime?"

"No, but it should be." Milo mussed my hair. "Good luck. I'm off to the Burger Barn. Breakfast came too early this morning."

Watching my husband lope away though the rotunda lobby, I pushed the elevator button again. The second car's door opened immediately. Two minutes later I was in Unit Six, a small but surprisingly cozy room where I found Ren huddled under a colorful quilt. Her eyes were half closed, but flickered open when I pulled up the only chair in the room.

"Good," she murmured. "Do you know the sheriff? He just left."

I didn't want to waste time on my personal life. It was more important to keep Ren focused. "Yes, I've known Dodge for years. He's a fine person, with great integrity. Was he able to help you?"

She rolled over onto her back, resting a hand on her forehead. "He was very kind. But he doesn't understand. He can't, of course."

For once, I didn't blame Milo for being baffled. "What should he understand?"

Ren's eyes widened. "My mother. She's here. I haven't seen her, but I can sense it."

"You mean . . ." I, too, was baffled. "She's a patient here?"

Ren's hand drifted from her forehead to lie like a wounded sparrow on the quilt. "I don't know. Is madness hereditary?"

"That depends," I replied. "There are probably genetic strains carried from parents to children when it comes to emotional stability."

"That makes sense." She smiled wanly. "It's good that something makes sense. Not much does since I came to Alpine."

"You've been on a bit of a roller coaster," I remarked. "I'm sorry you didn't get to see more of Donna's gallery. She sells mainly regional items, including works by a local painter who's very talented."

"Oh?" Ren's blue eyes widened. "Who?"

"His name's Craig Laurentis. I own one of his paintings. It's called *Sky Autumn*. Have you heard of him?"

Ren frowned. "Yes, I think I have. I don't know if I've ever seen his work, though. What does he paint?"

"The scene I have is quite realistic, a rushing river around here," I explained. "It's very visceral—to me, anyway. His style has changed in the last few years, though. More abstract is the best way I can describe it."

Ren nodded solemnly. "He's experimenting. That means he's growing as an artist. That's good."

Pleased that Ren was making sense, I didn't tell her that Craig's more recent work had failed to move me. "Donna's sold several of his paintings," I said. "He also deals with other galleries in the region."

"I'd like to meet him." Ren propped herself up on the pillow. "When I feel better, I mean. But some artists don't like talking about their work."

"Craig's a bit of a recluse. He's very kind, though," I added.

"Some people aren't," Ren asserted, frowning. "I wish I knew who is trying to kill me. Then I could tell the sheriff. Wouldn't he have to arrest whoever it is?"

"Well . . . he'd have to get some evidence first, but," I went on quickly, seeing Ren's alarmed expression, "he might find a reason for questioning whoever the person might be. I gather you don't know, right?"

"That's true." Her face turned wistful. "I think it's someone who doesn't want me to find out what happened to my mother. And maybe to my father." She blinked several times as tears welled up in her eyes.

"Have you experienced any actual . . ." I paused, trying not to further upset Ren. "Actual menace?"

She shook her head. "I sense the danger, though. It's there in the shadows. I wish I knew why my mother seems so close to me here. It's as if she's trying to protect me. Does that make sense?"

I hesitated. "That's a hard question to answer. Maybe you know something that you don't realize, something that's important about why your mother left you in the first place."

The tears had slipped down Ren's pale cheeks, though her voice was strong when she spoke. "How could I know anything like that?"

I handed Ren a tissue I'd pulled out of the box on the stand by the bed. "That's the problem. You don't recognize it, but something will come along that will trigger the memory." *And Skykomish County will become the must-see hot spot for international visitors.* To be fair to my big mouth, I knew that memory can play strange tricks.

Ren dabbed at her eyes. "You're so nice. I can't think why." She sank back down under the quilt. "I'm suddenly very tired. Would you mind staying until I go to sleep?"

I did mind, as I was starting to get hungry, but I wouldn't leave Ren alone. "Of course not," I said. "A nap is a good idea."

She smiled faintly. "Thank you."

Two minutes later, Ren was asleep. She was still smiling.

I caught up with Milo at the Burger Barn just as he was polishing off his standard cheeseburger, fries, and

a green salad. Before I could say anything, he leaned
forward and spoke in a low voice.

"Vida's in the booth behind me. Her frozen smile felt
kind of good on a hot day. She's nailing Marje Blatt to
the wall."

"For what?" I whispered.

My husband shrugged. "The latest medical records.
What else?"

"Speaking of that sort of thing," I said, keeping my
voice down, "Ren actually made some sense when we
started talking about art."

"Art who?" Milo asked in his normal tone.

"As in paintings," I said, deciding I might as well
speak up, too. "Craig Laurentis's work, mainly. I think
Donna may still have one of his new paintings for sale.
Ren has heard of him."

"They'd make a good pair," the sheriff remarked,
lighting a cigarette despite the NO SMOKING sign.
"Maybe she'd like to move in with him to his cave or
shack or wherever he holes up in the forest."

Kinsey came to take my order. Like my husband, I
lacked imagination. I asked for my standard plain
burger-fries-salad. Not that there was much choice.
With only three places serving a sit-down lunch in the
commercial area, the Burger Barn had never felt a need
to expand its menu. Their version of fish and chips
smelled like bullhead—I'd eaten it once and that was
enough. The most exotic item was a weekly special,
usually some kind of chicken on a bun. It hadn't ever
appealed to me—or to the sheriff.

After refilling Milo's mug, a quartet of boisterous
teenagers sat down across from us. There was no need
to lower my voice when I asked Milo for details of his
visit with Ren. Even Vida's keen hearing couldn't pick
up on what we were saying.

My better half scowled at me. "Why do you think?

She wanted me to put a deputy on watch at RestHaven to make sure she didn't get killed. I told her I couldn't. I don't have the staff, especially with a holiday weekend coming up. Anyway, I didn't think Dr. Woo would approve."

"How did she take that?" I inquired, now raising my voice to be heard over the raucous foursome a few feet away.

"She started to cry," Milo replied, darting a sharp look at the clueless kids. "I told her I knew RestHaven's security chief and he was topnotch. Hell, for all I know, Sid Almquist doesn't know his ass from his elbow. But Ren stopped crying."

"She cried when I was there, too." I winced as a menu turned into a paper airplane sailed past me. The sheriff got to his feet and loomed over the teens, who apparently were too self-absorbed to notice the big guy in uniform across the aisle.

"Any of you got a driver's license?" Milo asked in his laid-back laconic manner.

I had to lean to look around my husband, but I could see only one couple, a towheaded boy and a ginger-haired girl. They both appeared appropriately startled.

"I do," replied the male teen who was out of my line of sight. "We're from Sultan. Jeb's got a license, too. We never even got a ticket so far. Just a caution for Jeb. Danielle and Josie got learner permits. They just turned sixteen. We're here for a project."

His rapid, lengthy delivery indicated he was nervous. I tried not to smile. Long before I married Milo, I enjoyed watching him make people squirm. The enjoyment stopped, however, when I was the object of his official inquiry.

The sheriff took his time studying the license. "Okay, Alex. But tone it down. What's your project?"

The girl in my line of sight looked up at my husband.

"Are you the sheriff? If you are, maybe you can help us."

"Oh? How's that?"

I recognized the faint note of impatience in Milo's voice. I, however, sensed a news story. So did Vida, who suddenly appeared in the aisle with Marje Blatt trailing like a reluctant caboose. My House & Home editor ignored me, but acknowledged the sheriff with a curt nod. She didn't speak, but waited tensely for Milo to finish with the teenagers.

"We got a summer assignment for our junior year," the ginger-haired girl replied. "Our social studies teacher asked us to investigate something. It could be anything, just so it was something nobody else has figured out. We heard about the dead dude who was dug up here in Alpine, so we decided that'd be our project. Can we come to your office to ask some questions?"

"Call first," Milo said curtly. "Meanwhile, stay out of trouble."

He swerved around, almost bumping into Vida's imposing bust. "Hi, Vida. They're all yours," he said before addressing me. "I'm out of here. You got enough money to pay for lunch?"

"Yes!" I yipped. "I haven't even gotten my lunch yet. Maybe I'll bring it over to your office just to annoy you."

"Don't even think about it," he said. "I'm going into seclusion." The sheriff dumped a dollar and two quarters on the table, picked up his bill, and stalked off down the aisle.

Vida, meanwhile, was interrogating the teenagers. Marje stood patiently waiting for her aunt, giving me an occasional weary glance. Not seeing any sign of Kinsey, I decided to vacate the premises and see if I could take my lunch back to the office. It was going on one and I had to be at Des Ellerbee's cabin by two. By the time I collected my order at the service counter and paid for it, Vida apparently was still interviewing the Sultan teens. Maybe there *was* a story in their assignment. As I headed for the front door, I saw Marje leave just ahead of me. I assumed she'd given up waiting for Aunt Vida.

When I exited, I spotted Vida's niece lingering at the corner of Fourth by the bank. I usually would've crossed at Third, but decided I might as well stay on the south side of Front lest she think I was avoiding her.

"Hi," I greeted her. "Are you waiting for Vida?"

"No," Marje said, her once pretty face fading as she approached middle age. "I hoped you'd come this way. I'm worried about Aunt Vida. I suggested a checkup with Doc Dewey just now, but she fobbed me off. I really don't think it's physical, but that mess my idiot cousin Roger left for her to deal with. How is she at work?"

"Sour," I replied as we continued on across Fourth. "She's not speaking to me unless it's strictly business. I don't know what to do. I keep hoping somebody—Buck Bardeen, namely—can get her to stop blaming the world for Roger's imprisonment."

"Buck's stumped," Marje said as we passed the Chamber of Commerce office in the Alpine Building. "He's very fond of Aunt Vida. I think he'd like to marry her, but even before all this happened, she wasn't keen on the idea. She's too independent."

I smiled wryly. "I thought I was, too. I was wrong."

"Aunt Vida's never admitted being wrong," Marje said sadly. "Nobody in the family—except maybe Aunt Mary Lou—has ever been able to stand up to her. We all hoped Buck was made of sterner stuff. Has she talked about Roger since he went to jail?"

"Never," I replied. "She's too embarrassed. It's stupid. Everybody knows what happened. Deep down, I think the worst part of it is that she knows she's guilty of spoiling him rotten. I hate to say it, but Amy and Ted did a poor job of parenting."

"We all knew that from the start," Marje said as we reached the corner by the Whistling Marmot Movie Theatre. "She hasn't seen Roger since he went to the Shelton facility. I offered to go with her a couple of weeks ago, but she refused, saying she didn't want to see him caged like an animal with all those real criminals."

I couldn't help it. I laughed. "He's always been sort of *un*real."

Marje smiled ironically. "I can't tell you how many family get-togethers he's ruined with his bad behavior." She stopped at the corner. "I've gone out of my way to get back to the clinic, but I knew Aunt Vida was heading in the same direction toward the gym. She's writing up the Golden Agers program they're starting in the fall. Maybe she should sign up and work through her problems on the new equipment."

"I'd pay to see that," I asserted.

Marje shrugged. "It won't happen. She'd rather internalize." In an uncharacteristic gesture, she put a hand on my arm. "I feel as if I'm bad-mouthing Aunt Vida. But the truth is, she's the heart and soul of our family. Oh, the others might complain and not always agree with her, but . . . she's the source of our strength in so many ways. We feel rudderless when she's not acting like herself."

"Tell me about it," I said, glancing across the street at the *Advocate* office. "I'm starting to feel as if I'm the skipper of a sinking ship."

Marje nodded. "I understand. At least it's too hot for an iceberg."

That, I thought, as Vida's niece went on her way, was cold comfort.

* * *

The cabin that had once been owned by Crystal Bird looked much the same as I remembered it. Tucked into the woods off Highway 2, it seemed to have weathered nicely. Yet I couldn't help shuddering as I went up to the small front porch. Even though I hadn't been the one to find Crystal's body floating in the hot tub, that was where I'd left her on the night that she'd been killed. I'm not fanciful, but I sensed an unease hovering over the setting, as if the dead owner haunted the place.

Des's cheerful smile dispelled the feeling. "The local publisher," he said, stepping aside to let me in. "I hope you won't ask to see what I've written so far. I'm still in the concept stage."

"Don't worry," I assured him, recognizing a rocker and a faux kerosene lamp I recalled from my previous visit. "Who did you rent from? I lost track of the ownership some years ago."

"One Aaron Conley," Des said, indicating I should sit on a cut-velvet Victorian settee that wasn't part of the previous decor. "Everything was done online or over the phone. I gather he moved some time ago."

I nodded. "He and the previous owner were separated but hadn't divorced. He lived here for at least a short time."

"Right." Des chuckled, reminding me of Rosemary's initial impression. He was no love god, but his pleasant face crinkled nicely and his blue eyes had a humorous glint. "He struck me as an aging activist," my host continued, "keen on the environment. And music, given some of his comments."

"Aaron had a band when I knew him," I said. "Maybe he still does." I'd let Rosemary fill in Des about Crystal's murder. I doubted it would spook him. He seemed well grounded, and as a writer, he'd probably be intrigued. I launched into my role as interviewer. Des's background was the same as what Rosemary had told me, though he gave more detail about his early years in the movie business.

"Until recently," he continued after taking a break to make us each an iced mocha frappe, "I've been more of a script doctor than a writer of original screenplays. Oh, I've dabbled, working with my own concepts, but this is the first full-length, non-spec script I've done. I decided to do it on location, as it were. I'd never heard of Skykomish or Alpine until I started looking for rentals in the area." He paused to make a comical face. "So here I am, in the forest next to a couple of old logging towns."

After he'd served the frappes, we moved out to sit by the hot tub. I tried not to visualize Crystal at our last—and only—meeting, stark naked and contemptuous in the warm water. She'd defied the snowy night, but couldn't deter her killer. I forced myself to focus on my next question, asking Des if he had any characters in mind.

"I do," he replied, fingering his dimpled chin. "I learned Alpine was founded in 1910. Oh, the drama of the nearby train tragedy that killed over ninety people occurred at Wellington soon after Carl Clemans set up shop would make a great opening visual. Especially since news of the wreck was sent out from Alpine. Or Nippon, as it was still called before the name was changed. But I wanted the town to be already established, if raw." He paused to sip his drink.

"That makes sense," I remarked, realizing he'd done his homework, maybe on his first visit to the logging museum.

"Thus," Des continued, "I thought I'd start the story in 1915, focusing on two loggers—one from Norway and one from Georgia. A contrast of two men with very different backgrounds, and yet both risk takers. I gather that's part of the logging mentality."

I asked more about his process, a buzzword I loathed, but felt was necessary to prove I wasn't a small-town dinosaur.

Des waxed eloquently for the next few minutes while I jotted down words and phrases that might capture his exuberance. It was getting very warm under the mid-afternoon sun and all I could think of was that Milo and I would never nod off in the backyard again. We'd been shortchanged on sleep. Furthermore, I itched in several places, no doubt from the bugs that had attacked me during the night.

Shortly before three, Des wound down. I felt as if I'd gotten enough for a lively feature. If nothing else, he was semi-exotic compared to most of SkyCo's summer visitors. As he saw me out, he suddenly snapped his fingers. "I've got it!" he exclaimed. "A hook for the film! I knew it'd come."

"Dare I ask what it is?"

He smiled enigmatically. "Secrets. Everybody has them."

I smiled back. "I suppose so."

I left, wondering what secrets Des had. He seemed very open. But I'd been fooled before. For Rosemary's sake, I hoped I wasn't playing the fool this time around.

Chapter Thirteen

THE LONG DAY wound down without incident. At a quarter to five, I realized I didn't know if Milo planned on going to Bellevue for dinner at Tricia's. I needed to find out because I didn't have anything on hand that was easy to cook in what had to be eighty-five-degree weather.

"We're not," he informed me over the phone. "Everybody on the road is screwing up. We've had four wrecks this afternoon, including one possible fatality. Laskey already knows—he heard the sirens. Where've you been?"

"I've been sequestered, hiding from Vida and writing a so-called sprightly feature for next week," I replied. "Does the veto of tonight mean we'll go tomorrow instead?"

"Maybe. Let's see how everything plays out. Can you cook pork chops on the grill?"

"No, but you can," I said—and hung up on him for a change.

I looked into the newsroom. I saw only Leo and it appeared he was bailing out. He caught my eye as his face grew sheepish.

"I'm catching a late plane to L.A.," he said when I went out to join him. "With the three-day weekend I might as well make it a family event. I can take the red-eye back Tuesday morning and be here by nine. I've got everything pretty well in hand for the next edition. Is that okay?"

"Sure," I said. "It's probably cooler in Santa Maria than it is here."

"It is, actually," Leo said. "Averages in the low seventies this time of year. Maybe we can revive our family fireworks tradition. We had to stop it when the only thing that really got lit up on the Fourth was dear old Dad. I damned near blew out an eye the last time I shot off one of those big rockets. I hear traffic's a bitch. I hope I get to Sea-Tac on time."

I wished him luck and a happy visit. And, as I always did when Leo was reuniting with his ex-wife and the rest of the family, wondered how long he'd remain on the job. I decided I was done with work for the day. After bidding Alison a happy weekend, I set out for the Grocery Basket to buy pork chops and several packages of disposable diapers for my namesake. On the way home I stopped at Parc Pines to drop off the baby gift. Walt Hanson came to the door, but said both Amanda and little Emma were sleeping. That was fine with me. I was tired—and hot.

Milo arrived home five minutes after I did. "Let's eat out again," he said, tossing his regulation hat somewhere in the vicinity of the peg by the door. "My freaking fan broke and Harvey hasn't got his new supply in yet. I'll dig one out of the basement of my house tomorrow."

"Mine's been broken all week, jackass," I yipped. "Don't kiss me."

My husband looked vaguely dismayed. "Why not?"

"You're all sweaty. I'm all sweaty. Besides, you forgot. You were too busy shooting off your face."

"Hey . . ." he began, looking dejected. Or rejected. I couldn't tell the difference and I didn't really care. But he stopped. "I'll change, then we can head for the ski lodge."

"But I already bought the damned pork chops!" I yelled after him.

"I don't give a shit if you bought the whole hog. We're eating out." He and his voice disappeared into the bedroom.

I flopped down on the sofa. Maybe I should change, too. Before I could make up my mind, Milo reappeared, half undressed. "Hey, let's take a shower together. That might be fun."

"Are you insane? We're both so clumsy we'd kill ourselves."

He thought for a moment. "You're right. Never mind. Unless you want me to bathe you in the sink. You're small enough, you ornery little twerp." He disappeared again.

I couldn't help myself. I laughed. I never could stay mad at the sheriff, not even when we were just friends. On rare occasions, I wondered what would have happened if I'd married Tom. Despite having had a son together, despite reuniting infrequently over the years, despite deluding myself that he was the love of my life, I never really knew him. I had enough distance now after six years to realize that I might have been bored to tears. If Milo had nothing else to offer—and he certainly did—he was never boring.

I told him so when he came out into the living room.

"What brought that on?" he inquired, taking my hands and lifting me to my feet.

"Just thinking how glad I am I married you instead of Tom," I replied. "Of course he'd have made reservations ahead of time at Le Gourmand."

"Bullshit," Milo said after kissing the top of my head. "Even if he had, he probably wouldn't have showed up. There'd have been some kind of family crisis and he'd have taken off."

"You're right," I agreed as he let me go. "The man was utterly unreliable. Let me change, okay? I feel grubby."

"You feel fine to me," my husband said with a shrug. "I'll wait in the Yukon with the AC turned on."

I was out of my work clothes and into a simple cotton sheath within five minutes. After climbing into the SUV, I asked if the possible fatality had survived and if he or she was a local. My reporting skills seemed to have faded into the heat haze that hung over Alpine Baldy.

"I don't know," Milo replied. "It was a younger guy from British Columbia. They took him into Monroe. The damned fool tried to pass on that narrow stretch just the other side of Deception Falls."

"Was he alone?" I asked as we headed along Alpine Way to the Tonga Road turnoff.

"Yeah. Why do you care?"

"I don't, really. My brain's fried. Why can't we just drive around with the AC on?"

Milo let out an exasperated sigh. "Because, dopey, the ski lodge has AC and they have food. Not to mention that using the AC in the Yukon cuts down on gas mileage."

"I thought that was a myth."

My husband didn't comment. It was just as well. We were crossing the little bridge over Burl Creek before the bend in the road and the ski lodge parking lot. After rounding the curve, we saw that the parking lot was jammed.

"Shit!" Milo exclaimed. "Are all these people in town for the Fourth or is everybody eating here because of the AC?"

"Oh, I forgot!" I cried. "Henry Bardeen is having a holiday smorgasbord this weekend. He took out a quarter-of-a-page ad."

"You mean we have to dish up our own food?"

"Well . . . maybe it's only in the main dining room. I forget."

Milo pulled into the NO PARKING slot by the entrance. "And I forgot what a total dumb-cluck you are in hot weather. Do you want me to carry you inside, you little twit?"

"No!" I pulled away as far as I could without falling out the door I'd already opened.

Somehow we both reached the lobby without saying or doing anything to further aggravate each other. To prove I wasn't mad at him, but at the weather, I slipped my hand into his. He gave it a squeeze, acknowledging the unspoken apology. After sixteen years, we didn't always need words.

Sure enough, there was a line for the dining room and the coffee shop. We went straight to the bar, where Heather Bardeen Bavich told us there'd be a ten-minute wait unless we wanted to have a drink first. Milo told her that's what we'd do. Heather had to ask a man who was by himself to move down so Milo and I could sit together.

The young bartender who'd been on duty earlier in the week wore a name tag that read ROB. My husband got his attention and ordered our drinks. To my surprise, the middle-aged man with the shaved head sitting next to me turned and held out his hand.

"Howdy," he said in a semi-raspy voice, "I'm Glenn— two *n*'s—from Puyallup."

Milo leaned over before I could say anything. "I'm Sheriff Dodge and this is Mrs. Dodge." His tone was much colder than the AC.

"I'll be darned," Glenn said with a grin. "I'm a U.S. Marshal. I planned to see you this afternoon, but I got stuck in traffic." He reached around me to shake Milo's hand.

"I'm off the clock," my husband informed him, his hazel eyes chilly.

"No problem," Glenn asserted cheerfully. "It's my kick-back night."

The sheriff didn't respond. He was lighting a cigarette and nodding at Rob. "Where's that ashtray Heather found in the broom closet?"

"Coming up, sir," Rob said. A moment later he set down a small plate imprinted with Loki, the Norse god of mischief and chaos. If I thought Henry Bardeen had a sense of humor, I would have congratulated him. Alas, the ski lodge manager was the serious type.

"Let me tell you about Des," I said, trying not to look at Marshal Glenn, who was chatting up Bianca, the latest blond bar waitress.

"Des who?" Milo inquired.

"Rosemary's new boyfriend. I interviewed him this afternoon."

"I can wait to read it."

"You won't. You never read the *Advocate*."

"Yes, I do. At least I skim it."

"I think I'll write an editorial saying you're a lousy sheriff. If you don't try to strangle me, I'll know you never read it."

"Didn't you already write one of those a long time ago?"

"I wanted to, but I didn't. You were being uncooperative about an investigation. Instead, I was a trifle snide in my news article. You didn't complain, so I figured you'd never seen it."

"I didn't. Mullins told me what you wrote." Milo's eyes sparked as he took a deep drink of Scotch. "He and Nina had one of their discussions about it. She felt my deputies might be too sensitive to put up with your bitchy attitude. They didn't give a shit."

"I can't even remember who the murder vic was," I admitted. "You must've arrested somebody."

Milo shrugged. "Probably. I hope it wasn't one of the times you fingered the wrong killer."

"Don't remind me," I murmured.

Heather informed us our table was ready. Bianca was back to serving drinks and Glenn was talking to Forest Ranger Bunky Smythe, who was at the end of the bar.

"Okay," I said after we were seated between two couples neither of us recognized, "what put you off about Glenn?"

My husband had ordered another round of drinks and was already looking at the menu. "Why does Henry put some of this stuff in Norwegian? What the hell is *suppelapskaus*?"

"How would I know? I'm not Norwegian. Ask Bianca."

"No thanks. I know what halibut is and that's what I'm having."

"Me, too." I put my menu aside. "Answer the question, Dodge."

Milo scowled. "What kind of federal agent announces his job in a crowded bar? Those guys are tough, but they're usually smoother than that. Yeah, I opened my mouth and told him I was the sheriff so he'd buzz off. But he should've slipped me a card, not broadcast his job. I wonder how many drinks he had before we showed up. His eyes weren't very focused—except on your chest."

We stopped talking to give Bianca our orders. "Is he a phony?" I asked after she left us.

"The regular U.S. Marshals can deputize citizens under certain conditions," Milo explained. "A manhunt, for instance. But there's no big deal going on around here. I suspect this guy is just passing through. I don't expect him to show up on the doorstep tomorrow."

"Maybe he's headed for east of the mountains," I suggested.

"Maybe." Milo offered me a cigarette and I was stupid enough to accept. He'd brought the makeshift ashtray with him. "Are you sure you want to go to Bellevue tomorrow if I can get away?"

"Yes." I leaned a bit closer. "I want Tricia to move on the annulment. Ben and Adam are nagging. She has to understand, this is very important to me."

"Damn." My husband grimaced. "We *are* married, you know."

"I know that, but my religion is an important part of my life. It always has been, it's the way I was raised, it's what I believe." I put my hand on his. "Why would Tricia care, really? She's not getting you back."

Milo put his free hand over mine. "Hell, she's just making trouble because she doesn't want to see me happy. She thinks you want a big church wedding because you've never had one. That pisses her off."

I pulled my hand away and sat up. "I don't give a rat's ass about a big wedding. In fact, I don't want one. After the annulment's granted, we can have our marriage blessed by a priest in about five minutes."

Milo stared at me. "You mean I won't have to buy a damned suit?"

It was my turn to stare back at him—and laugh.

The house seemed to have cooled off a bit by the time we got home. I felt much improved and not just because the sun was setting behind the mountains. I felt I'd made my point with Milo about Tricia and the annulment. The truth was that I hadn't thought beyond the goal of getting her to cooperate. The concept of a church wedding had been tucked away in a corner of my mind, but only when I trotted it out at dinner had I realized it sounded silly—and expensive.

We'd gone to bed early—just after ten—when Milo informed me he was going fishing early in the morning. Did I want to meet him for breakfast around nine at the Venison Inn? I told him I would—if he made it nine-thirty. He agreed.

I surprised myself by waking up a little after eight-thirty. The house felt cooler, though it was another sunny day. Milo had plugged in the coffeemaker, so after showering and getting dressed, I poured a mug to sip while I glanced through *The Seattle Times*. I'd finished reading the comics when someone rang the new doorbell Milo had recently installed. Peering through the equally new peephole, I recognized Marshal Glenn. I mulled. My husband had warned me about opening the door to strangers after an ugly incident I'd had with a drunk from the Nelson house next door. He pressed the doorbell again. He couldn't have seen me inside because I'd left the living room drapes closed against the sun. I held my breath, waiting for him to go away.

After what seemed like at least two minutes, I looked again to see him heading for a black sedan parked on the verge by the front yard. I watched until he was in the car and had driven off. Then I opened the front door. There was a business card tucked under the mat. I frowned, trying to make out the handwritten note: *Sheriff—call me at this number. Urgent matter to discuss.* He'd jotted down what was probably a cell phone number. The card identified him as Glenn S. McElroy, U.S. Marshal for the Western Washington District, headquartered in Seattle.

With a sigh of resignation, I went out to the Honda and headed for the Venison Inn. I hoped Milo had caught some trout. Otherwise, he was going to be in a bad mood when he saw Glenn's message. I wouldn't show it to him until we'd finished breakfast.

I wasn't surprised to find the sheriff already seated—

and eating a waffle, eggs, and sausage. "Any luck?" I asked hopefully.

"Two," he replied. "Barely above the legal limit. I'm surprised I got anything. But it was good to get out on the river."

"I'm glad for you," I said, deciding between buttermilk and Swedish pancakes. I'd dined Norwegian last night, so I decided to stick with the Scandinavians. After giving my order, I asked Milo where he'd fished.

He grinned. "I like your attitude. Mulehide never gave a damn and she'd have me fixing the hot water heater as soon as I got in the house."

"I think you exaggerate sometimes," I said.

"Only the last five, six years," he responded. "It was after Michelle was born that things went south. Our third kid came as a surprise—and not a good one for Mulehide. She wanted out of the house."

"Irony there," I remarked. "I would've loved to stay home instead of having to work as a single mother. I missed so much with Adam. He was good about it, though. He knew we had to eat."

We spent the rest of breakfast musing on our past and present lives. After we got home around ten-fifteen, I showed him Glenn's card. "Don't worry," I said. "Even though he did show up on our doorstep, I didn't let him in. You've warned me enough times about allowing strange men to come here when you're not around."

"Damn!" Milo exclaimed. "This guy seems to be real. What the hell kind of urgent business is he talking about? Or is this a touch-the-bases kind of thing?"

"Don't ask me. I'm just the messenger."

"I'll bet he tried to call my cell while I was fishing," my husband muttered. "I'm glad I turn it off when I'm on the river." He went into the kitchen and poured himself a mug of coffee.

"Are you going to call the number he wrote on his card?"

Milo sat down at the kitchen table. "Yeah, I guess I should." Reluctantly, he got out his own cell. Glenn took his time answering.

"Dodge here," Milo said gruffly. "What's urgent?"

I watched my husband's face change from rigid to perplexed. "Right, I remember the guy, but it's been a long time." He paused to look at his watch. "Okay, around eleven-fifteen. I'll see you there." He clicked off. "Does the name Aaron Conley ring a bell?" he asked me.

"Of course," I replied. "Rosemary's new boyfriend is living in his cabin. I was talking about him to Des yesterday."

"You were?" Milo frowned. "How come?"

"Des is renting the cabin from him," I said. "Aaron still owns it."

The sheriff leaned back in the chair. "Damn. This is weird. The Feds are trying to find him. He's wanted for forgery in at least three states. Do you mean he's still around here somewhere?"

"I don't know. They made the arrangements over the phone. You'd better talk to Des. He has to send his rent somewhere. I have his phone number. I'll get it for you."

Milo checked his watch. "It's ten-thirty. I wonder if I should drive over to his place before I meet McElroy."

"McEl . . . oh, Glenn. Can't you just call Des?"

My husband had stood up, fingering his chin. "Yeah, I could. It makes sense. That cabin was Conley's last known address, according to McElroy. Frankly, I'd like to check *him* out first. He still strikes me as a little odd. I'd better head for the office. Can you keep out of trouble?"

I made a face at my better half. "What do you expect me to do? I plan to weed the garden before it gets too hot."

He tipped up my chin. "What you say you'll do and what you really do are often two different things, little Emma. You worry me."

"Quit calling me 'little'!" I shrieked. "I'm almost average!"

"For a squirt," he said, flicking my nose with his finger. "Stay put and figure out how you're going to deal with Vida come Tuesday." He headed for the door to the garage.

The last thing I wanted to do was dwell on my House & Home editor. Still, I couldn't help but wonder how she was spending the long weekend. Maybe she'd left town to visit one of her other daughters—Beth in Tacoma or Meg in Bellingham. Certainly there'd be no danger on this holiday of Roger's blowing up himself and the rest of the family with illegal fireworks. Oddly enough, the thought made me a little sad.

By eleven, I was ready to go out into the garden. Having switched mental gears to Aaron Conley, I thought back to what I remembered about him, other than his being a musician, smoking a lot of weed, and maybe doing other drugs. He'd briefly been a suspect in his estranged wife's murder, but that was about the extent of my knowledge, other than that he'd inherited the cabin as part of the state's community-property laws. I put him out of my mind as I started to focus on gardening. Of course the phone rang just as I was at the back door.

"Emma," the timorous voice asked, "do you know where Mom is?"

"Amy?" I said.

"Yes. I haven't been able to reach her since yesterday afternoon," Vida's daughter replied. "Buck doesn't know where she is, either. Is she on an out-of-town assignment?"

"No," I replied. "Have you been to her house?"

"Yes, Ted drove by last night and this morning. There's no sign of her or her car. She wouldn't leave Cupcake overnight without telling us. She always lets us know where she's going." Amy started to sob.

"I've no idea," I said. "If I had to guess, I'd say maybe she went to visit Roger. It's a long drive. She may've spent the night somewhere."

"No!" Amy exclaimed in a choking voice. "She wouldn't do that! Should I call the sheriff?"

I held my head. "Technically, he can't do anything until a person's been missing for forty-eight hours. If her car's gone, she's taken it somewhere. Have you talked to Dot Parker? If anybody knows where your mother is, it'd be her. They're very close friends."

"Oh. Yes." Amy seemed to have gotten control of herself. "I didn't think of Mrs. Parker. I'll check with her now. Thank you, Emma." She hung up before I could ask her to let me know if and when she found out where her mother had gone.

I took the phone with me out into the backyard. Despite Amy's protestations, I sensed that Roger was the reason for Vida's disappearance. Even in jail, the wretch could create chaos. For all I knew, his grandmother might've headed for Olympia to beg the governor for clemency. But I still worried about her.

Not long after noon, the sun was in my eyes as I worked the patch out front next to Viv and Val Marsdens' property. They appeared to be gone for the day, maybe visiting their recently arrived grandson. I was going to the front door when Milo pulled into the garage. I met him in the kitchen, where he bestowed a quick kiss on the top of my head and reached for the coffeemaker.

"You should've been there," he grumbled. "You remember more about Conley than I do. The only thing I recall is interrogating him about Crystal Bird's murder and busting him for forging checks. I guess he didn't learn his lesson."

I poured out the last of the coffee into my own mug. "Did Aaron ever do jail time after you let him out?"

"Not according to McElroy," Milo replied, sitting down. "He always made restitution and somehow wriggled out of staying in the slammer. What's weird is that not only is the Baring cabin his last known address, but there's no trace of him for the past four, five years until now, when a bunch of bad checks showed up in California, Oregon, and Washington."

I joined him at the table. "Maybe he's been abroad," I suggested.

"Only to Canada and Mexico," the sheriff said. "No passport on file. His last visit to B.C. was six years ago."

Maybe the sunshine had gotten to my brain. I had one of my weird ideas buzzing inside my head. "Does McLeroy have any leads on Conley?"

"It's *McElroy*," Milo said, then scowled at me. "You don't usually mess up names. What now, little Emma?"

Why didn't I marry some guy with a job that didn't require mind-reading? Milo knew me too well after sixteen years. "Damnit," I said. "What if I told you I was having a sexual fantasy about Harvey Adcock?"

"I'd ship you off to RestHaven. Well? What is it?"

I hesitated. Milo might be able to read my mind, but he didn't always like what was on it. "What if the dump-site body is Conley?"

To my surprise, he merely winced. "It occurred to me, but I didn't say so to McElroy. We could make a match if we found Conley's DNA at the cabin." He paused, growing serious. "Of course it'd mean whoever made the deal is an impostor. That seems far-fetched. What's the point?"

I didn't know. We dropped the subject. But unlike the nameless corpse, we couldn't bury it.

Chapter Fourteen

AMY WAS CRYING again. "The Parkers aren't home. They didn't answer the phone, so Ted finally went up there and the car was gone. I didn't think Dot drove anymore."

"Maybe they sold it," I said. "Durwood's license was pulled a couple of years ago. If neither of them drives, why have a car?"

"B-b-but they didn't p-p-pick up when I called. Twice," Amy blubbered. "Where c-c-could Mom be? I'm frantic!"

"Maybe she took the Parkers somewhere," I suggested. "If they both really have given up driving—and Durwood should've done that years ago, being so reckless at the wheel—then she may be taking them on errands. If she's been in a wreck, Milo would know."

Amy blew her nose before she spoke again. "Mom hasn't been herself lately. What if she had a stroke and drove into the river?"

"Somebody would notice that," I said. "It's a sunny day. People are outside. Probably some of them are already *in* the river."

"Not every part of it," Amy argued.

Of the three Runkel daughters, I only know Amy fairly well. But while they all resembled their mother in height and build, none of them had inherited her force of will. It was as if the gene pool had run dry with Vida.

Or maybe there just wasn't enough spine to go around. I asked Amy if her mother might have gone to visit one of her sisters.

"I already called Meg and Beth," Amy sniveled. "Now they're worried, too. Neither of them have spoken with her since earlier in the week. Even Dippy seems out of sorts."

"Be reasonable," I said, knowing the advice wouldn't be taken. "Your mother is a very competent person. Are you absolutely certain she didn't leave a message on your phone or a note by the door?"

"I get a signal when I have a message," Amy replied, no longer crying but sounding peevish. "No one's left any messages lately. Mom wouldn't write a note. Why would she? I haven't been out of the house since yesterday morning."

At least Amy could be as stubborn as her mother. I surrendered. "She'll show up. Your mom would never leave Cupcake untended."

"That's what I mean!" Amy screeched. "Unless she told one of the Gustavson relations who live across the street from her."

"Do you have a key to her house?"

"Yes. Somewhere. You know how Mom is—she rarely leaves Alpine."

True enough. "Okay, but let me know when you hear from her."

Amy promised she would. I put the phone down and joined Milo out in the backyard, where he was digging up a bunch of roots that had grown under the fence from my rotten Nelson neighbors' property.

"I should've waited until either Doyle Nelson or his kids got out of prison and let them do this," Milo griped. "Hell, if I had a big enough jail, they could've stayed in town so I could put them on a work release program to do the job." He leaned on the shovel and looked at me. "What now? You look worried."

"Well . . . a little." I explained to him about Amy's concern over Vida's alleged disappearance. "I still think she went to see Roger," I added.

"Not your problem on a weekend. Oh—Mulehide called. The dinner's off. Zach's in the ER. She's there with him, holding his hand. Or foot. He fell off his bike and broke something."

"How old is this new boyfriend?" I inquired.

"No clue. But you know how everybody rides bikes in and around Seattle. It's supposed to help traffic, but instead it creates more problems with drivers trying to avoid hitting the bicyclists when they're pedaling outside the bike lanes or on residential streets."

I regarded my husband with a bemused expression. "How am I ever going to get you into Seattle for a cultural event?"

"You'll have to drug me," Milo replied. "Take Fleetwood with you. He likes that stuff. You've gone with him to concerts."

"Once, a long time ago. It was *The Messiah*. He had free tickets. You were jealous."

"I sure as hell was. You spent the night there with him."

"Not *with* him. We had separate rooms."

The hazel eyes glared at me. "You never told me that at the time."

"It was none of your damned business. You and I weren't a couple."

"We were sleeping together. Sometimes."

I laughed. "We often were. Honestly, Milo, why didn't you save us both a lot of trouble and sweep me off my feet when I first met you?"

"Mulehide had scarred me and you scared me." He let the shovel fall to the ground and took me in his arms.

"I didn't know what to make of you. I've told you that. All I knew was that you were damned cute, and before I could do anything about it, Cavanaugh showed up. I saw how you looked at him and realized I didn't stand a chance. That's when I met Honoria. The rest is history, most of it goofy."

I looked up at him. "You left out the years I was being an idiot. That was then and this is now. Did you check McElroy's status?"

"Yeah, as much as I could without fingerprinting him. Being a Saturday and an official holiday weekend, even the Feds aren't around in the Seattle office. They definitely have a guy by that name and he's active, as they put it. When I met with him today he seemed all business. I guess he was winding down last night."

I traced Milo's profile. He just missed biting my finger. "I've still got the pork chops," I said. "Can you barbecue them?"

"Sure." He kissed me lightly and let go. "Hell, I'm relieved we aren't going into Bellevue. Even if Highway 2 isn't clogged today, traffic is always a hassle on the Eastside."

By three o'clock, it was too hot to work in the garden even under the shade of the evergreens. Milo had already settled into a chair on the patio. I noticed he was staring off into space. "What's wrong?" I asked, brushing dirt from my knees.

"I should go over to . . . what's Des's last name?"

"Ellerbee. You mean to look for DNA?"

"Yeah. I should've done that after I left the office, but I couldn't remember the new boyfriend's name. Do you think he'd be around this afternoon or would he be out somewhere with Rosemary?"

"I've no idea," I said. "Do you want me to go with you?"

My husband started to scowl, but stopped. "Hell,

why not? You already know the guy. I'll deputize you, and you can help me look for anything that might belong to Conley. You're good at that kind of stuff."

"Gee, thanks, Sheriff. I thought you'd never ask."

"Neither did I," Milo muttered, getting out of the chair. "You want to change? You're kind of a mess."

"Thanks," I called over my shoulder. "I wouldn't have thought of that all by myself."

Ten minutes later, we were on Highway 2 in reasonably sparse traffic for a holiday weekend. Milo remarked that it was better than driving I-405 into Bellevue. I didn't argue. After sixteen years in Alpine and the explosive growth in the Seattle metro area during the last decades of the twentieth century, I'd almost stopped missing city life. Or maybe I'd merely grown content with age—and being married.

Milo didn't have to be reminded of how to get to the Baring cabin. Pulling up behind the Avalon, he remarked that Rosemary seemed to have arrived early. I informed him that she and Des not only owned the same model car, but that was how they met.

"That's a start," he noted. "At least they have the same taste in cars. You had to show up in a used Jag when you arrived in town."

"My dream car," I said. "The repair jobs were a nightmare."

As we approached the cabin, I noticed that the front door was closed. That struck me as odd, given the hot weather. Then I realized there was no screen door. Des must've been trying to keep out the bugs that flitted among the wild salmonberry and thimbleberry vines by the porch. I stared at the glass inset with its calla lily motif that Crystal had added to the otherwise austere door. The native plant was highly toxic—and prophetic. My former nemesis had been poisoned.

Despite Milo's hard knocking, it took a couple of

minutes before the door opened. "Hello," Des greeted us, looking surprised, no doubt wondering who my companion was. "Have you come to show me the draft of your story about my humble status as a screen-writer?"

"No," I said. "This is my husband, Sheriff Milo Dodge."

Des looked even more startled as he looked up at Milo. "Is something wrong? Or is everyone from L.A. a suspicious character?"

Milo put out a big hand. I winced, knowing that Des was about to get his bones crushed. "No big deal," my husband said. "I'm out of uniform, but on the job. I'm checking on the cabin's owner, Aaron Conley. It's not a local issue, but an outside request."

Des tucked his mangled hand in his Dockers and stepped aside. "By all means, come in. I trust Conley isn't wanted by the FBI?"

"It's a routine inquiry," Milo replied as we went in-side. "Emma says you never met him face-to-face."

"That's true," Des said. "Would you care for a drink?"

Milo shook his head. "No, thanks. I need Conley's DNA. Do you know of anything he left behind that might have it?"

Des grinned. "Ah! Just like the movies and TV. This is a first for me. Research on the premises. Let me think . . ." He stood in the middle of the small living room, tapping his dimpled chin. "A hairbrush would be ideal, I suppose. Unfortunately, I haven't yet come across one. Feel free to look around. Offhand, I don't recall any personal items."

The sheriff merely nodded again before heading into the bedroom. I'd only been in the kitchen and living room on previous occasions, but guessed from the exte-rior that there was probably only one bedroom and a bath off the open area, which was divided by a counter.

"I'll start in the kitchen," I told Des. "How was your dinner with Rosemary last night?"

"Enchanting." His eyes twinkled. "She's returning the favor tonight at her condo. Grilled yearling oysters from south Puget Sound. They sound exquisite. I told her that would be even better than what I called my California cool collation."

I wondered what Milo was thinking about Des's entrée. Not much, I figured, from his grim expression. But I merely smiled and started for the kitchen drawers. There was nothing of interest: maps, campsite information, a small 1999 almanac, a couple of flyers advertising Conley's band, which had been renamed Tye Dyed. I noted that the dates were from 1997 and 1998. The venues were in Monroe and at Lake Chelan. I opened five other drawers, but they all held kitchen utensils and bakeware. A glance in the cupboards showed canned goods, china, and more cooking items.

"Any luck?" Des inquired.

"Not really. How did you learn about the cabin?"

"Via the Internet," Des replied. "Craigslist, to be precise. I wanted the western Washington ambience. I'd visited up this way a few times. When I read the cabin's description, I was captivated, especially since Alpine and Skykomish are former logging towns. I immediately contacted Conley via email. Meeting the delightful Rosemary turned out to be a bonus."

"She's smart, too." It almost sounded as if I were giving Des a warning. "Where do you work?" I asked, moving to the living room.

Des pointed to a side table by the little fireplace. "My laptop. It's many things to me, including my muse."

I smiled. "Of course." Frankly, I wasn't sure what he meant.

The living room was also a bust. The bookcase looked as if most of its contents had been owned by Crystal

Bird. There were several tomes on women's issues and liberal politics, a few novels—none of which I'd read—and the standard reference works. Aaron hadn't left much of an imprint on the cabin. I said as much to Des.

"Maybe," he replied, "Conley travels light."

"Did he mention if he'd rented this place before?"

Des shook his head. "I didn't ask. It was clean, except for cobwebs and dust. I assumed he usually only rented it in summer."

Before I could mention that ski season might also attract renters, Milo reappeared. "Zip," he said, looking glum and gazing at our host. "You got a phone number for Conley?"

"Yes." Des frowned. "It's stored in my cell." He went out to the patio by the hot tub. "Here," he said, showing the screen to the sheriff.

Milo took a small notepad out of his pocket. "Thanks." He jotted down the number. "Where do you send the rent for the cabin?"

"Conley wanted to be paid in advance," Des replied. "I mailed a money order to a PO box in Edmonds. I gather that's near Seattle?"

"Just north of the city," Milo said. "Sorry for the interruption. Have a nice evening." Putting a big paw on my back he steered me to the door.

I waited to speak until we were back in the Yukon and the front door was closed. "Well?"

"I already said I couldn't find a damned thing that might've belonged to Conley. All the stuff in the bathroom was new, same with the bedroom. No sign of the guy. If somebody's impersonating Aaron, he's doing a damned good job of it." My husband backed out far enough to turn around. "I take it you didn't have any luck, either."

"Right. But," I went on as Milo waited for two cars and a truck to pass before pulling onto the highway, "what little I found in the kitchen drawer that probably belonged to Aaron was from six, seven years ago. Doesn't that tell you something?"

"Hell, yes, but I still can't prove the stiff is him. There is a gap between his front teeth. Do you remember if Conley had one?"

"He did. He also must have had a family," I said as we headed for the turnoff to Alpine. "Besides Crystal, I mean. Hey, maybe Dean Ramsey would know."

My husband darted me a quick glance. "Ramsey? The county extension agent?" His memory snapped into place. "That's right, he was Crystal's first husband, who posted bail for Conley after the forged check bust. That was damned weird, frankly. Hell, you should've mentioned him before. He might recognize that belt buckle."

"Hey, you're the sheriff. I'm just a humble journalist."

Milo seemed to purposely take the turn off Highway 2 a mite too sharply. "You were never humble. If you were, you might not be such a pain in the ass."

I punched him in the upper arm. "Why don't you arrest yourself for reckless driving?"

"Why don't you call Ramsey? Didn't the daughter he had with Crystal stay with you before he moved the rest of his new family here?"

"It took him a long time to get settled," I said, recalling the chaos Amber Ramsey and her son had caused during their extended visit. "For a flake, she was a good mother, but lazy. Gosh, her kid—Danny—must be in third grade by now. Amber married a guy from Woodinville and moved there a couple of years ago. Vida wrote up the wedding."

Milo headed straight up Alpine Way. "Did he look like as big a geek as I did in my wedding picture?"

"I don't remember if there was a picture," I replied. "You've improved remarkably over the years."

"You should've seen me in high school," he said, taking a left onto Fir. "No, you shouldn't. You'd have run for your life."

"Hey, I was no teen queen," I retorted. "I was lucky I got guys to go with me to the Blanchet Winter Ball and senior prom."

"You must've changed fast if you caught Cavanaugh's eye when you were in college. You were engaged before that. Or am I mixed up?"

"I met Tom after I got engaged to Don," I replied as we pulled into the garage. "That's when I broke the engagement." Milo already knew I'd said yes to Don when he proposed not long after my parents were killed in a car accident. Ben had just been ordained and I was alone. At twenty, I needed to belong to somebody. Don was older and rather serious, finishing his engineering degree after doing his stint in the military. He seemed like sanctuary. Then I met Tom. I thought I'd found the love of my life. Poor Don was collateral damage.

After opening all the doors to let in some air, I confronted Milo in the living room. "I had a thought while we were calling on Des. I didn't want to mention it until we got home."

Milo looked up at the beamed ceiling. "Good God. What now?"

"If the body is Conley, is it possible he's Ren's father?"

My husband lowered his head and rubbed at the spot between his eyebrows. "Yes, it's possible. He could also be Amelia Earhart in drag. Or Elvis. I think I'll go sit outside now."

"Rats," I said under my breath. This was when I needed Vida. She wouldn't have scoffed at my nutty idea. Even if it was a wild guess, Vida would have examined it closely, turned it this way and that, seen its merits—small as they might be—and at least considered the possibility. Now I wasn't merely mad at her for being mad at me, but for defecting over a long weekend. On a whim, I picked up the phone and dialed Amy.

"Just checking," I said. "Any word from your mother?"

"No," Amy replied glumly. "Maybe she did go to Shelton. There'd be a lot of traffic, so she might've stayed somewhere overnight. I've tried to call her cell, but she won't pick up if she's driving. Sometimes she doesn't think to recharge it. Mom doesn't really care for cell phones, you know. They cut out on her too often. She thinks, as she puts it, 'they're all for show and not much for go.'"

I didn't know that, thinking that any form of human communication including smoke signals or notes washed up in a glass bottle would suit Vida just fine, since she always has to know everything. "She might've decided to stay the weekend visiting . . . your son," I suggested. It was hard for me to mention Roger's name without gagging. "Have you spoken to him recently?"

Amy's voice dropped. "No. He's only allowed so many calls."

"She may stay two nights as long as she's there," I babbled for lack of anything more comforting to tell her daughter. "She might have had car trouble and is waiting to have the problem fixed." Maybe she was trying to help Roger escape and they'd both been arrested. I kept that thought to myself. "Her Buick has quite a few miles on it by now."

"Not really," Amy said disconsolately. "You know she doesn't leave Alpine often except to visit my sisters and then sometimes we drive."

"Look," I began, sounding stern, "if anything happened to your mother, you'd hear about it. Aren't you listed as an emergency contact?"

"Yes, and Beth and Meg," Amy replied. "But what if she's been kidnapped?"

I leaned back on the sofa. "Ah . . . that's not likely." The picture of anyone insane enough to try to make off with Vida was so bizarre that I had to force myself not to laugh. Naturally, O. Henry's "The Ransom of Red Chief" came to mind. "Really, Amy, if there's been a serious problem, you'd hear about it from your mother or . . . someone calling for her." I didn't want to say "the authorities." That sounded a bit grim.

Amy finally rang off. Briefly, I felt sorry for Ted, but he was just as big a ninny—to use one of Vida's own words—as his wife. If they hadn't been a pair of ninnies, Roger might've survived his grandmother's spoiling without turning to a life of crime.

I joined my husband on the patio. "Disconnected," he said as I sat down next to him.

"Huh?"

"Conley's cell," Milo clarified. "If it was Conley, which I doubt."

I stared at him wide-eyed. "You're speculating."

"Well . . ." He ran a hand through his graying sandy hair. "It does fit. You know I like things to fit."

"Do you think he was murdered?"

Milo uttered a brief sigh. "Why else would anybody bury him at the dump? An outside shot is a drugged-up Conley breaking into a house, getting himself killed, and the owner panicking. It can happen."

I touched his arm. "Then you've got an unsolved murder."

Milo stared at me. "Right, from at least five years ago. Where do I start?"

"Am I still deputized?"

"Yeah," the sheriff replied, leaning back in the chair. "Call Ramsey. Do your newspaper thing. Tell him you're writing a story about his job."

"I can't say that," I said. "I'd have to actually write it. The county extension agency doesn't do much that's newsworthy, with so few farms around here. The last time we had a story out of there was a warning about bad cheese."

"You'll think of something," Milo asserted complacently. "God knows you've practiced enough bullshit on me over the years to wring out information."

I narrowed my eyes at him. "Often to no avail. You're a hard case, Dodge. I rarely had much luck with you."

His hazel eyes sparked. "Oh?"

"Never mind." I got up. "I'll call Ramsey now. Maybe he's got some new fireworks warnings we can put online."

I couldn't find Dean's home phone in the SkyCo directory. Then I remembered that after a deal in Alpine had fallen through, he'd bought a house in his hometown of Sultan, thirty miles west of Alpine. I had to call Directory Assistance for the number. It felt so warm inside that I was too lazy to dial the number and paid the extra charge to let the operator connect me.

A woman answered. If I'd ever known Dean's wife's name, I'd forgotten it. "Mrs. Ramsey?" I said. "This is Emma Lord from *The Alpine Advocate*. Is Dean home?"

"Is something wrong?" she asked in a startled voice.

I was also too overheated to bother lying. "No, I have a question for him about the background on someone he once knew many years ago. A man," I added, in case she thought I was asking about an old flame of her husband's.

"Just a minute," she said. "He's outside."

After a few seconds passed, I heard her call Dean's name. Any exchange between them was muffled. I guessed that Mrs. Ramsey had put her hand over the mouthpiece.

"Hi, Emma," Dean said in his pleasant voice. "Has the courthouse caught fire?"

"Not yet," I replied, deciding to get straight to the point. "This coming week there's an article about a screenwriter who's renting the cabin Aaron Conley inherited. I'm taking a trip down Memory Lane. Do you know where Aaron went after he moved from Baring?"

"Gee," Dean said after a long pause, "I haven't thought about Conley in years. I didn't know he was still around. I don't think I've seen him since he was let out of jail to attend Crystal's funeral."

"He was released not long after that." The truth was that I couldn't remember the exact sequence of events. My main impression of Aaron was that when he wasn't in custody, he was high on something, but basically harmless. "Except for the funeral, did you see him at any other point back then?"

"How do you mean?" Dean sounded wary.

I had started to perspire. *To hell with it,* I thought. *Milo should be making this call.* "Did you read this week's *Advocate*?"

"Yes, I always go through it," Dean answered stiltedly.

"Then you know about the dump-site body," I said, having unpeeled myself from the sofa to go back outside. "The sheriff has no way of knowing who it is. Could the belt buckle belong to Conley?"

"Didn't the picture of the buckle have a peace symbol on it?" Dean asked, sounding less tense. I told him it did—and having reached the patio, I shoved the phone at Milo. "You're on, Dodge. It's Dean."

With a glower for me, he spoke into the phone, "I can't keep the remains forever. If it is Conley, we should try to track down any relatives. Do you know if he had family?"

I'd sat down, watching Milo scowl.

"Okay," he continued, "I thought maybe you knew him better than that. You did post bond for Aaron after

I busted him on the bum checks rap. Thanks. I may be in touch with you later."

I watched Milo ring off. "Dare I ask why?"

He shrugged. "There's still something off about the Ramsey-Conley connection. I sure as hell never bonded with Mulehide's latest ex."

"I don't think Crystal dumped Dean for Aaron," I pointed out. "Dean sounded scared."

Milo was lighting a cigarette. "Oh?" He flicked the lighter before he spoke again. "Maybe he has a reason."

I hadn't thought about that.

Chapter Fifteen

Along about five, Milo suggested we drive into Monroe for dinner and stop off to visit Tricia's parents in Sultan as we'd planned to do when we thought we were going to Bellevue.

"I'm trying to remember what Conley was like," I said, "at least when he wasn't high. I vaguely remember his hair was about the color of those strands on the corpse. Frankly, he was kind of nondescript. You think he got into it with his drug dealer?"

Milo shrugged. "That's as good a guess as any. Or a fight with another druggie. That's the trouble with that stuff. It leads to a lot of other bad things. Getting high doesn't always make you mellow."

I considered my husband's words. "Can you offer an educated guess and ID him?"

The sheriff shot me a baleful look. "I don't guess. You know that. But if were a betting man, I'd say it's him. And I'd only say it to my wife."

"Okay," I said, getting up. "Forget the ID and let's get in the SUV with the AC and head on out. It'll be six by the time we get to Sultan."

Milo, who had started to doze off a few moments earlier, seemed reluctant to get out of the chair. "Let's eat in Monroe first."

That was fine with me. We were on the road by five-thirty. Traffic still wasn't too bad, though it worsened the closer we got to Sultan and Monroe. Maybe Vida was right about the exploding population creeping up on us. We'd just turned off Highway 2 and were on Frye-lands Boulevard by Lake Tye when Milo's cell rang.

My husband swore. "What now?" He hit the gas and pulled into the restaurant parking lot. "Dodge," he barked into the cell before shutting off the ignition.

I watched his jaw set as I heard a high-pitched woman's voice at the other end. "Look, Amy," Milo finally said, "it doesn't matter if Fuzzy Baugh's missing, it's forty-eight hours before I can put out an APB."

Amy lowered her voice, but I could still hear her, though I couldn't make out what she was saying. "Okay," the sheriff responded wearily, "here's what I'll do. If she hasn't shown up tomorrow by six o'clock *in the evening*, call my office and have . . ." He paused, apparently trying to remember who'd be on duty. ". . . Doe Jamison put out the APB." He waited for Amy to speak, making a *blah-blah* gesture with his free hand. "I get all that, Amy, but we receive traffic advisories and conditions from everywhere in the state. Your mother's not some addled old lady. Even if you don't know where she is, I'm damned sure she does. I have to hang up now. I'm working on an investigation out of town. What? No, it has nothing to do with your mom. Take it easy. You're working yourself into a fit." He clicked off and looked at me. "Dumb ass. Where do you think Vida is?"

"Visiting Roger," I replied. "If she has to make the three-hundred-and-fifty-mile round-trip in all the holiday traffic, she might as well spend the long weekend in Shelton. To my knowledge, Vida hasn't seen him since he was shipped to the facility there."

"Did she mention anything about leaving town to you or to any of the rest of your crew?"

"She's not really speaking to me, remember," I replied. "If she told Leo or anyone else, I never heard about it. And I probably would, if Vida said she was going to see Roger."

"She might not admit it," Milo said, opening the door. "Let's get out of here. It's heating up with the AC turned off."

The restaurant had its own AC. Either out of habit or needing a drink after talking to Amy, Milo headed for the bar. "They serve food in there," he informed me, steering me in that direction. "I ate here last month when I had to attend that law enforcement meeting and got stuck with a couple of the Skagit County guys I've known forever."

"Right," I drawled. "And you didn't call me until almost six to let me know you weren't coming home for dinner."

"I didn't know that until . . . never mind. There's a spot for two in front of the bar."

For a change of pace, I ordered a screwdriver. Milo stuck to Scotch. I admired the simple yet pleasing decor. "I saw some brave souls sitting out on the terrace," I remarked.

"Tourists," my husband said, cradling his glass. "Probably from some part of the country that has plenty of hot, even humid, weather."

We sat in comfortable silence, the hum of conversation enveloping us like so many grasshoppers out in the backyard. Except when I thought about it, I hadn't yet seen a grasshopper this summer. After a couple of minutes had passed, I noted that Milo looked worried.

"What's wrong?" I asked.

He took a quick nip from his drink and leaned forward. "Where *is* Vida? I don't think she went to see Roger. She would've told Amy and Ted if she had. Have they visited him since he went to Shelton?"

"I don't know," I admitted. "She never talks about

him." Milo's doubts bothered me. "But where else would she go?"

"Buck Bardeen doesn't know?"

I shook my head. "It *is* worrisome."

"Damn." Milo reached for his cigarettes, noticed there were no ashtrays, and decided against brazening it out. He was, after all, out of uniform and out of his jurisdiction. "Maybe," he said, "it's an attention getter, like a cry for help. You keep telling me she's not herself, which is sometimes bad enough."

That idea jarred me. "But where would she go? She can't be just driving around in weekend traffic."

Milo ran a hand through his hair. "How the hell would I know? Doesn't she know people up and down the Highway 2 corridor? You've talked about her and the colonel getting together with out-of-towners."

"I suppose Buck would check with them," I said. "She hasn't talked about him much lately. He might've criticized Roger and made her mad. He probably still thinks the kid should have joined the military."

"Maybe I should talk to him," Milo muttered. "I don't really know the guy, though I've met him a couple of times. He seems like a stand-up type. Typical ex–air force."

We both were silent again. Vida almost seemed to be in the bar with us—as unlikely as that might sound. But so commanding was her presence, she had that effect even when she was nowhere in sight. When we spoke again, it was of other things, including an equally depressing topic: the Mariners' seventh loss in a row earlier in the day. Milo had listened to some of the broadcast outside on the radio. No wonder he'd started to nod off by the ninth inning.

After we finished dinner—Alaska King salmon for my husband, clam chowder and a salad for my heat-deadened appetite—we found a phone directory to look up Dean Ramsey's address. They lived on Elm Street, which struck me as odd.

"Elms aren't native," I quibbled. "Do they have a Palmetto Drive?"

Milo shot me a sideways glance. "You're kind of picky, aren't you? If somebody plants an elm, they can grow in this climate. At least this far down from the mountains."

I turned mulish. "I still think it sounds weird. I'll bet Tricia's parents live on Orange Blossom Avenue."

"They're on Cedar," my husband replied, taking a sharp left off Highway 2 onto Main Street in Sultan. "Does that make you feel better?"

"I feel fine now. I don't suppose the Ramseys have AC."

Milo didn't comment, obviously preoccupied with finding Elm Street and the Ramsey residence. It was easy to do, with GPS and Sultan being about the same size as Alpine. Their older, frame house was painted a dull red, with a well-kept garden and a brick fireplace.

The front door was open, but we didn't see anyone inside, so Milo banged the brass knocker. A faintly harried-looking woman with graying dark hair appeared from a room off a short hallway. She regarded us with alarm. "Can I help you?" she asked in an uncertain voice.

Milo didn't offer his hand, but instead held out his wallet to show his official sheriff's ID. "I spoke to your husband earlier today," he explained. "My wife and I happened to be in Sultan so I thought I'd stop by to clarify a couple of things about the body we found."

Obvious relief swept over Mrs. Ramsey's plain yet pleasant features. "Oh, gosh, he isn't here. He just left with our kids for something going on at the fairgrounds in Monroe. Is there anything I can do?"

"Probably not," Milo replied, putting the wallet back in his pants pocket. "I may be in touch with him later."

"I'll tell him." Mrs. Ramsey's soft brown eyes widened. "Is this about that Conley person?"

"Right," Milo said. "Did you know him?"

"No." She paused. "Would you like to come in? It must be hot out on the porch in the western sun."

"Sure," I said, maybe to prove I existed. I was beginning to feel as if I might as well be with Vida, playing the stooge as I usually did when she dominated conversations. "I don't think we've met. I'm Emma Dodge."

"I'm Jeanine," she informed us as we entered a small but well-furnished living room. She gestured at the blue-and-white plaid sofa; I wondered if it was the Ramsey clan tartan. "Dean told me about your call," she explained, sitting in a matching armchair by the hearth. "He remembered he had a photo of Crystal and Aaron that was taken after they were married. My husband and Crystal parted amicably. It was a youthful marriage between people who hadn't yet found themselves. Very hard on their daughter, Amber. At least she finally settled down and is doing quite well. Would you like to see the picture?"

"Yes," Milo said in a more relaxed tone. "Is it handy?"

Jeanine virtually sprang out of the armchair. "It's in the kitchen. I'll be right back. May I get you something to drink?"

"No, thanks," the sheriff replied. "We just had dinner in Monroe."

Jeanine went off through the dining room and disappeared. Milo pinched my nose—gently. "Having fun?"

"It could be a story," I retorted.

"But you're Mrs. Dodge."

"I'm versatile. Watch me turn into Lois Lane."

Jeanine returned with a standard black-and-white

snapshot. "I think this was taken in Portland," she said, handing the photo to Milo.

"It is," I agreed, leaning closer to take a look. "That's the Japanese Garden at Washington Park. It's a wonderful place. They have an international rose test garden there along with the zoo and a children's museum. I lived in Portland for many years."

"I'm from Salem," Jeanine said. "I met Dean there after he took a job with Marion County. I worked for the state health department."

I sensed that Milo was growing impatient. "Could I borrow this picture?" he asked in what I knew was feigned deference.

"Well, I suppose so," Jeanine replied. "I don't think Dean would mind. After all, it's been a long time since Crystal meant anything to him. Of course he didn't really know Aaron at all."

The sheriff stood up. "I'll have a copy made and give the original back to Dean. Probably Tuesday, with the holiday."

"That's fine," Jeanine said, seeing us out. "I'm sorry Dean wasn't home. He'll be disappointed to have missed you."

We left. "Sorry, my ass," Milo grumbled after we were in the SUV. "I bet Dean's glad he was gone. He might've been hiding in the bushes."

"Is the picture any help?" I asked.

My husband shot me a sharp glance as he made a U-turn in the middle of Elm Street. "If you hadn't turned into an ad for the Portland Chamber of Commerce, you'd have noticed more about Conley. Take another look, Lois Lane. He's wearing that hippie belt."

"Gleep," I said weakly, staring at the photo. "Hey, I was going for camaraderie, getting Jeanine to loosen up. It works for Vida."

"You're not Vida. Thank God," Milo added under his breath.

I put the picture aside. "Crystal's smiling, but she still looks mean. Will you make an official ID now?"

"I can't base that on a buckle. We'll have to try for family members. I'll put Mullins on it. Holiday weekends screw up everything official. What I'd like to know is who the hell is impersonating Conley. And why?"

"Can you use the Internet to track down relatives?" I asked.

Milo turned a corner; I noticed a sign for Cedar Street. "Conley isn't an uncommon name. But we'll give it a shot. Too bad we don't know who played in his band. Do you remember what it was called?"

"I don't recall the original name," I replied, "but there was a flyer in the drawer at the cabin. Aaron had changed it to Tye Dyed after he moved into the cabin. For the river, I suppose. That suggests he intended to stick around."

We'd stopped in front of an older, two-story dark green house. Milo smiled faintly. "I guess the Stanleys aren't ready for a retirement home yet. They painted the place since I was here last winter. It used to be white. Let's do it."

Unlike the Ramsey house, the front door was closed. My husband pushed the buzzer in the door frame. No response. He pushed again. Still nothing. He swore under his breath, then muttered, "They must be out."

"Clever deduction, Sheriff," I remarked, following his long, loping strides as he went around to the side of the house.

"Their Nissan Maxima's gone," Milo said—and grinned. "I'll be damned—Ralph bought himself a new red Frontier pickup."

"What did he do for a living?"

"He ran a truck repair business," my husband re-

plied, taking my hand as we walked back to the Yukon.
"He made a good living off of it. Let's go home. I'm
tired of talking to people. You can tell me more about
the Portland zoo while I nod off."

"Fine. I'm going to think about Conley. He had a
beard back then."

"So? No way the ME could tell that," Milo said. "He
might've shaved it later."

I was quiet until we were past Gold Bar. "Maybe
whoever killed Aaron wanted the cabin," I remarked.
"Who kills for a roof?"

"Are you kidding?" my husband shot back. "That's
not a bad motive these days. Especially in Seattle. Ever
look at the real estate ads in the *Times*?"

I nodded. "It's crazy. But you're right. Especially with
the kind of people Conley probably hung out with. Musicians, mainly. The Hoods!"

"Not all musicians are druggies or troublemakers,"
Milo said.

"No, I mean Aaron's band," I explained. "That's
what it was called when he met Crystal in Oregon. It
was named for Mount Hood, not for crooks. But that
band broke up then. I think."

"That's not a lot of help," my husband muttered as we
followed the Skykomish River and began to gain altitude.

I decided to shut up and enjoy the AC. And the scenery. It was that golden time of evening when the sun
filtered in misty shafts among the vine maples, alders,
and evergreens along the highway. As traffic diminished, Milo exceeded the speed limit. I figured he could
drive the often hazardous road in his sleep. I glanced at
him to make sure he wasn't doing just that. He was
wide awake, but frowning slightly.

"Why the pensive look?" I asked.

"We just passed Baring a couple of miles back," he

replied. "I suppose Rosie and Des are getting better acquainted."

"Probably," I agreed. "He seems like a decent sort."

"I hope so," Milo allowed. "She's a nice woman. Good-looking, too."

"Oh?"

My husband grinned at me. "No, I'm not lusting after her. Jeez, Emma, stop fussing."

"I'm not. Really. You could've gone after her a long time ago."

"Not my type." He reached out to muss my hair. "She's too nice. I knew what I wanted and it was you."

"Keep both hands on the wheel," I warned him. "You're going almost seventy-five. We're not in SkyCo yet. Do you want to get busted by a SnoCo patrol officer?"

"They know me," Milo replied complacently. "I could always put on the flashing light."

"So what were you thinking about besides Rosemary and Des's budding romance?"

He sighed. "Ellerbee. He's an L.A. type. He forks out a few grand for a place he's never seen to somebody he's never met? It doesn't matter that he wouldn't know Aaron Conley if he fell into that hot tub. Even if Conley's still alive and drugged up in Edmonds, it sounds damned odd."

I explained what Des had told me about choosing Crystal's—and Aaron's—former home. "I think you're naturally suspicious of Californians. You're almost as bad as Vida."

Milo shot me another glance. "What did California ever do for you?"

"Okay," I admitted, "Tom was based in San Francisco for years. But being dead, he's not uppermost in my mind anymore. Thank God. Leo is from *Southern* California and I like him."

"As much as I like Rosie?"

"Yes, that's about right. Now we're even."

"Leo didn't always wish otherwise, did he?"

"He did not. But he got over it. The last thing I needed was a romance with one of my employees." I gritted my teeth. "Are you really going to pass that truck?"

"Yeah. Watch me. How the hell do you think I chase down speeders on this stretch of highway?"

"I don't want to think about it," I retorted, closing my eyes. When I opened them, we were passing by Skykomish. The little town was bathed in the mellow setting sun as a half-dozen people strolled between the old Skykomish Hotel and Maloney's Store. The river ran low, Prussian blue, with white riffles over the big boulders. A moment later I could see Mount Sawyer, rising above Tonga Ridge.

It took only five minutes before we turned off to Alpine. I could sense my husband relax. And slow down—which was a good thing. Just as the old green truss bridge was in sight, the railroad crossing bells rang and the safety bars started to lower.

"Damn!" Milo cussed, looking at the dashboard clock. "The *Empire Builder*'s fifteen minutes late. It's eight o'clock. Where did we pass it?"

"We didn't. It probably went by while we were in Sultan."

Unlike the long BNSF freight trains, the *Empire Builder* was relatively short. I envied the passengers who sat in comfort, gazing out the windows, especially the ones in the two sleeper cars and the dining car. "Let's take a train trip this fall," I said.

Milo was drumming his fingers on the steering wheel. "Where?"

"Across the country. Or Canada."

He thought for a moment. "Canada. I'll bet the scenery's better."

"Well . . . parts of it, maybe. Do you really want to go?"

Milo mulled again as the train moved out of view. "It'd take over two weeks to go both ways. That's a long time to be away from the job."

"We could fly one way and go by train the other way," I suggested.

The safety guards began to lift. "I wouldn't mind seeing Newfoundland and Nova Scotia," the sheriff said, waiting for a VW and a panel truck to move. "There's supposed to be some good fishing there."

I envisioned downtown Halifax with quaint shops. "How far east have you ever been?" I asked.

"Montana," Milo replied as we crossed the tracks. "It was after the divorce was final and I wanted to get away. I fished the Jefferson River south of Bozeman. Got some nice cutthroat and rainbows."

"Did the trip make you feel better?"

"Not really. But at least it was a change."

"I wish I'd been there," I said as we continued up Alpine Way.

Milo chuckled. "I wish you had, too." He sobered just before turning off onto Fir. "No, I don't. I needed that time to figure out how to live on my own. Even at that, it took me another five, six years to really recover. By then, you showed up. That helped."

"You were so low-key when we met, very different from—" I stopped, staring at our front yard, where four figures stood by the porch.

"Damn!" Milo grimaced. "It's those kids from the Burger Barn." He pulled into the driveway, stopped short of the garage, and all but exploded out onto the lawn. I scrambled from the SUV to join him.

"Slow down," I heard the sheriff bark at the teens. "One at a time."

"Like Jeb just said," the dark-haired boy with the

mullet asserted. I assumed he was Alex, who had been blocked from my sight at the Burger Barn. "What we found at the dump site is an old painting in a frame with glass over it. Is there a reward for that?"

"No," Milo snapped. "Somebody tossed it. It's a *dump site*."

"Hey, wait," the ginger-haired girl protested. "Me and Danielle seen on TV where a lady found a picture at a garage sale done by some famous guy and it was worth megabucks. What if this one's like that? Shouldn't somebody check it out? It's in the car."

The sheriff started to say something, thought better of it, and turned to me. "Is Donna's gallery open this weekend?"

"I don't know," I admitted. "She'd be closed now, but she might open up for part of tomorrow because of tourists coming through town."

My husband mulled briefly. "Show it to Mrs. Dodge," he finally said. "She knows something about art."

Jeb and Josie took off down the drive. For the first time, I noticed an older dark green sedan parked on the verge halfway between my property and the Marsdens'. It took them only a minute to come back with a Safeway grocery bag.

Milo addressed Alex. "Did you kids get permission from my office to search the dump site?"

"No," Alex replied. "Does it matter?"

"Yes," Milo said curtly. "Didn't you see the crime scene tape?"

"Sure," Alex responded. "That's why we went there. I mean, like if we're supposed to solve a puzzle, that's why we wanted a look."

Danielle's dark eyes were wide. "We saw the hole where the body was found. That really creeped out Josie. But we did some digging of our own. Let Jeb show you what we got."

Jeb offered the grocery bag to Milo. "Here. Take a look."

The sheriff removed the framed picture. I stood at his side—and gaped in amazement. The glass-covered painting of a river or creek was crude yet realistic. It appeared that the artist had been experimenting with rudimentary style. It also looked very much like an early rendering of *Sky Autumn*. Somehow, I stifled a cry of shock.

Chapter Sixteen

APPARENTLY, MILO ALSO saw the similarity and ordered the teens to come inside. He went ahead to open the front door; I followed behind him. The kids straggled in, the boys trying to show some bravado while the girls tried not to giggle. Maybe it was suppressed nervous laughter. Or they thought they'd really unearthed a gold mine.

"First," Milo said, having commandeered the easy chair, "don't ever tamper with a crime scene again. You got that?" His hazel eyes could have ignited a fire in the newly upholstered sofa the girls were sitting on.

"Yeah, but . . ." Jeb began, then thought better of it as my husband leaned slightly forward.

"Second," Milo went on, "how much digging did you do at the dump?"

The boys, who were sprawled by the coffee table in front of the sofa, exchanged glances. "Not much," Alex finally replied. "It was hot this afternoon. We sort of messed around in that creek."

The sheriff leaned back in the easy chair. "No other discoveries?"

Both boys shook their heads vehemently. "No," Jeb asserted. "We thought we was lucky to find what we did on the first try."

Josie spoke up. "Is it worth anything?"

"That's up to the local gallery owner to decide," Milo

responded. "I want your names, addresses, phone numbers." He looked at me. "You got something handy for them to write on?"

"I think so," I said in my meekest fake voice and smiled benignly at the teens. "Be right back."

From the kitchen, I could hear Milo ask how long the kids planned to stay in town. Jeb thought they'd hang out for a few more days. It depended on which parent had a spare car he or Alex could drive.

"We don't have to turn our report stuff in until we go back to school in September," Danielle was saying as I handed Josie a tablet and a couple of pens. "When can we have the picture back? I mean, to show we found something that's maybe worth money."

"That's up to Mrs. Wickstrom," Milo replied. "She's the art expert."

Josie looked at me. "I thought you knew about art."

"Not as much as Donna Wickstrom does," I said, not having to fake humility this time.

It took the teens five minutes to write down their information, pausing to confer with each other a few times. Apparently at least one or two of them had parents at different addresses. When they'd finished, Milo stood up.

"Thanks," he began. "When you come here the next time, report to my office first. There's always someone on duty. You got that?"

Alex said yes and the others nodded. I half-expected my husband to shoo them out the door, but they left without further ado.

"Were my kids that clueless?" he asked, leaning against the open door. "Was Adam?"

"Adam was stupefyingly vague," I said. "But he used proper grammar around me. Usually. When he wasn't mumbling."

"Maybe I shouldn't be sorry I missed a lot of my kids'

teen years," Milo muttered. "When I did see them, they seemed . . . normal. For kids."

I went over to him and put my hands on his shoulders. "I always figured you were relieved not to have to deal with their adolescent stuff."

My husband winced. "I was. But Mulehide always dumped on me anyway. At least it was usually after the fact. Hell, they're my kids. But I felt her taking them off to Bellevue meant they were mostly out of my control." He covered my hands with his. "Want to go sit outside?"

"Sure," I replied—just as the phone rang. I was closest, so I went to the end table by the sofa to pick up.

"If that's Amy . . ." Milo started to say.

"Yes, Glenn, he's here," I said, glaring at the sheriff. "Hold on."

My husband sank back down into the easy chair. "What's up?" he asked, trying not to sound irked. I returned the tablet and the pens to the kitchen. By the time I'd opened the back and the garage doors, Milo was concluding what he'd found out about Aaron Conley. I picked up the painting from the dump site and compared it to Craig Laurentis's *Sky Autumn*. There were definite similarities, though looking at them together, the differences seemed more pronounced. A river painting is still a river. Most of the streams that flow westward from the Cascades look alike if there are no recognizable objects or geography in the background.

"Hey," Milo said into the phone, "Conley doesn't want to be found. Work it out. If you can shake more out of Ellerbee, let me know." He paused, frowning. "Okay, fine. Maybe I'll give Ramsey one more shot, but meanwhile I'm trying to follow up on the family angle. You sure you don't have any relatives for him in your background check?" Another, longer pause. "That's possible, especially for a musician. Let me know what you find out. . . . Will do." Milo rang off and stared at me. "McElroy can't trace Conley further back than Baring. He thinks it may not be his real name."

"Good grief!" I exclaimed. "That never occurred to me. But he could've changed it years ago when he started his band. He might really be Helmut Glubbermuckel."

"I hope not," Milo said, getting up. "I'd hate to see what Dwight Gould would do if he had to put that down in the log. Let's go outside before somebody else shows up. It's too warm in here, and the sun should be starting to go down."

"It usually does," I murmured, taking the phone with me just in case. "I'm grabbing a Pepsi. You want anything to drink?"

"Just ice water. I'll get it."

"If," I said, taking a Pepsi can out of the fridge, "Conley isn't his real name, wouldn't he have had to use it when he married Crystal?"

Milo finished pouring water into a glass. "He would if he had to show ID. But would he and Crystal have gone the conventional route?"

"Good point. Maybe not." I started for the back door. "Are you going to put the Yukon in the garage?"

"Damn. I forgot." Milo headed out through the side door.

By the time he joined me, I was anxious to broach the subject of the painting. He agreed that it reminded him of Craig's work.

"The question," I concluded, "is why it was buried in the dump and not thrown out with whatever else might've been disposed of. Doesn't that suggest deliberate hiding of the picture, no matter who painted it?"

"Could be." Milo took out his cell and punched in a number. "Hey, Dustman, where are you?" He waited for a response. "Okay, the next time you swing around by Carroll Creek and the dump site, take a look at a hole some idiot kids dug there. Let me know how deep and how far it is from where we found the stiff. . . . Yeah, I'm at home with the Little Woman." He clicked off.

I grabbed his arm. "I told you never, ever to call me that!"

Milo laughed. "You know I'm teasing."

I shook his arm "I know it, but does Dustin? Or do you refer to me like that at work?"

My husband looked innocent. "You're Ms. Lord at work."

"Only Dustin—who has excellent manners—calls me that," I shot back. "I'm Emma to everybody else. Except Dwight, who I'm not sure has ever called me anything."

"That's probably something to be thankful for," Milo said calmly. "You prefer 'my old lady'?"

"Ohhh!" I punched him in the shoulder. "You're impossible!"

The sheriff gazed around him. "I feel a breeze. Want to roll around on the grass?"

"Not until you convince me you don't call me the Little Woman when I'm not around."

Milo turned serious. "Hell, you know I wouldn't do that. I never called Mulehide anything but my wife, even when she was pretending I didn't actually exist. Get serious. Do you really think that painting is by your favorite recluse?"

I removed my hand and drank some Pepsi. "I'm not sure. I do think Donna would be able to tell us."

Milo rubbed his chin. "If the gallery isn't open tomorrow I'll take it over to their house. Want to tag along, my little ball and chain?"

Before I could snarl back at him, his cell rang. "That's

close enough," he said to the caller. "How deep? . . . Sounds about right. Thanks, Dustman." Milo disconnected and sighed. "Less than a yard away, toward the creek. Damn."

I leaned closer. "What do you mean?"

"I don't like coincidences," Milo asserted. "You know that. But the painting being buried so near the body makes me suspicious. What if they were buried at the same time? And why?"

I admitted I didn't know. "It may not be Craig's work," I pointed out. "It's not a very good painting, at least not as good as he'd later become. I do wonder why anyone would bother to frame it. It strikes me more as something an amateur would want to show off. If the frame is removed, the artist may have signed it."

Milo kept staring into space. "Okay," he finally said. "I'd better have it taken apart by an expert—like Donna. I don't want to screw it up. Speaking of which . . ." He gestured at the expanse of grass behind us.

"No. I'm still too hot and crabby."

My husband stood up and pulled me to my feet. "Good. Then take it out on me."

"You're an asshole!" I shrieked. "I hate you!"

"Good start," he murmured, lifting me into his arms. "You're even better when you're ornery. This should be fun."

And so it was.

I left Milo reading Sunday's *Seattle Times* at ten to nine as I headed off for Mass. The lower parts of St. Mildred's windows were open and I heard, if not felt, a faint breeze ruffling the trees outside. The pew in front of me creaked as Ed Bronsky and his family tried to get more comfortable. A younger couple had arrived late, squeezing in next to Ed, Shirley, and their five chunky offspring. I didn't recognize the newcomers. If some of SkyCo's Catholics had left town for the holiday weekend, visitors had taken up the slack. Father Den had returned from his vacation, and his homily was on peace, according to the gospel of the day. He spoke about the difference between inner peace and temporal peace, a suitable subject on the eve of our country's birth. As usual, his words were well crafted, befitting a former seminary teacher, and thus slightly sleep inducing. Den, like my brother, knew that sermons weren't his strong suit, and never went over ten minutes. On this warm July morning, he cut it to seven. In the brief silence that followed, Ed apparently sat on the visiting young woman's purse and let out a stifled "oof!" The nonresidents were able to ignore him, a talent I seemed to lack. Maybe I should pray for it. On the other hand, it'd be un-Christian to ask for Ed to evaporate.

After Mass, I managed to elude Ed by being fleet of foot—and the Bronskys still being wedged into the pew by the couple, who were probably trying to assess the damage done to the woman's purse. I did pause to greet Jake and Betsy O'Toole and Francine and Warren Wells. Even the usually chic Mrs. Wells looked a trifle wilted in our unseasonable weather. Her women's clothing shop didn't have AC.

Milo had migrated to the backyard, apparently having read the Sunday paper, which lay in my chair.

"Do the Wickstroms go to church?" he asked.

"I think so," I replied, moving the *Times* so I could sit down. "Lutherans. They stick fairly close to a traditional liturgy, except maybe Pastor Nielsen gives longer sermons. I gather he's a better speaker than most of the local clergy. If memory serves from their weekly ad, the main service is at ten."

Milo stretched and yawned. "Okay. Why don't we go see them around noon?"

I grinned at him. "You really want to take your old lady along?"

"Why not? I kind of like her." He stood up. "Where's your coffee?"

"I was so excited to see you that I forgot to pour it," I said drily. "I've had enough coffee. While you're up, grab me a Pepsi."

"That's got caffeine, too, you know."

"So? I *like* caffeine. It keeps me alert."

"It makes you hyper," he called over his shoulder. "That's why you crash into walls and stumble over your own feet."

I didn't respond. I'd heard it all before. My husband might be right. He'd had to pick up the pieces a few times over the years after I'd trashed my clumsy self. Somehow I'd managed to keep upright since we'd been married. Or maybe I was just getting older—and slower.

Shortly before noon, we arrived at the Wickstroms' well-kept house on First Hill. Their Dodge Durango was in the driveway, indicating they were home. Steve Wickstrom responded to the door chime, looking surprised to see us. He put out his hand to Milo.

"Are we under arrest?" he asked with a faint smile, then noticed the Safeway bag in my husband's hand. "Or did you bring brunch?"

"I've got a question for the local art maven," the sheriff replied as we entered directly into the living room. "Is Donna busy?"

"Donna's always busy," Steve replied, "but I insisted she take off today and tomorrow. She wears herself out, between the day care and the gallery. Not to mention keeping up with the house and our two younger kids. Karen's home from the UDub for the summer, but she's working at the public pool as a lifeguard. Have a seat. Coffee?"

We both declined. Donna emerged from the kitchen.

"Hi," she greeted us, looking surprised. "Is this a social visit? Or—"

Milo hugged Donna. They had a history that bonded them, but it wasn't romantic. Her first husband, Deputy Art Fremstad, had been killed in the line of duty. Karen was the daughter Art and Donna had had together. I was already sitting down, so I merely waved at our hostess.

Milo remained standing, sliding the painting from the paper bag. "Take a look at this. You may want to remove it from the frame." He joined me on the sofa.

"I guess I don't have to worry about fingerprints," Donna murmured, holding the picture out in front of her. "Steve, can you get me some tools so I can pry off the back of the frame?"

Steve headed back the same way his wife had come. Donna had gone to the big window that overlooked the front yard. She didn't speak until her husband returned with a coffee can full of various items, including a small screwdriver that seemed to be Donna's choice of implement. She set the painting on the floor and knelt down beside it.

"I have a feeling I know where you two are going with this," she said softly. "Frankly, it's sort of exciting."

Steve got down on his haunches to watch his wife, their heads close together. I smiled to myself. I'd met Donna a few years after Art had been killed and was glad she'd found another good man. Steve had been teaching at the high school for only a year when they started seeing each other not long before I moved to Alpine. I'd never known Art, but Milo and Donna had both held him in high esteem.

"It's not signed," Donna announced, taking the painting itself back to the window. "It was done in a bit of a rush, as if the artist had a deadline. Or," she added, coming over to sit between Milo and me, "he wanted to please someone."

"He?" I echoed.

Donna's smile was ironic. "You're thinking Craig, right? So am I."

"Nothing on the back?" Milo asked.

Donna shook her head. "The fact that it's in a frame indicates he did it for someone. This is very raw, only suggestive of Craig's real talent. I'd guess he painted this in his late teens or early twenties, just as he was discovering himself."

My husband frowned. "Damn. How do you get in touch with Laurentis?"

"I call him on his cell," Donna replied, carefully setting the picture on the coffee table before standing up. "Craig does have means of communication. He doesn't ever pick up, but eventually he calls back. Is there some reason you need to talk to him?"

"Well . . ." Milo rubbed at the back of his head, then gestured at the painting. "This was dug up yesterday at the dump site where the body was found last week. You heard about that, I suppose?"

Both Wickstroms nodded, though it was Steve who spoke. "Any idea who it is?"

"We're working on it," Milo replied. "If there's a connection between the picture and the body, and if Laurentis is the painter, he might be able to help us with our investigation. I know, it's a lot of 'if's."

It was Donna's turn to make a face. "You realize Craig is anti-authority? I mean, any kind of government person."

Milo nodded. "That's where you—and Emma—come in."

Donna and I exchanged looks. "I think we just got Dodge-smacked," I said. "Have you heard from Craig since you sold his painting?"

"No," Donna replied. "That usually means he's being very intense about what he's currently working on. No one has seen him in town—at least no one has mentioned it—since early spring. But that's typical."

I hadn't seen Craig since he'd been recovering from a gunshot wound in late November. He always came to Alpine by stealth, usually at night. I wondered if he lived mostly off the land, somehow foraging enough to stay healthy. But for all I knew, he ordered food online and had it delivered to some pickup destination.

Milo was more interested in how to get to Craig. "Any way you can lure him into town, Donna?"

"I send his money to his Wells Fargo account in Monroe," she said. "The only way he'd show up is—maybe—if I coaxed him into bringing his new painting. I have no idea when it'll be finished. Sometimes he'll work on one painting, then abandon it for months, even years, and start something else."

I could sense that under his laconic pose, the sheriff was frustrated. "I guess we'll have to set a trap for him." He poked me in the shoulder. "You're good at that sort of thing. Work it out."

Steve and Donna laughed. I didn't.

"You're a beast," I informed Milo after we left the Wickstrom house. "If Donna can't get Craig into town, how the hell can I?"

"How'd you meet him the first time?" my husband asked. "Didn't you fall on your ass or some damned thing?"

"Yes." I stared straight ahead. "Maybe I could fake my own death."

"See? That's a start."

I heaved a big sigh. "I'd love to interview him, but he wouldn't go for it," I finally said after we were almost home. "If I could think of an angle that would appeal to his artistic sensibilities rather than anything personal . . . something that would challenge him."

Milo pulled into the driveway. "Keep thinking."

As soon as we got inside our not-so-little log cabin, I called RestHaven to inquire after Ren Rawlings. A brisk female voice informed me Ren was resting. I asked if this would be a good time to visit her.

"Please try again later," the voice said.

"Why?" I asked. "Is she asleep?"

"Yes. Call back this evening. Have a pleasant afternoon." The hang-up seemed to echo in my ear.

I started for the backyard, where Milo had headed as soon as we got home. But my husband was now stalking into the kitchen, the cell at his ear, and a thunderous expression on his face. "Have you seen their car?" he growled at whoever was on the other end. "I'm not sure what year, damnit. Hold on." He turned to me as I paused by the sink. "You got any idea how old that Subaru the kids were driving might be?"

"I didn't remember it was a Subaru," I admitted. "What's wrong?"

He gave an impatient shake of his head. "I'm guessing a 1994," he informed his caller. "You've got the license number. Maybe they camped out. Ask Mrs. Van Doren if they had any gear. And make damned sure the other parents besides her are on board with this. I got the impression a couple of them may've split up. . . . Right. Keep me posted." He clicked off and stuffed the cell into his shirt pocket. "That was Sam Heppner. As you have deduced, my little sleuth, the Sultan kids have gone missing."

I waited for Milo to grab a beer out of the fridge before following him back outside. "You mean they didn't come home last night?"

"That's right. Josie's mother called the SnoCo sheriff's office and they told her to call us. I don't think

Mrs. Van Doren knows we're in a different county. Her brain may be in a different world."

"Has Sam been looking for them?" I asked.

"Only in town," Milo replied, sitting down in the patio chair. "I told him to pull in Doe early if he needs her. She's got those Muckleshoot instincts for finding things—and people. It'll mean overtime for her, but I'm betting those kids went off on a logging road and got stuck. Or lost. Sam's already alerted the park rangers."

"The kids must have cell phones," I pointed out.

"They do, but they aren't answering. The dumb asses probably forgot to charge them." Milo popped the top on his Budweiser. "Maybe they'll find Vida. What's for lunch?"

"Whatever you can fix," I replied. "I'm not eating. This weather ruins my appetite."

Milo shot me a look of mock dismay. "You'll get so small I won't be able to find you in the dark."

"Dubious." My response was halfhearted. "I'm worried about Ren. She isn't able to talk on the phone."

"Not your problem," my husband said. "You can't take on everybody else's troubles. You don't really know the woman."

I scowled at Milo. "You went to see her."

He folded his arms and sighed. "So I did. But that's because she thought someone was trying to kill her."

"Can you guarantee someone isn't?"

"Hell, I can't guarantee somebody isn't trying to kill *me*." He took my hand. "I don't want to see you worrying about people all the time, okay? You want to get wrinkles?"

"I've already got turkey neck," I said.

"You don't look like a turkey to me." He squeezed my hand. Gently. "You look like a cute little baby chick—"

The sheriff's cell rang. "Now what?" he muttered, dropping my hand and yanking the cell out of his pocket. "Dodge." His long face grew increasingly annoyed as he listened to whoever was on the other end. Then his shoulders slumped. "Okay, Sam, I'll take over."

I heard sirens in the distance. "What?" I asked as Milo clicked off and stood up.

"Doe's in Seattle at some family gathering," he replied. "Gould's on the desk, Fong worked the night shift, and I forgot Blatt had a vacation day and took Tanya over to Lake Chelan. They like it over there, but I'll bet it's at least ninety degrees. There's a big wreck out by the road into Alpine Falls, so I've got to help look for those dumb-shit kids. Betsy O'Toole spotted the lurker outside their house and got a vague description of the guy. If he shows up here, don't offer him one of my Budweisers. And stay put, okay? I'd better change into my uniform. I'll grab some takeout at the Burger Barn."

Disconsolately, I watched my husband lope back into the house. It crossed my mind to ask if I could tag along, but I knew he'd say no. I sat staring at our house, still not quite used to the new addition out back. After I heard the Yukon leave the garage, I felt antsy. Somewhere nearby, fireworks were going off, probably in the cul-de-sac down the street. I hoped the dry shrubs and trees wouldn't be set ablaze by careless Fourth of July celebrants.

But I refused to sit outside and mope. So what if I'd only read the sports section of the *Times* before leaving for Mass? I could finish the rest of the paper later. After securing the house, I got into the Honda and drove to RestHaven. It was exactly one o'clock. Milo probably wouldn't be home until Doe came on duty at five.

I avoided Front Street, thinking it would be busy. But a glance to my left by the Icicle Creek Development showed that downtown was semi-deserted. I continued on to River Road, noting that the sky seemed to have dropped another couple of inches since Friday. Some preteen children were in the river, shrieking happily as they tossed a couple of inner tubes back and forth. I heard more fireworks after I got out of the Honda and was walking under the porte cochere to RestHaven's entrance. Inside, I blessed the AC as I moved more briskly toward the elevators. The receptionist desk was vacant, but Kay Burns was entering the rotunda from a side door that had once led to the Bronsky drawing room. It was there that Ed's family had dined on their TV dinners at a Louis XV marble-topped table.

"Emma!" Kay exclaimed. "What are you doing here?"

"I want to see how Ren Rawlings is getting along," I said. "How come you're working today?"

Kay's smile didn't reach her deep blue eyes. "I'm attending a conference in Palo Alto at the end of the month. I don't have much spare time during the workweek to do the research I need for a panel I'll be on. Are you working, too?"

I shook my head. "I know Ren's all alone up here and I felt I should see her. Not to mention that this place is air-conditioned."

"Oh." Kay frowned. "I happened to be in the psych ward a few minutes ago. You should've saved yourself the trip. I overheard that she's been sedated."

I didn't hide my surprise. "Why? Did she get violent?"

"No, no," Kay assured me. "Just very . . . distraught. Or so I gathered. Dr. Reed was afraid she'd make herself ill. Physically, that is."

"Poor Ren." I shrugged. "I suppose I might as well go home. Oh!" I clapped a hand to my cheek. "Is Sid Almquist here today? We should do an article about his new job."

"I'm not sure," Kay replied. "You might ask at the

front desk. Nice to see you, Emma. I'm going home to collapse." She headed for the double doors.

I'd wandered halfway back to the reception area but stopped, making sure Kay had left the building. As soon as she made her exit, I returned to the elevators. A minute later, I was on the second floor, turning left to Unit Six. I could hear voices, but didn't see anyone. The door to Ren's room was closed but unlocked. I stepped inside. Ren was under the colorful quilt, her eyes shut and her face pale. Whatever tan she might've had when we first met had faded. If I couldn't see that she was breathing, I would've thought she was dead.

I called her name, but there was no response. She simply lay there as if she'd been drained of blood. Her slim hands were on the quilt. I carefully picked up the right one. It felt cold, almost clammy. Was that normal? I looked around for a chart but didn't see any patient information. Despite the coziness I'd felt on my earlier visit, the room now seemed more like a tomb. There was nothing personal, not even a glass of water on the stand next to the bed. I patted her hand—an irrelevant gesture—and left.

Entering the hall, I saw Iain Farrell coming my way. His step halted as he saw me, but he kept walking. I nodded and tried to smile, assuming he'd pass me by. But he stopped, his eyes narrowing. "What are you doing here, Ms. Lord?" he inquired with an ominous expression.

"I came to see Ren Rawlings," I replied. "Is she all right?"

"What do you mean?" he asked as if I'd posed a conundrum.

"Physically," I replied.

"Of course," he responded, crossing his arms. It struck me as a defensive gesture. "Her physical health isn't the problem."

I wouldn't give up. "Then what is?"

Farrell grew patronizing, a tight smile on his thin lips. "Ms. Lord—do you have a degree in mental health or behavioral sciences?"

My perverse nature came to the fore. "Yes. I majored in clinical psychology at the University of Oregon. Very helpful for a journalist in understanding human behavior."

"The Oregon school has no such curriculum," Farrell shot back.

"Oh yes, it does," I asserted. "It was accredited by the American Psychological Association in 1958." The only reason I knew that was because I'd written some articles about the psych department for the *Daily Emerald,* the student newspaper.

Farrell unfolded his arms and made a dismissive gesture. "Your education is of no consequence. I can't discuss Ms. Rawlings's condition with you because of patient confidentiality. As both a clinical psychology major and a working journalist, you surely understand." He nimbly sidestepped me and moved on down the hall.

I had no choice except to keep going to the elevators. My feet dragged. I didn't like leaving Ren, and not just because I felt sorry for her. I was leaving her alone—at RestHaven. She might be resting, but the facility didn't seem like a haven. Despite the AC, it felt more like hell.

Chapter Seventeen

As long as I was in the car, I decided to do some grocery shopping. Even though we'd eaten out twice during the week, I was getting low on basics. I especially needed more easy-to-cook items. The first person I saw inside the Grocery Basket was Grace Grundle, the retired schoolteacher who had reported one of the lurkings. She was in the express lane at the checkout stand, her cart loaded down with cat food and other assorted items. Six people were already in line behind her. Pretending I didn't notice Grace, I started for the ATM, but she called my name in the same sharp manner that she'd no doubt used on three generations of Alpine students. To my dismay, she was next in line to be waited on by Kenny O'Toole, Betsy and Jake's nephew.

I approached her. "Let me help you unload," I offered with a smile.

"No, no," Grace said. "I prefer doing it myself. I have a certain routine with my groceries." She began to take out the cat-food cans one by one, placing each tin separately on the conveyor belt. "I'm so relieved to run into you, Emma," she continued, reading each label before letting go of the can. "Has the sheriff found that man who has been terrorizing us for the past week?"

"Not yet," I admitted. "He's been very busy trying to identify the skeleton that was dug up at the dump site. In fact, he's working today."

Grace frowned. "Whoever it is has been dead for some time. Milo should be more concerned with the living. But then, he always took his time handing in his schoolwork. I do wish he'd been more eager to speak out in class. He was such a quiet boy, not at all like his brother, Clinton. Very bright, outgoing, very cheerful. He still sends me a Christmas card every year from Dallas."

I managed to keep a straight face. "Thoughtful of him," I murmured, noting that the long line now reached Fresh Produce. "Did you get a good look at the person who frightened you?"

Grace shook her head. "I'd taken off my glasses. He was just a blur. But his manner was very sinister. I was shaking so badly that I could barely dial the telephone."

"I thought it was Marlowe Whipp who'd been in your garden," I said as Grace finally emptied her cart.

"Well, perhaps it was Marlowe who trampled my poor flowers, but it certainly wasn't him I saw prowling about earlier. Marlowe came much later. He was always late for class, too. He has no sense of time. I just talked to Betsy. She saw the same dreadful person this morning. He must be caught." Her gaze indicated that nothing short of hanging the guy in Old Mill Park would satisfy Grace.

"I should speak to Betsy," I said. "I'll do it now before I shop."

"My, yes." She stared at Kenny, who had just informed her that the total came to thirty-one dollars and fifty-eight cents. "Goodness, but that's quite high," Grace said. "I might have to go to the cash machine. Would you mind rechecking those items?"

I virtually bolted off, knowing that Grace would also try to make exact change. Someday she'd cause a riot at the store. I didn't want to be there when it happened. I also decided to skip the ATM, lest she need more money.

I'd write a check instead. Heck, I'd shoplift the stuff to avoid another conversation with Grace.

I found Betsy in Canned Vegetables, replenishing the peas. She looked frazzled, more so than usual after talking to Grace.

"I didn't think you'd be working today," I said in greeting. "The store doesn't seem all that busy—except for the express line."

"Grace," Betsy groaned, her attractive face looking more tired than usual. "She does that every time. I don't think she can see very well."

"She can't ID the lurker," I said, "but Milo heard you got something of a description."

Betsy shrugged. "I couldn't pick him out of a lineup, but at least I got a vague idea. I was still half asleep when I saw him in the backyard around seven. He's average height, maybe a little more, average weight, wore pants and a shirt, medium-colored hair, somewhere between thirty and fifty. How's that for vague?"

"It's better than a blur," I noted. "Did he see you and run off?"

"I don't think so," Betsy said. "I didn't go outside. He was wandering around by the vegetable garden next to the garage. Then something—a car, maybe—seemed to make him hurry off and go over through the Carlsons' yard. They weren't up yet."

"Apparently he hasn't tried to get into anybody's house," I remarked. "Nor has he done anything threatening, unless you believe Grace Grundle or Ella Hinshaw Blatt."

Betsy gave me a tired smile. "Poor old ladies. They're both a bit addled in different ways. But you're right, now that I think about it. If I hadn't known about the other prowler reports, I might've gone out and asked if he was lost. Jake and I wondered if it's somebody from

RestHaven. I mean, a patient who's allowed to leave the premises?"

The idea hadn't occurred to me. "I've never heard that they permit that sort of thing. But trying to get any kind of patient information out of that bunch is like pounding on a cast-iron door."

Betsy smiled at an elderly man with a cane who was pushing a cart filled only with home health aids. "Could Milo find out?" she asked.

"I'm not sure they'd tell him," I replied. "I'd better let you get back to work. Are you off tomorrow?"

"Are you kidding? Buzzy and Laura won't be back until Wednesday. Which reminds me—I have to check Buzzy's produce section. One of these days," she said over her shoulder, "Jake and I are taking a *real* vacation!"

I didn't quite believe Betsy. The only big trip they'd taken was to Europe six years ago when they decided to splurge after inheriting money from Jake and Buzzy's sister, Ursula. They'd planned on staying for two months but had come home in three weeks. The English were snobbish, the French were rude, the Germans were gruff, and worst of all, the Irish never heard of corned beef. Or so the O'Tooles claimed. Betsy and Jake weren't married just to each other, but to the store his father had founded after returning from serving in the navy during World War Two.

After I got home and had put all of the hundred and twenty dollars' worth of items away, I realized I hadn't yet seen my namesake. I called Amanda to ask if they'd mind if I stopped by. She informed me that Walt's mother and his stepfather were arriving from Boise later that afternoon, but to come ahead now. I left a note for Milo, in case he came home while I was gone and thought I'd run off with the lurker.

I kept my visit fairly brief. Little Emma was a sweet-looking baby, but she had very strong lungs. Despite Amanda and Walt taking turns trying to comfort her, Emma wouldn't shut up. Her parents were obviously frazzled. I offered to hold her, but the wee one took a look at me and howled even louder. Maybe, I suggested, she didn't like her name. Walt said he'd tried calling her Little Mouse, but she hadn't liked that, either. I left shortly after three-thirty, recalling the first weeks after Adam's birth. He'd had colic and nearly driven me nuts. I'd cursed his father's absence for almost a month. By that time I figured his loony wife had given birth to their own baby and they'd be as miserable as I was. But they'd suffered together. I was alone.

As I was leaving Parc Pines, Buck Bardeen was coming in. He'd sold his house in Sultan and moved to Alpine, apparently to be closer to Vida. We met by the mailboxes in the foyer. The tall, robust retired air force colonel smiled at me and shook my hand. I hadn't seen him in a couple of months. He asked how Milo and I were enjoying marriage.

"We like it," I assured him, "especially now that the disruptions of the remodel are over. We must have you and Vida to dinner."

His smile faded. "Kind of you to offer. I haven't seen much of her lately. Busy with family, I guess. Maybe you can talk her into an outing."

Despite his longtime relationship with Vida, I didn't know Buck all that well. But I had the impression he was a man of great integrity and very down-to-earth— even when he was flying a plane. "She's not acting like herself these days," I said. "I'm afraid we've had a bit of a falling-out this past week. Has she mentioned it to you?"

The furrows in his high forehead deepened. "No. We haven't talked for a while. Vida seems—as she would put it—on the peck."

I had to ask the question. "Do you think it's because of Roger?"

Buck's keen blue eyes gazed at the ceiling. "No doubt. She refuses to discuss his jail sentence. Can't seem to accept what's happened. I could see it coming from a mile away. Just a matter of time."

"I know," I said sadly. "She's in denial. Maybe Vida's convinced he was framed. I don't suppose you know where she is this weekend?"

"No." His gaze was again on me and he looked faintly dismayed. "Amy already asked me."

"She's really worried," I told him. "I gather nobody's seen Vida since she left work Friday. My guess is she went to see Roger, but Amy insists she wouldn't do that. Has she spoken to you about Roger since his arrest? She hasn't mentioned his name to me."

Buck briefly closed his eyes and rubbed at the bridge of his blunt nose. "I tried to talk to her about the whole sorry mess, but she didn't want to hear it. Told me I didn't understand young people. After all my years in the service dealing with kids who were still wet behind the ears and didn't know their ass from a . . . Sorry, Emma," he apologized, his tanned face growing darker. "I don't use that kind of rough language around Vida. You can be sure of that."

I managed to smile. "Forget it. I'm married to the sheriff."

Buck nodded. "Good man. Solid. He should've put Roger away the first time. Oh, I know Dodge was in a bind. Munkie-Runkie . . . I mean, *Vida*," he went on, though I knew his pet name for her, "is a force to be reckoned with. One of her many virtues. But now you've got me worried."

I was beginning to think my belief that Vida had gone to see Roger was a pipe dream. Too many people had too many reasons for her not doing that. "Amy wants

Milo to put out an APB on her by six o'clock. I have doubts about doing that. What do you think?"

"Well . . ." He rubbed his chin. "If she's gone somewhere over the long weekend, that'd make her mad enough to chew nails and spit rivets. On the other hand . . . I don't know what to say. Wait another day? She'll probably be back by tomorrow night."

"Good point," I said. "If you think of anywhere Vida might've gone, let me—or Amy—know."

"I'll do that." He patted my shoulder. "Take care, Emma. I can't imagine Vida running into any trouble she couldn't handle."

I smiled faintly. I couldn't imagine it, either. But as indomitable as she might be, Vida was still human.

Milo wasn't home yet when I pulled into the garage. I put dinner together before going outside to sit in the backyard. Like it or not, my husband was going to eat a salad for dinner. I'd bought cooked prawns, so he couldn't gripe about trying to find the "frigging microscopic shrimp" I'd used the last time I'd made a seafood salad. My husband insisted he used bigger bait with periwinkles when he went trout fishing. I'd told him if that was true, he should catch bigger trout.

I heard more sirens in the distance just as Milo arrived shortly after five. "Are you fleeing another wreck?" I inquired as he collapsed into the patio chair next to me and took off his regulation hat.

"No," he replied, looking hot and tired. "That's for those idiot kids. Bunky Smythe and one of the rangers from Skykomish found them on a logging road near Anthracite Creek. Their car broke down last night, so they slept in it. Then Jeb and Josie thought they must be near the highway so they tried to hike out, but he fell and may've broken his ankle. They're all being checked out at the hospital. Dumb kids."

"I assume the parents have been notified?" I asked.

Milo nodded. "The ones Heppner could track down. Damn, what's wrong with people these days? What's the point of having cells if they don't keep them charged? They didn't even have a compass. Jeb and Josie were walking the wrong way. They were only a couple of hundred yards from Highway 2 and almost right across from the Skykomish Ranger Station."

I put my hand on Milo's shoulder. "Maybe they'll give up the dump-site search now. That should please you."

"I should be so lucky." He looked at me, evincing surprise. "You stayed put. Are you sick?"

I briefly recounted my afternoon, including my conversation with Buck. "Let me make our drinks," I said when I finished. "I assume you want to change clothes."

"Yeah. But I want to sit for a minute. I've been driving all over logging roads most of the afternoon. I stayed closer to town. Sam and I didn't think the kids would go too far away."

"What were they looking for? Another corpse?"

"They'd stopped at the Icicle Creek mini-mart," Milo replied. "The kid who works there told them about your hermit pal. The Sultan gang decided they should try to find him. I wish they had. You thought up a scheme to lure Laurentis into town?"

"No," I confessed. "This weather affects my brain."

"Give it a shot. I left a note at the office for Doe to run a background check on him. She's intrigued by the guy. His back-to-nature thing appeals to her." Milo stretched and yawned before he stood up. "I'd better change before I nod off."

I followed him into the house. "I'll make the drinks now," I said, a bit too cheerfully.

My husband turned in the kitchen doorway to look at

me. "Don't tell me Vida showed up and brought you one of her ptomaine casseroles."

"Let's call it a change of pace." I smiled angelically.

"Oh God." Milo continued on his way.

The phone rang just as I was putting ice cubes in the glasses. Racing out to the living room, I heard Amy's anguished voice on the other end when I picked up. "Is Milo there?" she asked. I could hear Dippy screaming in the background. When Amy spoke again, it was to her husband. "Ted! Get him out of the sink!"

"What is it, Amy?" I asked, trying to control my impatience.

"It's been such a horrible day," she replied, on the verge of more tears. "I have to talk to Milo to tell him to put out the APB."

"He's not here," I lied. "He was called out this afternoon to find some missing children. Luckily, they were found. By the way, I ran into the Colonel at Parc Pines. He thinks an APB is a bad idea."

"What does *he* know?" Amy shot back. "He's always meddling in our family's business. No wonder Mom's upset with him. Be sure and have Milo call back as soon as he gets home. I've got to hang up. Dippy cut his finger and he's bleeding. What next? I'm a nervous—" She hung up before finishing the sentence.

My husband ambled into the living room. "Amy, huh?"

"You were listening in the hall," I accused him.

"You bet. Thanks for lying through your teeth." He leaned down to kiss the top of my head. "Turn off the ringer. Otherwise, Amy'll drive us nuts. Bardeen's right. If Vida's still missing by tomorrow night, I'll do it. Otherwise . . ." He shrugged.

"Amy won't give up. She'll call our cells. She'll call Doe at headquarters. She'll drive us all insane. What if

Ben or Adam call me?" I asked, moving back to the kitchen.

"They'll try again. Doesn't Adam only call when he's away from his frozen Alaska village with the screwed-up reception? Where's dinner?"

I opened the refrigerator. "You ate a late lunch, so . . ." I held up my hands. "Ta-da! See the big blue bowl? That's dinner."

"Shit. Are you trying to starve me? What next? Tofu?"

"I'm trying to keep you healthy. And strong," I added in a breathy voice, sidling up to him. "You have no gall-bladder, remember?"

Milo put his arms around me. "The things I have to do to keep you satisfied. It's too bad you're worth it."

"Hey," I said, looking up at him, "I saw Grace Grundle at the grocery store. She mentioned your brother. Does he know we're married?"

"No. I usually only hear from him a couple of times a year. That's fine with me. He always was full of himself and he only gets worse with age. He emailed me some goofy Internet card for my birthday. I emailed him back with a brief thanks, but that was it. I didn't ask if he and Pootsie were really coming up this way in the fall. He'd said something about doing that in his ego trip of a Christmas letter."

"Pootsie?" I said as Milo let me go.

"Right." He started pouring our drinks. "Her real name is Patricia—same as Mulehide, except she was known as Patti—with an *i*. Pootsie was a cheerleader at Wazzu. That's where they met. I never cared much for her, either. She has a more ear-splitting giggle than your former reporter Carla. And don't ask why Clint calls her Pootsie. I'd rather not know."

We'd migrated to the patio. "Did you and Clint get along as kids?"

"We had to," Milo replied. "Pa couldn't stand 'squabbling,' as he called it. But Clint was the family star. Good grades, into all the activities, popular kind of kid. I was none of those things. Clint was the eldest, then Emily, then me. Emily was more like Clint, but nicer."

"I'm trying to picture you as a baby," I said, smiling. "You must've been a big—"

Milo's cell rang. Reluctantly, he took it out of his pocket. "It's Doe," he murmured, clicking on the call. "Dodge. What's up? . . . You're sure you got the right spelling? . . . Right. Okay, thanks. In a way, I'm not surprised."

"What was that?" I inquired after my husband rang off.

"Doe's search for Laurentis came up empty," Milo informed me. "It seems as if your recluse artist doesn't exist. Turn on your brain. What do you think that means?"

Chapter Eighteen

"CRAIG'S AN ARTIST," I finally said after a pause. "Maybe his real name is weird or too common. I think his name fits him. Changing it to something else doesn't mean he's a crook."

"I'm not saying he is," Milo replied. "It just muddies the waters. Call me crazy, but I like it better when people are who they say they are."

"It *is* odd," I said after a brief silence. "We're running into a lot of people lately who may be using aliases. Ren's mother, the minister who married you and Tricia, now Craig." A wild thought came to me. I grabbed Milo's arm. "What if Craig is the Reverend J. C. Peace?"

"Huh?" Milo looked puzzled. "Oh—you mean . . . Damn. I don't know if he *couldn't* be. Last fall when Laurentis was in the hospital after he got shot, they cut his hair and shaved his beard to get rid of any wildlife he might've had living in that mess. When I tried to interview him about the shooting, I had an odd feeling when I saw him up close. His unusual green eyes, maybe. I'd never spotted him on his rare trips to town."

"But you didn't know why you reacted that way?"

"No. I forgot about it until now." Milo sipped his drink. "I dismissed it as seeing what the legendary recluse looked like. And why," he added wryly, "you seemed so taken with him. I suppose I was kind of jealous. He didn't seem to be your type."

"Neither did you," I said. "But we've got to find Craig. If he's J. C. Peace and he was never a certified minister, that's grounds for the annulment. I told you that. We wouldn't need to keep badgering Tricia."

Milo sighed. "I don't know where to start. Judging from the times you've seen him in the woods or coming out of them, it's always been from the south. Remember when Laurentis was still known only as the crazy hermit and was a suspect in the Rafferty house fire a couple of years ago? Vida—and Roger—put together a search party. They supposedly scoured that area and came up with zip."

"I doubt any of them were very thorough," I said. "Roger never went farther than Fir Street."

"Some of them did," Milo reminded me. "I talked to one of the Gustavsons and Norm Carlson's daughters. They got as far as Jewel Lakes at the four-thousand-foot level. Another group went to the end of the logging road by Fisher Creek. That's quite a ways into the forest."

I nodded. "Craig has to live by a creek. He needs water. Did any of them search around Sawyer Creek before the road ends?"

"Not that I know of." He grinned at me. "I know that turf from when I was a kid and hiked all over that part of the county. Burn Creek, even Alpine Creek, are possibilities, though that's getting close to the ski run up from the lodge and then the Foss River Campground. If tomorrow's quiet, I may send somebody to look around the area. There are only so many creeks, especially this time of year, with such a piddling runoff from Mount Sawyer."

"Make sure whoever you send doesn't wear a uniform," I cautioned. "Craig can probably sniff the law."

"Then the uniform doesn't matter." Staring off into space, my husband sipped more of his drink before speaking again. "Hell," he finally said, "he likes you. You're still deputized. You and I'll go looking for him."

"But he knows you're the sheriff," I protested. "If he sees me with you he'll hide."

"No, he won't. He was juiced up on meds when I tried to talk to him in the hospital. He probably doesn't remember what I look like."

"You're kind of hard to forget," I said. "Being tall, I mean. And Craig has an artist's eye."

"He was damned near cross-eyed when I tried to get him to talk. If he remembers anything, it's the uniform. I never took off my hat."

"Up close, he'd sense you were the Law."

"I could hide behind a tree."

"A *big* tree." I remained dubious. But I couldn't refuse. "Okay, but I don't like our chances."

"You like to take chances," Milo said. "I don't like you doing that, but this time you'll be with me. We'll do this not only for the investigation, but to find out if he's J. C. Peace, right?"

I couldn't argue about that.

Somehow, we got through the evening without further interruptions, visitors, or calls to duty. To our relief, we didn't hear from Amy again. Maybe she'd decided Buck—and Milo—knew what they were talking about when they stated that jumping the gun on an APB for Vida was a bad idea.

We left on our quest just after ten o'clock Monday morning, driving up past the Icicle Creek Ranger Station and onto a gravel track that became increasingly dicey as we climbed up Tonga Ridge. Milo found a place to turn off just before we reached the old logging road.

I posed a question to my husband. "Aren't we too close to civilization for Craig's tastes?"

"You prefer parachuting into the forest? We have to start somewhere. Fisher Creek is a short walk from here." Milo glanced at my feet. "I expected you to wear hiking boots, not sporty shoes that look like you'd use them on an art crawl in Seattle."

"I don't own any hiking boots, as you should know by now. Where would I put them? Your feet are so damned big that all your foot gear takes up most of the space, remodeled closet or not."

"You don't want a man who can fill big shoes?" Milo shot back. "Get out of the vehicle. You're stalling."

"Am not," I mumbled, having trouble with the door. "Hey—it's locked!"

"Oh, right." My husband clicked the doors open.

I got out, staring up at the thick stands of Douglas fir, western hemlock, and Sitka spruce. "I don't think I've ever been this high up," I said. "Where are we?"

"Alaska," Milo retorted. "You want to look for Adam? Come on, let's head for the creek."

"I'm glad you know where we're going," I muttered. "You *do* know, right?"

"Hell, yes." He'd led the way and glanced back at me. "Try not to fall down, okay?"

A moment later, we'd reached Fisher Creek. It wasn't very impressive, with only a narrow ribbon of water languidly gliding over its rocky bed. "That's not a good sign," I remarked. "Where does it go?"

"Into Deception Creek. It comes out of Fisher Lake."

"I wouldn't think Craig would live that close to Deception Creek because of the hikers."

"That's right," Milo agreed, now several yards ahead of me. "We're going in the other direction."

"Oh." I decided to shut up and focus on walking faster.

After twenty minutes, more great stands of conifers, and an annoying amount of various bugs, I was certain we were lost. "Are you sure this is a trail?" I called to my husband.

He paused by a couple of firs that had apparently been toppled in a winter storm. Their gnarled roots reminded me of Medusa's head with snakes for hair. Except the roots were more appealing, curling outward as if begging for help.

"Yeah, I'm sure," Milo replied, stopping by an aging cedar stump. "The trail maintenance people haven't gotten around to it yet. Global warming has put them off their usual schedule. In the past, this area would still be under a foot of snow."

I didn't comment. My mind was elsewhere. "Maybe Craig wouldn't use a trail," I finally blurted. "We'll never find him this way."

"He has to have a route," Milo asserted. "He can't spend an entire winter holed up in the forest. The guy's lived up here for thirty years. Back when he arrived, we had some pretty severe winters. With eight, ten feet of snow, he had to be sure of his way in and out. Nobody else would be using the trails because they couldn't see them."

We resumed walking. I wouldn't admit it, but my feet hurt. I hadn't worn my sturdy shoes for a long time. Years, maybe. I felt foolish. The footing was often rocky, but then we were traversing a mountainside. I tried to focus on identifying the lush types of ferns that lined the alleged trail. I stumbled twice and decided I'd better watch my step instead of admiring the flora. Sniffing at the air, I savored the heady, primal scent of the forest. In town, I lived at the edge of these endless woods, but civilization thwarted the senses, even in a small town.

We kept walking. And walking. Finally we were in a meadow. It was too soon for most of the wildflowers to be in bloom, but I sensed the peace of this lush, emerald swath amid the mountain grandeur.

"Are we lost yet?" I asked Milo as we paused to admire the scenery.

"Hell no," he replied. "I haven't been up this way in years. I brought Mulehide here for a picnic before we got engaged."

"And she married you anyway?"

"She liked the outdoors. She wasn't a city girl. Like some women I know," he added archly. "She owned hiking boots."

"Good for her," I muttered, checking my watch. "We've been wandering around for over an hour. I haven't seen any sign of human life, let alone of Craig."

Milo seemed to be drinking in the mountain air. Or maybe he was ignoring me. But when he finally spoke, he asked a question. "Has your recluse ever done a meadow painting?"

"Not that I know of," I admitted. "You're right—this is a perfect subject, even better in August when the flora blooms."

"If you could tell what it was," my husband remarked. "Didn't you say his recent paintings were weird?"

"He's gone to a different style," I said. "It's more . . . abstract."

"You mean they look like one of Vida's casseroles?"

"They're more attractive than that, but it's not a bad description. Can we go home now?"

"Hell no. We just got started. Move, woman."

I moved—grudgingly. We went back into the forest where the trail—if it was a trail—was pitched at such an angle that I felt like a mountain goat. I knew we were still at about the same altitude because the trees grew close together. The sun was almost overhead, filtering hazily through the thick, towering evergreens.

Half an hour later, we came upon another creek.

"Where are we?" I asked, dragging myself to Milo's side.

He kicked at some pebbles and looked amused. "Carroll Creek. You've never seen it from up here?"

"No. You mean if I followed the creek I'd end up at the dump site?"

"That's right. We're about fifty yards from the logging road—but not where we left the Yukon." He bent down on his haunches. "I'll be damned," he murmured, standing up. "Take a look at this." He'd fished out something from the creek. "It's a penny, dated 1994. Didn't somebody say Laurentis carried a lot of change in his pockets?"

"Yes, but it could be from a hiker who was here last year."

He shook his head. "No. It would've been washed away in the earlier runoff. We're on your artist's turf. You want to keep going?"

I didn't want to admit I had blisters. "Well . . . we want to find Craig."

Milo looked down at my feet. "You're limping. I think we've nailed Laurentis's usual route—at least one of them. We'll go back to the logging road, then I'll get the Yukon and collect you."

I felt chagrined. "I'm sorry."

My husband grinned at me and took my hand. "We did what we set out to do. You can't help being a tenderfoot city girl. Don't budge after I leave you alone. It shouldn't take more than ten minutes for me to come back to collect my battered bride."

Five minutes later, I was alone, leaning against a Sitka spruce next to the road, staring at clumps of lavender yarrow. The same species grew on the verge of my street. In town, yarrow was a weed; in the forest, it was a flower. I smiled at the difference.

And heard a voice call my name.

I turned around to see Craig coming toward me. His gray beard and hair had grown out since I'd seen him in the hospital seven months ago. I smiled as he moved in his quick yet stealthy manner.

"You're trying to find me, I think," he said with the familiar slight rasp in his voice from lack of human conversation.

"We are," I confessed. "I'm so glad to see you're well."

He nodded. "Nature heals. Why are you looking for me?" The forest-green eyes were probing—and amused.

I couldn't help myself. "Are you J. C. Peace?"

His expression grew quizzical. "What a peculiar question. Why do you ask? Is this a query for your newspaper?"

"No. It's personal."

"Then why is the sheriff looking for me?"

"He's my husband now. Did you know that?"

Craig hesitated. "I know he lives with you. I didn't know you were married. Are you content?"

How like Craig to ask not about happiness, but contentment, I thought. "Yes. Very." I smiled, as if I had to prove it to him.

"I'm glad." He opened his mouth to say something, but stopped and suddenly looked tense. "I must go. Take care, Emma."

"Craig . . ." I held out my hand as if to stop him, but he moved quickly on bare feet. There was something wraithlike about him, disappearing behind the first big cedar and evaporating as if he'd merged into the mountain air.

I leaned back against the spruce and sighed. *Damn.* I'd blown my chance. I was still cursing myself two minutes later when the Yukon appeared from around a sharp bend in the road. Milo came to a stop and I limped around to the passenger side, realizing that Craig had heard—or sensed—the SUV approaching.

"What's wrong?" my husband asked after I flopped into the seat. "You looked pissed. I came as fast as I could."

"Craig was watching us," I said. "I blew it for both of us."

Milo darted a quick glance at me, but he had to stay focused on the narrow, rugged road. "You talked to Nature Boy?"

"Yes. Briefly. He realized you were coming to meet me."

"Shit!" The sheriff started to say something else, but stopped. While I sulked, he didn't speak again until we were almost back on the Icicle Creek Road.

"What the hell did you talk about? His latest frigging masterpiece?"

"No. I did ask if he was J. C. Peace, but he wouldn't answer. He seemed . . . bemused by the question."

Milo just shook his head.

"He wanted to know if I was content with you," I said after a long pause as we passed the ranger station.

"Jesus."

"He didn't ask about Jesus."

"You're un-deputized."

"Good. I don't like working for you. You're a jackass as a boss."

"You're damned lippy for a deputy. Worse than Mullins."

"I'm furious with myself for flunking the test," I asserted. "You think I didn't want him to admit he was J. C. Peace?"

Milo was now able to look at me. "Do you think he is? Was?"

I slumped even further into the seat. "I don't know.

Maybe. He didn't deny it." I reconsidered the encounter. "The question didn't seem to surprise him, though."

"Did you ask him if he was Craig Laurentis?"

"No. I don't think we talked for more than a minute or two. How are you going to question him about that painting from the dump?"

"Maybe Donna can ask him," Milo said. "It'd be a natural question coming from her. She might be able to sell it for him."

I admitted that was a good idea. "But would he tell her the background of the painting, as in who might have owned it?"

Milo shrugged. "It's worth a shot. I'll call her tomorrow."

We'd reached Fir Street, with our log cabin almost in sight. "I hope Vida gets home this afternoon or early this evening. Otherwise, Amy'll go nuts. I wonder if she's checked in again with her sisters. It's possible that Vida stopped off to call on Beth in Tacoma. It'd be easy to pull off coming from Shelton to see her family."

"I thought you changed your mind about her visiting Roger in Shelton," Milo said.

"Well . . . where else would she go for a long weekend? Buck didn't suggest she'd visit friends or shirttail relations along Highway 2. I doubt she'd stay overnight with any of them, being so close to home."

"She'll show up." My husband pulled into our garage. "Charging rhinos couldn't stop Vida."

After we opened the doors and windows to air out the house, I noticed that the red message light was blinking on the phone. As soon as I heard the words, "Hi, Mom," I beamed and forgot about my blisters as I immediately called my son back.

"Adam! Where are you?" I cried, trying to kick off my shoes without untying the laces.

"Fairbanks," he replied. "I got in about an hour ago

for a big meeting with the bishop of northern Alaska. I'll be here until Wednesday. We had the longest day of the year about ten days ago. Did you notice?"

"I thought of you. It wasn't so long here, but it started to warm up about then. It's probably well over eighty by now."

"Gosh, it was above fifty when I left the village," Adam said in mock dismay. "I almost said Mass in shorts. What are you and the sheriff up to for the holiday weekend?"

"Nothing exciting," I fibbed. "We just got back from a little hike."

"You went hiking? Where to? Francine's dress shop?"

"Up on Tonga Ridge above town. What's the meeting for?"

"The usual." Adam sounded blasé. "Morale booster, keep the faith, try not to kiss a walrus during mating season. Ever since the Jesuits got themselves into trouble up here, the bishop figures the rest of us need a boost. I talked to Uncle Ben earlier and he told me to go look in the mirror. If I wasn't wearing prison garb, everything was fine."

"I'm glad they don't ask your uncle to speak at those meetings," I said. "Of course, he's realistic about his vocation. So are you. Dare I ask if you plan to shop while you're in the Big City?"

"Funny you should mention that," Adam responded. "Even funnier that I haven't lost your spare debit card. I'll try to keep it under four figures, okay?"

"You have no choice," I declared. "I'm never too far from being maxed out. You have needs, not merely wants, correct?"

"Dodge isn't covering you in diamonds and furs? Wait—it's eighty degrees in Alpine. You'd pass out. Say, one of my needs is a new cell. This one's practically ready for the Smithsonian."

"Okay," I agreed. "Try not to buy one that can reach Jupiter in bad weather."

"Mars is closer," Adam said. "Or is it? Did I take astronomy in college?"

"I never really knew what you did in college," I replied, thinking back to my son's irresponsible younger years. "Other than taking out girls and taking in half-racks to your dorm."

"Long time ago." Did he sound wistful? I couldn't be sure. "Hey, here comes Paul McMillan from Barrow. He tells the worst anti-Catholic jokes, but half the time he forgets the punch line. Love and peace, Mom. You'll be able to tell what I'm up to when you get your VISA statement."

With a bittersweet feeling, I set down the phone. It rang before I could get off the sofa. "Yes?" I said assuming, it was Adam who had forgotten to mention one of his needs.

"Emma?"

"Kip?" I said.

"Right. Are you okay?"

I laughed in a strangled sort of way. "Yes, I thought you were Adam calling me back. We just hung up. What's going on?"

"No work-related problems," he replied. "Chili and I went to see her sister, Jenni, in the hospital. She had an emergency appendectomy last night. She's fine, probably coming home tomorrow, but Amy Hibbert was admitted last night, too. Do you know what's wrong with her? We didn't want to ask the nurses. They looked busy."

I leaned back against the sofa. "Nerves, I'll bet. She's made herself sick worrying about her mother, who's been gone since Friday after work. You didn't hear Vida mention taking a trip, did you?"

"No," Kip said. "I didn't talk much to her Friday.

She's been kind of grim lately. I keep my distance when she's like that."

"Did you see Ted while you were there?" I asked.

"I didn't even see Amy," Kip replied. "Chili saw her on the way out, but didn't stop. She doesn't know the Hibberts that well. Heck, I don't either, except through Vida."

"Same here. Amy lacks her mother's spunk. I'll call Ted or the hospital to check on her. Thanks for the heads-up."

We rang off. I'd managed to remove my shoes, wincing at the blisters on both heels. After applying Band-Aids, I went barefoot to join my husband on the patio.

"Want to eat out again tonight?" he asked.

"I thought you might have to work crowd control at the picnic in Old Mill Park," I said. "We probably should show up for the sake of our public images."

"Hell. I suppose you're right. They should have some decent fried chicken. Potato salad, too." He looked at my feet and laughed. "Serves you right. Why don't you buy some *real* shoes?"

"Because I don't like what you consider 'real' shoes. They're ugly and clunky." I changed the subject and told him about Amy.

"I'm not surprised," Milo said. "It's too bad, though. Amy always was the nervous type. She was a year behind me in school. She got kidded a lot because she had such big feet."

"Did you tease her?"

"I wasn't into teasing girls. They scared me."

"I don't believe you."

"I was. Kind of. In seventh grade, Amy was taller than I was. She's damned near as tall as Vida."

"All the Runkel girls came within an inch of their mother—and a foot shorter on spine, as far as I can tell. Not as imposing, either."

"Not even close." Milo mussed my hair. A twig fell out. "Good God, woman," he said, "did you bring back part of the landscape with you?"

"I left enough so Craig could paint it."

"How will we be able to tell what it really is?" My husband turned serious. "I don't like the idea of tricking the guy, but I have to talk to him. He must know who had that painting. Too bad he won't stop in for some free food at the park."

I cringed at the thought of Craig socializing, especially on a federal holiday. His anti-government stance would erupt all over the hot dogs. As the lazy afternoon meandered on to the picnic's start at three, we could hear more fireworks going off. Some of them sounded annoyingly close.

Around four, I poked Milo, who had somehow managed to doze off despite the noise. "Are those firecrackers over at the loathsome Nelsons' place? I thought their awful kids were still locked up."

My husband sat up and rubbed his eyes. "Isn't there a younger kid living there with Grandma Nelson?"

"That kid," I said, "is a toddler. Don't you remember when the older one you busted showed up at headquarters with his wife and baby? Her name's Chloe."

"Oh, right. Was that when I slammed you with the door and you ran away because you thought I did it on purpose?"

"That's not exactly what happened, but yes, that was Chloe. She's still too young to set off fireworks."

"Not if she's a Nelson. They get started young." Milo got up to amble over to the property line. "Not them. They're coming from across the street. Or in the street. You want to head for the park? I'm hungry."

"I have to change. Why didn't you get dirty on our hike like I did?"

"Because I wasn't walking on my knees. Did you fall down when I wasn't looking?"

I didn't deign to answer the sheriff. But flouncing off indignantly wasn't easy with blisters.

It was hotter in Old Mill Park than it had been in our backyard. Milo and I traded beleaguered looks as we prepared to mingle with the over two hundred people who were laughing, talking, and, judging from some angry expressions, arguing.

"Where's the food?" my husband asked, dragging me by the arm. More firecrackers went off, almost drowning out the high school band.

"It may not all be out yet." I gestured with my free hand toward the area where the cookstove was located. "It's usually over there."

"Where's Mullins?" the sheriff asked, using his height advantage to survey the gathering. "He's supposed to be on duty here."

I spotted Jack's wife, Nina, talking to fellow parishioners Buddy and Roseanna Bayard. As usual, Nina was the epitome of calm amid the semi-frenzied Fourth. She saw us and smiled sweetly just as someone threw a firecracker at Brendan Shaw, the local insurance agent, who jumped out of the way. The big man thumped into Darla Puckett, knocking off her glasses. A fox terrier raced over to pick them up in his teeth and headed for the river. Darla screamed.

"Shit," Milo muttered. "Nina!" he called. "Where's Jack?"

The deputy's wife looked like a startled doe. "I'm not sure," she replied, never one to raise her voice. At least it sounded like what she said. It was hard to tell with all the noise going on around us.

"Stay put," my husband said. "I'll find Mullins so he can find the damned dog."

I intended to join Nina and the Bayards, but several young children got in my way. I guessed them to be Bourgettes, since Rosemary and Des seemed to be chasing them.

"Hi, Emma!" Rosemary shouted—and kept going.

I was about to join Marisa Foxx and a couple I recognized from the poker group I'd joined for a short time. I'd soon discovered I couldn't afford to play Texas Hold 'Em with well-heeled attorneys. But my path was barred again by the majestic figure of Mary Lou Blatt.

"Well," she began, looking smug, "I understand my self-righteous sister-in-law's done a disappearing act and put her idiot daughter in the hospital. Complete nervous breakdown. Tsk, tsk."

"Is that an official diagnosis?" I asked.

"Close enough," Mary Lou replied, all but smacking her lips. "Nancy Dewey is the source. I know how to translate medical mumbo-jumbo. Doc's wife told Lila Blatt, who told me. She's Episcopalian, like the Deweys. Other than that, Lila's a sensible person, unlike you-know-who. In any event, I say good riddance."

The spate of words from Mary Lou's acid tongue was hard to follow with nearby firecrackers going off, the crowd's raucous chatter, and the band playing the rousing finale of John Philip Sousa's *El Capitan* march.

"What," I shouted, "do you mean by 'good riddance'?"

"I mean," Mary Lou responded with evil glee, "Vida's gone for good. I thought you knew."

Chapter Nineteen

I DIDN'T KNOW WHAT to think about Mary Lou Blatt's statement. I wanted to ask, but the Bourgette children and a half-dozen other little ones had marched straight toward us. I'd seen them coming, but Mary Lou's back was turned. She was almost toppled by a chubby toddler who tromped between her legs. Naturally, she charged after the offender. In an attempt to escape whatever mayhem was about to ensue, I sought sanctuary with Milo, who was heading for the food table.

"This was not a good idea," I hissed at him. "Where did you go?"

"To find Mullins," he replied, elbowing his way through the crowd. "He was hiding in the can. I don't blame him. Where the hell's the chicken?"

"It's probably been poisoned by Mary Lou Blatt," I said, wincing as a beach ball bounced off my rear. "She's a witch."

"I can't hear you," my husband bellowed.

I shut up. Five minutes later we'd dished up some semblance of food. To my horror, I saw Ed Bronsky driving a golf cart through the crowd and honking a *a-oo-ga* horn. He was towing a wagon filled with what I assumed were Casa de Bronska souvenirs. Milo had spotted him, too.

"Holy crap," my husband muttered, "let's get out of here."

Like a couple of burglars, we sneaked around to the other side of the campstove area. The band was taking a break and the noise had diminished a few decibels. My chicken tasted like putty. I marveled that Vida hadn't cooked it. I was finally able to tell my husband what Mary Lou had said about her sister-in-law taking a one-way trip.

"That's bullshit," Milo declared. "Vida would never desert Alpine."

"I know that, but it bothers me that Mary Lou would pass on that rumor. She's malicious."

My husband shrugged. "She's always been that way. Especially when it comes to taking digs at Vida. I'm surprised she didn't tell you Vida had run off with Crazy Eights Neffel."

I gave up on the chicken. It was too hard to chew. "You must've found Jake's take-out kind," I said.

Milo nodded. "I know my chicken. Yours is better than Jake's, though. I lived on his deli chicken for the first month after Mulehide left."

My watch said it was after five. "Will you put out an APB on Vida?"

"No. If Amy had a breakdown, she won't be bugging me about it."

"I'm uneasy, though," I admitted. "Maybe I should go see Amy."

"That's the dumbest idea you've had since you wore party shoes to go hiking," Milo declared. "You know damned well Amy will moan and groan about her mother being ass-end up in a ditch somewhere."

"I suppose," I murmured. But I was still uneasy.

Vida wasn't in the office when I arrived Tuesday morning.

"Is it her day to bring the pastry?" I inquired of Mitch.

"No," he replied, pouring a cup of coffee. "She brought

those damned muffins Friday. Why? Do you think she quit in a fit of pique?"

I was loath to tell my reporter about Amy's concern for her mother, so I kept quiet. Instead, I asked about his weekend.

"We went to see Troy on Saturday," Mitch replied. "Then we spent Sunday in Seattle fighting traffic. We stopped again on the way back to see Troy yesterday afternoon. He's put on some weight working out in the gym there. He looks good."

"I'm glad to hear that," I said.

Mitch, being Mitch, frowned and ran a hand through his thick gray hair. Good news was never good enough. "Brenda worries about how he'll manage once he's released from prison. She's afraid it'll be hard for him to make the adjustment to life outside."

"He won't have been in that long, really," I pointed out. "Doesn't he have only a year to go?"

"A year come August," Mitch said. "No chance of him being released early because of the two escapes. It seems like forever since he's been locked up. And not just to him, but to Brenda and me."

"This last year has certainly gone fast." It was a stupid thing to say, but my brain is never in gear until I've had massive amounts of caffeine. I tried to rectify that by pouring myself some coffee.

"I wouldn't be working here if Troy hadn't been put away at the Monroe facility," Mitch reminded me.

"Well," I said, "I'm glad you are." That much was true.

"It beats early retirement from the *Free Press* in Detroit," Mitch allowed, gazing around the newsroom. "Where is everybody?"

"Kip has the bakery run," I said, suddenly remembering. "Leo told me he'd be late. He took the red-eye from L.A. Vida went out of town for the weekend."

"Oh. Leo's lucky his kids didn't get themselves into big trouble. Especially since he and his wife were divorced."

"They had their own problems," I said. "But you're right. He counts himself fortunate that things never got any worse than they did."

Mitch's spirits were lifted by the sight of Kip carrying the lavender Upper Crust bakery box. "Cinnamon rolls, twisters, and bear claws," he announced. "I already ate a twister. Chili and I overslept, so I didn't have breakfast." He glanced around the newsroom. "No Vida? No Leo?"

I explained again about Leo's late arrival into Sea-Tac. "Vida should be here soon," I said, not wanting to set off any alarms. "She took off for the weekend, too."

Neither Kip nor Mitch—who was scarfing down the first bear claw out of the box—seemed concerned. But I was. I took a twister into my office and realized I hadn't given my editorial any serious thought. I had to come up with a fresh idea. Realizing that Milo and I had missed the usual speeches at the picnic because we'd arrived late, I didn't know if Fuzzy had announced the date for the special election. I hurried out to the newsroom, asking Mitch to find out.

"You were out of town," I told him, "so you have a good excuse not to have been on hand. I don't. If the mayor did confirm the date, that's two, three inches on page one."

Leo showed up a little after nine, catching me by surprise as I stared at my Sky Dairy calendar, seeking editorial inspiration. "Earth to Emma," he said, grinning.

I jumped. "Leo! How was your visit?"

"Good." He sat down, but stopped grinning. "Except for Brian threatening to quit his job at Raytheon in Santa Barbara. He doesn't get along with his superiors. Kids these days . . ." Leo shook his head.

"How does his fiancée feel about that?" I asked.

"Shannon's laid-back," Leo replied. "Being a free-lance illustrator, if they have to move, that's fine with her. She's an army brat who's used to living in different places. Liza would hate to see them move out of Southern California, though. Rosemary and her boyfriend are talking about settling in Denver. That's where he's from. Katie seems content in L.A. Westwood, actually. She's finishing her PhD in history at UCLA."

I felt stupid. "Which one has the grandson?" I asked.

"Brian and Shannon," Leo said. "That's why they decided to get married. When they first started living together, Liza was so embarrassed that she told me they were already married. It's a different world, Emma."

"You've forgotten that Tom and I weren't married when I had Adam?"

Leo looked faintly embarrassed. "God no! Somehow, that was different. That happened before I knew either of you." He turned to glance into the newsroom. "Where's the Duchess? I didn't see her Buick parked outside. Is she off on her rounds?"

Having seen Mitch leave earlier, I didn't have to lower my voice. "Vida's been gone all weekend. Nobody, including her daughter, Amy, knows where she went. In fact, Amy had a meltdown yesterday and is—"

I stopped speaking. Vida was tromping into the newsroom, wearing something on her head that looked like a small bathtub. "Traffic!" she exclaimed, heading toward us. "I thought I'd avoid it by getting an early start over the pass." She sat down in the other visitor chair. "Really—where do all these people come from?"

"Where," I asked, relief flooding over me, "did *you* come from? Amy's been so worried that she got sick."

"What?" Vida was dismayed. "Didn't Ella tell her where I'd gone?"

"Ella?" I echoed as Leo got up, patted Vida's shoulder, and went off in search of coffee.

"Yes, Ella, that ninny," Vida said. "What do you mean, Amy's sick?"

I grimaced. "She's in the hospital. It's not serious," I added quickly. "Nerves, I gather. She was so upset about where you'd gone that—"

Vida threw up her hands. "Gracious! I called Amy before I left Friday, but something's wrong with her answering machine. It has been for the past few months. I told her that a dozen times. I asked Ella to call Amy for me, but she's so addled that she obviously forgot. I must go see my silly daughter at once. Where is her spunk?" Vida stood up, holding the bathtub in place with one hand. While she was seated, I'd noticed the inside was full of paper forget-me-nots. "I'll tell you about my weekend with Faith Lambrecht in Spokane when I get back. Most inspiring."

Leo sauntered in with his coffee and a cinnamon roll. "Missing Mrs. Runkel mystery solved, I take it. Who's Faith Lambrecht?"

"The mother of the new Bank of Alpine president. Didn't you catch Vida's Cupboard last Thursday when she talked about Bob Lambrecht's wife and his mother?"

"I missed it," Leo confessed. "Don't tell Vida. Liza phoned just before seven to ask when I'd arrive so she could meet me at the airport."

I promised not to rat him out. After Leo headed to his desk, I called Milo to let him know Vida had landed.

"Spokane?" he said. "God, I don't remember Vida going that far from Alpine in the last ten years. Why didn't she tell Amy?"

"You don't want to know. It's complicated. I suspect Roger removed the Hibberts' phone message capabilities before he went to jail. No doubt there was incriminating evidence involved. I'll spare you the details now."

"Keep it to yourself," Milo responded. "I've got problems of my own."

Any time the sheriff had problems, I smelled news. It was after nine-thirty. Mitch should return soon unless the mayor had launched into one of his long-winded explanations. Vida had recently told me that years ago Marius Vandeventer and former sheriff Eeeny Moroni had an agreement to downplay the seamier aspects of Alpine life. Maybe it was time to put a spotlight on those bad old days, if only to create enthusiasm for a change in SkyCo's government. I settled in, digging deep to find my most self-righteous stance. I'd gotten as far as three feeble leads—all deleted—when Mitch showed up.

"Just the usual," he said. "The mayor verified that the vote on his plan will be held Tuesday, September sixth. If Blackwell doesn't shoot Fuzzy first. Oh—did you know about the break-in at your church?"

"No," I replied, startled. "Was anything valuable taken?"

"Apparently not," Mitch replied. "The only way Father Kelly knew someone had broken in was because the lock was jimmied when he returned from his trip Saturday night."

"That's a relief," I said. "Maybe it was kids horsing around." I decided not to mention something might've occurred at the sheriff's office after my reporter had gone over to the courthouse. If my editorial writing skills didn't improve, I'd pay a call on Milo. For reasons I've never understood, the sheriff and his deputies were indifferent when it came to anything that smacked of a headline, big or small.

By ten o'clock, my wellspring of inspiration had run dry. Vida still hadn't returned from checking on Amy, so I headed off down Front Street, already feeling the sun's heat.

Dustin Fong was in charge of the reception desk, greeting me in his usual polite manner. "Mr. Laskey was already here," he said. "You probably already knew about the wrecks and those kids who got lost."

"Do you have an update on the one who broke his ankle?" I asked.

"No." Dustin looked apologetic. "You'll have to call the hospital. After they were rescued, the situation was out of our hands."

Dwight Gould appeared from the hallway. "It's not a crime to break an ankle, you know."

I glared at Dwight. "No kidding. How come you're not on patrol?"

He returned the glare. "I just got back. We had another wreck out by Cass Pond. Three injured, all taken to the hospital in Monroe. They're full up here. Damned three-day weekends. Firecracker injuries, domestic brawls, a fight at the Icicle Creek Tavern. Didn't Laskey tell you?"

I wouldn't admit he hadn't. "He's used to it. He's from Detroit."

"Detroit," Dwight sneered as he headed out the door. "No wonder he moved here."

"Is there anything I can do for you?" Dustin inquired.

"I had a question for the sheriff. I assume he's not too busy?"

"He left," Dustin said. "I guess you didn't notice the Yukon's gone."

I wouldn't admit I hadn't done that, either. "I figured . . ." Lori had hung up the phone and was staring at me with a puzzled expression. "Okay, I sensed news. What's going on?"

Dustin glanced at Lori, who shrugged. "Honest, Ms. Lord," the deputy said, never having called me by my first name in the ten years I'd known him, "we're not sure yet." He paused, frowning. "I can only say—

since it was logged after Mitch left—we got a call from RestHaven. They have some kind of problem up there."

I smiled. "Okay. I'm sure Mitch will hear about it later. I'll go back to the office and drink more coffee. I'm not really awake yet."

"You can have some of ours," Lori offered.

"No!" I cried. "I mean, we have plenty of our own." And ours doesn't taste like toxic waste. "Thanks, though." I was out the door, hurrying as if the sheriff's coffee could follow me down Front Street like a bad dream.

I had no intention of going back to the *Advocate,* however. Seeing that Vida's Buick and Mitch's Taurus were both gone, I got into my Honda and headed for RestHaven. Reminding myself that I wasn't fully alert, I exercised caution on the route to River Road. Traffic— such as it is in Alpine—was light. Maybe some people were still on vacation. Or they were in the hospital. That was a story in itself. I couldn't recall a time when they'd run out of beds in all the years I'd lived in the Valley of the Sky.

I spotted the Yukon and a cruiser parked by Rest-Haven's main entrance. The sheriff wouldn't be glad to see me, but we both accepted the adversarial nature of our jobs. I got out of the car, took a deep breath, and marched into the rotunda.

I didn't get far. A lean man of average height with hollows under his cheekbones blocked my way before I took a half-dozen steps inside. "Ma'am," he said in a soft voice, "may I see your RestHaven ID?"

He wasn't in uniform, but despite the gray slacks and navy blue summer shirt, I guessed him to be Sid Almquist. "I'm Emma Lord from the *Advocate.* I don't think we've ever met, Sid, but I know who you are."

Sid flinched. "This isn't a good time to visit, Ms. Lord."

"That's why I'm here. I just came from the sheriff's office."

He looked puzzled. "You work for the sheriff *and* the newspaper?"

I felt like saying I certainly did, since I had to feed Mr. Law Enforcement. Briefly, I argued with myself: Truth or Dare? "I'm here to see Ren Rawlings. I know where her room is. I've visited her before."

"I'm afraid that's not possible right now," Sid said. "We're in the middle of a patient reorganization."

"You mean you're moving patients around?"

Sid looked uncomfortable. "It's an internal process. Tomorrow might be a better time to call on your . . . friend."

"Okay." I smiled. "As long as I'm here, is Kay Burns free? I have some PR-related queries for her."

"She's in a staff meeting," Sid replied, not looking me in the eye. "Sorry. Maybe you can phone her this afternoon."

I had no choice but to surrender. "Thanks, Sid. See you later." I left the building. But I had no intention of leaving the premises. I got in the Honda and drove from the parking area to where Milo had left the Yukon under the porte cochere. Unless he wanted to move the cruiser and then reverse all the way back down to River Road, he wasn't getting away without telling me what was going on. I almost laughed, an indication that I was finally waking up.

But ten minutes later, I was growing impatient. Seeing Fleetwood's BMW pull in, I got out of the Honda. "You're late," I called to him. "If you get past security, I'm going with you. Or has Rosalie already told you all?"

Spence looked as irked as I felt. "The lovely Rosalie is incommunicado," he declared, checking his Movado watch. "I've got twenty-five minutes before the hour-turn news at eleven. I'd better get something by then. Sleeping with our sources isn't doing us much good. Maybe we should deny them the pleasure of our company."

"I can't," I responded. "I'm legally wed."

"Alas, you are. I don't understand your taste in men. You're a woman of culture. Don't you long for a night of Verdi or Brahms or—" Mr. Radio stopped speaking as the sheriff hauled Iain Farrell out of the building while Jack Mullins rushed to open the cruiser's back door.

"What the hell?" Milo yelled, spotting Fleetwood and me. "Move those vehicles! Now!"

"See you at headquarters," Spence murmured, hurrying to the Beamer.

I got into the Honda, waiting for Spence to get out of my way. Milo and Jack were behind their respective wheels. I could practically feel sparks flying out of my husband's hazel eyes. But my foot almost slipped off the accelerator when I saw Jack Blackwell exit RestHaven. Without a glance at any of us, he strode toward the parking lot.

Spence had pulled onto the verge at the bottom of the sloping driveway. Maybe he figured Milo and Mullins were going to turn on the sirens. I followed Mr. Radio's lead, but there were no warning sounds as the Yukon and the cruiser went by us.

As we reached the arterial at the Icicle Creek Road, I noticed Blackwell's new silver Lexus was behind me. To my surprise, he followed us to the sheriff's instead of heading for his mill. When we all arrived at once, several curious pedestrians stopped to gawk.

"Where's your camera?" Spence asked after we got out of our cars.

"You know Milo won't let us take pictures," I said,

noting that the sheriff had entered his domain. "Besides, I'm a lousy photographer."

"We might as well wait until they get Farrell inside," Spence said. "What's with Blackwell? He's getting out here, too."

"Ask him," I suggested. "He probably won't insult you."

"I think I will." Spence moved onto the sidewalk. "Jack, my good man, are you making news or just being another interested observer?"

I felt like gagging at Mr. KSKY's unctuous approach. Jack turned to speak but didn't break his stride. I noticed the right side of his face was bruised and swollen. He kept moving. "That bastard Farrell attacked me," he called to Spence. "I'm filing a complaint. And no, I don't want to be on the radio. Go comfort your girlfriend. He slugged her, too."

My media colleague staggered slightly. "What?" But Blackwell had gone inside. "Jesus, Emma," Spence said. "I should check on Rosalie. Damn, why didn't I stay put?"

"Can you call her?" I asked.

"Yes, yes, I'll do that now." He turned away and got out his cell.

I decided I might as well beard the lion's den. There wasn't anything I could do to help Spence. I paused to see if Mitch's car was parked by the *Advocate,* but a FedEx truck blocked my view. The news was happening in the sheriff's office and I was on the scene.

Milo, Mullins, and Farrell were nowhere in sight. Dustin looked bemused as he listened to Blackwell. Lori seemed agog.

"Are you bringing charges?" the deputy asked Black Jack.

"You bet your ass I am," Jack replied. "Why do you

think Dodge busted the SOB? He took a swing at your boss, too."

Dustin handed over a form. "If you'd like to sit, sir, you can—"

Jack made a slashing motion with his hand. "I can do this standing up." He glanced at me. "I'll bet she can do some things standing up, too. But Dodge already knows all her moves."

That did it. I stomped over to Jack and didn't give a damn that he was more than half a foot taller and at least fifty pounds heavier. "Thanks, Blackwell. You just inspired this week's editorial. I'm going to write about how you treat the women in your life. Patti Marsh may be too chicken to complain about you beating the crap out of her, but I'm not. Go ahead, sue me. I'll see you in court. I'd love to see you try to deny the truth in public. We won't need a humor piece in this week's edition. You'll provide all the laughs from Alpine Baldy to Mount Sawyer."

The bruise wasn't the only thing that turned color on Blackwell's face. He actually bordered on puce. I didn't care. I was so mad that I was almost shaking. I wished he *would* hit me. But I knew he didn't dare. I made a clucking sound and whirled away from the world-class abuser.

Milo entered from the hallway as if on cue. He stopped before coming into the area behind the curving counter. "What's going on?" he inquired, glancing from Blackwell to me and finally to Dustin.

"Ask Jack," I said. "He's the one with a complaint. I feel *good*."

But Blackwell had snatched up the form and was storming out the door. Dustin expelled a big breath of relief. Lori started to giggle.

The sheriff, however, did not looked pleased. "Come into my office, Ms. Lord," he said in a chilly voice.

I obeyed, though I suddenly felt a bit wobbly. I couldn't recall when I'd been so infuriated. But anger is depleting. I practically fell into one of the visitor chairs. I noticed Milo had left the door open.

"Well?" he asked, looking very business-like.

"Blackwell insulted me—again." I paused to rub at my forehead. "I told him I was going to write an editorial about how he beats up women."

"Are you?"

"Maybe." I felt foolish and self-righteous at the same time. "I should. It's not right. How many women got beat up around here over the three-day weekend?" I was regrouping and gathering steam. "We did a series on abuse earlier this year. Maybe it's time to do a follow-up. Dwight mentioned several domestic brawls in the last few days."

"Four," Milo said without inflection.

"Four reported," I countered.

The sheriff just looked at me.

"What?" I yipped. "You expect me to let that asshole say terrible things to me and I should act like mealy-mouthed Patti Marsh?"

Milo seemed to relax. "Hell, I almost got into it with him at RestHaven. He's looking for a way to can me before the county commissioners are history. You know Jack and I've never gotten along."

I scowled. "Are you telling me what to write in my newspaper?"

He considered the question. "Yeah, I guess I am. I shouldn't do that. I don't like it when you tell me how to do my job."

"Maybe my threat will make Jack think twice before he shoves Patti's head into a wall the next time he gets mad at her."

"Dubious." Milo drummed his fingers on the desk.

"It's a habit. Hard to break—like smoking." He reached for his cigarettes. "Want one?"

"Yes, please," I said meekly. "I didn't mean to cause you a problem, but I couldn't stop myself."

"He ever make a pass at you?" Milo asked after lighting cigarettes for both of us.

"Never." I shook my head a half-dozen times. "Oh, ugh, what a grotesque thought. Are you mad at me?"

"No." He chuckled. "I heard most of it. You brought your A game. I hope you never get really mad at me. At least not for more than—what's your record?"

"Eleven minutes." I set the cigarette in the ashtray. "Please tell me more about what went down at Rest-Haven. All I've got are bits and pieces. Did Farrell really hit Blackwell and Rosalie?"

Milo ran a hand through his hair. "I'm still not sure what started it. Blackwell came to see Kay Burns. He's been taking part in some charity deal for the Alzheimer's-wing kickoff. Kay's not as fond of her second ex as she is of Dwight. Farrell interrupted the meeting and got into it with Kay—or maybe Jack. Rosalie went to see what was going on. Farrell tried to slug Jack, hit Rosalie instead, and then took another swing at Jack and connected. We busted Farrell on assault-and-battery charges."

"I'm . . . flummoxed," I admitted. "What started the fight in the first place? The mere presence of Blackwell?"

"Lot of 'he said,' 'she said,'" Milo replied. "Kay and Rosalie will have to give statements as soon as they get their acts together. Kay was semi-hysterical and Rosalie was in a state of shock. Hell, maybe she always looks like that. I'm guessing Fleetwood went off to comfort her."

"I assume so," I agreed. "Is Farrell giving a statement in his cell?"

"He will be, once he calms down," my husband said. "After he does that, he can post bail and beat it. I don't want that prick hanging around here. *I* might end up slugging *him*. Are you posting any of this online?"

I considered my options. "You've officially charged Farrell, but I'd like to wait to see why he hit Blackwell. Jack's complaint should fill in that gap. There are two sides to any fight."

"Let's hope so." Milo made a shooing motion with his hand. "Now beat it, Emma. I've got work to do."

I stood up. "You will keep me informed, won't you?"

"Yeah, sure. By the way, if you're going to Pie-in-the-Sky, why don't you pick me up a roast beef—"

I didn't stick around to hear the rest of the sheriff's order. Frankly, he was lucky I hadn't slugged *him*.

Mitch felt out of the loop. "I missed all that while I was interviewing Simon Doukas?" he exclaimed after I'd related what had gone on at RestHaven. "I got cheated. Doukas isn't a lively feature subject."

I refrained from saying that Simon was dead to me. "He's an attorney. You were expecting Clarence Darrow or Johnnie Cochran?"

Mitch shrugged. "He's dry as dust, but he gave me background on the Doukas clan. Grandpa Deeky—Demetrius Doukas—came here from Greece before World War One. He was seeking gold, bragged he'd found some, but worked as a logger. After Carl Clemans closed the mill, Deeky started buying up land. Maybe he did strike it rich."

"If I ever heard that, I forgot," I said. "Oddly enough, an old gold mine was involved in one of the first big stories I covered here."

"A Golden Fleece theme," Mitch murmured. "Simon's aunt converted to Catholicism. He made her sound like a traitor to the clan."

"What aunt? I never heard that before." Maybe Simon thought all Catholic women had loose morals.

"Cassandra," Mitch replied. "She married a Barton. Isn't that the family that owns the shoe store?"

"Yes, Clancy Barton. He must be Cassandra's son. The dad was before my time here. His sister, Mimi, works in the office at St. Mildred's. Kay Burns is the other sister. I don't recall ever seeing Kay in church."

"Simon didn't elaborate on them," Mitch said. "Are you sure you want me to take on this RestHaven brawl instead of going after the French connection with Buddy Bayard?"

"No rush on the ethnic feature. I want to detach myself from Blackwell and Farrell for personal reasons. I don't get along with either of them. You can take a neutral stance."

"I'll wait for Dodge to get things sorted out." He nodded at Vida's vacant desk. "The Duchess hasn't come back since she left earlier this morning. She must be making up for lost time."

"Probably," I murmured. "It *is* deadline day."

Mitch returned to his desk. I headed for the rest room. When I came out, Vida was entering the front office. "Emma!" she called. "We must have lunch. Let's leave early to get a window seat at the Venison Inn. A quarter of?"

I joined her and Alison at the front desk. "Sure. How's Amy?"

"Doc sent her home," Vida informed me, adjusting the bathtub on her head. "Nerves, worrying about me. Ella's mind has deteriorated since her fall. She'd forgotten I was visiting Faith. No wonder Amy was upset. I must finish all those advice letters. Dear me!"

I smiled at Alison as Vida tromped off to her desk. She'd described her visit as "inspiring." Maybe the minister's widow had miraculous powers. The Spokane trip seemed to have cured our House & Home editor of her irascible mood. It was too bad Faith's influence couldn't sail across the state and over the Cascade Mountains to stop some of our bellicose Alpiners from declaring war on each other.

I was still smiling when I heard the phone ringing in my office.

"Emma?" Milo said.

"Hey—I am not going to Pie-in—"

"Glenn McElroy's body was found this morning near Grotto. He'd been shot. I'll get more details later."

Chapter Twenty

I'D SHOVED GLENN McELROY to the back of my memory. Of course he was the federal marshal looking for Aaron Conley, but only Milo and I knew that. Maybe I should cover this latest blast of bad news. Peeking into the newsroom where Mitch was hunched over his keyboard, I realized I'd have to alert him if he was going to see the sheriff after lunch.

I stuck to the bare bones, however. Milo wouldn't want me blabbing about McElroy's reasons for being in SkyCo. The marshal's search for Conley had never been made official. Mitch would have to handle the story on a need-to-know basis. I didn't tell him that the murdered man was a U.S. Marshal.

But of course my reporter was curious. "Another out-of-towner gets whacked?" he said in surprise. "That's not good for the tourist trade."

"It helps fill up the front page," I said.

Mitch nodded. "In Detroit, it'd take up about an inch. I'll call on the sheriff after I have lunch with Brenda."

I returned to the conundrum of my editorial. *Violence*. That was always a solid topic. I could weave in criminal and domestic violence. I considered tying in the Fourth of July by leading off with how our country had been conceived in a violent revolution. But tossing a bunch of overtaxed tea into Boston Harbor didn't suit the modern era. I cut to the chase, trying to avoid clichés. By eleven-forty, I'd finished a rough draft. Very rough. I winced as I hit SAVE.

"You may not believe this," Vida said. standing in my doorway, "but after Spokane, it feels quite cool in Alpine. It was over ninety there! Faith has window fans, but they can only do so much. Are you coming? I didn't take time for breakfast and I'm famished."

I grabbed my purse and followed Vida like a good little stooge. "I'm so glad you're back," I said as she led the way out the door and to the Venison Inn. "I was worried, too."

"Ridiculous!" Vida exclaimed, her gray eyes darting every which way as if to absorb each nook and cranny of her beloved hometown. I wondered if she'd gone through withdrawal in Spokane. "If only Ella had a brain." She paused at the restaurant entrance, sniffing the air. "So fragrant. So refreshing after the smell of a city."

By the time we'd made the usual Runkel Royal Progress through the VI's front section, we settled into a window booth that looked out onto Front Street. Nicole, a dark-haired member of the Gustavson branch of Vida's family, hurried to greet us.

"Aunt Vida!" she cried. "We thought you'd run away from home!"

Vida put a hand to her imposing bust. "Oh, good heavens! Such a fuss! I was only gone two full days. Spokane seems like another world, but it *is* in the same state. Now tell me what the special is. I haven't eaten since last night. My old friend Faith is frugal when it comes to preparing meals. A Presbyterian virtue, of course."

"Meat loaf," Nicole replied. "Very hearty, with a side of mashed potatoes and a small salad."

I tried not to blanch. The special didn't strike me as warm-weather fare. Vida, however, was undaunted.

"Hmmm," she murmured. "With gravy?" She saw her niece nod. "Good. But a *small* salad? That's doesn't sound right for a hearty entrée. Could you bring a regular salad portion? And the bigger boat of ranch dressing. Tea, of course. Oh—a roll with an extra pat or two of butter?"

Nicole promised to fulfill her aunt's requests. She started to hurry off, apparently forgetting my existence. Obviously embarrassed, she backtracked and apologized.

"Sorry, Ms. Lord," she said. "I haven't worked the lunch shift since I enrolled in night classes at the college during summer quarter."

"No problem," I responded. "I'll have the prawns and chips with the small salad. Roquefort dressing. And a Pepsi, please."

Nicole dashed away. Vida watched her go, smiling fondly. "I do hope she carries through with her journalism major, though I don't understand why she wants to blog. Whatever is the purpose?"

"It's sort of a cross between a journal and an op-ed piece," I ventured. "People have a chance to air their views on life."

Vida looked skeptical. "Most people have very little to say that's worth knowing. That is, in terms of their life philosophy. If anyone should blog, it's Faith. Of course her view is that of a sincere Christian woman. She certainly opened my eyes this weekend." Vida paused, looking a trifle sheepish. "I've been rather cross lately. With Amy, especially, fretting about Roger being away for a while. But it's a good lesson for him to learn about associating with wicked people. Youngsters can be very naive."

I realized that was how Vida was coping with Roger's jail term: the innocent lamb had been led astray. Why not, if it made his grandmother feel better? He still had to serve his sentence. Maybe it'd help him grow up.

"Or," Vida continued, "perhaps it's the unseasonable weather. But after the heat of Spokane and the wisdom of Faith, I feel quite rejuvenated. I hope I convinced her she must move here. I also hope you'll dismiss my silly ramblings of last week."

"Of course," I asserted, smiling. "I've been off my feed, too. I assume Amy feels better now that you're home?"

"My, yes! My daughters tend to overreact." Vida paused as Nicole showed up with our salads and beverages. "Oh dear—I was hoping there'd be hard-boiled eggs in the salad. So slimming, you know. Do you think you could find some in the kitchen?"

"I'll try," Nicole said, no longer smiling so brightly. Maybe she'd have to dash out to the Overholt farm and find a couple of eggs to boil.

Vida, however, hadn't seemed to notice her niece's change of expression. She leaned toward me. "Now do catch me up on the news."

"We've got a dead body," I said. "Milo called about a half-hour ago to report an apparent homicide."

Vida almost dropped the three sugar packets she was dumping into her tea. "No! Who is it?"

"Someone from out of town," I replied.

"Oh." Her interest level plummeted. "A vagrant, perhaps."

I didn't elaborate. Instead, I asked if Miriam and Bob Lambrecht were coming to town today. If so, we'd need a photo and a brief article.

"No, alas," Vida replied. "They won't arrive until the weekend. They have so much to do winding up things in Seattle. You can imagine how difficult it is to deal with business and personal matters in the city."

I thought back to my leave-taking from Portland sixteen years ago. The worst part had been wresting Adam away from his current girlfriend, Coco Crawley. They'd gone together for only six weeks, but Coco had insisted she couldn't live without him. I'd been afraid she might follow my son to Alpine, but instead, she'd eloped with her yoga instructor a month later. To my relief, Adam had forgotten about her by the time he heard the news. In fact, only then did he reveal that her name wasn't Coco, but Cordelia ... or Cornelia. He wasn't sure which.

As soon as Vida and I returned to the office, I got a phone message from Mitch saying he was going directly from his lunch at home to see the sheriff. Even without the Lambrecht coverage, the front page was filling up. I conferred with Kip about the color fireworks photo. It was, he assured me, really eye-catching since we'd hired Buddy Bayard to take it. We hadn't had much choice with Mitch and Vida gone for the weekend.

My reporter didn't get back until going on two. "Dodge took a late lunch," he told me, putting a foot on one of my visitor chairs. "I didn't want to bother him at the Burger Barn."

I didn't comment. Instead, I asked what he'd learned about the murdered man.

"Glenn McElroy, forty-nine, from Puyallup." Mitch paused. "Did I say the town's name right?"

"Close enough," I replied.

"Some of the local place-names are tongue twisters. Anyway, he was shot through the head and neck at fairly close range. McElroy was found by his car just off Highway 2 in Grotto. A local resident called it in. Guy wouldn't give his name. It sounds as if he was pretty badly shaken. Body to SnoCo for a full autopsy, but Dr. Sung did a prelim, so that much is official. I suspect the final results won't get back to Dodge until the end of the week, especially after a holiday."

"Right. Has next of kin been notified?"

"Fong was working on that," Mitch said. "Apparently the vic was some kind of civil servant."

I told Mitch to write up what he knew, subject to change by press time. He grinned at me. "With stories like this, you're close to the source during the off-hours."

I gave him a dark look. "Guess again. That's when the sheriff takes the phone out to the garage and shuts the door."

I couldn't tell my reporter that I intended to take the back-door approach on McElroy. Obviously, Milo was opting for discretion until he touched based with the Feds. I'd give the sheriff another half-hour before I dropped in on him.

A few minutes later, Leo stopped in to see me. "Blackwell pulled his standing ad. What's up with that?"

I supposed I shouldn't have been surprised—but I was. "Does he want a refund for the month of July?"

"You bet." Leo rapped his knuckles on the door frame. "I told him it was a bad idea to cancel the ad. It could start a rumor that he was closing the mill and his logging operations. He told me what I could do with my advice. But the ads will run. Jack signed off on them. Does this have something to do with his feud with Dodge?"

"I doubt it," I replied. "He got pissed off with me over Fuzzy's government reorganization plan and today he got into some kind of dustup at RestHaven. Don't ask. I'm still waiting for clarification from Dodge."

"Does hot weather really make everybody nuts around here?" My ad manager didn't wait for an answer. "At least the Duchess is acting more like herself. What happened?"

"She got religion," I said. "I'll tell you about it later. She could be back any minute from wherever she went."

Vida, in fact, came through the door almost as soon as Leo went to his desk. To my dismay, she was holding Dippy by the hand and heading my way. "Amy is so exhausted from her distress over my so-called disappearance that I insisted on taking Dippy off her hands. Ted had to take the morning off to care for him while Amy was in the hospital. Such a tempest in a teapot! Is Ed's old clip-art file still around? I thought Dippy might like some of the pictures."

"Ask Leo," I advised as Dippy eyed me with suspicion. "Mitch could use your help with the Doukas family tree. I don't recall anything about Eeeny's dad finding gold."

"Gold?" Dippy echoed, gazing up at Vida with his curious gray eyes. "You have gold teeth, Grams."

"They're crowns, dearest," Vida informed him, beaming. "Dr. Starr put them in for me. Some day you'll visit him. He's a very kind dentist."

Dippy bared his own teeth. I was afraid he might try to bite me. "I'm off to . . . Parker's Pharmacy," I announced. "I need shampoo." I thought it best not to let Mitch know I was going to see the sheriff, since he might consider it a breach of his turf.

"Your hair looks funny," Dippy said as I sidled past him.

"That's why I need shampoo," I informed him with a half-baked smile. Maybe he'd suggest I needed toothpaste, too.

Stepping outside, it felt like mid-eighties. If Harvey Adcock hadn't gotten more fans, maybe Parker's had some. I really could use more shampoo, too. My husband seemed to wash his hair every time he showered. At least he still had his hair. I supposed I should be grateful for that.

Tara Wesley, who owned the pharmacy along with her husband, Garth, greeted me as I came in the door.

"Your namesake was in here with Amanda about half an hour ago."

"Have they run out of diapers already?" I asked.

"No, but she had to buy formula," Tara replied. "Trying to nurse didn't work for her."

"I flunked that, too," I said. "Now I need fans. From giving birth to post-menopause. You got any?"

"Menopause? Been there and done that." Tara laughed. "We've only got a couple of smaller fans left. Will they help?"

"Having you come to the office and blow on me would help," I told her. "Yes. And let me browse. I didn't make a list."

Tara nodded toward the next aisle and lowered her voice. "Dixie Ridley just told me they had a window peeper this morning. Rip chased him away, but he tripped over the hose and sprained his ankle."

"Did they report it to the sheriff?"

Tara shook her head. "Rip was too embarrassed. Being a macho football coach, he didn't want to admit he fell flat on his face. But they got a fairly good look at the guy. He's not a kid, according to Dixie."

"They should notify Milo," I said. "The descriptions he's received are vague."

Tara shrugged. "Tell your husband you heard it through the grapevine. Uh-oh. Here comes Ed Bronsky to pick up his prescriptions. I'm off to the pharmacy. Grab those fans on aisle two before somebody else does."

I briefly mused on what meds Ed was taking. I couldn't think of anything that would cure him of self-absorption. Apparently, he hadn't seen me, which was good. With any luck, I could stay hidden in the Housewares aisle. Ed wouldn't dream of buying an item that smacked of chores.

Ten minutes later as I exited Parker's, I almost literally ran into Dennis Kelly. Not having lingered after Sunday Mass, I asked him about his trip. It had been enjoyable, he informed me, even if some of his relatives were politically unenlightened.

"How," he remarked, "can my brother Pat—who was so outspoken on civil rights when it came to racial matters—not understand equality when it comes to gays? I finally told him I thought one of the Apostles was gay. He wanted to know which one, and when I wouldn't answer, he decided it had to be Judas." My pastor shook his head.

I laughed. "Say—I heard somebody broke into the church, but nothing was taken. Is that accurate?"

Den shook his head. "It was the rectory, but Mimi Barton was so upset that she told the sheriff's office it was the church. She's an efficient secretary, but . . . emotional." He smiled wryly. "The only sign of anyone getting inside was that some of the books in my study seemed to be out of order. Maybe whoever broke in thought we were the library."

"It might've been Crazy Eights Neffel," I suggested. "He may've decided to stop driving Edna Mae crazy. His current fetish could be books."

We parted on that whimsical note. It was after two-thirty by the time I reached the sheriff's office. All appeared to be calm, with Dustin talking on the phone and Lori at her computer. She smiled at me wanly and asked if I'd be at her grandmother's funeral.

"I'll have to see what's going on with the newspaper," I hedged. "It's a short workweek. I'm sure Vida will be there, though."

Lori looked peeved. "Mrs. Runkel was very late to Grandpa's funeral. We were all surprised. She's usually so punctual."

I assumed Lori had forgotten that Milo and I were escaping death just before Alf Cobb's services began.

Doc Dewey had been called away from the Baptist Church to tend to me, and Vida had come with him. "We were in crisis mode that day," I said. "Is your boss busy?"

She sighed. "He always is. But go ahead. He probably won't mind if it's you. A man was shot, you know."

"Yes, that's why I'm here. Mitch is involved in another story," I added, lest Lori think I was co-opting my reporter's assignment.

The sheriff looked up from some of the paperwork he despised. "Why are you loaded down?" he asked, noting my heavy shopping bags. "You look like the village peddler."

"Better than the village idiot," I muttered, slumping into a chair. "I've been buying household supplies. Mitch's information on McElroy is vague. When can we elaborate?"

"When I get it all sorted out with the frigging Feds in Seattle," Milo replied. "They're sending somebody up here." He checked his watch. "Whoever it is should've arrived by now. He probably got stuck on the Evergreen Point Bridge. And no, you can't be here to meet him."

"Did I ask?"

"You were thinking about it."

"Stop reading my mind. Sometimes you're wrong."

"Not often. You want to eat out tonight? Somebody said it could hit ninety. We could drive down to the Cascadia for a change of pace."

I considered the suggestion. "You sure you want to drive there and back after a busy day?"

Milo shrugged. "I can avoid the locals bugging me with a bunch of dumb questions about McElroy."

"You're avoiding *my* questions, Sheriff."

"So I am. Why don't you leave that stuff with me? I'll put it in the Yukon. Your little arms might fall off if you have to carry it to your office."

"You're trying to get rid of me," I asserted. "I have news for you."

"About how much you spent at Parker's? Skip—"

"About the Ridleys. The lurker showed up at their place and they got a good look at him. If you want a description, call Rip. He doesn't want to admit he fell down trying to catch the guy."

Milo chuckled. "Sounds like Coach Two-and-Ten. I'll call him. I like giving Rip a hard time. Maybe I'll buy him a beer after work. That's it?"

"Yes. Did you ask Donna to leave a message for Craig?"

My husband grimaced. "Damn. I forgot. Good-bye, Little Emma."

"Stop calling me 'little'!" I yelled. But I left. At least I'd gotten rid of the blasted shopping bags.

I'd forgotten to ask Milo if Dr. Reed and Kay Burns had given their statements about the set-to at Rest-Haven. I told Mitch to follow up on that part of the story. Meanwhile, I decided to write two brief editorials instead of a longer one. The first would be Fuzzy putting his plan before the electorate and the other on violence, both abroad and on the home front. Naturally, I was opposed. I wondered if I came out with a pro-violence stance, more people might actually read my editorials. Probably not.

Vida and Dippy weren't around when I returned. Alison told me they'd gone to the retirement home so she could catch up on news from the weekend. I shuddered at the havoc Dippy might create. Many of the residents, of course, were from the Greatest Generation. They'd need all of their Depression-era and World War II skills to survive the little terror.

I called Milo at four-thirty. Kay Burns was stopping by his office when she got off work at five. Rosalie was still recovering from being hit by Farrell. She'd release her statement after conferring with Dr. Woo and Kay in the morning. I couldn't use one statement without the other. Their versions could be very different. Mitch agreed, and he had to write the story. We were stuck with the bare facts in the current edition.

When I started out of the office, Vida informed me that she—and Dippy—were staying late to get her copy in before deadline. "By the way," she said, oblivious to her great-grandson, who was up on the table by the unplugged coffee urn, "Mitch and Leo were both gone over the weekend so I'm short on 'Scene' items. Do give me something for my column."

As usual, I initially drew a blank. "Oh—Rosemary Bourgette and her new boyfriend, Des Ellerbee, chasing small children at the picnic."

"Rosemary has a new beau?" Vida wrinkled her nose. "How could I not know that?"

"Well, I guess it happened while you were being . . . cross," I said. "You can read about him in the feature I did for this week."

"I certainly will," Vida murmured. "More, please."

"Sultan teens in town—"

She cut me off. "I already have that. I was at the Burger Barn, as you may recall."

"Okay. Darla Puckett released from the hospital after a brief stay?"

"Marje gave me that item for my 'Ailing Alpiners' report. Do try for one more."

As much as I hated to mention it, I told her about Ed trying to sell his Casa de Bronska souvenirs at the picnic. With a resigned expression, Vida decided to use it. "Really," she said, "I should never leave town. That is, I'm glad I did just this once, but still . . . it's amazing how people don't notice what goes on around them."

Edging toward the door, I glanced at Dippy, who was

trying to dismantle the coffee urn. "You might want to make sure your great-grandson doesn't electrocute himself. I think Alison has already prepared the coffee for tomorrow. Have a good weekend."

I kept going. It had to be ninety degrees. The car felt like a sauna. I turned on the AC. To heck with gas mileage. I wanted comfort, at least for the brief drive to our too-warm house.

Assuming we'd eat out, I opened all the windows and doors before heading outside. When Milo hadn't shown up by five-thirty, I decided to make myself a drink. When he hadn't arrived by six-fifty, I began to worry. But five minutes later when I went indoors to check in with Kip, I saw the Yukon pull into the driveway.

"What happened?" I asked as my husband loped inside.

"No big news for you," Milo replied, bestowing a quick kiss on me. "Rip figures they'll have a five-hundred season. He's dreaming."

"You've been out guzzling beer!" I yipped.

My husband looked puzzled. "I told you I was going to do that."

I made a face. "I thought you were kidding." I put my arms around him. "I sound like a . . . wife."

"Occupational hazard," he said, hugging me. "Try paying attention when I tell you something, okay?"

I looked up at him. "Did the Fed from Seattle show up?"

Milo frowned and let go of me. "No. His car broke down by Woodinville. He had to get towed and by then it was too late with all the damned traffic. He'll be here tomorrow."

"Do you think he'd let Mitch . . . never mind," I mumbled. The Fed wouldn't cooperate with a small-town weekly. Milo had already gone off to change. I soothed myself by looking at *Sky Autumn*. It never failed to lighten my mood. It also gave me an idea.

I was still in the living room when my husband came out from the hall. "We should've run a picture of that painting in the paper. Where is it? It's not too late."

"It's at headquarters." Milo looked pained. "You don't really want me to go get it, do you?"

"I'll go in to get it," I said. "Then we can drop it off for Kip before we go to dinner. Someone may recognize it."

"Nobody recognized the stiff."

"But you've probably ID'd him anyway. I can have Kip put the painting next to the story about the body. Or maybe inside . . . the front page is full . . . we could pull—"

"Damn! Quit dithering. Let's just do it before I decide the Cascadia's a bad idea."

"Fine. I'm ready. Let's go." I stomped off to the garage. I was inside the Yukon when I realized Milo hadn't followed me. I leaned over and honked the horn. A full minute passed before he came out of the house.

"What's with you?" he bellowed. "You didn't bother to close the doors. Have you got something going on with the lurker?"

I held my head. "No. I'm sorry. This weather makes me crazy."

"You can't change the weather." Angrily, he turned the ignition key and backed out at warp speed. We pulled up at headquarters in less than two minutes. I think I held my breath for almost half the time. "Go get the frigging painting. Tell Mullins I okayed it."

Jack looked amused when I entered. "Has the big bad boss sent you to tell me I'm fired? Whoa—you look fit to spit."

"I'm hot," I declared, trying to collect my wits.

"The boss obviously thinks so." Jack sobered. "How can I help?"

"I have his approval to remove the picture found at the dump site," I said, regaining my aplomb. "Do you know where it's stashed?"

"It's gone," Jack replied.

"Gone?" I goggled at him. "What do you mean?"

"Kay Burns came in a while ago to give her statement about the brawl at RestHaven," Jack replied. "Lori couldn't figure out if the picture was actual evidence, so she'd left it on the counter. Kay claimed it belonged to her. I thought she was full of it, so I asked her what the other side of the frame looked like. She had to think about it, but when she finally said it didn't have wires, but a brass hanger, I decided it must be hers." He shrugged. "Does Dodge want it back?"

"No." I frowned. "If he does, he can talk to Kay."

I wanted to talk to her, too. But I wasn't sure how to approach Kay. The questions I had for her were the type that might make *her* slug *me*.

Chapter Twenty-one

"WELL?" MILO SAID when I got back in the Yukon. "Did Mullins pull one of his dumb stunts and refuse to hand over the painting? Do I have to go in and kick his ass?"

I explained about Kay taking it. "She could describe the back of the frame."

"Shit. Now I'll have to talk to her." He pulled away from the curb. "We're skipping the Cascadia. After we eat, I'm calling on Ms. Burns."

I opened my mouth to ask if I could go with him, but thought better of it. To my surprise, my husband told me I could come along.

"You and Donna think it's a Laurentis. Kay probably figures I don't know squat about art. She's right. You can even ask some questions. Does that cheer you up, my ornery little twerp?"

"I'm stunned. And I told you I'm almost average," I added.

Milo ignored the comment as he took the turn to the ski lodge. "Let's just hope she's not getting it on with Gould when we show up. That could be embarrassing. It's still kind of unbelievable."

"Have you been to her townhouse?" I asked.

"Nope. Why would I?"

We ate in the coffee shop, having already had our pre-prandial beverages. We both ordered the steak sandwiches. By seven-fifteen, we were on our way to Kay's townhouse on Second Hill. To our surprise, Vida's Buick was parked out front.

"What's she doing here?" Milo muttered.

"Don't ask me. I'm merely her boss."

My husband sighed. "Hell. Let's do it. At least we won't be walking in on a three-way with Vida, Gould, and Kay."

"Don't say things like that," I scolded. "I've got a vivid imagination and it just scared me."

After we got out of the Yukon, Milo hit the buzzer while I admired Kay's small garden plot of asters and various kinds of daisies. I don't think either of us was really surprised when Vida opened the door.

"My, my!" she exclaimed with her toothy grin. "I was just leaving. Good night, Kay," she called over her shoulder. "Clam," Vida whispered as she stalked past us. "Honestly!"

Kay was smiling, albeit not convincingly. "Suddenly I'm very popular. I can't think why. Or did I make a hash of my statement?"

"I haven't seen it yet," Milo replied, parking himself on the sleek dark green sofa. I joined him. "Mullins says that painting from the dump site belongs to you. Where did you get it?"

Kay sat down in the matching armchair. "You mean originally?"

"Right."

Kay was no longer smiling. "It was a gift from a friend. Years ago, actually. He was an amateur painter. Dwight told me about some teenagers who found it at the dump site. It sounded familiar. I asked to see it when I was at headquarters earlier this evening. To my astonishment, it was the one that had gone missing somewhere in between my moves over the years. A minor miracle, really."

I felt Milo lean back and realized I was supposed to speak. "Who painted it?" I asked, trying to sound casual.

"His name was Bob Jenkins," Kay replied and uttered a small laugh. "I suppose it still is. I lost touch with him thirty years ago. That was after I moved to Seattle. He lived in the University District. Typical grad student."

"I knew a Bob Jenkins when I was at the UDub," I said. It was true, though he wasn't a student, but had been a high school friend of Ben's. "What did he look like?"

Kay gazed up at the ceiling. "He was a little over average height, dark hair, kind of long, majoring in . . . fine arts, I think. Very much into Buddhism back then. In fact, he got me interested in the subject, including haiku poetry. Does that ring a bell?"

"No," I replied. "The Bob Jenkins I knew was short, redheaded, and had no interest in the arts. It's not an uncommon name. Did you have it framed?"

She nodded. "I took it to one of those U-Frame It places."

"Will you hang up the painting?" I asked.

"Oh . . . I don't know." Her eyes darted around the room. The only art Kay had on the walls was a couple of retro posters of Paris. "I'll see. I suppose the only value is sentimental. Not that I had a thing for Bob, but I did like him. He was very soulful, in his way."

Milo got to his feet. "Thanks, Kay. Just in case, don't toss the picture. It should've been in the evidence room, though I can't see how it ties in to the dead man."

Kay and I had also stood. She looked faintly alarmed as she turned to the sheriff. "I gather you know who he is."

"We think so," he replied. "We're trying to track down relatives. Mullins is working on that this evening."

"Oh," I said at the door, "I didn't get a chance to ask Vida why she was here. Is she doing an article on you?"

Kay smiled diffidently. "She's helping your Mr. Laskey with his stories on different ethnic groups. Apparently my cousin Simon didn't offer much information about our side of the family. Typical of him, of course. He doesn't approve of so-called defectors. Not that he often takes the trouble to attend Greek Orthodox services out of town."

"I suppose he'd have to go to Seattle to do that," I said, despite not liking to defend Simon under any circumstances.

We made our farewells and left. Starting back down Second Hill, we passed the Dithers sisters' horse pasture. I noticed they'd painted their barn purple. I should phone that in for Vida's "Scene."

"Kay's lying," Milo said as we turned on to Disappointment Avenue. "But I'm not sure what she's lying about."

"Why would she lie?"

"How the hell do I know?" He glanced at me, slowing for the zigzag across Spark Plug Road on to Fir Street by the high school. "I suppose you're wondering if Laurentis is Bob Jenkins."

"I am," I admitted. "I wonder if we could check through the UDub. We might be able to prove if he isn't, but not if he is."

"I think that almost makes sense. Maybe we've been together long enough that I'm figuring out how to understand whatever language you sometimes speak that sounds a lot like English."

"You always were kind of slow on the uptake," I said.

"Deliberate," Milo murmured. "I like that better. I remember when you thought I was dumb."

"I never thought that! But sometimes it took you a long time to . . . deliberate over stuff."

My husband chuckled. "I kind of liked seeing you squirm around while I deliberated over what you asked me. You never could sit still for very long. It was like watching a kitten try to catch a bug."

"Jackass," I muttered as we pulled into the garage. "Will you check with Mullins to see if he found out anything about Conley's family?"

"Maybe I should, just to see if he's awake," Milo replied after we'd gravitated to the patio.

As it turned out, Jack hadn't had much luck. There were lots of Aaron Conleys, along with variations of the last name. "No mention of one who had a band," my husband informed me. "The only time his name came up was in the *Advocate* when I busted him for bum checks."

"*The Oregonian* or the *Statesman Journal* in Salem should have references," I said, "but probably only listings of where Aaron's band was playing. Those items wouldn't be archived. Have Jack check for Aaron and Crystal's marriage license in Salem, Marion County."

Milo held out a big hand. "See? You're trying to tell me how to do my job. You still think I'm dumb."

"I do not! We talked about this before. Now you're the one who's not paying attention to things I tell you."

The sheriff stood up. "I can do it myself. I'll go get my laptop."

I smiled as I watched him amble off to his den. Maybe it was because the sun was going down and I was cooling off. Or because Vida was not only back in town, but being herself again. It could be marriage to Milo. Whatever the reason, I felt much better. I'd called Kip and everything was going smoothly in the back shop. That was always good news. I'd considered checking in with Vida about her visit to Kay, but I could catch up on that in the morning.

I was still musing when Milo returned. "It's getting

dark earlier," he murmured. "We should put in some patio lights. Why didn't I think of that before?"

"Because you're dumb?"

"That must be it." He peered at the laptop. "What year?"

"What . . . oh, when Crystal and Aaron got married. Let me think. Mid-nineties. It wasn't long before she moved here in . . . ninety-eight?"

"That sounds right," Milo agreed. "I'll try ninety-four."

"Her last name would've been Ramsey, not Bird."

Milo looked at me. "That's right—she was married to Dean Ramsey first. Could he and Conley have been more different? I'm surprised she didn't keep her maiden name. I thought she was an All-World Feminist."

"Not back then. That came later."

"No luck . . . I'll go back . . . ah! Crystal Ramsey and—" He stared at the screen. "Wesley Ellerbee. What the hell . . . ?"

"*Wesley* Ellerbee?" I repeated. "No!"

"See for yourself," he said, handing me the laptop as his cell rang.

I was incredulous. But the disturbed look on my husband's face alarmed me as he talked to his deputy. "That's not good. I'd better go see her. You sit tight, Jack."

"What?" I asked, almost letting the laptop slip out of my grasp.

"It's Rosemary. The boyfriend's causing a problem. I'm out of here."

"Not without me," I said, clutching the laptop and following Milo. "Rosemary's my friend."

"Damnit . . ." Milo sighed. "Fine, just don't get in the way. Lose the laptop and lock up the house. I'll be in the driveway."

I wouldn't put it past my husband to ditch me and

take off. But he was waiting in the drive when I flew out of the house. To my surprise, he didn't turn left on Fir to head for Parc Pines, but to the right.

"Where are we going?" I asked. "Rosemary's in the other direction."

"She's at the courthouse, working late," Milo replied. "Or so I gathered. She was kind of incoherent when she called Mullins."

"This is creepy," I declared. "Could Des and Wes Ellerbee be related? Is this the link to Aaron Conley?"

The sheriff turned onto Second Street. "Don't ask questions now, okay? I'm working."

Milo pulled in behind the courthouse, using his master key to go through the rear entrance. He punched in the button for the freight elevator, which opened immediately. It creaked and shuddered, however, as it moved from the basement to the second floor. We ended up in a section I'd never seen before, but after hurrying through what looked like a delivery area, we were out in the hall and heading past the offices of Dean Ramsey and County Clerk Eleanor Jessup, another of Vida's shirttail relations—and a source of information.

Sam Heppner stood in the doorway to Rosemary's cramped quarters. "She's okay," he said. "Just shaken up. She won't let me call Doc."

Milo entered the office, Sam at his heels, and me taking up the rear. Rosemary was seated at her desk, hands covering her face. Her client chair was overturned; books, papers, and a legal pad lay on the floor.

"I'm a mess!" she declared, letting her hands fall to her sides. "This is all so crazy!"

"Crazy's not your fault," Milo said in his laconic manner. "Take it easy. Do you want me to send out for a stiff shot of Scotch?"

Rosemary leaned her head back. "I could use it. Heppner should've asked you to bring some. God, but I feel like a fool!"

"Do you want to talk about it here or . . . ?" The sheriff let the question dangle.

Rosemary sat up straight, looking as if she hadn't noticed I was with Milo. "Emma," she said. "Can I come to your house? I want to get out of here."

"Sure," I replied. "We've got Scotch."

She looked at Milo. "Is that okay? Can I fill out a report later?"

"No problem," my husband replied. "Sam, can you do your job of cleanup around here?"

Sam said he could. I sensed that the sheriff implied the office should be processed, just in case it ended up being a crime scene. It took Rosemary a minute to get herself and her belongings together. "Wouldn't you know I have a court appearance tomorrow? That's why I was working late."

We bade good-bye to Sam and left the way we had come. None of us spoke on the short ride back home. But Rosemary was the first to speak after getting out of the Yukon.

"I should call my parents," she murmured as Milo opened the side door for us. "They'll think I'm nuts."

I stayed in the kitchen to make the drinks, but I could overhear Rosemary telling Milo what had happened. She'd finished preparing her judicial request, but had decided to look into Charles and Janice Ellison's query about suing the school district for not locating their daughter, Samantha, after she went off with her boyfriend and got involved in Roger's solicitation caper. It was a frivolous request, since Mrs. Ellison had seemed unconcerned at the time. But while Rosemary was reading through their complaint, Des had showed up.

"He knew I was working late," Rosemary said as I handed her a glass of Scotch. "He glimpsed the Ellison file. Somehow, Des thought it was 'Ellerbee,' and accused me of checking up on him. I tried to reason with him, showed him their full names, but he just went ballistic. I honestly believed he was going to get violent. I got scared. I told him I was calling the sheriff. He just looked at me—and ran."

Milo had his Scotch in hand and I'd sat down next to Rosemary on the sofa with my Canadian Club. "He didn't touch you?" my husband asked in a calm, quiet voice.

She shook her head. "But I thought he would. Did I overreact?"

"No." Milo sipped from his drink, letting the single word sink into Rosemary's brain. "It appears he made some violent gestures or there wouldn't have been stuff on the floor, right?"

"Yes, he was kind of flailing away, but he kept on the other side of the desk." Rosemary leaned her head back against the sofa. "He seemed so nice, so normal. I feel like a fool."

Milo shrugged. "You're not a mind reader. Did he threaten you?"

Rosemary shut her eyes. "I . . . I'm not sure. I mean, if I had to testify in court, I couldn't swear to it. But I *felt* threatened—physically."

"That's enough." My husband stood up. "I'm going to have Heppner try to locate him. Are you willing to bring charges?"

Rosemary made eye contact again. "Do I have to decide now?"

"No."

She smiled faintly. "Thanks, Milo."

"You need time to collect yourself," he said. "I'm going to check in with Heppner." The sheriff ambled off to the garage out of hearing range.

Rosemary gave me a bleak look. "Have you ever dated dumb?"

"Are you kidding?" I shot back. "I lived dumb for thirty years, waiting for Adam's father to marry me. Meanwhile, I failed to notice I was really in love with that big dude with the badge. Try doing dumb for decades. You can't top that."

"That's . . . pretty dumb," Rosemary said, and laughed. "Didn't I say you and Dodge were icons?"

"Icons of dumbness," I muttered. "It would've helped if Milo had been a little more . . . aggressive, so to speak. But never mind that. The important thing is that you got enlightened tonight."

"I'll never hear the end of this from Terri," Rosemary said. "Maybe I'll spend the night with my folks. Mom and Dad will pitch a fit if they don't find out about this before it leaks all over town."

The sheriff came back inside and sat down again in the easy chair. "Has Des ever mentioned any family?"

"His parents," Rosemary responded. "They still live in Montana. He has a brother there, too, and a sister who married and moved to Idaho. I don't think his family is all that close. He's mentioned how much he admires our clan." She lowered her eyes. "I suppose that's hogwash."

"We'll check," Milo said without expression.

"Rosie's staying at her folks tonight," I put in. "I think that's good."

Milo nodded. "Sure. I've already got Heppner checking your place, but it's pretty secure. Unless you gave Des the code to get into Parc Pines."

"No," she replied. "I hadn't gotten that far with him yet."

"Just as well," my husband said. "Finish your drink and I'll take you over to Dick and Mary Jane's. You can come in tomorrow to do whatever paperwork is required."

Rosemary gulped down the rest of her drink. "Let's go now. If I have any more Scotch, I might pass out. I usually drink wine. You're a generous bartender, Emma."

We hugged before she left. I stood in the doorway as Milo pulled out of the drive. It felt much cooler outside. I closed the front door and locked it. I had no idea if Des knew where I lived or if it would occur to him that Rosemary might be here. But this was one time when I didn't want to take any chances.

"Well?" I said when Milo returned twenty minutes later. "Did you stop in to see the Bourgettes?"

"Yeah," he replied wearily. "I thought it might help Rosie feel better if I gave Dick and Mary Jane my official version first."

I put my hands on his shoulders. "You're a good guy, Sheriff."

He shrugged, putting his hands over mine. "It's part of the job."

"How did they take it?"

"No muss, no fuss. They're solid people." He leaned down to kiss the top of my head. "Let's go outside and just sit."

We did just that for about ten minutes, listening to the welcome wind in the evergreens and watching the sky turn from pale gold to gray as the sun slipped down over our mountain aerie. Finally, after a long silence, I asked the burning question.

"Wes and Des Ellerbee—what does that suggest?"

Milo glanced at me. "Is this a riddle?"

"No, but it can't be a coincidence," I said. I waited for an answer and didn't get one. "Can it?"

"Damn, but you're persistent," Milo muttered. "Can't

you stash that curiosity of yours for a while and just take it easy?"

"It's not my style," I asserted. "You should know that by now."

"I do. Unfortunately." My husband sighed. "Go get the laptop and do the work. I *can* just sit here. Do you realize I haven't had a real day off for over two weeks?"

Dolt that I was, I hadn't thought about it. I put my hand on Milo's arm. "I'm worse than Tricia. I'm only looking at things from my point of view. Maybe she wasn't interested in your job, but that doesn't make me any less selfish."

He chuckled. "I've never been sure which is worse. But I'm used to it. You've been that way since I first met you. Face it, you're a real nag when it comes to your job of reporting on my office. But I get it, okay? Now take your hand off my arm before we both do something that might give me a heart attack about now."

I complied and stood up. "I'll get the laptop and play with that instead. Okay?"

Milo merely nodded. I paused inside to grab a can of Pepsi. Before I got through the kitchen my husband came inside with the cell at his ear. He looked as if he were about to explode. "Yeah, I can hear it now," he growled. "I'll be there. Follow up on the other crisis. You got that?" He clicked off.

"What's happening?" I asked as I suddenly heard sirens in the distance.

"Heppner went to Ellerbee's house and the place was on fire. He called it in. Engines and medics have been sent from Skykomish and Alpine. I've got to head to the fire site."

"Why you?" I asked. "Why not a deputy?"

"I had Sam alert Doe," he replied, his hand on the door to the garage. "It's quicker if I go to the cabin.

Damnit, you'd better come with me. I'm not leaving you alone if Ellerbee's on the loose."

"But he doesn't know where I . . ."

"Don't argue. *You* don't know what Ellerbee knows. Let's go. The reason I called in Doe is because we've got another problem. Jack Blackwell beat the crap out of Kay Burns. She's in the ER. Move, woman. We're in crisis mode."

Chapter Twenty-two

"WHAT," I ASKED, "can you do if the cabin's burning down?"

Milo, who was waiting for a van to get out of the way before turning onto Fir, shrugged. "Find out if anyone was inside."

I shuddered, remembering another fire two years earlier that had burned a local young man to a cinder. "I wonder how it started," I said. "I hope they can contain it before it gets to the forest."

My husband didn't comment. He had obviously kicked into full sheriff mode. I felt as if I might as well have been a suitcase he had on the seat next to him. It was only when his cell rang just as we were about to turn onto Highway 2 that he spoke.

"Grab the damned thing out of my shirt and answer it, okay? I've got to focus on cutting into cross-state traffic."

I plucked the cell out of his shirt pocket. "Emma?" Sam Heppner said at the other end. "Tell Dodge that Doe's at the fire scene. Mullins thinks it'd be better if the boss goes to headquarters. Blackwell's raising hell."

I told Sam I'd convey the message.

"Shit!" Milo bellowed. "Kay must be filing charges. That horse's ass Blackwell can't post bail because there's no bondsman open."

I tensed as the sheriff executed a dangerous U-turn

just after we'd crossed the bridge over the Skykomish River. Maybe I'd have been safer if I'd stayed home. I could've locked the doors and gotten out my father's gun to defend myself against Des Ellerbee. Worse yet, I'd have to face another encounter with Black Jack. At least he wouldn't dare vilify me in front of Milo. Unless, of course, he'd want to incite the sheriff to violence so he could sue him.

I was still mulling when we pulled up in front of head-quarters.

"Stay put," Milo ordered. "I don't need any more aggravation. Neither do you." He stalked off to his official lair.

The SUV was parked in its usual spot in front of the entrance. My view inside was limited to what I could see through the glass in the double doors. Though there were windows that ran almost the width of the building, the bottom halves were frosted and at night the shades were drawn from the top. After a couple of minutes, I couldn't see anything except an occasional glimpse of Jack Mullins behind the curving counter. He looked unusually somber.

I was, as usual, curious. I decided I could see more if I got out of the Yukon to peek through the double doors. Approaching cautiously, I didn't dare go farther than halfway under the overhang. I saw part of Blackwell, who was making incisive gestures. He was turned toward someone I presumed was Milo. There was just enough traffic to drown out the voices on the other side of the doors.

Black Jack disappeared from view just as the Whistling Marmot let out across Front Street. *Bewitched* had drawn quite a crowd for a Tuesday night. Maybe the theater's AC was part of the attraction. I moved closer to the Yukon to get out of the way to call Kip.

"Where are you?" he asked. "Did I hear a car horn honk?"

I explained that I was outside of the sheriff's office, waiting to see if Blackwell was going to spend the night in jail.

"No!" Kip exclaimed in an uncharacteristic burst of excitement. "What'd he do? Slug Dodge?"

"Not yet," I replied before ringing off and ducking out of sight. Fuzzy and Irene Baugh, Harvey and Darlene Adcock, and a half-dozen other people were heading my way. I didn't want to explain why I was standing in the gutter in front of my husband's headquarters. If I weren't the *Advocate*'s editor, that tidbit might end up in Vida's "Scene."

I was still waiting for the passersby to move off when the sheriff strode outside. "What . . . ?" he began, seeing me leaning against the Yukon. "Skip it. Blackwell's locked up, so you can come inside."

"Is he pitching a fit?" I asked, hurrying to keep up.

"You bet." Milo opened the door for me. "He asked to call his attorney in Everett. Mullins let him do it. The guy wasn't home."

Deputy Jack grinned at me. "You'd have liked seeing Blackwell get apoplectic. I honest-to-God thought he'd have a stroke." The grin faded. "Oh, no! Here comes Patti Marsh."

Milo, who had been studying some paperwork on the counter, grabbed my arm. "You're deputized. I'm not taking on . . ." As Patti made her entrance, the sheriff headed for his office.

"Hey," Patti called after the sheriff, "come back here, you big jerk! Where's my guy?"

Milo kept going and slammed the door behind him. Worse yet for me, the phone rang and Mullins answered it. I was stuck.

"Hi, Patti," I said, as if we'd run into each other at the mall. "What's up?"

"My dander," Patti shot back. "Where's Jack?"

"Mullins?" I responded. "Right here, working the desk."

She stood toe-to-toe with me. I couldn't move unless I back-flipped over the counter. "You know who I mean!" she yelled. "Where is he?"

As usual, Patti smelled like a distillery. "He's in a cell," I informed her. "This may shock you, but your guy beats up women. He did it once too often with somebody who had the courage to file charges. Go home, Patti. Your Jack isn't going anywhere until tomorrow."

Patti's face sagged under heavy makeup. She looked old—and pitiful. But she had pluck. "What're you talking about? Who filed what?"

"Ask Mullins," I said.

Jack had hung up the phone, but looked at me, not Patti. "No corpse found at the fire scene. I better tell the boss." He got to his feet and headed for Milo's office.

"What fire?" Patti asked, edging away from me.

"A cabin near Baring," I replied.

She looked alarmed. "Was my guy there when it happened?"

"No, Patti," I said. "It has nothing to do with Jack."

"So who complained about him?"

I glanced at the paperwork on the counter. "Here. It's official. You can see for yourself."

"Let me get my cheaters," she murmured, digging into her small sequined shoulder bag. Putting on a pair of bejeweled half-glasses, her lips moved as she read through the document. "Shit! Kay! What's wrong with her? Jack was done with that skank thirty years ago!" She tossed the complaint at the counter. It missed, sailing over the top to land on Lori's desk. "How can she

still be causing trouble after so long? Let the past be."
She obviously didn't expect a comment. "Can I see my
guy?"

"You'll have to ask Jack. Mullins, I mean. Here he
is."

Patti posed the question. "Why not?" he said to her.
"No conjugal visiting, though." He winked.

Patti preened. "You'd be surprised at what my guy
can do, you dumb mick. I call him Mr. Versatility." She
sashayed around the end of the counter and into the hallway that led to the cells. "Hey!" she yelled. "The door's
locked!"

"We dumb micks aren't allowed to have a key," Jack
called after her. "You better go home, Patti."

"Prick," she muttered, almost running out the door.

Jack sighed. "That's one thing about Patti—she's eas-
ily deterred."

I leaned on the counter. "Dare I ask what's deterring
the sheriff from going home? It's going on ten."

"For one thing," Jack replied, "there's a jurisdic-
tional problem about who's in charge of the McElroy
investigation—SkyCo or the Feds. For all I know, the
boss won't find out until tomorrow."

"Great. Any idea about Ellerbee? Do you know where
he is?"

Jack shook his head. "What's with that guy? Is he
nuts? Hey, you want to sit down? Take Lori's chair,
Emma."

"Thanks, I will." I opened the swinging half-door in
the counter and parked myself in Lori's place. "Don't
ask me about Des. For all I know, he's a privacy freak.
Or a phony."

"Poor Rosie." Mullins lit a cigarette. "You want
one?"

"No, thanks. I've already fallen off the No Smoking

Wagon today. Do you know why Blackwell beat up Kay?"

Jack shrugged. "No, but Dodge wonders if it didn't start with the RestHaven mess. He'll probably clue you in when he gets out of here."

"Surely you jest," I muttered.

He laughed. "I know the boss well enough to realize he could stonewall even you. Heck, he's had sixteen years of practice. I've always gotten a kick out of how you two would go round and—" Jack shut up as Milo came out of his office.

"Don't even think about it," the sheriff growled.

Jack looked bewildered. "What, boss? I'm trying to entertain Mrs. Dodge. Or is she Ms. Lord tonight?"

"She's Mrs. Sleepy," Milo replied. He took my arm and hoisted me out of the chair. "I'm taking the Little Woman home. Don't screw off, Mullins. We've got a possible creep on the loose."

"Yes, sir, I'm all over it," Jack replied.

"You're full of it," the sheriff muttered as we made our exit.

"If you *ever* call me the Little—" I began.

"Stop. I said that to keep you from one of your chatty farewells. How did you get rid of Patti Marsh?"

"Mullins did that," I said. "Give him credit. He's no dope. Now please tell me why Blackwell beat up poor Kay and how is she?"

"Doc patched her up and sent her home a few minutes ago," Milo answered, driving up Third Street. "Jennifer Hood was coming to spend the night with her. Not only is Jennifer a nurse, but I guess Kay and Jennifer are friends off the job. Maybe they bonded because both of them were dumb enough to marry Blackwell. I suppose I should've alerted Gould, but I was afraid he'd show up at headquarters and shoot Black Jack. I'd rather not be around when Dwight finds out what's happened."

"Gee," I said, "I got who, what, where, and when, but no why. Well?"

My husband grimaced. "That's because I'm not sure. The only thing Kay and Blackwell agree on is not saying what started the row."

"That's weird," I murmured. "Maybe I'll go see Kay tomorrow. It's Wednesday, so I'll have some free time."

"Kay might not want company," Milo said, pulling into the garage. "She's going to look kind of gruesome. Besides, it's Gould's turn to be on patrol tomorrow. I'd be surprised if he didn't park his cruiser at her place to make sure Blackwell doesn't show up. The SOB will post bail first thing, even if he has to have Patti do it for him."

"I hope he gets out before you go to work," I said after we were inside the house.

"Dubious. I don't think he can get bail before nine." Milo hooked an arm around my neck. "Promise you won't do anything dumb tomorrow?"

I looked up at him with wide eyes. "Visiting Kay is dumb?"

"It could be." The hazel eyes were solemn. "I worry about you. The only time I know you're safe is when you're with me."

I leaned my head against his chest. "I always feel safe with you. I always have."

"You must have felt safe with Cavanaugh."

"Safe?" I looked up at my husband again. "How could I feel safe with Tom when I never knew if he'd be there when I woke up?"

"Good point. If I'm not there, you know I've gone fishing."

I smiled. My mind went back in time to over a decade when I'd compared Tom's and Milo's virtues. I'd given the sheriff an edge for being dependable. But even then I'd shortchanged him—and myself.

* * *

To my relief, Vida was still back to normal in the morning. Naturally, she was agog about what had happened the previous evening. Just as naturally, her pipelines to Marje and Bill Blatt, Eleanor Jessup, and whoever she'd pumped on her Presbyterian Telephone Tree had kept her virtually up to speed.

"If you intend to call on Kay Burns," she said with one eye on Leo, who was filling the pastry tray, "I may go with you. She was going to find a picture with her grandchildren in Leavenworth."

"Sure," I replied. "If Blackwell shows up, you can hit him with your hat. What's it made of? I've never seen it before."

"Cork," Vida responded. "Meg bought it for me at a rummage sale in Fairhaven, that older section of Bellingham. Isn't it rather ingenious? It's supposed to resemble an eighteenth-century frigate, perhaps one of Captain Cook's ships. Or was it Captain Vancouver?"

"Cork floats," I said, "so I suppose that's apt. But isn't it . . . heavy?"

"My, no!" she exclaimed. "Cork's light. That's *why* it floats."

I nodded. "I don't think I'm awake yet. I need coffee."

After filling a mug and grabbing a maple bar, I summoned Mitch into my office to bring him up to speed before he left on his morning rounds. He devoured a cinnamon roll and an apple tart while I relayed the evening's events.

"You should've called me," he said when I finished. "I feel left out."

"I had no idea what would happen," I explained. "If Milo hadn't been worried about me being home alone, I wouldn't have been at his office. In fact, I had to wait in the SUV until Blackwell was in a cell. Besides, I don't like calling you out and your leaving Brenda at night."

"As I mentioned, she's improving," he murmured, still apparently disappointed over missing a news opportunity. "So nobody knows where this Ellerbee has gone?"

"Maybe he took off for California. Which reminds me," I went on, "when you're at the courthouse, check with Dean Ramsey for ideas about dealing with food in hot weather. That's his department as county extension agent. Any news about Blackwell is yours. You know martial arts and I don't."

Mitch frowned. "We don't run domestic abuse items with names."

"This involves charges," I said. "I'm referring to fallout. It wouldn't surprise me if Black Jack threatens to sue the sheriff."

My reporter still seemed dubious. "Fine, I'll inquire about him." He rose from the visitor chair and left my office.

Kip came to see me five minutes later. "I wanted to let you know I pulled the item from 'Scene' about Rosemary and the writer guy chasing kids at the picnic. But I ran your feature on him. Is that a problem?"

"No," I replied. "I wanted to spare Rosie's feelings and use the Dithers paint job instead. My Ellerbee piece doesn't mention her. For all I know, he is what he says he is. There are lots of odd movie types. It's possible he's a bit of a Hollywood prima donna."

"Some day Chili and I'll have to go to Disneyland," Kip said. "Would you believe I've never been south of Portland?"

I smiled. "There's a lot of country to see out there, Kip."

He looked skeptical. "It can't be any prettier than Alpine."

"Well . . ." I paused. "Not by much," I said. And

marveled at my own words. It seemed that marriage had curbed my big-city bias.

Shortly after nine-thirty, Vida asked if I wanted to call on Kay. I demurred, thinking it might be too early. "She got home fairly late," I said. "Let's wait until eleven. Then we can have lunch."

"Very well," Vida agreed, then looked thoughtful. "I could get one of my casseroles out of the freezer. I'm sure Kay would enjoy a tasty home-cooked meal."

"Of course." I wanted to add that Vida's casserole wouldn't qualify, but didn't. *Peace at any price,* I thought, as she went into the newsroom.

Mitch called me a few minutes later. "We've got breaking news," he announced in an unusually excited voice. "Apparently there's a hostage situation at the courthouse."

My initial fear was for Rosemary. "In the prosecutor's office?"

"No," Mitch replied. "It's the county extension agent who's being menaced. It looks like Ramsey's finally making some real news for us."

I was stupefied. "Where are you?"

"In front of the courthouse," he replied. "The building's in lockdown. Dodge went inside a few minutes ago. The emergency vehicles are manned now, but staying put out back."

I was stunned. "Milo went inside? What's going on?"

"I don't know," Mitch admitted. "I'd gone over to the post office to get some stamps before I went to the courthouse, and after I came out, I saw Dodge hurrying over there. That's not his style, as you know. I sensed news, so I went back to his office. Blatt said Eleanor Jessup called to say she'd tried to see Dean Ramsey, but he couldn't talk to her. He had someone with him who wouldn't let him open the door."

"Did he say who it was?"

"He either couldn't or wouldn't," Mitch said. "That's when Eleanor called the sheriff."

I was too upset to stay in my own office. "I'll join you," I told my reporter. "Find out if Milo's office is in contact with their boss."

The newsroom was empty. Vida must have gone to fetch her casserole and Leo was on his advertising rounds. Alison was helping a man I vaguely recognized with a classified ad, so I merely waved before going outside. I wanted to run, but my feet felt like lead. Besides, I didn't want people staring at me. At the corner of Third, I had to wait for a Sears truck to go by. As soon as it turned onto Front, I could see Mitch going into the sheriff's office. I'd meet him there.

Bill and Lori were behind the counter. They both looked anxious. Before I could speak, Bill said they hadn't heard from the sheriff since he'd gone into the courthouse.

"Why," Mitch asked, "would anybody hold the county extension agent hostage? Is the 4H Club in revolt?"

Bill lifted his hands in a helpless gesture. "No idea. Eleanor told us that Ramsey was late getting to work. Her office is right by the county extension agent and she swears nobody went in there after the main door was opened at eight."

"What about the back way by the freight elevator?" I asked.

"They hadn't unlocked it yet," Bill replied. "They aren't expecting any deliveries this morning so they don't unlock that door until somebody goes outside to smoke."

My fear for Rosemary hadn't quite been quelled. I asked the deputy if she'd come to work.

"I suppose so," he replied, looking puzzled. "Why wouldn't she?"

"Just curious," I said, realizing Milo had kept Rosemary's scare to himself until she filed a complaint. "Is the courthouse really sealed off?"

Bill nodded, his fair skin flushing slightly. "Crazy, huh? At least nobody's phoned in a bomb threat."

Lori stared at her coworker. "Don't say things like that! I'm already a wreck with Grandma's funeral tomorrow. My poor dad feels lost with both his parents gone."

I kept from saying Myron Cobb should be able to cope by now, being in his seventies. I didn't speak at all as Spence made his entrance.

"Ah!" he exclaimed, "the doughty Deputy Blatt, the lovely Lori, and half the staff of the *Advocate* are already here. No wonder I sense news. Is it true that Mayor Baugh is being held hostage by Jack Blackwell?"

That had never occurred to me. I gaped at Bill. "Has Black Jack been released?" I asked.

Bill nodded again. "About half an hour ago. He's still fit to spit."

Spence looked annoyed. "Blackwell was arrested? What for? Is this tied in to what happened at Rest-Haven?"

I leaned closer to Mitch. "Stick around," I whispered. "I'm heading for the courthouse."

My reporter seemed puzzled. "But—"

I kept going. If there was danger to the sheriff, I had to be there. My mind was racing as I crossed Second and waited for traffic on Front. Inspiration struck when I saw Leo coming out of the Clemans Building. He saw me and waited on the corner.

"I just got Doukas Realty to take out—" he began.

"Never mind. Call the courthouse and tell them there's a priority FedEx delivery out back."

"Emma . . ." Leo began, but apparently realized I was not only sane, but serious.

"Okay." He took out his cell. "Mine is not to reason why. . . . Hello? Urgent FedEx at the rear entrance," he said and immediately disconnected.

"Thanks!" I called over my shoulder as I crossed Second and headed straight for the rear of the courthouse. To my dismay, Medics Del Amundson and Vic Thorstensen were standing by their vehicle. I tried to ignore them, but Del called to me.

"Hey, Emma, you can't go in there!"

The door was opened by the bailiff, Gus Tolberg. He was about the last person I wanted to see. "What the hell . . . ?" he uttered in confusion.

"The sheriff!" I shouted, somehow managing to edge past Gus.

He came after me just as I entered the freight elevator and poked the second-floor button. "Do you want to get arrested?" Gus demanded, barely getting his burly body inside before the door closed on him.

I glared at Gus. "If the sheriff arrests me, he'll have to get his own dinner tonight," I declared. "In case you've forgotten, you were one of the witnesses at our wedding here last February."

Gus simmered down, but he still looked grumpy. He always did. "Oh, yeah, along with Ms. Bourgette as the other witness."

"Is she here today?" I asked just before the elevator stopped on the second floor.

"Haven't seen her." He remained in place and pushed the button for the main floor. "I have to go back to court. If Dodge doesn't bust you, I hope he tells you you're a real pain in the butt."

"He often does," I mumbled, starting through the delivery area.

I was about to turn the corner into the hallway when a voice called out. "Stop! Who goes there?"

"Your wife," I shouted. "Don't shoot me."

"Christ!" Milo, who had his hand on his weapon, looked as if he was tempted to kick, if not shoot, me. "How the hell . . . Damnit, Emma, why can't you stay put?"

"I'm on the job," I replied innocently. "I heard you were making news at the courthouse."

"The last thing I need is to worry about you," he growled, leading the way down the hall. "Go into Rosie's office. She's not here yet. Which is good, under the circumstances."

"Which are?" I inquired.

The sheriff, whose hand finally fell away from the King Cobra Magnum, yanked open the prosecutor's door. "Never mind," he said in a low, adamant tone. "Get in there. Now."

I knew what that glint in his hazel eyes meant. I scooted through the door. Milo closed it behind me. I wondered if he'd locked it. After I recovered from being intimidated, it occurred to me that I might as well have stayed in my own office instead of being stuck in Rosemary's. I tested the knob. It moved.

"Knock it off!" I heard my husband yell.

I looked around, noticing that the room looked exactly as I'd seen it the previous night. If Rosemary hadn't yet filed an official complaint against Des, it probably hadn't been processed. I didn't dare touch anything. Milo might bust me for tampering with evidence.

To hell with it, I thought, and opened the door an inch. "Who's in there with Ramsey?" I whispered.

My husband shot me a disgusted look. "He won't say."

"It's got to be Des," I asserted. "I'll bet he never left last night."

"Maybe." Milo seemed to relax slightly.

"Any demands?" I asked.

He shook his head, his eyes fixed on the door across the hall.

I remained standing on watch. About all I could see was the sheriff's broad back, but that was a comfort. After a couple of minutes, he shifted from one foot to the other. I knew his patience was running out. Maybe he'd sent out for tear gas. It couldn't be any worse than the coffee they served at his headquarters. To my dismay, I began to giggle.

"What the . . . ?" Milo glanced back at me. "Pipe down!" he hissed between clenched teeth.

Suddenly sounds erupted from across the hall. I heard someone let out an agonized cry. A couple of thudding noises followed. The sheriff's hand had automatically gone back to his weapon. An ominous silence enveloped the hallway. I had to force myself to stay rooted to the floor.

Just beyond Milo, the door to the county extension office opened. A ghostly faced Dean Ramsey leaned against the frame. "Call the medics," he said in a ragged voice. "I just stabbed someone." Dean passed out at the sheriff's feet.

As usual, I didn't have a camera. But I could call Mitch and tell him to come to the courthouse. "If you can't get in," I said hurriedly, "go to the back and get a shot of the ambulance taking away a wounded man. Don't ask for details. I can't talk." To prove it, I rang off.

Milo was still on his cell, apparently having already called in the emergency crew and now was talking to one of his deputies. I still didn't dare leave Rosemary's office, especially with Dean lying halfway into the hall. Then I heard the medics before I saw them.

"Never mind this one," the sheriff told Del and Vic. "Check out the guy in the office who's been stabbed."

Del glanced at me. "Hi, again, Emma," he said, before disappearing with the gurney. Somehow, the long-time medic could remain cheerful under even the grimmest of circumstances. I supposed that's how he survived the harrowing nature of his job.

The sheriff was out of sight, having gone into the county extension office. I threw caution to the wind and went into the hall, where Dean was coming to. "Emma?" he whimpered, looking disoriented.

"Yes," I said, helping Dean sit up. "We have to get out of the way. Can you stand?"

He seemed bewildered. "I don't know." Dean stared at the open door to his office. "Dang. Now I'm going to jail."

"Why?" I asked stupidly.

He gestured at his office. "I stabbed that man with my Boy Scout knife. Besides, I . . ." He paused as Del and Vic wheeled Des Ellerbee out into the hall.

"He's moving," I said, "so he's not dead." I shut up as Dwight Gould and Bill Blatt came down the hall from the regular elevators. The sheriff obviously was waiting for them at the scene of whatever crime may or may not have been committed. Both deputies nodded at me as they passed by. If they were surprised by my presence, they didn't show it.

Dean seemed oblivious to Dwight and Bill's arrival. His eyes had widened. "The guy won't die? I got him in the ribs."

"That's not necessarily fatal," I asserted. "Do you know who he was?"

"I do now," Dean replied in a miserable tone. "He finally told me his name. What did I ever do to him?"

I didn't know how to respond. "Did you two talk much?"

"He talked. He sounded kind of crazy. Who is he? Besides Des Whoever? He jabbered about movies and logging and all kinds of stuff. How'd he get into my office in the first place? He was hiding under the desk when I got to work."

"Did he seem to know you?"

The question obviously puzzled Dean. "Well, he knew I was the county extension agent."

That wasn't what I'd meant. "Then I assume he didn't know you from somewhere else."

Dean looked flabbergasted. "Heck, no. Isn't he from California?"

"That's what he told me," I replied. "Maybe he is. He may be Aaron Conley's brother."

Dean's face sagged. "What?"

"Aaron wasn't really Aaron," I said quietly. "That was his name as a musician. He was probably Ellerbee's brother and I think Des killed the man we knew as Aaron."

"Oh, no!" Dean cried, covering his face with his hands just as Milo stepped out into the hall and looked down at me.

"Does Ramsey need medical help?" he asked.

"He's really upset," I replied. "There's something I have to tell you about who killed Aaron or Wes or whatever his name—"

Dean scrambled around me to grab the sheriff's pants leg. "Des didn't kill Aaron, Sheriff! I did! I never meant to! Go ahead, arrest me. I can't take it anymore."

It's unusual for the sheriff and me to be speechless at the same time. But we both stared at Dean and then at each other. "Dean," the sheriff finally said in his laconic manner, "I think you could use a look-see from the medics."

Dean kept protesting, but Milo told Dwight to have the medics return after they dumped off Ellerbee in the

ER. "You and Jack keep an eye on Ramsey," he continued. "I have to interrogate another witness."

Jack poked his head out from around the other side
of Dean's office door. "Who is it?" He saw I was still
crouched on the floor by Dean. "Oh. Right. The Little
Woman."

Milo hauled me to my feet as the deputies came into
the hall. I glared at Jack instead of Dwight for a change.
The sheriff then pulled me into Dean's office. To my
surprise, he slammed the door behind us.

"Take a seat," he growled, going around Dean's desk
to sit in his office chair. "What in hell is up with
Ramsey?"

"Ask him," I retorted. "Did you hear his so-called
confession?"

"Yeah." Milo sat back and lighted a cigarette. "You
want one?"

"Yes, but you'll have to bust both of us for smoking in
the federal courthouse."

"Good. I don't know about you, but I could use a little peace and quiet about now." He lighted a cigarette
and handed it to me. "We can use Ramsey's coffee mug
for an ashtray. Okay, unload, you little pain in the ass."

"I don't know any more than you do. Really. I figured
Des killed Wes, but that'd mean he was up here several
years ago. In fact, he told me he'd been in the area before, but claimed he didn't know about Alpine until he
read the cabin ad."

My husband rubbed at the bridge of his nose. "I can't
question Ellerbee in the ER or talk to Ramsey until he
calms down. He may be in shock. He may be crazy.
Why would Dean kill Conley?"

"If he's telling the truth," I said slowly, trying to
reconstruct the distraught man's spate of words, "it
may've been an accident. I suppose they met some-

where, maybe at the cabin. They had Crystal in common."

"Or they got into it over her," Milo murmured. "Even dead, Crystal could cause problems." He paused. "How come you first fingered Des?"

"Even if Des told me he didn't know about Alpine, I suspected he'd been here when his brother was living at the cabin. Someone must know if the place has been vacant for all these years. It certainly hasn't changed much since Crystal died. I guessed Des came up here a few years after the murder and the brothers quarreled. Aaron ended up dead and a panicky Des buried him at the dump site."

"Emma's wacky theories survive." The sheriff stared at the ceiling. "Go on. This might start making sense."

"Fine. I'm getting to the revised part."

"Revisionist history. Why not?" Milo was still staring at the ceiling.

"If Dean's not crazy and really killed Aaron, that scenario still plays. Des wouldn't know his brother was dead. He shows up at some point, can't find him, steals his credit cards, and takes off. We should've checked into Des's background."

Milo nodded slowly and finally looked at me. "He may be wanted in several states as Aaron Conley, not as Desmond Ellerbee. I'll check that out. Somebody should have him on a surveillance camera." He paused, listening. "I think the medics are back. Let's stay here and make out."

"Milo . . ."

"I'm kidding," he said. "I've got to go to the hospital and check on both patients. Maybe one of them will be lucid. And no, you can't come with me." He put out his cigarette in the mug and stood up. "I'd ask how you got in the building, but I really don't want to know."

I'd let my cigarette burn down so far that it had gone

out on its own. "You're not mad at me?" I asked, pulling at his short-sleeved regulation shirt.

"Hey," Milo said, putting his hand over mine, "if you can't stay mad at me, how the hell can I stay mad at you? But move that hand before it touches my brawny arm, okay? I've got work to do."

I found Mitch out in the hall with the deputies. Apparently the courthouse had been reopened. "I got good outside shots of the medics leaving and reloading. The deputies have been filling me in," he added with a touch of reproach.

"I'm sorry," I said. "I honestly couldn't talk. I was trying to help Dean Ramsey. He was the second one headed for the hospital."

"Mullins told me," Mitch said. "This is your story, I assume."

"This story is such a mess that we'll both work on it," I assured him. "Are you going back to the office?"

Mitch checked his watch. "I can't. I've got a date at ten-thirty with the Bartons. The ethnic series, with their Irish and Greek backgrounds."

"Okay. I'll see you later." I walked away, feeling as if I was departing from a Greek tragedy with comic Irish overtones. There really are times in life when you don't know whether to laugh or cry.

Chapter Twenty-three

NATURALLY, VIDA POUNCED on me when I returned to the office. "How could I miss all the excitement? Alison had no idea where you'd gone. Nor could I reach Billy. I called Lori, but she's such a sad sack lately, and insisted she didn't know what was happening at the courthouse."

I summed up what had occurred as if I were writing the lead paragraph. If I could remember what I said, maybe I could use it in print.

"How very odd," Vida murmured, adjusting the cork hat. "My, I'd almost forgotten how much trouble Crystal caused in the first place. I never met her after she moved back to this area. I feel remiss. How soon do you want to leave for Kay's? I already fetched my casserole. As I recall, it has pork, sweet pickles, potato puffs, and . . . I forget. Very hearty."

I avoided wincing. "I can't visit Kay," I said. "At least not before lunch. I have to get this story online."

"That's fine," Vida responded. "The casserole hasn't yet thawed, though it will in this weather. Just as well, if Kay wants it for supper."

Sometimes it's better to say nothing at all, especially about Vida's cooking. "By the way," I inquired, "has Mitch asked for help with his ethnic roots series?"

"He mentioned it yesterday," Vida replied. "I told him the Doukas family that lived near the old Camp

Two site had moved some years ago to Cle Elum. I don't
recall why they did such a thing. The family still owns
Doukas Realty."

Unable to provide a reason for what Vida no doubt
considered irrational behavior, I went into my office. I
had to hedge about what had gone down at the courthouse. No one yet had been charged with a crime. The
only hard news out of the sheriff's office was Kay's
charge against Blackwell. I wouldn't go online with
that, despite my threat to make Black Jack's abuses public. I'd wait for our next edition, as I always did when an
official complaint was lodged.

I was still mulling when I saw Spence come into the
newsroom, pausing to make his obeisance to Vida. A
few moments later, he was in my office, sitting down in
a visitor chair.

"I come as a humble beggar," he announced, not
looking even faintly meek. "I'm at sea about the courthouse lockdown. Lori informs me you may have some
knowledge. She's apparently in the dark."

"Funny you should ask," I said. "I was just trying to
sort through it to see how I could post what went on.
Let's call it unsubstantiated."

"That doesn't help me with the eleven o'clock hour
turn," Spence retorted. "An intelligent inkling might
suffice."

" 'L.A. screenwriter locks county extension agent in
his office after his cabin burns down'?"

Spence stroked his hawklike nose. "And both men
end up in the ER? I believe you omitted something."

"Dean Ramsey didn't want to be locked in his office."
I sighed. "Okay, here's what happened and good luck if
you can sort it out."

When I finished, Mr. Radio looked bemused. "A pity
I wasn't around when this Crystal person got whacked.
Are you taking Ramsey's confession seriously?"

"As I told you, he did mention the word 'accident.' For all I know, the guy we knew as Conley may have passed out from his drug habit and Dean accidentally backed over him with his car."

"It'd all be simpler if the dump-site corpse had been Myrtle Everson," Spence remarked. "Oh, well. I suppose I could use the word 'rumpus' to describe what went on at the courthouse. As for the confession, I await official word from the bellicose love of your life. I'm told he's gone to the hospital."

I nodded. "I guess we both wait, though everybody in the county must be asking why the courthouse was closed down."

"Rumors abound," Spence said. "Delivery of small-pox samples stolen from a lab in the Distant East. Eleanor Jessup having a hair-pulling match with Bobbi Olson. Mayor Baugh being throttled by Jack Blackwell. And so on." He made a spinning gesture with his index finger.

"No bomb scare?" I asked.

"Too common, as are deranged people shooting innocent victims. Let's give the locals credit for some imagination, however . . . localized. Except for the Distant East, of course." He stood up. "I suppose I could go with an apparent hostage situation. No demands, obviously."

"Good luck. I like your 'rumpus' description. Maybe I'll steal it."

Spence looked disdainful. "It's mine. You can use 'ruckus.'" He sketched a bow and left, whistling.

Mitch returned just after eleven. "Simon Doukas was ailing, so his wife, Cece, filled in. Did you know Mimi Barton and Kay Barton Burns were given Greek first names in an effort to placate Neeny Doukas?"

"No. What are their real names? Aphrodite and Hera?"

"Nothing so heroic," he said, leaning on a visitor chair. "Mimi is Mercia, meaning 'compassion' or 'forbearance.' Does that suit her?"

"She's very kind," I said. "Mimi put up with my brother when he subbed for Father Den, so I consider that forbearing on her part."

Mitch smiled faintly. "I was gone when your brother was here at Christmas." He looked at his notes. "Given Kay's marital history, her name doesn't suit her as well. It's Kassia, which means 'purity.'"

I started to laugh, but stopped. "Kassia?" I repeated.

"Right." He frowned. "What's wrong?"

"Nothing," I said hastily. "I've heard that name recently in another context. Odd how that happens with an unfamiliar name or word."

"Then it doesn't turn up again for a long time," Mitch remarked. "I'm seeing the Bartons about their Irish roots at four, so I'll go home from there. What can I do with the courthouse story?"

"Not much," I said. "I won't post anything online until we get official word from the sheriff's office. Can you check in with them before lunch?"

Mitch seemed to brighten, though it was always hard to tell. "Sure. I'll stop in on my way home to lunch with Brenda. I'll call if I find out anything useful you can post."

"Thanks," I replied, smiling. "I gather rumors are rampant."

He shrugged. "In Detroit, the incident would be a mere kerfuffle."

I didn't remind Mitch that he wasn't in Detroit. I had other things to consider—such as Kassia Barton aka Kay Burns. Vida was on the phone. I'd suggest an early lunch, but I didn't want to miss Mitch's call from the sheriff's office. I thought about calling Milo, but he'd still be at the hospital or coping with the paperwork he loathed so much.

A few minutes later, Vida stopped by, looking vexed. "Amy still feels puny. She's suffered from migraines since the fall, you know."

"I didn't know," I said. Maybe they'd been brought on by Roger's first serious brush with the law back in October. He'd certainly given me headaches over the years. "Is she having a migraine now?"

"Yes, and it's quite severe," Vida replied, scowling. "Ted can't leave work, so I must take care of Dippy and see what I can do for Amy. Really, mind over matter can cure a great many ills. My daughter would've benefited from Faith's good sense and Christian ethic. In any event, I won't be able to go to lunch."

"That's okay," I assured her. "But can you wait five minutes?"

"Well now . . . of course." She sat down. "Is something wrong?"

"No. What was the last name of Kay Burns's third husband?"

Vida counted to three on her fingers. "Arthur. I don't recall his first name. She met and married him in Seattle. He was later killed in a vehicular accident. He fathered the son who lives in Leavenworth."

"That's sort of what I remembered," I said—and followed up with what Milo would have called one of my wild and wacky theories.

Vida, however, grew thoughtful. "Oh, my," she finally said softly, "doesn't that beat all? Why, if your conclusion proves to be true, then Kay is Ren Rawlings's mother. Do you intend to confront Kay? Or suggest such a thing to Ren?"

"I don't know what to do," I admitted. "Ren's so fragile and Kay might laugh in my face. The odd thing is that Ren told me she sensed her mother was nearby at RestHaven. Maybe she is."

Somewhat reluctantly, Vida rose from the chair. "Kay as a hippie? Well, having left to live in the city, heaven only knows what madcap ideas she might've gotten. She was still in her twenties back then. Oh, my! But," she went on, her gray eyes glinting behind the big glasses, "who is Ren's father?"

"Mr. Arthur?" I suggested.

Vida frowned. "Perhaps. We were sent wedding announcements of her marriage to him a year or so later. I merely mailed a nice card. Kay's matrimonial adventures were an unwelcome expense. She didn't have the nerve to send any notification when she later married Mr. Burns. I really must dash. Poor Dippy will be wanting his lunch. Maybe I'll take the casserole to Amy instead of to Kay. My family may appreciate it more than she would."

They may even have an antidote, I thought. But I beamed at Vida and wished her well. It was almost eleven-thirty. Mitch had just gone out, so I took a chance and called Milo.

He was in, but according to Lori, unavailable. "He only got back about ten minutes ago," she explained. "He closed his door and told me to hold all calls. In fact, I can see from the console that he's on the phone right now. Mr. Fleetwood's waiting for him."

Great, I thought. I was about to get scooped on my husband's news by KSKY's noon report. I thanked Lori and rang off. I didn't dare usurp Mitch's duties by showing up at headquarters. My only hope was that Milo hadn't yet made anything official.

At five to twelve, that hope was dashed, though not as I'd expected. "Here's what Dodge told me—and Fleetwood," Mitch said over the phone. "Ramsey's being brought in for questioning about a possible assault on

Ellerbee. Dean will be released from the hospital ASAP. According to the sheriff, the county extension agent's suffering from being a jackass, but don't quote him on that."

"I won't," I asserted. "I want to maintain a happy home. Is that it?"

"No. Dodge will bring Ellerbee in for questioning in Aaron Conley's disappearance. His wound's superficial, so he'll be released soon."

"Wait," I said. "If Dean confessed to killing Conley— who was really Wes Ellerbee—why isn't the sheriff questioning him about that?"

"He will be," my reporter responded. "But you know Dodge goes by the book. One thing at a time."

"Of course," I murmured. "I wish my husband would sometimes consider his wife's responsibilities. At least we're not up against a publishing deadline. Is there anything else I should know?"

"Not according to the sheriff," Mitch said.

"That figures. Thanks." I hung up and headed for the back shop to post my reporter's latest news.

There was no point seeing Milo in person. However, I could call on Kay Burns. Vida might not be pleased at being left out, but family was her priority. Not having much appetite for various reasons, including the weather, I got in the Honda and drove to Second Hill.

After what seemed like a long, hot wait outside the townhouse, Kay finally opened the door. "Emma!" she exclaimed. "What a nice surprise. What brings you here?"

"My curiosity," I replied, following her kimono-clad figure inside. "That's about all that can send a journalist out in the midday sun."

This time, Kay gestured to the green armchair while she sat down on the sofa. She wasn't wearing any makeup and the bruise on her cheekbone was ugly. For the first time, I realized she looked her age.

"I was thinking about going in to work this afternoon," she said, "but I'd rather not show up looking so ghastly. I might frighten the patients. There's already been enough disruption at RestHaven."

"Does it still hurt?" I asked.

She lightly touched her face. "Not much. I've been icing it. If you're here to ask if I'm sorry I pressed charges against Jack, I'm not."

"I don't blame you," I said, "but that's not the reason. It's something quite different. My visit has nothing to do with the newspaper. Please don't be offended. I feel sorry for Ren Rawlings, who, as you may know, came to see me when she first arrived in town."

Kay again put a hand to her cheek. "Oh. Well, she is a fragile creature. But Dr. Reed is hopeful that with proper medication she can soon be discharged."

"That must please you," I said, smiling. "As her mother, I mean."

The little color in Kay's face turned to chalk. "Oh. Oh, my." The words were barely audible.

"Kay, relax, please. I bore a child out of wedlock. I'd be the last person to think ill of you."

"Well . . ." She passed a hand over her forehead. "Dare I ask how . . . what did Ren tell you?"

"Almost nothing except your name, Kassia Arthur," I replied. "She had—maybe still has—no idea what became of her mother. In fact, she thinks she was murdered here in Alpine. Are you the one who called the *Advocate* a week ago Tuesday?"

She nodded. "I'd called Edna Mae about a book I wanted reserved. You know how she chatters. She mentioned Ren was there, talking about a Kassia Arthur. I was stunned. I called the paper later to find out if she'd made inquiries there, but whoever answered didn't know what I was talking about when I asked for Kassia Arthur. Later, I asked Iain Farrell to call and inquire after Ren—same response." She smiled diffidently. "Everyone thinks Iain is so intimidating, but he's really rather sweet. I've become quite fond of him."

That figured. Farrell was single. Maybe he'd end up as Husband Number Five. It would also explain how he'd gotten into it with Blackwell. I felt like saying Iain had fooled me, but Kay had continued talking.

"I'd lost track of Ren after she was adopted. Once she had a real home, I backed off." Tears glinted in Kay's eyes. "I didn't recognize her when she came to Rest-Haven. It was like a miracle."

"All she had was some of your poetry and a postcard from Alpine," I said. "The name Aurea was on the back of the postcard."

"Aurea?" Kay looked puzzled. "Oh—maybe it was Ourea. It's a reference to the primeval gods of the mountains in Greece. I was writing a poem about them, I suppose." She grimaced. "I wrote some really awful poetry. If you read any of it, you know that."

"I only heard some quotes Ren mentioned to Vida when she visited her in the hospital," I replied.

"I merely dabbled at poetry. My late husband, Ross, was the PR creative force. I handled the business side and dealt with clients."

"Mr. Burns," I remarked, making sure I had Kay's mates lined up correctly. I posed an awkward query. "Was Mr. Arthur Ren's father?"

"No." Kay seemed amused. "I'd met Matthew Arthur while I was carrying Ren. He offered to marry me, but I felt it'd be wrong for him to take on a child who wasn't his. Oh, he argued, but my divorce from Jack wasn't final and wouldn't be for another couple of months. There were problems to be worked out."

I recalled Milo telling me about his own breakup and

that it had taken almost two years to finalize his divorce. "I understand," I murmured. "This may seem like an odd question, but there is something I have to know. Is Bob Jenkins actually Craig Laurentis?"

Kay gaped at me. "You mean the recluse who's also an artist?"

She seemed sincere in her surprise. "Donna sells his paintings at her gallery."

"I've never gone in there. I'm not really into art." Kay gestured at the Paris wall posters. "That's as much of an art lover as I am. I like those because they have romance and the lure of a glamorous lifestyle." She laughed self-consciously. "I've been to Europe twice, but I didn't visit museums. I don't know anything about the recluse. I've never seen him. I don't think he was around when I lived here."

"No," I said in a dull tone. "I don't think he was, either. Do you know what became of Bob Jenkins?"

Kay shook her head. "I lost track of him after I married Matt. He was probably off on one of his protests or demonstrations. I did admire him for his political activism, of course. It was a big part of our times."

So much for that line of inquiry. But I wasn't done with Kay. "Donna thinks that painting is an early Craig Laurentis," I said. "Apparently, he changed his name for artistic purposes."

Kay smiled. "More likely to avoid the draft. He did talk about moving to Canada."

"That fits," I agreed. "In any event, you should have Donna appraise the painting, if only for insurance purposes."

"Really?" Kay looked flummoxed. "Maybe I will. How did it end up at the dump site? I thought I left it in the apartment when I moved out after marrying Matt Arthur."

"I've no idea," I admitted. Maybe Bob—or Craig—

had come to see Kay and found she'd left without the painting. Maybe he'd taken it with him—and eventually buried it as a bad memory. The young man might have felt either he or his art had been rejected. Maybe both.

"I never thought Bob was that good," Kay was saying. "I have no appreciation or understanding of art. I left some of Bob's sketches with Ren. Rivers, waterfalls, streams—Pacific Northwest scenery. If she kept them, they might be of value to her. One was of the Olympics. Bob sketched it while I worked on a poem about the Ourea. My apartment on Seattle's First Hill looked to the west. I literally wanted to put the Cascades behind me."

"Ren may still have them," I said, standing up. "Are you going to tell her the truth?"

Kay was also on her feet. "Should I?" She seemed to be speaking to herself rather than to me.

"Wouldn't it be the right thing to do? For both of you?"

The tears returned to her blue—"cerulean blue"— eyes. "I'm not sure."

"Is that because Bob was her father?"

"Bob?" Kay looked stupefied. "Heavens, no!" She took a deep breath. "I was pregnant when I left Alpine. Ren's father is Jack Blackwell." She touched her face. "I finally told him I'd had his baby and given her away. That's why he hit me."

I didn't offer Kay any more advice. That was a decision only she could make. After saying as much and assuring her any secrets were safe with me, I left. On a whim, I dropped down to Alpine's First Hill to call on Donna Wickstrom. She was feeding lunch to her daycare charges.

"I just put the Overholt baby down for a nap," she

said. "Are you here to find out if Craig's dropped off a new work?"

"No, but it's Craig-related," I replied, not taking time to mention that I'd seen him over the weekend. "Have you got a brochure here?"

"Yes," she replied, smiling. "Are you browsing?"

"I'm afraid not," I admitted. "I've never seen your brochure. You didn't need a sales pitch to get me hooked on *Sky Autumn*."

"The easiest sale I ever made," Donna said with a laugh as she went to a drawer in the china closet. "Here. This needs updating, though. You can handle the job in your back shop, right?"

"Yes, talk to Kip." I flipped through the pages—and stopped to stare at a Laurentis I'd never seen. "When did you sell this one?"

Donna glanced at a mountain scene. "That's the first of his I sold—over two years ago. You can tell it's the Olympics from a distance."

I nodded. "I'll bet he painted this some time ago."

"Probably. You know how he works. It takes him years to get everything the way he wants it. I suspect he did it from memory." Donna gave a little shrug. "Don't ask me why. For one thing, it's the only thing of his I've ever seen that's from a distant perspective."

I handed over the brochure. "I'm sure you're right. Who bought it?"

"Tourists," Donna replied. "They were passing through on their way from Banff and Lake Louise. They live on the Oregon coast. I guess they were tired of seascapes. Is that early effort of Craig's still in custody?"

I made a face. "It got liberated. The owner claimed it."

Donna was wide-eyed. "You're kidding!"

"Not really. I'm sworn to secrecy, but I have a feeling

you'll find out soon enough. If not, you can torture me until I squeal."

"Well! That's intriguing. . . ." She spun around as shrieks erupted from the kitchen. A fair-haired little girl came racing into the living room. "What's wrong, Savannah?" Donna inquired.

"Jordan put pudding in my hair!" she cried, throwing her arms around Donna's legs. "He needs a time-out!"

"I think," I said, "that's my cue to leave you in . . . chaos."

"I'm used to it," Donna said. "I'll be waiting for the Laurentis owner. Meanwhile, I'll check out Savannah's complaint against Jordan."

I wished her luck and made my exit. Now I knew why Ren had passed out when she'd seen the brochure. Maybe she'd seen an earlier version of the Olympics that had been left behind by her mother. I was vaguely sorry that Craig wasn't Ren's father. Just about any local except Crazy Eights Neffel would be an improvement over Black Jack.

Leo was the only staffer in the newsroom when I got back around one. "Guess what," he said, looking puckish, but not waiting for me to speak. "Brian sorted out things with his bosses at Raytheon and asked for a transfer. He got it—to their operation in Tukwila."

"Tukwila!" I gasped. "You know that's just south of Seattle."

Leo grinned. "Sure. I drove by it going and coming from the L.A. flight. Brian won't start there until after Labor Day, though. In fact, they're going to Hawaii for their honeymoon and think maybe they'll come back via Sea-Tac and look for a place to live in the area."

"How does Liza feel about this?" I asked.

"Not good," Leo replied, no longer smiling. "She tried to convince Brian he could find another, better job in the L.A. area, but this is also a promotion. I told her it's not as if they're moving to Saudi Arabia."

"Do you think she'd consider moving up here?"

"I doubt it," Leo replied. "Liza's a real California girl."

I dreaded asking the next question. "Does this change your own plans about retirement?"

"I just found out ten minutes ago," he replied.

I let the subject drop. Leo had to live his life the way he saw fit. Vida called an hour later to say she was using the Hibberts' computer to work on her page. "I'm already behind," she told me in an exasperated tone. "Losing Monday to the long weekend has put me in a bit of a hole."

"You'll dig your way out," I assured her. "How's Amy?"

"Wan," she replied. "I told her I'd phone in a prescription for gumption. That made her cry. Really now! Oh—I must see to Dippy. He's getting into the oven."

Shortly after three-thirty, I felt as if *I* were in an oven. I'd put one fan in the newsroom and the other by my desk. It was too small to do more than riffle a few pages of press releases. My office still felt stuffy and I'd become restless. Having no further word from the sheriff's office, I decided to pester my husband in person.

"Maybe," Lori said when I arrived, "you can cheer him up. He's kind of grouchy."

I feigned shock. "Dodge is grouchy?"

"Maybe I shouldn't have asked him if he was going to Grandma's funeral tomorrow," Lori murmured. "You better knock first."

I did. Milo barked back. I assumed he meant I should come in.

"Oh," he said, "it's you."

"Don't sound so thrilled about it," I retorted, shutting the door behind me. "At least you've got big fans in here. I forgot to bring my new one to the office."

"You came here to bitch?"

"No. I came here to annoy you. And to tell you that Jack Blackwell is Ren Rawlings's father. I bet you didn't know that, Sheriff."

"Shit." He shook his head. "So that's what happened with him and Kay? Or was it just reflex on his part? And how did you find out?"

"Kay told me," I replied. "She's Ren's mother."

"Oh, Christ!" Milo half-spun around in his chair. "No wonder their kid's half nuts. Do I want to know how you figured all this out?"

"No," I asserted. "Because I only got the Kay part right. I was wrong about Craig being Ren's father. Blackwell's her father."

My husband paused to collect himself. "You can tell me the gruesome details later after I've got a Scotch in hand. I've spent two hours listening to Ellerbee and Ramsey spill their guts. Before it slips what's left of my mind, Ellerbee confessed he's the lurker, and yes, he's Wes's brother. We tracked down the family members in Montana, who claimed to have lost track of both Wes and Des years ago. Maybe that's true. I don't blame them. Des has also been known as Aaron Conley. He's got a California rap sheet for window peeking. No assaults, no showing off his anatomy. He just likes to look. He claims he's curious, doing research for his movie script. But he's going down this time for the murder of Glenn McElroy."

I gaped at the sheriff. "Are you sure?"

Milo sat up straight and gave me an arch look. "Ellerbee owned a Colt forty-five. I saw it when I searched the cabin. He also had a carry permit, so there was no reason to ask him about it. When I took Rosemary home last night she mentioned McElroy had been nosing around. That gave Ellerbee a motive to get rid of McElroy. Now the Feds will take over. Their agent, some guy named Smith, takes over now. He's legit. But I've got a call in to the state arson squad. They can't be here until tomorrow. Ellerbee's out of my hands, even if he is in my jail."

I was momentarily overcome, "Poor Rosie. What about Dean?"

"That went down with Conley the way we figured," Milo replied, lighting a cigarette. "Ramsey was being a nice guy and checked in with Conley now and then to see how he was getting along. But the last time—the spring of ninety-nine—Conley was really cranked up on something and got violent. He charged at Dean, yelling and screaming. There was a scuffle, Conley fell, hitting his head on the fireplace tools. The pointed end of the shovel went through his ear and killed him. That's why Doc and the Everett ME couldn't find any apparent skull damage. Freak accident, but Ramsey can't stop blaming himself."

"What did Dean do then? Drive the body to the dump site?"

"He swears he doesn't remember much about the aftermath except digging a hole after it got dark." Milo nodded at his SkyCo map. "I asked if he knew about the dump by Carroll Creek. He was vague, said he'd heard it mentioned, but had never gone there. He probably hasn't, except for burying Conley. Why would he? He doesn't live in Alpine."

I was silent for a moment. "So no charges against him re Conley?"

"What could I charge him with? The stabbing this morning is another matter." Milo put out his cigarette and stretched. "It's iffy, though. Ramsey was trying to unlock the door to get out. Ellerbee tried to stop him. I'll go with some half-assed assault charge."

"I can't quote that in the news," I said with a dirty look.

"The paper doesn't come out until next week," the sheriff responded. "Your deadline's . . . Tuesday, right?" He looked uncertain.

"You know damned well when our deadline is," I declared. "I'm talking about posting it online, jackass."

"That's *Sheriff* Jackass to you, Ms. Lord," he said sternly.

We glared at each other. Then we stared at each other.

"God, I'm glad I married you," he muttered.

I smiled. "I'm glad you did, too."

I left him then. I was still smiling.

Dinner. I couldn't bear to turn on the stove. I hated to ask Milo to barbecue. I knew he was not only hot, but he'd put in a rougher day than I had. I wondered if I could set off the charcoal. I'd probably incinerate myself and set our log cabin on fire. Then the arson squad would have two jobs. I stopped at the Grocery Basket to peruse their deli items. Having skipped lunch, I was hungry. I also lacked imagination, so I bought fried chicken, a green salad, baked potatoes, and an apple pie.

After opening up the house, I headed for the patio. I got as far as the back door when I saw a book lying on the cement near the door.

I didn't recognize the cover. Picking it up, I noted the title: *Catholic Christianity: A Complete Catechism of Catholic Church Beliefs*. Puzzled, I realized a piece of paper was barely peeking out at the top of the cover. I carefully removed it and read the semilegible handwriting:

I borrowed this from your priest. I'm not conversant with Catholic doctrine. This book told me what I needed to know, so I'm telling you what you need to know. Yes, I once called myself J. C. Peace. I conducted the marriage ceremony between your husband and his first wife. I was not and never have been ordained nor have I had any other official capacity as a minister. If you need legal documentation, I can provide that. You don't have to contact me. I will know. Peace, Craig.

I gazed out into the forest that surrounded my tiny patch of the wider world. How often did Craig slip among the evergreens and vine maples and wild berry vines to glimpse the rest of us in what he considered our mundane, even crass routine? Maybe I should have resented that. Most people would consider it spying, voyeurism, even akin to Des Ellerbee's lurking. But I disagreed. It was more like having a guardian angel. Craig would laugh at that idea. I sensed he didn't consider himself religious, at least not by conventional standards. I recalled something about life not being about the destination, but the journey. A Zen belief, remembered from my brother talking about Thomas Merton's *The Seven Storey Mountain*. I'd tried to read it to please Ben, but it was too deep for me. Yet there are some things that are instinctive.

A sound made me turn around. I saw Milo coming toward me. I knew where I was going. Our journey had started sixteen years ago. The path we'd traveled, alone and together, had been marked with laughter and tears, anger and intimacy, business and pleasure, loss and love. The next step in my journey was to walk into my husband's arms. He met me halfway.

That's what makes a marriage.